TWO FRIDAYS IN APRIL

Roisin Meaney was born in Listowel, County Kerry. She has lived in the US, Canada, Africa and Europe but is now based in Limerick city. She is the author of numerous bestselling novels, including *Love in the Making*, *One Summer* and *Something in Common*, and has also written several children's books, two of which have been published so far. On the first Saturday of each month, she tells stories to toddlers and their teddies in her local library.

Her motto is 'Have laptop, will travel', and she regularly packs her bags and relocates somewhere new in search of writing inspiration. She is also a fan of the Random Acts of Kindness movement: 'They make me feel as good as the person on the receiving end'.

www.roisinmeaney.com
@roisinmeaney
www.facebook.com/roisin.meaney

ALSO BY ROISIN MEANEY

After the Wedding
Something in Common
One Summer
The Things We Do For Love
Love in the Making
Half Seven on a Thursday
The People Next Door
The Last Week of May
Putting Out the Stars
The Daisy Picker

Children's Books:
Don't Even Think About It
See If I Care

Roisin MEANEY

Two Fridays in April

HACHETTE
BOOKS
IRELAND

First published in Ireland in 2015 by HACHETTE BOOKS IRELAND
First published in paperback in 2015

2

Cataloguing in Publication Data is available from the British Library

ISBN 978 1 444 799552

Typeset in Bembo Book ST by Bookends Publishing Services, Dublin
Printed and bound in Great Britain by Clays Ltd, St Ives plc

Hachette Books Ireland policy is to use papers that are natural, renewable
and recyclable products and made from wood grown in sustainable forests.
The logging and manufacturing processes are expected to conform to the
environmental regulations of the country of origin.

Hachette Books Ireland
8 Castlecourt Centre
Castleknock
Dublin 15, Ireland

A division of Hachette UK Ltd
Carmelite House, 50 Victoria Embankment, London EC4Y 0DZ
www.hachette.ie

This book is dedicated to random acts of kindness,
and the excellent people who commit them

As he pulls down the security grille he hears a wolf whistle. 'Stop that now,' he says, not turning around, crouching instead to stab the key into its lock.

A second whistle. Longer, with more feeling. He shakes his head, smiling. 'Cut that out.' He straightens up and looks to his left and sees Sean Daly planted in the doorway of the neighbouring butcher's shop, arms folded.

'Suits you,' Sean says, eyeing the lavender bicycle. Grin on his puss.

'Una's birthday present.' He swings a leg over the saddle. 'Easiest way to deliver it.'

'What's this she is now?'

'Sixteen today.'

Sean shakes his head. 'Doesn't be long passing. Haven't seen her around here for a while.'

'No – she gave that up.'

He still misses the muffled thump on the shop's rear door that heralded her arrival each weekday afternoon, her bike propped next to his against the back wall as soon as he let her in. He misses the way she'd fling her schoolbag on the floor and lean against the counter to tell him about her day, smelling of the apple shampoo she's grown out of now too.

He misses their cycle home together at closing time, after she'd done her homework in the little room behind the shop, after he'd bagged the takings and put them in the safe. All in the past, since she decided she'd prefer to go down the town with her pals after school than hang around with her old man. As it should be, but still he misses it.

'Won't feel it,' Sean says, 'till she's bringing home the boys.'

'Jesus, the fun'll begin then.' He pushes off, raising a hand. 'Be good, see you tomorrow.'

But of course he won't. He'll never see Sean again.

It's bright and crisp today, just the way he likes it. He's the polar opposite to Daphne, who can't get enough of the heat, who packs a picnic anytime it looks like there might be a bit of sunshine on the way. Hot weather seeps the energy out of him, leaves him sweaty and wilting. This is the kind of day he loves: cool enough to fog your breath, but nicely lit by a watery sun. Perfect day for a cycle.

He whizzes past the crawling rush-hour vehicles, weaving with ease, despite the too-small bike, around the various obstacles he encounters: the odd pedestrian straying onto the road, a discarded splayed umbrella, the scattered mushy remains of someone's bag of chips in the gutter.

Passing parked cars, he watches for signs of an imminently opening door, reminded as he always is of the day he and Daphne met. Her face when it happened, the shock on it, as if she'd been the one to go flying instead of him.

He wonders if he's been forgiven since the morning, and thinks he probably has: she's not one to stay mad for long. She didn't ring him back, though – she must have seen the missed call, heard the message he left. Busy, probably – or letting him stew a bit longer. He wonders if she's doing a lemon cake for the birthday, his favourite. Although Una prefers chocolate, so he hasn't much hope.

He's conscious of the comical figure he must cut, astride a bicycle clearly the wrong size for him, like a huge man squeezed behind the wheel of a Mini. His knees jut out, denied the space to straighten as he pumps the pedals. And the colour of it, not exactly manly. Who cares though? Soon be home. Might give someone a laugh, no harm.

He zooms past a travel agency, thinking of the surprise he's planning for the end of the month, and his heart does a small skitter. She won't be mad then – she'll be far from mad when he breaks it to her. Be nice for them to get away on their own, his mother on standby to move in with Una for the few nights, sworn to secrecy.

He turns off the main road, circles the green, tips a hand to his forehead as he passes the church. Five minutes he'll be landed. Una gone bowling with pals, not due home till later, he'll give the bike a bit of a rub with the chamois before she sees it. Leave it in the hall so it's the first thing she claps eyes on. Daphne might have a bit of ribbon to tie around the handlebars for a laugh.

He approaches the corner shop, thinks about stopping for a bar of the Turkish Delight she loves – peace offering, in case he needs one. But then he decides against it: forgot to bring a lock for the bike, better not chance leaving it outside. He can always duck back on foot if she's still a bit frosty.

He whirrs around the corner, onto their road.

A bin lorry roars towards him.

A cat comes flying out from Buckley's garden.

The bark of the dog that's chasing it is the last thing he hears.

FRIDAY, 2 APRIL
(ONE YEAR LATER)

DAPHNE DARLING

The day he died, they had a row about the butter. Afterwards, when the horror of it all wouldn't stop replaying itself in her head, like some forgotten reel of film endlessly and uselessly looping back on itself in a silent projection room, it was that final stupid argument, it was her snapped *Why can't you ever remember?* that caused her insides to curl and wither with anguish. She fought with him on the day he died.

She pours tea from a yellow pot and adds milk. She stirs, lifts the cup and sips. It's not quite eight o'clock. She woke before the alarm this morning, and her toes are cold inside their navy wool socks – she *hates* the cold – but she heard the thrum of the boiler starting up in the utility room a few minutes earlier. Heat is on the way.

As if the butter mattered a damn. As if his forgetting to leave it out of the fridge the night before should have merited a comment, let alone annoyed her. As if it should have stopped her reaching up on tiptoe to press her lips briefly to his, to cradle his face between her palms for a second like she always did just before she left for work – but it *had* stopped her, it had.

There was no goodbye kiss that day, no tenderness at all between them, the day she looked at his living face for the last time. She picked up the beautiful vintage leather briefcase he'd got her for Christmas and left the kitchen – did she even say goodbye? – and he made no attempt to follow her.

She still can't remember when they last kissed. It kills her; it just plain kills her.

Mo never once offered sympathy. Mo wouldn't know sympathy if it hopped up and bit her on the behind. Of course she was grieving herself, but she didn't have to sound so uncaring. *Cut that out right now*, she would order sharply when Daphne was drowning in remorse. *It was a row; married couples row all the time. You think I never had words with Leo? Get some sense. You weren't to know – how could you know what was going to happen?*

And unfeeling as her tone was, not a trace of softness in it, Daphne would clutch at the words and pull what comfort she could from them – *married couples row all the time, you weren't to know* – and she would manage somehow not to go under.

The toasted bread jumps up, causing a corresponding jolt in

her chest. She doesn't want breakfast, she never feels like it now, but every morning she makes it and eats it because that's what people do. She goes through the motions, sleepwalking her way through life since he left. She lifts out the toast, drops it onto a plate, reaches for the butter.

The morning of his funeral an envelope addressed to him slid through the letterbox and landed face up on the hall floor. The sight of his name brought a wash of despair so intense she thought she was literally going to fall apart, to disintegrate into small bloodied chunks of bone and flesh. She sank onto the bottom step of the stairs, clammy and nauseous with grief, hugging her knees with frozen hands, heedless of her crumpling black dress.

When she eventually managed to open the envelope she found a receipt inside from a holiday company. She looked at it uncomprehendingly, saw their two names, and Rome, and flight times. It meant nothing to her. They'd made no travel plans.

And then she noticed the departure date, 29 April, and it suddenly made sense. A surprise gift for her birthday, and what would have been their third wedding anniversary. She'd never been to Rome. *I'll take you sometime*, he'd promised – and here it was, his final present to her. Heartbreak layered on top of heartbreak.

The marmalade jar is almost empty. She gets to her feet and crosses the room and scribbles on the blackboard that's screwed to the wall beside the shelf of cookery books. *Floor cleaner* is already there, and *toothpaste* and *coffee*. *Marmalade*, she writes, the chalk clacking over the surface like a cockroach.

As she returns to the table she hears sounds from the room above: the soft bump of footsteps crossing the floor, the rattle of curtains along their pole, a door clicking open. She slots two more slices of bread into the toaster and pushes down the lever.

Mo moved in with Daphne and Una the day after Finn was buried. She didn't even phone to say she was on the way, just turned up on the doorstep in the middle of the morning, her face shiny with tears or with rain, someone's unwanted handbag wedged under her arm, someone else's battered blue suitcase sitting on the path beside her.

I thought I might stay here for a while, she said, her voice hard and steady despite her wet face, despite the fact that her only son, her only child, had been lowered the day before into a hole in the ground – and Daphne was too numb, too stiff with grief, to find a way to say no, so she lifted the case and brought it inside, and Mo followed.

And there the three of them were: his daughter, his mother, his wife, living under the same roof but connected only by their loss of him, broken with misery, stumbling as best they could through the unimaginably deep void he'd left behind.

And five days later, Mo had moved herself out as abruptly as she'd arrived, again offering no explanation. She simply materialised on the threshold of the sitting room one afternoon, the blue case all packed up again.

I'll be off home now, she said. *I'll give a ring, see how you're doing* – and Daphne stopped shovelling ashes from the fireplace and sat back on her heels and regarded the rigid little figure in the doorway. Blue scarf wrapped tightly around her neck, black quilted jacket, burnt-orange sneakers below grey tracksuit bottoms.

You don't have to go, she told her – what did it matter who lived where now? – but Mo went anyway.

For the first few agonising weeks and months Daphne would lie in bed each night and think, *How did I get here? How did I end up in this life?* She would imagine the days stretching endlessly ahead, each one beginning with a fresh wallop of misery that left her empty and flaccid as a pricked balloon, and she wondered how many more she was expected to endure.

Time played tricks. An hour would seem never-ending, a month would pass in a blink. She would find herself in a supermarket with no recollection of having travelled there, or sitting in a queue of cars with no clue as to where she was headed. She would stand at crossroads for unknown periods of time, lost in her grief, heedless of the green man that lit up every so often across the street.

Along with the almost unbearable pain of losing Finn, there was the added anguish of all that had to be done in the aftermath of his death. Closing his bank account, applying for his death certificate, switching bills and health insurance into her name, cancelling his standing orders and his cycling club membership and his magazine subscriptions.

Tidying up the life he had abandoned, smoothing it over like it had never happened. Each task was like driving another nail into his coffin; each form added insult to injury by forcing her to tick *widowed* instead of *married*. How she'd adored being married, being someone's wife. Now she was nothing, she was nobody's.

She didn't ask for Mo's help with any of it, and Mo didn't offer. When they began to meet regularly again, when Daphne finally felt able to reinstate Mo's weekly invitation to dinner that had been in place while Finn was alive, his name rarely came up. They talked about everything but the man they'd lost.

In February, ten months after his death, Daphne opened an envelope from the city council and found a cheque for a substantial sum paper-clipped to a brief typewritten note of condolence. It stung as painfully as an unexpected hard slap across her face.

It wasn't the amount of the compensation; that hardly registered with her. It was the implication that money, that a number followed by a series of noughts on a cheque, could somehow lessen her sorrow.

Sorry about one of our lorries killing your husband, it said to her. *Buy yourself a new handbag, go on a little cruise, you'll be grand.* She wanted to rip up the cheque and send it back to them, or set fire to it and watch it turn to ash – but it was Mo, brisk, unsentimental Mo, who forbade it.

Don't be stupid, she said. *Put it in the bank, forget about it, pretend it's not there. Some day you'll be glad of it, or Una will.* So to keep the peace a new account was opened and the cheque lodged, and there it sits gathering dust, and Daphne would rather crawl across a mile of broken glass than touch a cent of it.

The bicycle shop didn't reopen. In the past year not one of them has gone near it. From time to time Daphne pictures the brand-new bicycles still lined up inside, coated by now with dust no doubt, their shine completely gone. The accessories lying in drawers or hanging on hooks, the helmets and pumps and locks and lights and puncture-repair kits that nobody can buy. The bell above the door that had as much music in it as a twanging rubber band is still and silent now, a ghost herald with no arrivals to announce.

Their neglect of the premises disconcerts her whenever she thinks of it, scratches at her like rough wool against her skin. They should do something with it, the family business founded by Leo nearly fifty years ago, but she lacks the energy or the will to figure something out. And there's never a mention of it from Mo, so presumably she feels equally unable to make a decision about it.

And today is the second of April again, and it is their three hundred and sixty-fifth day without him, and Daphne is trying very hard not to let the memories of a year ago rise up and swamp her. And so far, barely half an hour into her day, she is having no success at all with that.

The kitchen door opens.

'Morning,' Daphne says, summoning a smile. 'Happy birthday.'

Una shoots her a look she can't read and mumbles something, pushing her hair from her face as she crosses to the worktop that holds the toaster and the kettle. Wonderful hair she has, the warm sheen of burnished old gold, falling past her shoulders in a glorious tumbling, curling mass. It's damp: she must have washed it in the shower.

'There's toast on,' Daphne says – and as if it heard her, up it pops. Una takes it out without comment and clicks the kettle on, yawning. She opens the fridge, finds the peanut butter.

Seventeen today, her birthday tainted now by association:

hardly surprising that she shows little enthusiasm for it. Both
their birthdays ruined from now on, Una's because of his death,
Daphne's because of her wedding on the day she turned thirty-
two, and the heartless anniversaries that will keep coming
around now without him, reappearing every so often like a
painted grinning horse on a carousel, forever reminding her of
her loss.

Una spoons instant coffee into a mug. Never touched coffee
until Finn died: now she starts each day with it, presumably
because he did too. As she takes her seat Daphne notes her
lightly flushed face, the puffy skin around her eyes. Crying for
him, like Daphne had cried earlier. Instinctively she reaches for
the girl's hand — but Una moves it smoothly towards the milk
jug before contact is made, leaving Daphne feeling hurt and
foolish. *She's a child; let it go.*

She indicates instead the package on the table by Una's plate.
'I got you something small. I have the receipt if you want to
change it.'

Bought a few days earlier in a little boutique near the estate
agency, the amount on the price tag not that small, but worth it
if Una likes it. Of course it might never be worn or exchanged,
its non-appearance serving as another unspoken rejection.

Una glances at the package, wrapped in yellow paper.
'Thanks,' she says, making no move to open it. She twists the
lid off the peanut butter, dips in her knife and slathers a glob of
it onto the toast. Only a year and a bit away from her Leaving
Cert, noncommittal about future plans. Showing some artistic
flair certainly, but seeming uninterested in taking it further.

Have you thought about college? Daphne asked her a few months ago. *Any idea what you want to do when you leave school?* But Una just shrugged and said she hadn't decided, and Daphne backed off and hasn't brought it up since.

What has happened to them? It's like they've gone back to the bad old days when they were first introduced to one another, a month or so after Daphne met Finn. Una was twelve: Daphne could sense her wariness, and it made her apprehensive in turn. If she and Finn ended up together – and already he was becoming frighteningly important to her – how would she cope? She knew nothing at all about twelve-year-old girls, least of all how to be a mother, or stepmother, to one of them.

But when she eventually confided her fears to Finn, shortly after he'd proposed and she'd accepted, he brushed them aside. *It's been just the two of us for a long time*, he said. *She's got used to it, that's all. She'll come round, wait and see. She's had it tough, her mum dying when she was so young, and then the bombshell I had to drop when she was old enough. Poor kid, she's been through a lot.*

So they married – and like Finn had promised, Una eventually accepted Daphne's presence in their lives, and things were fine, if not always perfect. They were never like a real mother and daughter, that would have been too much to expect – but Daphne did the best she could, and it seemed to be enough.

To her relief, she wasn't called on to teach the facts of life; when she forced herself, after weeks of procrastination, to bring up the subject, Una immediately headed her off, telling her they'd learnt it in school – but Daphne provided sanitary towels when the need arose, she brought Una shopping for her first bra, she persuaded Finn to allow a mobile phone when the girl was begging him for it.

Of course it went without saying that Una had a stronger bond with Finn than with Daphne – but she and Daphne were friends, weren't they? Connected through Finn, united by their mutual attachment to him, but friends too in their own right. They had plenty of good times, the three of them.

And then Finn had died, and Una retreated to her room, emerging only when bullied downstairs at mealtimes by Mo in those first few days. After Mo packed up and went home, Daphne forced herself to keep up the routine and put some kind of a dinner on the table each evening. She and her stepdaughter sat silently across from one another, shell-shocked with misery, bereft without him, and totally unable to communicate their heartbreak to one another.

And in the year since his death, not a lot has changed. A trembling kind of harmony has settled between them, but they may as well be fellow patients in a doctor's waiting room for all the intimacies or confidences they exchange these days.

Daphne does her best, attends the parent-teacher meetings, gives pocket money on Friday, feeds and clothes this child, this almost-woman who's ended up in her care, but beneath their polite, meaningless interaction the cold, ugly truth exists: they didn't choose one another. Their only connection was through Finn, and now he's gone. And while Daphne does feel a fondness for Una – how could she not have grown attached to the girl who played such an important part in Finn's life? – she feels unable to demonstrate that fondness in the face of Una's nonchalance.

She knows virtually nothing about Una's life. Friends who would have called to the house in the past – Ciara, Jennifer,

Emma – haven't appeared since Finn died. Una has dinner in one or other of their houses at least once a week, but she keeps turning down Daphne's offers to feed them in return. There's no sign of a boyfriend either, which is not to say he doesn't exist.

The two of them need to talk, that's what they need to do. They need to sit down some evening and really talk, really open up to one another, break down whatever wall has grown up between them – but Daphne simply can't bring herself to broach the subject. She's afraid of the rejection her approach might well be greeted with, afraid of being hurt any more.

So she never ventures far, never takes it beyond where she feels safe. 'You OK?' she asks now, because Una cried alone upstairs this morning, and because it's her birthday.

'Yeah.'

A short silence falls, broken only by the muted tick of the clock above the sink, and the tiny sound of Una chewing and swallowing.

'Today will be tough,' Daphne dares to say eventually. 'Try not to dwell too much on it.'

Something she can't define – an uncertainty, a mild alarm – flits across the girl's face. 'I'll be fine,' she replies shortly, thrusting her chair back as she gets to her feet, the movement making Daphne feel like she's the one who's being pushed away.

'You haven't finished.' Barely half a slice of toast gone, her coffee mug still three-quarters full.

'I'm not hungry.'

'You forgot your present.'

Una scoops up the package wordlessly. At least she's taken it. School shoes thump on the stairs. Daphne stands and begins to clear the table. Twenty-five to nine, nearly time they were going anyway.

◆

They never mention it, there's never a comment. Every morning she drives past the spot where his life came to an end – not fifty yards from the house, seconds away from her – and neither of them remarks on it.

But every morning Daphne feels the horror of it. Every single time they pass Buckley's – there, just there – she's thrown back to that awful day. The images that have seared themselves into her head insist on flipping one after another into view, like a series of playing cards flashed for an instant before a magician's rapt audience.

Annie and Hugh Moloney's stunned expressions when she opened the door to them, apron still on, her smile fading as Hugh began to speak—

The buckled wheels, the cracked handlebars of the unfamiliar lavender-coloured bicycle propped against Buckley's wall, a curl of matching mudguard lying nearby—

The bald circle in the bowed head of the bin-lorry driver, who sat on the edge of the path, the slop and wobble of the tea in the red mug that was clamped between his hands—

The clutches of neighbours on the road, elbows nudging, heads swivelling at her approach, the muffled gasps of someone's sobs—

Finn's tan shoe poking from the grey blanket someone had

covered him with, his half-open, unseeing eyes when she pulled the blanket away to look at him, the bright crimson patch he left behind on the road when they lifted him onto the stretcher—

Mo's blank face in the morgue, Finn stretched out between them on a slab; a slight shifting of her jaw, a small twitch of her mouth, no more, when the attendant lifted the sheet so she could look down at her son's dead face—

'Thanks for the present.'

The memories scatter. Daphne glances at Una. 'What?'

'The top, it's nice.'

'Really, you like it? Because I have the receipt if you want—'

'No, it's fine. I do like it.'

'It fits OK? I wasn't sure whether to get ten or—'

'Ten is fine.'

'That's good. I'm glad you like it.'

She flicks on the indicator, makes a turn. *Enough*, she thinks. *Enough sadness.* She's so tired of sadness; she's exhausted from it snatching the joy away, day after day after day. When will it stop?

They pass the corner shop that sells the Macaroon bars Mo likes.

'I told you Mo is coming to dinner tonight, didn't I? She didn't want to miss your birthday.'

'Yeah, you told me.'

Mo would probably have been just fine about missing Una's birthday but they'll paint on smiles for her, try to make the day less awful than it is. Even if the girl doesn't feel like celebrating – which of course she doesn't – they have to mark it; they can't ignore it.

'What are you doing after school? Any plans?'

'… Not sure yet.'

'Well, don't be late, OK? I told Mo dinner at eight.'

'OK.'

She thinks of the chocolate cake she ordered from a bakery that opened just a few months ago. It looked busy anytime she passed; she figured that had to be a good sign, so she called in on Monday and told them she wanted a chocolate cake for Friday. *Happy Birthday Una*, it'll say, in gold script on treacle-coloured icing.

She was in the middle of baking Una's cake last year when Annie and Hugh rang the doorbell. She remembers the abandoned bowl of mix still sitting on the table in the kitchen when they finally got home from Mo's house, not long before midnight. The place littered with eggshells and scattered chocolate drops and torn butter paper, a pale dusting of flour and cocoa over everything.

She remembers sitting in the middle of the mess, still frozen with shock, her mind refusing to take in what had happened, as her father and George cleaned up. She recalls the wash of their conversation – not the words, she has no idea what the words were – as they tried unsuccessfully to drown out the wails of Una's grief from the room above.

The price they quoted her for the cake in the new bakery was astronomical but she paid up, grateful to have someone else, anyone else, making it this year. She'll collect it on the way home from work.

They reach the school. She pulls up and takes out the ten-euro note that's been sitting in her pocket. 'Here,' she says, 'in case you go someplace after school.'

Una looks at the money.

'Take it,' Daphne urges, pressing it into her hand. 'Go on. Treat yourself to … ice-cream, or something.'

Ice-cream, on a day as cold as this. Ice-cream, as if she's seven instead of seventeen.

But Una takes it, not meeting Daphne's eye as she stows it away. 'Thanks,' she says, getting out, slinging her rucksack across a shoulder. 'See you later,' she says, pushing the door closed and turning to merge into the groups of teenagers making their way to the big iron gates.

Daphne watches her walk off. Poor lost creature, everyone abandoning her until she's finally left with someone who can hardly look after herself, let alone anyone else. A stepmother is all the family she has now, apart from a pair of grandparents who barely acknowledge her existence, and an acquired other grandmother not exactly given to displays of affection.

When the head of gold curls has vanished from view Daphne pulls out into the line of cars and makes her way to work. Traffic is heavy, like it is every Friday. Next week the roads will be quieter, schools closed for Easter and the children still in bed.

She parks her car in the little yard behind the office. As she takes out her briefcase she becomes aware of a distant droning noise. She looks up and sees a small plane crossing the sky, trailing a white banner that reads *Congratulations Charlotte and Brian* in dark lettering.

A wedding, more than likely. She watches it crossing the sky, imagines Charlotte, whoever she is, looking up too and clapping with delight. About to marry Brian, already getting into the dress, or having her hair done. The future stretching ahead of them, all the possibilities yet to come.

Inevitably, her own wedding day slides into her head, less than four years ago. Her birthday making it even more special, her happiness almost tangible for the entire day, so gorgeously real it felt. Everything splashed with it, every minute drenched in happy.

She recalls waking early that morning, lying in bed thinking, *This is the last time I wake up as Daphne Carroll: tomorrow morning I'll be Daphne Darling.* Such a perfect name, like something out of a book, a name for a heroine. Daphne Darling, fearless righter of wrongs, blazer of trails.

She remembers the sausages her father fried for them – *We can't be walking up that aisle on an empty stomach* – and the knee-length cream dress she wore. Not exactly bridal, nothing fancy about it at all really, but catching her eye on the rail in a little boutique a few weeks before, when she hardly knew what she was looking for. Tiny orange and pink embroidered flowers scattered willy-nilly through the outer layer of cream net. Pink sandals on her feet, a posy of orange and red daisies, not quite matching the ones on the dress but the closest she could find.

She thinks of her mother and Alex meeting them in the church porch before the ceremony, the awkward, terribly polite little conversation the four of them had. She remembers her relief when the organ struck up in the church, their signal for things to get moving. The slow walk up the aisle beside her father, her throat unexpectedly tight, her legs trembling a little. Finn waiting for her at the—

No, too painful. She locks the car and makes her way inside.

❖

Mr Donnelly doesn't remember the significance of today – or if he does, he gives no sign.

'This came in yesterday,' he says, sliding a page across his desk. 'You might check it out this afternoon.'

His office smells as it always does of the clove-drop sweets he loves. Bags of them he goes through, always an open one sitting by his phone. 'Bridestone Avenue,' he says, 'small little cul-de-sac somewhere behind the maternity hospital, as far as I can gather. Owner will give you proper directions.'

At Finn's funeral he had shaken her hand along with all the other mourners, squeezed her fingers painfully as he told her how sorry he was. His wife Barbara's eyes were red-rimmed. *I couldn't believe it when I heard*, she'd whispered, leaning in to press a hot cheek against Daphne's, bringing with her a faint waft of something chemical – TCP? Dettol? – but since she'd barely known Finn, and had never come across as particularly soft-hearted, Daphne had been inclined to put the red eyes down to hay fever.

'Tea?' she asks now, because she needs to give herself something else to think about, and because there's no reason why he should remember the anniversary, however raw and fresh and painful it is for her. 'I'm making a cup.'

'Lovely,' he replies, and she goes into the tiny kitchenette and fills the kettle, and dries the few mugs on the draining board while she waits for the water to boil. Busy, that's what she needs to be today. Busy following up on offers and keeping an eye on ongoing contracts and making sure her paperwork is up to date before the weekend.

Good that a new house has come in: give her something to fill up the afternoon. She likes checking out new properties, being the first to assess them, measuring and recording and giving them a thorough going over.

When the tea is made she adds a Hobnob to Mr Donnelly's saucer and delivers it to his office. Barbara wouldn't approve, always has him on some diet or other – and definitely wouldn't be impressed if she knew how many clove drops he puts away – but he enjoys a Hobnob, and life is too short.

At her desk she dials the number he gave her and listens to the soft, rhythmic burrs. The other two desks in the front office are unoccupied this morning, William and Joanna out and about. People buying and selling again, thank goodness, the market beginning to pick up at last after a few anxious years when they'd been forced to do three- and four-day weeks in rotation to keep Mr Donnelly from having to let any of them go.

The ringing stops with a click. She waits, glances down at the name on the page before her.

'Yes.' The word isn't a question. The voice is deep.

'Tom Wallace?'

'Yes.' Precisely the same measured tone.

'I'm Daphne from Donnelly and Co. You were in touch about putting a house up for sale with us.'

'Ah, yes.'

In the beat that follows she watches the steam curling slowly upwards from her cup. Finn always drank his tea black, wasn't a fan of dairy; she'd cut out her beloved blue cheese because he couldn't stomach the smell. Some weeks after he died she threw a wedge into her shopping trolley, trying to coax her appetite back to life, but the first taste, bringing with it the reminder that he could never again object to it, made her double up in anguish. She hasn't bought it since.

'Hello?'

She pulls herself back. 'Sorry – I'm ringing to arrange an appointment for a valuation. Would you be around this afternoon? I could—'

'Four o'clock would suit me.'

Later than she was going to suggest – she won't be finished before five now. Should still be OK, though: cemetery doesn't close till six, and dinner isn't until eight. Time enough.

'Four is fine,' she says. 'See you then. I think Bridestone Avenue is between—'

But he's gone, the deep voice replaced by the gentle rumble of a vacant line, leaving her to locate him and his house without his help. Man of few words.

As she hangs up, her mobile phone beeps in her desk drawer. She takes it out and sees George's name.

Thinking of you today, will call you later x

George, the closest thing she has to a real brother. Taking time out from his precious break – his ten minutes of sanity, he calls it – to let her know he hasn't forgotten. George, who arrived with a bottle of gin and strawberry ice-cream when he heard about Finn, who stayed with them through most of that first endless night, who helped her father to field phone calls and visitors the next day while Daphne lay woozy from Valium in her darkened bedroom, floating horribly between wakefulness and sleep, Finn's death slamming into her with every return to consciousness, flooring her again and again.

George, who had remembered what day it was.

Thank you, she types, adding an *x*. She'd invited him to Una's dinner, but there's some end-of-term thing on at his school tonight. Pity: he'd have livened up the evening a bit, and he and Una get on well enough.

She slides her phone back into the drawer, thinking, as she still so often does, of Finn's last voice message to her. *Am I forgiven? Hope so, see you later.*

Sent mid-afternoon on the day he died: she heard the phone ringing but ignored it, busy in the middle of a conversation with a couple of house-hunters. When she got a chance she listened to his message, was about to call him back when she was diverted by another call, and by the time she'd hung up it had slipped her mind.

She didn't think of him again until she was back home, and in the middle of baking Una's cake. She wiped her hands and called his number, but got only his voicemail. Glancing at the clock, she thought, *He's on the way home*, and hung up without leaving a message.

And before she'd had a chance to get back to the cake, the doorbell had rung.

In the nightmare days that had followed his death she replayed his message incessantly, pressing the phone to her ear, drinking in the last eight precious words he'd addressed to her, inhaling them through every pore. When the message was automatically deleted a week later she was flooded with fresh grief, as if he'd died all over again.

And to add to her anguish, there had been no baby.

I can't, he told her before they got married. She'd known Una wasn't his from the start; he'd never made a secret of that. *I've been reliably informed*, he said, *that I'll never be able to father a child* – and devastating as this news was, Daphne had gone ahead and married him anyway, because by then the idea of life without him was unthinkable. She'd put aside her yearning for a child because she loved him too much to be able to give him up.

She lifts her cup and drinks tea, and gets on with the day.

❧

At one o'clock precisely she hears the beep of a car horn outside: punctual as ever.

'Your chauffeur's here,' Joanna says, fingers continuing to fly across her laptop keyboard. Joanna joined the company a few months before the downturn, replacing Don who had retired. Late thirties, divorced and childless, with the bone structure to carry off her severely cropped marmalade-coloured hair, a tiny star tattooed inside her left ankle, and a younger boyfriend with some high-up job in Google, Joanna has a master's in marketing and an Italian grandmother, and happens to be very good at selling houses.

'See you later,' she says, as Daphne pulls on her jacket. No mention of the anniversary from her either: forgotten it, or decided to avoid it.

'Well,' Daphne's father says, sliding back into the traffic as she buckles her seat belt, 'you doing OK?'

'I am, not too bad.'

'We'll go home, yes?'

'Yes, please.'

He doesn't always bring her to his house when they meet

for lunch. Sometimes he parks the car and they walk down the street to Minihan's for a pot of tea and a baked potato. If the weather is good they might get a sandwich at the deli and take it to the nearby park. But today home sounds good: she's happy for the two of them to spend lunchtime in the house where she grew up, a five-minute drive from the estate agency.

He feeds her a soft poached egg sitting on a warm crumpet, their mutual comfort food of choice for years, and tells her about a woman he's teaching to drive who refuses to touch the gear stick or steering wheel before cleaning them both enthusiastically with a tissue soaked in some kind of antiseptic.

'Car smells like a hospital after her,' he says. 'I've tried spraying air freshener, but it hangs around for the rest of the day. Brings one of those wedge things too, to sit on. Says her chiropractor told her to get one.'

He's been a driving instructor all his life: it was how he and Daphne's mother, Isobel, had met. Taught her to drive when she was twenty-one, married her before her twenty-third birthday. Had his heart broken by her when she walked away from him eight years later, leaving six-year-old Daphne behind with him, deserting her daughter along with her husband.

'I'm going to value a house this afternoon,' Daphne tells him, dipping crumpet into the oozing egg yolk. 'Bridestone Avenue – you know it?'

Isobel had run off with Con Pierce, who had drilled and filled the teeth of Daphne's parents for several years until Isobel decided she preferred him to her husband. Mr Pierce the dentist, who'd visited Daphne's junior-infant classroom once to tell them about his job, who'd used a giant toothbrush and a big doll with enormous teeth and a head that flipped apart so he could show the class how to brush properly.

The runaways didn't last: before the year was out the dentist was reunited with his wife and children, back living in the house he still occupies today, separated by just three streets from Daphne and her father. Within a month or two of his return he was once again gainfully employed in a new dental practice, the scandal of the past ostensibly forgotten by him, or at any rate folded up and tucked into some little-used part of his mind, like a pair of deckchairs leaning all winter against a lawnmower in a corner of a shed.

For several months and years he was ashamed enough – or possibly cowardly enough – to cross the road if he spotted Daphne or her father approaching, but eventually this practice was put aside. Now he gives a noncommittal nod whenever their paths cross – and while she suspects her father might be more forgiving, Daphne has perfected the art of pretending not to see him. Why should she acknowledge him after the part he played in breaking up her parents' marriage? How dare he assume she'd want to interact in any way with him.

After the eggs are gone her father makes coffee.

'Pity you can't come to dinner,' she says, spooning in sugar. He's busy with lessons till nine, the brighter evenings extending his working day. 'Do drop in on your way home for cake.'

'I will,' he promises, and she knows he'll bring a present for Una. Doing the right thing like he always does, even if Una will hardly notice him there, even if she couldn't care less whether he appears or not.

Doing the right thing when his wife walked out all those

years ago, careful to say nothing to Daphne that might poison her mind against her mother. Never confronting Con Pierce on his return to the neighbourhood – never once entertaining the possibility, Daphne bet, of punching the face of the man who had stolen his wife.

Doing the right thing all his life, except when he married a woman who subsequently showed herself well capable of doing the wrong thing.

Isobel didn't come back when she and her fancy man parted company. She didn't come back but she made contact, a week or so after word of the dentist's return had reached Daphne and her father. There was a phone call one evening – he went downstairs to answer it in the middle of the bedtime story – and sometime after that there was an encounter that included Daphne, still aged six, wearing a green and white striped knitted dress. How does she recall it so clearly? She can see the white Peter Pan collar, the belt tied into a bow, the scalloped edge of its hem.

The meeting took place at a café in a newly constructed shopping centre on the far side of the city, almost four months after they had last laid eyes on Isobel. Apart from the dress, Daphne's memory of the occasion is haphazard. Did she and her mother embrace on coming face to face? Did Isobel reach down to hug her? That part is blank.

What she does remember from that day are incidentals: Isobel's over-bright smile whenever she caught Daphne's eye across the café table; the squiggle of shiny white icing across the top of the apple Danish that sat virtually untouched on a plate beside her father's mug the entire time; the wonderful softness of the unfamiliar rose-pink scarf draped across the seat of the vacant chair next to her mother, when Daphne reached a furtive hand across to stroke it; the warm fuzziness of the tea-scented air; the rise and fall of neighbouring conversations; the muted clink of cutlery; the splatter of occasional laughter.

Nothing threatening, nothing unnatural – and yet her abiding sense of that day, whenever she thinks of it now, is overlaid with a fingernail-along-a-blackboard shiver of anxiety. Her childish subconscious maybe, picking up on the tension that caused her father's nearside foot to jiggle ceaselessly during the half-hour or so that the three of them spent together.

She has no memory of what was discussed, just a faded impression of her parents' lowered voices going to and fro above her head as she licked sugar from her fingers and pulled apart the jam doughnut she'd been presented with – but from then on there was a weekly phone call to Daphne, and an afternoon spent with her mother on alternate Saturdays, just the two of them, in the town twenty miles down the motorway where Isobel now lived.

The running order of these encounters never varied. A walk to begin with, weather permitting, around the shops on the town's main street, during which a new hairband or book or toy would be purchased for Daphne: the rainy-day alternative to this was half an hour in the town's library, with her mother reading aloud to Daphne from various picture books, and using considerably less animation than Daphne's father. A visit to the cinema came next, to see whatever children's offering was showing, followed by a meal in the café at the bottom of the street.

Daphne found the fortnightly episodes challenging. Her

initial loneliness and longing for the woman who had vanished abruptly from her life had long since morphed into a baffled wariness, and being thrown back into contact with her, without the reassuring familiar presence of her father, filled her with unease.

Sitting in the darkened, too-loud cinema only increased her edginess – afterwards she could hardly recall the title of what they'd seen, let alone the plot – and her normally enthusiastic appetite would be nowhere in evidence when whatever dish she'd ordered in the café was placed in front of her.

As far as she can recall, her mother gave no sign of being put out by Daphne's lack of enthusiasm on these occasions; on the contrary, she seemed hardly to notice when her questions were met with monosyllabic replies. *So what have you been up to at school?* she would ask, and Daphne would scrabble around frantically for something to offer in response as her mother peered into a small mirror and dabbed with a napkin at the corners of her mouth, or thumbed a bright red crescent from the rim of her teacup, face turned towards the half-curtained café window.

There was never a suggestion of visiting Isobel's home, wherever it was: the meeting point was always under a shop awning in the town's square. Daphne never discovered – and neither, she assumed, did her father – what kind of living arrangements or lifestyle her mother enjoyed at that time. Similarly, the past was never mentioned: their conversations, such as they were, never travelled further back than the previous week, and largely involved Isobel asking questions and Daphne doing her best to answer them.

Her father invariably turned up to bring her home at precisely the time he had promised, and the sight of him standing at the café door, signalling the end of her ordeal, was always wonderfully welcome. To her enormous relief he never enquired about the afternoon as they travelled back to the city, but would usually suggest stopping on the way to feed the ducks at their local park – paper bag of bread already stowed in the glove compartment – or making a detour to the airport to watch the planes taking off and landing, something Daphne never tired of.

Her father was her constant. He had always been there, before and after Isobel's departure. Reading her a story, or three, before she went to sleep, dabbing cream on a grazed elbow or knee, kissing better a bump on her temple. Singing her awake in the mornings with his improvised version of 'Thank Heaven For Little Girls' – for years she thought the real words were *Thank Heaven for Daphne Carroll* – bringing her to the doctor and the dentist when the need arose.

There were others occasionally – Nana Carroll, Granny and Grandpa Kingston. They'd call with new clothes or shoes, or a doll in a box. They'd talk in mumbles with her father and raise their voices to enquire of Daphne how she was getting on in school, and if she liked her teacher, and who her friends were. And there was Jane, who minded her in the afternoons till Dad collected her. But she was happiest when it was just the two of them.

The fortnightly mother-daughter sessions eventually came to a stop. There was no revolt, no argument that signalled the end of their encounters, nothing as dramatic or final as that. It was more a gradual drawing back on Daphne's part, a cancellation now and again when a birthday party, or a holiday, or an illness prevented their meeting. Every other Saturday slid into once a month, and slowly became even more fluid – until seventeen-year-old Daphne realised one day that she hadn't come face to face with her mother in several weeks.

But the phone call survived, every Friday evening around eight or nine, and is still happening. They take it in turns to call one another now, and their conversations rarely last longer than ten minutes.

They meet occasionally for lunch too, always at Isobel's invitation, which Daphne feels duty-bound to accept. The awkwardness of these infrequent encounters, the unacknowledged tension that hovers like an over-attentive waiter, brings Daphne back to the every-other-Saturday ordeals of her childhood – except that these days she's rescued by work rather than her father.

It was at one of their lunches that Isobel revealed she was getting married again.

Alex, she said. *He's a lawyer, you'll like him* – and two things occurred simultaneously to twenty-six-year-old Daphne: she wondered what her father would say when he heard the news, and she marvelled that her mother could find two husbands, when she herself had yet to find one.

In the event, her father heard the news with equanimity. *Let's hope she's happy this time*, he said, and not for the first time Daphne wanted to shake him, wanted to hear him rage, and curse the woman who'd thrown him away, thrown both of them away, so easily.

It was to be another five years before Daphne met the man

she would marry, but she was introduced to her mother's fiancé just a few weeks after Isobel's revelation. Over the course of the lunch they shared she found Alex to be polite and well-spoken, and quite distant: before their coffees arrived she had come to the conclusion that he was as uninterested in her as she was in him, which didn't upset her in the least.

Isobel's second marriage took place, and she moved back to the city to live with Alex and his son, but apart from the fact that they now live closer to one another, relations have remained unaltered between her and Daphne.

Still the stiff little phone calls each week, still the less-frequent lunch dates. They discuss Isobel's part-time job and Daphne's full-time one, and Daphne enquires about Alex, and Isobel asks how Una is doing, and if Daphne has replaced the boiler yet.

They fill the time with talk, but there remains so much more unsaid between them.

After lunch her father drops her back to the office. Getting out of the car, she holds her jacket closed against the sharp-edged breeze that has begun to whip up. April can't be trusted: yesterday she was opening windows when she got home from work, and shaking out rugs in the sunshine. She checks the sky and sees a bank of dark grey clouds advancing. Rain on the way, by the look of it.

In the office Joanna is shrugging on her coat. 'I've got appointments all afternoon,' she says, slinging her bag over her shoulder. 'Have a good weekend, see you Monday.'

Mr Donnelly's door is closed, which means he's out of the

office. There's no sign of William, who handles their out-of-town business, and who might be missing in action for days at a time. With Joanna's departure, Daphne is left alone. She removes her jacket and sits at her desk, and watches the people passing by on the street outside.

She remembers how disconnected from everyone else she'd felt in the months after Finn's death, how locked away with her pain that it seemed like she'd stepped off some kind of conveyor belt and left everyone else to carry on without her. Grief made an alien of her: she would overhear a burst of laughter and literally wonder what the sound was. She'd see someone smile and it would hold no significance, none at all. Was she ever to feel happiness again, or take pleasure in anything?

And during those first few dreadful months, she'd been useless at work. She'd gone through the motions, unable to summon up enthusiasm when showing properties, often forgetting to return calls or follow up on possible sales. On one occasion she'd actually burst into tears in the middle of a house-viewing with a newly-wed couple who were clearly mad about one another. Poor Mr Donnelly must surely have felt tempted for a while to pay her off, give her anything just to go away – but thankfully he'd stuck it out.

It will get easier, she'd told herself, and it has. Hasn't it?

At half past three she closes her diary, switches off her computer, gives half a glass of water to the pink-leafed begonia George presented her with at Christmas. She checks her bag for a pen, and the glasses she's begun to need for small print.

About to leave, she picks up the silver-framed photo of Finn that she'd taken a fortnight before he died. She holds it close to her face, looks at the features she knew so well. Cheeks flushed and shining from what would turn out to be his last long bike ride. Pale brown hair pushed off his forehead a few seconds before, a gesture she had witnessed him making a thousand times.

The startling navy eyes, the first physical thing she noticed about him, despite her distress on the day they met. His father's eyes, he told her, when she commented on them a few weeks later. Mo's eyes are blue too, but much paler – the only facial feature she passed on to him was her longish nose.

Finn is smiling in the picture: bike rides did that to him. He wasn't a natural driver, jerky and ill at ease behind the wheel of his cumbersome grey Volvo, happier by far when he was whizzing along on two wheels. Daphne worried about him when he drove, never envisaging the horrible irony of his losing his life on a bicycle.

After he died she got her father to take away the Volvo, unable to bear the sight of it in the driveway. *Do what you want with it*, she told him. *Just get it out of here.* Finn's blue bicycle she left in the shop, together with all the new ones: unable to part with it, but too sad to contemplate seeing it without him.

Would it have made any difference if he'd cycled home on it that day? They'll never know. The inquest report was ambiguous, the bin-lorry driver's assertion that Finn had swerved into the path of his vehicle to avoid a cat unable to be corroborated or ruled out. Accidental death, the chairperson of the jury called it. Nobody wanting him dead, but he'd died all the same.

She sets down the photo and gathers her things together.

She locks up and walks down the alleyway to the yard where her red Beetle is parked and deposits her briefcase in the boot. Bridestone Avenue, according to her father – as good as Google Maps with all his driving – is located some two miles away, between the maternity hospital and the river. *You'd be better off leaving the car in Larkin Crescent, just off Bridestone*, he told her. *As far as I remember, Bridestone is pretty narrow; parking could be tricky*.

The streets are as busy as they were that morning, people already on the move for the weekend. Halfway to her destination Daphne realises she's forgotten the first name of the man she's going to meet. Something short, one syllable – Pat? Tim? John? As she turns onto Larkin Crescent, *Tom Wallace* pops abruptly into her head.

She drives slowly past neat houses, spots a small road off to the left. No cul-de-sac sign, but that must be it. She parks a little way beyond the turn and takes her briefcase from the back seat. Three minutes to four: she could hardly be more punctual.

She turns onto the narrow little road. Above her the sky is dark and heavy with cloud: rain on the way for sure. She remembers her umbrella, still presumably sitting in the boot of the car where she usually keeps it. She's definitely not thinking straight today. No matter: the owner will be there to meet her. They always are.

❖

He's not there.

After her third press of the bell goes unanswered, she leans her briefcase against the door and walks up and down the short cement path, rubbing her hands together. She should have worn her coat this morning. The wind is picking up; she can almost smell the rain. She debates going back to the car for her umbrella, and decides to chance it. He won't be long.

The minutes tick on. By a quarter past four she's had a good look around the outside. There's no back garden to speak of, just a metre-wide paved pathway between the house and a beautiful shoulder-high old stone wall that runs along the rear of the property.

A fairly well-tended shrubbery sits off to the side of the house: a young budding clematis making its way up the wall, a pair of dwarf apple trees covered with blossom, a bay and a lavender and what looks like a fuchsia, hard to tell with no flower coming yet. One or two other plants she can't identify, a few clutches of bluebells nestling under a graceful Japanese maple tree at the far end.

A small garage lies to the right of the property, a new-looking padlock on the door.

Twenty past four – where is he? At this rate it'll be well after five by the time she finishes: all she needs today, to be up against the clock. She'll ring him, tell him she's in a rush. Should have done it sooner.

She scrolls through her phone contacts, but there's no sign of him. No, that can't be – she always adds new clients to her phone as soon as they come in, keeps them there for as long as she needs to. She scrolls again, but he's definitely not there. Had she been so distracted by the anniversary that she'd forgotten to put him in?

Evidently she had – but surely she has the page Mr Donnelly

gave her with his number on it. She searches her bag but there's no sign of it either: great.

She calls the office – maybe he's rung to cancel. *One new message*, the answering machine tells her, *sent at three thirty-seven*. A few minutes after she left – must be him.

It is. *This is Tom Wallace for Daphne*, he says in the deep voice she remembers. *We have an appointment at four. I'm afraid I've been delayed, but I'll be there as soon as I can.*

As soon as he can, whenever that'll be. She'll give him another few minutes and then she'll go, drop into the office for his number after she's been to the cemetery, make a new appointment. Not the end of the world.

To distract herself she has another walk around. The house is built on an oddly shaped plot, roughly a quarter-acre in size, the daisy-speckled lawn petering almost to a point at one end where the front garden wall meets a straggled hedge. There's a tiny weather-beaten wooden shed tucked as far as possible into this narrow corner.

The shed door is unlocked but thoroughly stuck – anyone's guess when it was opened last. Through the little cobwebby window she makes out a hedge clippers and a rusting watering can dangling from hooks, a jumble of battered paint tins and a dented wheelbarrow into which has been piled a ramshackle heap of dust-covered bottles. Stacks of newspapers lean against the end wall, next to tottering towers of plastic plant pots. Has he never heard of recycling?

She turns and regards the house again. The front of it is pebble-dashed, with what looks like a relatively new red-tiled roof and three big windows, two of them bay, all shielded with heavily embossed net curtains that don't allow a look inside. The wooden front door has been painted dark blue, with a quartet of stained-glass panes set into the top third.

Around the back the windows are similarly veiled in net, giving her no clue as to the rooms within. The rear door is white uPVC with frosted-glass insets; she can make out shadowy shapes beyond them but no more.

She walks to the little wooden gate and looks out. The cul-de-sac is quiet, no sign or sound of life from the dozen or so houses that make it up, the residents presumably out at work. A couple of cars are parked in driveways, a few others pulled up close to garden walls.

She feels a wet splotch on her cheek, and then another: just what she needs. She heads back to the house and presses up against the front wall, but it provides next to no shelter. The drops quickly turn into a proper shower. Her jacket becomes patched with damp, and within a minute water is dripping from the ends of her hair.

This is ridiculous: she's waited long enough. She picks up her briefcase and is about to stride down the path when she hears a car turning into the cul-de-sac. Horrible timing — another half-minute and she would have been gone. Now she'll be watching the clock to finish, but she can hardly tell him to get lost.

She watches the car approach, waits while it pulls in close to the garden wall. Let's see what he has to say for himself.

'Sorry, I'm so sorry.' He scrambles out and slams the door. 'I called your work but I only got a machine, I'm really sorry, something came up.' He pushes open the gate and strides towards her, hand extended. 'Tom Wallace, you must be Daphne.'

Dark hair, grey suit, half a foot taller than her. A not-unpleasant waft of something woody as he approaches. She summons as much of a smile as she can and shakes his hand: much warmer than hers. Of course it is – sitting in his heated car while she stood shivering on his doorstep.

'God, you're frozen.' He stabs a key into the front-door lock. 'Come inside – I'm afraid there's no heat, but at least you'll be out of the elements.'

No heat: this afternoon is getting better. She follows him over the threshold and into a short, narrow hallway that smells strongly of tobacco.

'Hang on,' he says, vanishing around a corner. She takes in the awful flock wallpaper, the wide old wooden floorboards, the pine doors leading off to her left and right. The air is frigid with cold, no sign of a radiator – who has a house without central heating these days?

She presses a light switch, but the bulb suspended above her within its dusty fringed shade doesn't react. The tobacco smell is overpowering: he must smoke like a chimney. She'll have to do something about that if prospective buyers aren't to be put off right from the start.

The tips of her fingers are numb. Her wet hair clings unpleasantly to her head. Her trousers are stuck to her thighs. The last thing she feels like doing is going through this drab little house trying to find good things to say about it.

'Here.' He's back, passing her a blue towel, thin and hard. 'All I could find, I'm afraid, but at least it's dry.'

She takes it from him without a word, presses it to her face, gives her hair a brisk rub. Without a comb she must look a show, but he's hardly in a position to complain.

'So,' he says, 'how do you want us to do this?'

She hands him back the towel and clicks open her briefcase. She pulls out her tape measure and notebook. 'I can handle it,' she says crisply. 'I'll ask if I need any information.'

He nods, lips pressed together; she gets the impression he's trying not to smile. Has she said something amusing? Does he think it's funny that she's wet and cold because of him?

'Fine,' he says. 'I'll keep out of your way, then.'

Left alone, she opens her notebook, clamping her teeth together to stop them chattering. A miracle if she doesn't end up with pneumonia after this. She thinks longingly of a cup of tea – anything hot to wrap her hands around – but it looks like she'll have to do without it. He probably doesn't possess a kettle.

She begins to measure the hallway. This will be the fastest valuation in history.

●

It takes her just under an hour.

Very quickly she realises that the bungalow is in fact quite saleable, despite her negative first impression. Apart from a smallish dark stain at the bottom of one bedroom wall – which experience tells her probably isn't anything major – the place seems structurally sound. It's also quite well laid out, with two good-sized bedrooms, a bathroom between them that will have to be described as compact, a surprisingly light-filled kitchen that stretches the width of the house – undoubtedly one of its main selling points – and a small sitting room with a fireplace that she imagines would be cosy if anyone bothered to light a fire.

The décor is appalling – he has no clue – but that's easily fixed. The ancient wallpaper could be steamed off and replaced with paint, the flowery curtains binned, with their net partners, the old wooden floors sanded and varnished – they could be beautiful – and the furniture that looks like it's been there since the Flood consigned to a skip. And all of that would help to banish the cigarette smell that seems to have seeped into every pore of the place.

The house is pretty much empty of ornamentation. No table lamps anywhere, no vases, no knick-knacks, the sitting-room mantelpiece bare apart from a stilled dusty carriage clock. Little on the walls too – a few framed photos in the kitchen featuring various combinations of the same four people: the owner himself, a young woman with dark bobbed hair, a little brown-haired boy, two or three years old, and a frail-looking elderly man.

There's a picture of the Sacred Heart in the sitting room, complete with red lamp beneath – amazingly, still lit – and a Constable print in the larger of the two bedrooms, above a double bed whose mattress is covered only with a salmon-pink candlewick spread. No pillows, no sheets.

Clearly, he doesn't live here any more, and neither does anyone else. The wardrobes in both rooms are empty, not a single item of clothing to be found, nothing in the rather battered chest of drawers in the main bedroom. A folded grey towel, just as hard as the one she was given, rests alone in the small hotpress. No toothbrush in the bathroom, no razor, not even a sliver of soap.

She decides there's been a break-up. He's separated or divorced from the woman in the photos, and she moved out with their little boy. She broke his heart, and he can't bear to stay in the home they shared so he's moved out too, into temporary accommodation – a poky bedsit, probably – and he's selling up now and planning to find another house with no bad associations.

She has no evidence to prove any of this, of course, but it's a common enough scenario. If the walls could talk, she's pretty sure they'd corroborate her theory. She feels her annoyance dissipating as she considers his situation; for all she knows, he might have come from a fraught meeting with his ex. Trying to sort out custody of their little son, maybe.

'It's quiet around here,' she observes, packing her things away. 'I was never down this road before.'

'It's a peaceful spot,' he agrees. 'Not many people know it exists.'

He sat all the time with a newspaper in the chilly little sitting room and didn't attempt to get involved as she moved through the house. Thankfully he didn't produce a cigarette while she was there, although she suspects the smell will linger anyway in her clothes and hair when she leaves.

Her throat feels unpleasantly dry, as if she's been inhaling smoke all through her visit. Not even a glass of water was she offered, let alone a cup of tea. Then again, she doesn't remember noticing a glass, or any other crockery, in the kitchen.

'We'll be in touch,' she tells him. 'We'll get a sign erected on Monday.'

'That would be good.'

He walks to the door with her. The rain has stopped but the ground is puddled, the air still cool. He looks up the road. 'I take it you have a car somewhere.'

'Larkin Crescent.' She can't wait to get in and put the heat on full blast.

'Right so.' He puts out a hand, and she shakes it again, marvelling at its warmth after an hour in that house. 'Thanks for coming,' he says, 'and sorry again about the late start.'

He's not too bad. She'll forgive him the late start.

Outside the gate she checks her watch: nearly half five. The cemetery isn't that far but it's Friday and rush hour, no time to be lost.

She makes her way rapidly back along the cul-de-sac and turns left into Larkin Crescent. There's nobody about, no sign of activity.

She scans the street, doesn't see her red car. Didn't she park it just there, outside the blue gate? She looks left and right: the car is nowhere to be seen.

She feels a prickle of anxiety. It must be around the corner. She must have left it further away than she'd thought. She walks quickly to the bend, still sees no sign of the car. God, where is it?

She retraces her steps, more running than walking now, heart pitter-pattering, skin tight with apprehension. Don't let it be gone, please don't let it be gone. She goes to the opposite end of the crescent, scans the next road: nothing.

It's gone.

Her car is gone.

Her car has been stolen.

She returns, heart sinking, to where she left it. Definitely she parked here: she remembers the blue gate. She checks the road – no sign of broken glass. She pushes open the gate, marches up the path, jabs at the doorbell. She listens to it echoing within, hands clenched into fists. When nothing happens she rings it a second time, presses her ear to the door, finally hears approaching footsteps.

There's a fumbling, a rattle of metal on metal. The door is opened a few inches, as far as the security chain will allow.

'Yes?' The slice of face that peers out is female, and elderly. The voice is high, with a sharp edge to it. 'What do you want?'

'I'm sorry to bother you,' Daphne says in a rush. 'It's just that – my car, I parked it outside—'

'Have you ID?'

She stops, thrown. 'What? No, you don't—'

'I need ID, or I'm calling the guards.'

'What? My car's been *stolen*. I had it parked right outside your house for about—'

'You had no *right* to park there,' the woman says crossly. 'That parking space is for me and my—'

'Oh, forget it,' Daphne says, turning away, swiping at the tears that have sprung up. Trust her to park outside the house of possibly the least helpful person on the road – and why did it have to be stolen today, of all days?

The street remains deserted. The rain begins again, a sudden heavy fall. She ignores it, takes a deep breath and tries to think. What can she do? Who can help her?

Not her father, busy with driving lessons all afternoon.

George? No, she can't bother him – he'll be getting ready for his school thing. Mo: she's good in an emergency, she'll know what to do. But Mo's phone rings and rings, and remains unanswered.

She'll have to phone the police, of course, report the theft – but first she must get to the cemetery, she *must* get there today, and already it's gone twenty-five to six.

In the end she calls a taxi.

'Larkin Crescent,' she says, giving the number on the door of the house she just visited. 'To St Patrick's Cemetery. Please hurry.'

She hangs up, casting around for shelter and finding none. Can this day get any worse? The rain pelts down on her in earnest; her hair, her clothes, her shoes, everything is quickly soaked for the second time. She shouldn't have phoned a taxi, she should just have started walking. Maybe she could—

'Daphne?'

She starts. Tom Wallace's silver car has pulled up beside her. She never heard him coming.

'My car,' she says, the words tumbling out, her voice shaking ridiculously, 'it's been stolen. I need to get to St Patrick's Cemetery before it closes at six.'

He doesn't miss a beat. 'Hop in,' he says, reaching across to open the passenger door.

She gets in, pulls the door closed. Least he can do – this mess could well be down to him and his late arrival. His car is chilly, but the heat is already on – he switches the fan to full blast. 'Soon be warm,' he says. His wipers flick rapidly to and fro, sweeping water away. He moves off. 'Have you called the guards?'

'No – I'll do it after the cemetery.'

He glances at her. She wills him to keep quiet.

'Daphne, the sooner you—'

'*No*,' she snaps. 'I can't, I just can't think about that right now. I'll do it after. I *must* get to the cemetery.'

She can hear how irrational she sounds, but a phone call is completely beyond her right now. She wouldn't be able to concentrate, couldn't communicate with any degree of clarity. If he keeps going on about it she's in serious danger of exploding.

Thankfully he seems to sense how tightly wound she is. 'OK,' he says calmly, and they travel in silence after that.

She sits hunched forward, briefcase clasped to her chest, eyes fixed on the road ahead, seat belt straining around her. Water dribbles from her hair onto her face – she swipes it away, biting her cheek, forbidding the tears that are dangerously close. Her clothes cling to her, heavy as lead. The seat will be ruined after her – might as well have flung a bucket of water over it – but the condition of his car is the least of her concerns right now.

The traffic, once they reach the main road, is dismayingly heavy. They inch along, stopping and starting. Daphne closes her eyes briefly, yearning for Finn, longing for this horrible day to be over.

After an endless crawl the cemetery finally comes into view – she can see it half a block ahead as they sit waiting for a red light to change. She unbuckles her seat belt, unable to wait any longer. She's afraid to check the time.

'This is fine,' she says, reaching for the door handle. 'Thank you for the lift.'

'Daphne, I know someone—'

'*No*,' she says vehemently. 'You've done enough.' There: let him take that any way he wants.

She scrambles out and pushes the door closed before he has a chance to say more. She makes her way rapidly through the rain without a backward glance. At the intersection she darts across the street, dodging traffic. She runs the half-block, arrives at the cemetery gates.

They're closed. By her watch it's three minutes to six.

❀

The tea is blindingly hot, and very sweet. 'I'm sorry,' she repeats, reaching for another tissue, and again the policewoman tells her she has nothing to be sorry about.

'Drink the tea,' she tells Daphne, turning for the door. 'Take your time, no rush. I'll just put the form through, get the word out.'

Her name is Louise. She's younger than Daphne, somewhere in her middle-twenties. She smells of soap, or maybe shampoo, something clean and uncomplicated. Her nails are perfect shiny ovals, and she wears an identical thin silver ring on each of her index fingers. Her boyishly cut hair has the colour and sheen of new conkers. She looks vaguely familiar.

She'd reacted swiftly when Daphne began to crumble. She lifted the hatch that was set into the counter and ushered Daphne through to a room in the back before the scattering of people in the police station's reception area had much of a chance to see what was going on.

She found a box of tissues. She produced a mug of tea and a plate of Rich Tea biscuits — *All the budget will run to, I'm afraid*. She exchanged Daphne's sodden jacket for a dry navy fleece – *Throw it over your shoulders, it'll warm you up a bit. I'll put yours on the radiator.*

She'd taken a statement from Daphne, recorded her responses in a form. She didn't complain as Daphne wasted her time with tearful explanations about cemeteries and anniversaries and late arrivals.

What are the chances of getting the car back? Daphne had asked.

We'll do our best, she'd replied, *but a fifteen-year-old car would more than likely be targeted by youngsters looking for something to take for a joyride, and they're often found crashed or burnt out. We'll hope for the best, but it might be wise to expect the worst.*

The room is warm, if a little sparsely furnished. Two dull green couches are set opposite one another, a coffee table positioned between them, and what looks like a CCTV camera in a corner where the wall meets the ceiling. Big Brother watching Daphne falling to pieces.

A family room, Louise called it. *Part of our attempt to become more public-friendly. Big improvement on before – up to this, all we had were tiny interview rooms, or the cells.*

She makes an effort to compose herself before Louise gets back. She dreads to think what she must look like, all swollen eyes and bright red nose, hair all over the place. Probably just as well they didn't think to put a mirror in the family room.

She pictures her much-loved car – God knows where it is by now. It's the only one she's ever owned, the only thing she's ever won. The draw ticket bought absentmindedly and promptly forgotten, the thought that it might get pulled out never once crossing her mind. But then the letter, several weeks later: *Dear Miss Carroll, Congratulations!*

Twenty-one years old with a brand new VW Beetle, the first of her friends to have any car, let alone the one they'd all lusted after since its arrival in Ireland just a few months before. The envy of them all she'd been – and able to drive it right away, her father nagged into teaching her before her eighteenth birthday. The test passed first time, thanks to him.

And, of course, the car was what had brought her and Finn together – not that it had seemed like a good thing at the time. She'd parked and opened the door, her mind a million miles away, full of something she can't now for the life of her recall – and he'd cycled straight into it, and gone flying over the handlebars to land several feet ahead on the road.

She was shocked and mortified and apologetic; he was gracious and forgiving, and mercifully not seriously injured. She tried to persuade him to let her take him to hospital to get his cuts and bruises attended to, but he insisted he was fine – his bike shop wasn't far away; he'd see to them himself there. She watched him limping off, trying to steer a straight course despite his buckled front wheel, and she cursed her inattention.

She found herself thinking about him for the rest of the day. She baked a lemon cake when she went home: it was the least she could do to say sorry. A bicycle shop should be easy to find – and if his wife was behind the counter, so be it.

The shop was certainly easy to find, less than a hundred yards up the street from where the collision had occurred. She called in during her lunch hour the next day and met a woman who, unless he'd chosen someone considerably older than himself, was definitely not his wife.

Not the friendliest either. She listened to Daphne's

explanation, her face tight with disapproval. *He's not here right now*, she said curtly, looking with suspicion at the box that held the cake. *A miracle he was able to come to work at all today: he can hardly walk, he's so stiff.* Plain as day she was protective of him, and disapproving of Daphne's carelessness, not to mind her having the gall to show her face in the shop.

And just as Daphne was wondering whether to hand over the cake — would he ever see it? — the door opened and in he came, his face still scribbled with scratches, a purple-black bruise encircling one of his navy eyes.

It didn't take her long to fall in love. Just ten months later she walked up the aisle to him, a bride at last on her thirty-second birthday. And less than three years after that, another bicycle accident made a widow of her.

Two light taps on the door. Louise reappears, holding Daphne's jacket, damp and crumpled, and the form they completed earlier.

'Well,' she says, 'are you feeling a bit more human?'

Daphne sets down the mug, gets to her feet. 'Yes, thanks.' And, oddly, she does feel somewhat better. A little calmer, a bit less tightly wound, as if someone has opened a valve in her and let out some of the pressure. Marvellous what a good cry can do.

Louise taps the form as Daphne eases herself back into the jacket. 'One last thing we need to clear up. Something I should have asked earlier, and forgot: are you quite sure you locked the car?'

'Definitely. I always do.'

Louise nods. 'You have your key so.'

'I have, it's in my bag.'

Another nod. 'And just for the record, and to keep me happy, will you check that you have it?'

Daphne unzips the side pocket of her bag, where she always stows the key, and reaches in to pull it out.

It's not there.

'I must have ...' She rummages through the main section, finally upends the bag onto the coffee table, scrabbles among tissues and lipstick and wallet and gum and pens. Searches the pockets of her jacket.

No key. It's not possible.

It's in her briefcase then, it must be. She never normally puts it there, but today isn't normal.

The key is not in her briefcase.

She looks at Louise in bewilderment. 'I always lock it, I've never forgotten, not once ...'

She trails off, the awful reality dawning. No key, which must mean that she didn't lock the car. Not only did she not lock it, she left the key sitting in the ignition. There's no other possible explanation. How could she have been so thoughtless, so stupid?

'Daphne,' Louise says gently, 'it happens. Today was a tough day for you. Your mind was elsewhere. You were preoccupied. You're not the first.'

She can't believe it. The key in the ignition, an open invitation. It wouldn't have taken a second for someone to slip in and drive away, and she'd given them well over an hour.

Five minutes later she's heading home in a taxi. The rain has finally eased off. It's lightly misting now, blurring the edges of the trees and railings and buildings they pass. Daphne leans back, closes her eyes wearily. The day isn't over, there's still Una's birthday dinner to prepare.

Birthday.

Her eyes snap open.

The cake. She never collected the cake.

●

She arranges the parboiled potatoes around the chicken. She shakes the dish gently to make them skitter and dance, coating them in the hot, oily juices. She twists the salt mill and scatters garlic slivers and little snips of rosemary. She returns the dish to the oven and turns her attention to the cake she got in the corner shop. The plan-B cake.

Out of its box, it's even smaller than she'd thought. The top and sides are covered with flamingo-pink icing; anyone's guess what chemical has been used to achieve that particular shade, or what lies beneath the pink layer. A far cry from the fancy chocolate cake, but it was that or a jam swiss roll.

Nearly a quarter past seven. No sign of Una yet, wherever she went after school. Hopefully not moping on her own somewhere, hopefully out with a pal or two. Home soon: she knows she's expected.

A pink envelope sits on the table, addressed to Una. The Queen of England looking out from the stamp, the address of Una's maternal grandparents written in blue biro on the reverse. The usual tenner inside probably, tucked into a birthday card – their only contact with their granddaughter, apart from the same again every Christmas. Punishing her still for something that wasn't her fault.

Daphne crosses the room and sinks into the armchair by the patio doors, the one Mo donated to Finn when he was furnishing this house nearly thirty years ago. Started off by the fireplace in the sitting room, relegated to the kitchen when Finn had risen to a three-piece suite. A bit shabby by this but still here, and still comfortable. A tidy little wing-backed chair covered with heathery tweed, perfect for this corner.

Finn used to sit in it on summery evenings, when the sinking sun would throw a slanted beam across the tiles. He'd pore over his beloved cycling magazines, long legs stretched out, hair hiding his face from her until he shoved it back every so often, only for it to slide forward again within half a minute.

This was always his chair. When she sits in it now she imagines being cradled in his arms.

Her phone rings. She finds it in her bag and sees George's name on the screen.

'Hi.'

'Daphne, it's me. You OK?'

'I'm OK,' she tells him. She won't mention the car, can't face going into it now.

'You are? Really?'

'I am, really. And you? All set for your big performance?'

'As set as I can be. Hard to believe they're onstage for all of about two minutes – the hair I've pulled out to get them ready for it.'

'Ah, I bet they'll steal the show.'

He teaches junior infants, twenty-four of them in his care. She called to his classroom once to deliver a wallet he'd left at her house the evening before, and there he was, all six foot of him folded onto a low stool, giant storybook propped open on his knees, all his little charges perched on cushions that were scattered about the floor, everyone looking perfectly content.

'Is the birthday girl there?'

'She's not – she's due home any minute.'

'Give her my best.'

'I will.'

'By the way,' he says, 'I've decided to go house-hunting. Did you hear?'

'No I didn't, but it's high time.' At twenty-six he still lives at home with his father and Isobel. 'What are you looking for?'

'Oh, just something small and humble. You might keep an eye out.'

'I saw one, only this afternoon,' she tells him, the chilly little bungalow hopping into her head. 'It's new to the market: we'll be putting it on the books next week. Come over for lunch tomorrow and I'll tell you more.'

'Sounds good – around one?'

'Lovely.'

After hanging up she sits back and looks out at the garden, glistening and alive after all the rain. George was just seventeen when they'd met, nine years younger than Daphne but easily a foot taller. He'd worn a grey suit, the trousers barely making it all the way to the ends of his long legs, and he blushed anytime someone spoke to him.

His palm was damp when he shook hands with Daphne. His father Alex was marrying Daphne's mother Isobel, and he and Daphne were meeting for the first time.

'Good to finally have a brother,' she told him. 'I was getting a bit fed up with being an only child.'

He gave a weak smile, his cheeks reddening. She felt sorry for him – he was as peripheral to all this as she was, and clearly out of his comfort zone. Maybe he was there only because he had to be, like her.

'Are you allowed to have a glass of champagne?' she asked.

He shrugged, gave a shy smile. 'I don't think anyone would notice.'

She took two from a passing waiter's tray. They left the small gathering and found an empty couch in the hotel lobby, and she began the business of becoming acquainted with him.

She learned that he was in Leaving Cert year, and planning to be a teacher. 'My mother teaches English in a high school,' he told her, 'but I'd prefer primary. I love little kids – I love how they're so … honest.'

She thought it a peculiar word for him to choose. 'Where's your mother now?'

'In Canada, Vancouver. She's Canadian – she moved back after they split up.'

She thought it strange that he hadn't gone with her. Didn't mothers generally claim the children in the event of a marriage breakdown? Apart from *her* mother, of course.

'They gave me the choice,' he went on, as if she'd asked the question aloud. 'I wanted to stay here, at least until I finish school.'

A tough decision for a young boy to have to make. She wondered how he felt about his father remarrying, and what he thought of Isobel, his new stepmother, but he didn't volunteer this information.

She told him about her job. 'I like poking around other people's houses, so it suits me perfectly.'

'Did you ever want to do anything else?' he asked.

She laughed. 'When I was young I wanted to be a driving instructor, like Dad, but then when he taught me I changed my mind – I realised I wouldn't have half enough patience.'

As they'd talked, she found herself warming to him. They discovered a shared love of crosswords, and a mutual aversion to sudoku. Before they were summoned by George's uncle for the meal, they'd exchanged phone numbers and promised to keep in touch. And they had. They do.

He never moved to Canada. He trained as a teacher in Ireland and got a job here, in the school where he still teaches. He travels to Canada during the holidays, and his mother has been back to Ireland a couple of times. From what Daphne can gather, there's no communication between her and Alex. A bitter split, it would seem.

In the almost ten years they've known one another, George has never mentioned a girlfriend; she wonders if he's ever had one. It's none of her business, but it doesn't stop her wondering. Maybe he's gay, although she never got that sense from him. She'd love him to find someone, sad to think of him on his own. At least she'd had Finn, even if it was only for a short while.

She watches a sparrow pecking at something in the grass. Four weeks yesterday to her own birthday, the second last day of April. Her thirty-sixth coming up; she's still young. Finn, if he'd lived, would have been turning fifty-three in July. The age difference hadn't mattered a damn to either of them.

He'd had a life before he met her. At thirty-eight he married Susan; they'd spent just four years as man and wife. Susan died in her early forties, a fortnight after stepping on a rusty nail that sent its poison zinging through her bloodstream. Six years after that, a driver opened a car door and Finn Darling cycled straight into it.

It used to frighten Daphne, how accidental their meeting had been. What if she'd opened the door a few seconds earlier or later, or glanced in her wing mirror and spotted him in time to prevent the calamity, or simply parked further along the road? What if illness, or a dental appointment, had prevented her going to work that morning, or being on that street at that particular time? All the variables that might have stopped them coming into contact.

But maybe there *was* such a thing as destiny; maybe the Fates would have conspired to bring them together in some other way if that encounter hadn't happened. She might have twisted an ankle one day as she walked past his bicycle shop; they might have chosen neighbouring seats on a train, or stood next to one another in a checkout queue at the supermarket, or reached for the same magazine at the newsagent's.

She used to feel sorry for Susan. She used to think *They only had four years together; we'll have so much more*. But in the end Susan had had the longer marriage, and Susan had been spared the heartache of losing him.

They lie together now in the cemetery, he and Susan. Their mortal remains rest side by side in the plot Finn had bought when she'd died. It is a reality that Daphne must live with.

Her phone gives three shrill beeps. She takes it from her bag again. *Una*, it says. She opens the text message. *Sorry, having dinner at Ciaras, her dad will drive me home, hope thats OK, c u later.*

She reads the words, re-reads them. Not coming home, not putting in an appearance on her birthday? Could she have forgotten that Mo is due, that they're making a special effort? It doesn't seem possible.

She scans the short message for a third time. Of course Una hasn't forgotten, she's simply avoiding it. She's pretending it's not happening. So much for Daphne cooking her favourite dinner, so much for the pricey cake that wasn't even collected.

Mo will undoubtedly be put out when she arrives, but there's not a lot Daphne can do about that.

She should try, though. She presses the call button and listens to Una's phone ringing, and waits until the voicemail recording clicks on: *Sorry I missed you, please leave a message.*

She hangs up, half relieved. What could she say, after all, that Una would want to hear? Better, maybe, that the call went unanswered. Better to let her put this first painful birthday behind her, and hope she's stronger by the time the next one comes along.

Good that she's with Ciara this evening – always the most frequent caller in the days when Una's friends still came to the house. *They've known one another forever*, Finn had told Daphne once. *Bonded in junior infants, never looked back.* Good that she's with someone she feels close to.

The pink cake sits on the worktop. Una doesn't want it; none of them do. Why on earth did Daphne think they had to celebrate today? Why did she press on with this farce? She'll send the cake home with Mo tonight – and if Mo isn't interested she'll give it to George when he calls tomorrow.

Or maybe she'll do none of the above.

Suddenly she just wants rid of it. She slides it none too carefully back into its box, lifts the lid of the kitchen bin and deposits it inside. Terrible waste: she'll tell nobody. And she'll get Mo to collect the other one tomorrow – the bakery is just down the street from the charity shop, and the women who work with Mo would surely welcome a bit of cake at their break. It can be Daphne's contribution to charity.

She slides open the patio doors, stands on the threshold and inhales the damp, early-evening air. Still chilly, but she's warmer now after a hot shower, and dressed in dry jeans and a cosy sweater. On her feet are two pairs of the thick wool socks that used to belong to Finn and that she wears often around the house now. Better than any slippers.

The light is just beginning to wane at this hour, the longer day bringing a promise of summer. This time last year she couldn't have cared less what season it was, didn't give a damn that summer was coming. She can smell woodsmoke from someone's chimney, above the earthy freshness of damp grass.

She watches little brown birds flitting above the lawn, flying up to perch on the wooden fence that separates her from Sheila and Jim Redden. Hopefully their cat isn't on the prowl – nothing is safe with him around. She's glad when they take off again, drifting upwards where he can't get at them.

Something else in the sky catches her eye, fluttering higher than the birds. Two kites, tails trailing – years since she's seen kites. She follows their dips and swoops, and is reminded of the plane this morning with its message of congratulations for the couple whose names she's forgotten. Married by now, dancing maybe at this moment as man and wife.

At five to eight the doorbell rings. Not Una, she has her key.

'Smells good,' Mo says, handing a tinfoil-covered box to Daphne before unbuttoning her coat. 'That's for Una.'

'You look nice,' Daphne tells her. She's wearing make-up: when does Mo ever wear make-up? Awful blue eye shadow, lipstick, foundation. Amateurishly applied, the foundation too dark for Mo's skin tone – but still making an effort, presumably for Una. And no Una here to appreciate it.

She takes the coat from Mo and hangs it on the hallstand. It's olive green, with a half-belt and a line of brass buttons. It's all wrong on Mo – the hemline hits her mid-calf, swamping her tiny frame, and the colour washes the warmth from her face – but it's still the smartest thing she owns, and one of the few items of clothing that didn't come via the charity shop.

Beneath the coat she wears black trousers and a powder blue cardigan buttoned to the neck, and for once she's swapped the trainers for a pair of black lace-up shoes. The pearls have come out too, the ones Leo bought her for their thirtieth anniversary – definitely gone to some trouble for this evening. What will she say when she hears Una has decided not to show up?

Daphne leads the way into the kitchen, biding her time. She places the silver box on the worktop and opens a press. 'The dinner will be a bit later than advertised – I was delayed getting home. You'll have a drop of sherry.'

Mo isn't much of a drinker. According to Finn, she first tasted alcohol nine years ago, at the age of sixty-six. Since then she's never ventured beyond a small sweet sherry, or a very occasional Baileys.

'Where's Una? She dolling herself up?'

Daphne fills two glasses, hands one to Mo. Here goes. 'I'm afraid Una's not eating with us – I got a text a while ago.'

Mo frowns. 'What do you mean, not eating with us? Why not?'

'… I think she just couldn't face it.' *Please don't turn this into a battle*, she begs silently. The last thing she needs tonight.

'Face what? Isn't it her birthday? Didn't you tell her I was coming?'

'Mo, I think she decided it would be too hard to celebrate – under the circumstances.'

'Rubbish! Who said anything about celebrating? It's just dinner and a cake – it's not as if we're planning to pop open the champagne.'

'Mo, it's her *birthday*, and she's—'

'Where is she? Or did she bother telling you that?'

'She's in Ciara's house. She's eating with them.'

Mo snorts. 'Eating with *them* – does she think this is easy for any of us?'

She raises her glass, and Daphne bites back a sharp retort as she sees the tremor in the arthritic hand. Suffering every bit as much as Daphne and Una today, missing Finn just as acutely as they do – and missing Leo too, of course.

She searches for words of comfort, and finds none. 'What kind of a day had you?' she asks instead.

Mo flicks the question away with a toss of her head. 'The

usual,' she says curtly. 'Same day I always have. Same old ding dong.'

Where do you go from there? Daphne sets down her glass and fills a saucepan with water. She breaks the broccoli into florets and puts two dinner plates into the warming drawer, conscious of the charged silence in the room. She checks on the chicken; few more minutes.

'At least the rain has stopped,' she says. 'And the dinner should be good, even if it's only the two of us eating it.'

No response. Going to be a long evening.

❁

'I've been thinking,' Mo says.

They're well into the meal, almost finished it, and an uncharacteristic second sherry has gone some way towards softening her humour. All the same, the words trigger a small alarm bell in Daphne's head: her mother-in-law's thinking could go anywhere.

'It's about the shop,' Mo goes on, laying down her fork. She's left a small chunk of roast potato still impaled on a prong. 'We need to sort something out.'

The shop. The bicycle shop, she must mean. Two Wheels Good, owned equally by both women since Finn's death. Lord, what now?

'I think,' Mo says, watching Daphne's face carefully, 'that you – well, that we – should do something with it.'

The alarm bell grows shriller. Daphne's grip tightens on her cutlery. 'Do something with it? You mean ... sell it?'

'No, I do not mean sell it,' Mo says steadily. 'I mean open it up again.'

'Open it up? Who?'

'You and me,' Mo says tartly. 'The two of us. Who else?'

She has to be joking. She doesn't look like she's joking. Her mother-in-law is not known for her sense of humour.

'Mo,' Daphne begins carefully, 'are you seriously suggesting that we reopen the bike shop?'

'It wouldn't have to be bikes,' Mo says. 'It could be anything. Toys, or … a grocery shop. I don't know, I haven't worked that out.'

Toys. Her and Mo in a toy shop. The two of them behind the counter, surrounded by dolls and tubs of Lego and inflatable paddling pools. The idea is so ludicrous that Daphne would be tempted to laugh out loud if laughter was remotely on the agenda, which it isn't.

Instead she settles on the most obvious objection. 'Mo,' she says, in the same cautious tone, 'I already have a job.'

Mo nods grimly. 'You have, yes. And exactly how many houses have you sold in the past year?'

Daphne frowns. 'What? I don't see how that has anything—'

'You're an estate agent, aren't you?'

'Of course I am, but—'

'Estate agents sell houses. I'm asking how many you've sold in the past year. A dozen?'

'Mo, it doesn't work like—'

'Six? Have you sold six?'

'Oh, for God's sake, if you'd let me get a—'

'It's none, isn't it? You haven't sold a single house in the past year, have you?'

Daphne glares at her, feeling her face flush with anger. 'It's not as simple as that. You have no right—'

'I'm just saying that maybe it's time to make a change.'

'*What?* But I don't *want* a—'

'And one thing you could do, one thing the two of us could do, is open up some kind of a shop. It makes perfect sense.'

'How can you even—'

'We already have the premises, and you have the compensation money to invest in stock. It's the obvious thing to do.'

Daphne looks at her in fresh disbelief. 'Mo, you *know* I said I'd never touch that money.'

Mo waves an impatient hand. 'For God's sake, what good is it to anyone gathering dust in a bank? It should be *used*, and this is the obvious thing to do with it.'

The woman is insufferable. Daphne is rapidly running out of patience. 'Look, even if I wanted another job, which I don't, the last thing I'd look for is—'

'But are you *happy*?' Pushing her plate aside, planting her forearms on the table. 'Are you *happy*?' she repeats, staring fixedly at her daughter-in-law.

The question stops Daphne dead. Has the woman lost her wits? 'Happy? Of *course* I'm not happy. I'm heartbroken. How can you possibly—'

Mo shakes her head impatiently. 'I don't mean *that*. I mean are you happy in your work?'

'As happy as I can be right now, yes. I *love* my job.'

A short silence falls. They hold one another's gaze across the table, a few feet and a million miles apart, the remains of the meal nobody really wanted sitting between them. What a day, what a wretched, miserable day – but at least it's nearly over.

'Look,' Daphne says finally, 'I appreciate that you don't like seeing the shop shut up. Neither do I – but your idea makes no sense. It's one thing if *you* want to reopen it – maybe you could find people to staff it for you – but the idea of *me* being involved is absurd. I don't know the first thing about running a shop.' *And the last person I would choose to work with is you.*

Mo gives a snort. 'What's to know, apart from stocking it and keeping the accounts right and being pleasant to people?'

'It can't possibly be that—'

'Anyway, you'd have to be involved – how would we afford it otherwise? And as for bringing strangers in, you can forget about that. I'd do the books, obviously – and you'd be well able to deal with the customers, if you'd only pull yourself together.'

Pull yourself together – possibly the most infuriating and useless phrase in the English language. As if Daphne could decide to send her grief packing, dust herself down and move on, just like that. The injustice, the heartlessness of it stings her far more than Mo's earlier cross-examination. The last of her patience flies out the window.

'For your information,' she says levelly, 'I'm still in mourning for your son, so pulling myself together isn't exactly an option right now. You may have got over his death, but I haven't.'

Mo's face stiffens, and Daphne is instantly remorseful. What a horrible thing to say, like verbally slapping her. No call for that; no call, whatever the provocation.

'Mo, I'm sorry, I shouldn't have—'

And again, Mo breaks in. 'Now you listen to me,' she says sharply, finger jabbing on the table, swollen knuckles rising like hillocks. 'Just you listen to me for one minute. I *know* your heart is still broken, and mine is too, believe it or not – but do you think that's going to go away all by itself? You think you're going to magically wake up one day and not feel sad any more? You think *time* will heal you? Get some sense.'

'But I can't just *fix* myself – I just can't! I don't know how you expect me to do that.'

'You need to get some *purpose* into your life again,' Mo insists, still prodding the table. 'You need something that'll pull you out of the rut you've been in for the past year. We both need that. And even if you hate the thought of spending the money you got, it's giving you the chance to do just that. At least say you'll think about it.'

But everything in Daphne revolts against the idea. Pack in a job she's perfectly happy with to jump into the great unknown? Burn her bridges to risk falling flat on her face and end up with nothing at all, not to mention using the money she'd sworn she'd never touch? Working side by side with *Mo*, day after day? Out of the question.

She's been at Donnelly's for sixteen years: it's the only job she's ever had. Mr Donnelly is like a second father to her. And it's true she hasn't sold anything lately – well, for quite some time – but that's the swings-and-roundabouts nature of the estate-agency business, nothing to do with her.

What part of this whole hare-brained scheme could Mo possibly think would work? She's nothing more than a delusional old woman, trying to bully Daphne into going along with it.

'I'm sorry,' she says firmly, 'but I'm just not interested. It's not going to happen.'

Mo regards her angrily. 'You won't *let* it happen, you mean. You won't even think about it.'

'That's right. I won't.'

And as they regard one another in a defeated, furious silence, Daphne's phone rings, cutting shrilly into the tension. She picks it up, sees her mother's name.

'I have to take this,' she says curtly, getting to her feet. A conversation with Isobel is the last thing she feels like having right now, but it gives her a chance to escape. She leaves the room and closes the kitchen door, pressing the answer key as she walks upstairs.

'Daphne,' her mother says, 'how are you feeling?'

'My car was stolen,' Daphne tells her.

Give them something to talk about.

❖

At almost half past nine there's still no sign of Una. 'Ring her,' Mo says, refilling their three teacups, placing a second slice of cake on Daphne's father's plate.

'You're trying to fatten me up,' he says.

'I am indeed. Someone has to.'

They enjoy one another's company, always have. He has the knack of softening Mo's edges, however he does it.

'Give Una a ring,' she repeats, so Daphne calls the girl's mobile again, and for the second time that evening she gets only her voicemail message.

'Just wondering if you'll be home soon,' she says. 'Jack and Mo are here, we're having cake. We'd love to see you.'

The cake has been resurrected. It was sitting on a plate in the middle of the table when Daphne returned to the kitchen after her phone conversation with her mother. She stared at it.

Mo was doing the washing-up. 'See what I found,' she said, without turning from the sink.

'You took it out of the bin.'

'It was in a box. It's fine.' Her head swung around then, a bundle of dripping cutlery held in her rubber-gloved hand. 'What I'm wondering,' she said mildly, 'is how it ended up there.'

Daphne slipped her phone back into her bag. At least their earlier argument seemed to have been put aside. 'It seemed a bit ... pointless, when Una wasn't coming home to eat it.'

'So you just threw it in the bin. Even though there wasn't anything wrong with it.' But her voice held none of its earlier sharpness; she wasn't on the attack any more.

Daphne took the tea towel from its hook. 'I shouldn't have binned it, I know that. I was tired, and ... upset. I wasn't thinking straight.'

Mo set the cutlery on the draining board, peeled off the gloves. 'And I'm wondering what became of the one you ordered. I'm assuming this isn't it.'

'No, of course not – this one was four euro in Mulligan's. I never got to collect the other one.' She paused. 'I had other things on my mind,' she said. As briefly as she could, she recounted the events of the afternoon.

Mo was horrified. 'Your car was *stolen*? Why didn't you tell me? What did the guards say?'

'That it will probably turn up, but it might well be crashed or burnt out.'

'God above.' Mo lowered herself stiffly into a chair, looking suddenly old and defeated. Looking every bit of her seventy-five years.

Daphne dropped the damp tea towel onto the draining board and sat next to her. 'Mo, would you collect the other cake tomorrow and bring it to the charity shop for the tea break? It's already paid for and I'd hate it to go to waste.'

Mo looked doubtful. 'I'd have to give you something for it.'

If she knew how much it had cost, she'd faint. 'No need, I don't want money.' Before they could say any more about it the doorbell rang and it was Daphne's father, so they made tea and cut the pink cake and waited for Una.

And now it's nearly half nine, and still no sign of her.

'Who did you say she's with?' Mo asks.

'Ciara, one of her friends.'

'Have you a number for her, or an address?'

'No.'

After a year, Daphne can hardly recall what Ciara looks like – long auburn hair is all she can picture. It hits her that she has no way of getting in touch with Una, apart from a mobile phone that's proving useless. For the first time she feels a tiny twitch of apprehension. What if Una doesn't show up, and continues to ignore her phone? What then?

'What's Ciara's surname?' Jack asks. 'We could look them up in the phone book' – but again Daphne draws a blank.

'I don't remember ever hearing it,' she replies, knowing how pathetic it must sound to them. Una's best friend, and she doesn't even know her last name.

Finn knew it, of course. He knew where Ciara lived too – he'd often been at her house, either dropping her home or collecting Una from there. But Daphne had never thought to look for that information while he was alive, never imagined she'd need it.

It strikes her suddenly that she must have met Ciara's parents: they would certainly have come to Finn's funeral. They would have lined up and shaken her hand like everyone else; they might even have called to the house in those first nightmarish days – but her memories of that time are blessedly indistinct, all the hushed voices and clasped hands and bowed heads blurring together.

'What about the school principal?' her father suggests. 'They'd be able to tell you the surname, and maybe they'd know the address too.'

'The principal ...'

For a few seconds her mind refuses to supply a name, or even a gender, for whoever is in charge at the comprehensive. No, she knows this – she's been to events at the school, cake sales and parent-teacher meetings and end-of-term things. She *knows* this.

She racks her brain, aware of the other two looking expectantly at her, and finally remembers two Christmases ago, the school's annual variety concert, Una singing carols with a few others. The principal introduced it, acted as MC for the night – yes, a lanky, balding man in a tuxedo. Mr Dunphy – no, that's not right. And then all of a sudden it's there: Dunworth. John, or maybe Joseph, Dunworth.

It takes her three phone calls to locate him. A woman answers on the fifth ring.

'Who will I say is calling?' she asks, and when Daphne gives her name she goes off without further enquiry – resigned, maybe, to his being pestered by parents when he's off duty.

The principal pretends to remember her when he comes to the phone, although she doubts that he could. Did *he* attend Finn's funeral? She has no idea. If he's annoyed at being contacted outside school hours he gives no sign. He tells her immediately that Ciara's last name is O'Mahony, and that she lives on Morefield Terrace. A few hundred students in his care: can he possibly know where every one of them lives?

'I don't know the house number – all that information is at the school – but you should be able to find them in the phone book,' he says. 'Call me back if you have any problems.'

Daphne thanks him and hangs up. What must he think of her, not having contact details for Una's friends? It's probably one of the most basic rules of parenting.

For the second time she searches the phone book while Mo continues to try Una's mobile – and there the O'Mahonys are as promised, on Morefield Terrace. Daphne dials the number, wondering how Una will react to being checked up on. Her own fault for ignoring her phone, but she might still—

'Hello?' A man's voice.

'Mr O'Mahony?' She hasn't a clue what his first name is, only that his initial is B.

'Speaking.'

'Daphne Darling here, Una's stepmother. I was just—'

'Ah, Daphne — hello there. Everything all right?' From his tone they might have met yesterday.

'I just wanted a word with Una. I've tried her mobile a few times, but she's not answering.'

Pause. 'Una? I don't think— Hang on there a sec, Daphne, would you?' She hears the receiver being laid down, a distant exchange. She waits.

'Is she there?' Mo asks.

Daphne nods. 'He's getting her now.'

'Hello?' But it's not Una, it's a different female voice. 'Mrs Darling? It's Ciara — Una's not here.'

'Oh — she's left already? But she said your father was driving her home.'

'Um ... Una hasn't been here today, Mrs Darling.'

'Not *there*? Didn't she have dinner with you?'

'Um ... no.' Her voice filled with uncertainty now. 'I haven't seen her since yesterday.'

'What?' The conversation is making less and less sense to Daphne. She feels the tension of the afternoon returning, prickling her skin, tightening her jaw. She's aware of the other two listening intently. 'What are you talking about? Weren't you at school today?'

'Yes, but Una wasn't.'

'Of course she was. She was definitely there — I dropped her off myself.'

'Um ...'

'Are you in different classrooms?'

'Well, only when we split up for science and stuff – but we're in the same room for most things.'

'And you didn't see her at all?'

'No. I know it's her birthday and ... stuff, so I thought she just ... stayed home today.'

Daphne tries to make sense of it. Ciara didn't see her at school, but Una *was* there. She must have skipped some classes, maybe couldn't face meeting her friends today, which is probably understandable – but where did she go, and who was she with?

Suddenly a light dawns: she's not the right Ciara. Una must have two friends with the same name. There's nothing wrong, it's just a simple misunderstanding.

'Is there another Ciara? I mean, has Una got another friend called Ciara?'

'Um ... not that I know of. I'm the only one in school.'

Only one Ciara: of course there's only one. Daphne's palms have become damp. Was Una's earlier text a lie, then? If she wasn't in Ciara's house, where was she? Where *is* she? There must be some simple explanation.

'Ciara,' she says urgently, 'you're not making this up, are you? I mean, Una isn't putting you up to anything, is she? Playing a trick on us or something, a joke or something like that? Because if that's what this is, please stop. I'm really very worried.'

For a second, two seconds, there's silence. 'Um, Mrs Darling, I texted her this morning when she wasn't at school, and she texted back to say she was at home, sick.'

'What? What time was this?'

'About ... half nine.'

And as the words register, Daphne's insides begin to dissolve. No mistake then, no misunderstanding.

Una is missing. She's sixteen – no, barely seventeen, and she's missing.

'Daphne' – Ciara's father again – 'Bill O'Mahony here. Look, I've heard the gist of that. Sounds like you're having trouble tracking Una down. I think the best thing we can do is for me to get Ciara to ring around the pals, see if she's in anyone else's house … OK, Daphne?'

She becomes aware that she's nodding silently. 'Yes,' she says, her scalp tight, her mouth horribly dry. 'Yes, thank you.'

'And we'll get back to you as soon as that's done, OK? Give me your number there.'

She recites the number of her mobile phone in a voice that won't stop shaking. Una isn't in anyone else's house: they won't find her. The certainty of this is terrifying.

'Ciara will be as quick as she can,' he says. 'OK, Daphne?'

'Yes,' she says. 'Thank you.' She hangs up and turns to the others.

'They don't know,' she says. 'She wasn't at school, she sent Ciara a text—' She breaks off, unable to finish for the fear that has clutched her, for the sudden wave of nausea that washes over her.

'Could she be in the house?' Mo asks, rising. 'Have you checked her room?'

Her room. Una's room.

Daphne takes the stairs two at a time, comes to a halt outside the bedroom door, gripped by a new terror.

She wouldn't. She wouldn't do that. She's not like that.

She flings open the door. The room is empty. She slumps against the jamb, her whole body trembling, the facts slamming one after another into her head like the thump of a closed fist.

Una ran away from school.

It's almost ten o'clock.

She's been missing for the whole day.

She's Daphne's responsibility, and now she's lost.

She's seventeen. She's only seventeen.

MO DARLING

'**I**'m looking for a teddy,' the woman says. 'It's for my little boy – he's in a play at his school this evening. Well, not so much a play, just a musical thing. He's in junior infants, and they're doing "Ten in the Bed" – you know that song? He's the little one, the one that tells them all to roll over. He needs a teddy, but he refuses point blank to use his own – you know what they can be like at that age – so I thought I'd pick one up here.'

It's clear she doesn't remember Mo. She doesn't remember the first time they met, a year ago today.

He's dead, Mrs Darling. Saying what had to be said, no beating around the bush. *He was involved in a road accident this afternoon. He died instantly. Your daughter-in-law wanted to come and tell you, but she's in no fit state—*

And even as the horror of it, no, no, no, even as the horror beyond horror of it was crashing, no, no, no, like a tidal wave into Mo, even as the words were lancing through her like spears, whooshing the breath out of her, no, no, no, making her heart go insane inside her, making nothing right, nothing the same ever again, Mo was grateful for the woman's directness, for the way she didn't shilly-shally around the truth. The compassion plain in her drained face, the reluctance for her task evident. Standing on Mo's doorstep in her navy uniform beside her male colleague, looking much too young to be a guard, looking far too young to have to break such terrible news to anyone.

For the first time in her life, Mo fainted. Not even a real faint, just a brief darkness, like someone drawing a blind down in her head, only for it to shoot up again, consciousness restored within seconds, and she was half lying, half sitting on the hall floor, the male guard crouching awkwardly beside her, his arm around her shoulders, his navy trousers straining across his broad thighs. His breath, too close to her face, smelling of coffee.

Mrs Darling, he was saying, *you're all right, you just took a bit of a turn.* As if she'd suddenly become senile instead of childless.

I want to see him, she said to them, and they tried to talk her out of it. They wanted to call a neighbour, said she could wait and see him tomorrow, but she was having none of it, so they took her to the morgue, where she found an incoherent Daphne and a silent, white-faced Jack, and what was left of Finn.

Over an hour dead by this time, his beautiful face waxy and still. A scream wanting to erupt at the sight of him but not coming out because she didn't let it: she didn't dare in case it went on forever, so she kept her mouth closed and shoved it back down inside her.

And that night, that endless night after everyone had left, Daphne wanting her to come back to their place but Mo refusing. Sitting alone in her empty house that whole night, wrapped in a blanket as she kept vigil for him. Watching the moon as it came and went, as the stars shone down uncaringly on a world that didn't contain him any more. Unable to cry, still too broken apart with shock to cry.

The young guard phoned Mo the following week, a few days after the funeral. *Just checking in, Mrs Darling*, she said, *to see how you're doing*. Nice, that — even if Mo was doing abominably badly, even if all of Mo's seams were unravelling. The gesture still appreciated for all that.

The next time they met was several months after Finn's death, about a week after Mo had begun volunteering in the charity shop. The woman had come in with a little dark-haired boy; she'd smiled at Mo as they walked past the counter. Gave Mo a right land, the sight of her. Brought it all back, all the horror rushing right back, but she managed not to let on.

The woman had bought a table lamp that day, had paid for it and waited while Mo wrapped it. She and her little boy had stood beside Mo for at least two minutes, and she'd never given the smallest sign that she was aware she'd met Mo before. Why would she remember, though? Probably had to give plenty of people that kind of news: how was she to recall them all?

She knows Mo by sight now, of course. She drops into the shop every so often, sometimes with her boy, other times alone. The two women haven't exchanged names or made any conversation other than what's needed. Mo is a familiar face to her, that's all.

Plenty of people wouldn't be caught dead going into a charity shop, but it doesn't seem to bother her – and you'd think she could afford better on a guard's salary. Mo approves of that, appreciates the lack of snobbery it shows. She's been a fan of charity shops herself for years, hardly ever goes anywhere else to buy her clothes. So what if someone else wore it first, if it's still fit to wear?

'Soft toys in that box there,' she says, indicating, and the woman drops to a crouch and rummages among the jumble of sorry-looking offerings. Her hair has been cut since Mo last saw it: the reddish-brown bob has become a pixie crop. It suits her, makes her grey eyes appear larger, her face even younger than before. Instead of a wedding ring she wears a silver band, no wider than a piano wire, on each of her index fingers. They look wrong to Mo there; they jar like a picture crookedly hung. Those fingers weren't made for rings.

'This'll do.' The woman pulls out a rather raddled teddy, his toffee-coloured fur worn bald in several places. 'Looks well loved, don't you think?'

'Certainly does.'

Mo rings in fifty cents, even though the box is marked *Everything €1*. Couldn't ask for a euro for that shabby old thing.

But the woman insists on paying full price – 'No, no, it's cheap enough,' and Mo accepts, knowing she'd do the same herself.

A carrier bag is offered and turned down. 'Chilly today,' the woman says, stowing the toy in the black satchel that's slung over her shoulder. 'Big change from yesterday.'

'That's April for you,' Mo agrees. Yesterday had been warm enough to sit in the garden for an hour with the paper when she got home. April brings dangerous weather, every day more unpredictable than the last. Who was it called April the cruellest month? She's glad she put on her blue cardigan today, seven euro last week, a hundred per cent cashmere and not a mark on it, apart from a tiny stain on one of the cuffs.

'Bye now.' The woman zips her purse closed, lifts a hand in farewell. 'See you again.'

She strikes Mo as happy. Something bubbles within her, adding warmth to her eyes, giving her a ready, bright smile. Maybe she's in love. Mo remembers how that feels, oh, she remembers it well.

In the momentarily deserted shop she wanders back over the years to 1958; she sees the navy and white polka-dot dress she wore the first time Leo Darling took her to the cinema. She was nineteen years of age, in her second year of being an articled clerk at Twomey Accountants. It was three weeks since their first encounter, three weeks since she'd gone into Hadigan's to look at tennis racquets, and Leo Darling the assistant who'd attended to her. And that night at the pictures she knew, yes, she was certain that she loved him.

Four years her senior, not her first boyfriend but by far the most exciting. Pencil moustache that reminded her of Errol Flynn, wonderful dark blue eyes that Finn was to inherit. The marks of his comb still in the nut-brown hair that he swept straight up from his forehead like James Dean. Finn was to do that too, push his hair back in precisely the same style, but without Leo's Brylcreem it would never stay put.

I'm going to open my own shop some day, Leo told her, when the lights were on at the interval and she was eating the Palm Grove choc-ice he'd bought for her. *A bicycle shop*. And, even though she wondered where an assistant manager at Hadigan's Sporting Goods Store could possibly get the money for a shop of his own, she didn't doubt him for a second.

When the place went dark for the second half, and a few minutes later she felt the warmth of his arm across her shoulders, she thought, *I love him*, just like that. And for the rest of the evening the happiness hummed and glowed inside her, warm as a coal fire. She was in love.

And he did open the shop, after eight more years of him working all hours, even taking on a second job for a few months as night watchman at the railway station to put more money aside, snatching sleep where he could until Mo had put a stop to it, hating the pinched look on his face, his eyes sunk with tiredness into deep sockets.

Of course all the scrimping meant him and Mo, and later Finn, living for years in the cramped one-bedroom converted garage they leased for some tiny amount from his cousin, but she didn't mind – his dream had become her dream, and she grudged him nothing.

Two Wheels Good – the name inspired by *Animal Farm*, his favourite book – opened on a blustery June day in 1966. Mo had stood beside him, holding four-year-old Finn by the hand as the ribbon was cut by a well-known cyclist, whose name escapes her now. Fine figure of a man, won Rás Tailteann more than once. She remembers a clutch of giggling, shoving youngsters asking for his autograph, the brand new shop full of people. Leo wearing a wide, wide smile as he walked among them, his wish finally fulfilled. Happy times.

And later that year, when it looked like the business was going to survive, Mo handed in her notice at Twomey's and became his book-keeper. They were a team, right from the start.

The door opens to admit a pair of women. Mo checks the time: just gone half nine. Morning dragging already.

●

'Would it go with this jumper?' Gretta asks, draping a turquoise scarf across one Fair-Isled shoulder. Gretta is the longest running of the volunteers, been there well over thirty years, pricing the donations in the back room before sending them out to the shop floor. You wouldn't dream of asking her age, but Mo reckons she can't be far off ninety. One of those women who'll go on forever.

'Not bad. Be nice with your green tweed as well.'

'I'll buy it so.' She sets it aside, reaches into the black refuse bag again and pulls out a badly creased shirt. 'This'll need the iron, Martha.'

'I'm having my tea.'

'I know you are – I'm only sayin' you can do it after.'

Gretta throws Mo a look that Mo pretends not to catch. No love lost between those two these days, not since Gretta took home the peach curtains Martha had had her eye on. Stay out of it, best all round.

She takes a ginger-nut biscuit from the plate and dunks it in her tea. They don't know it's Finn's anniversary today; she hasn't let on. She wasn't working here when it happened – she didn't start till December, when he'd been dead for more than half a year. All they know is she had a son who died – she had no choice, they were enquiring about family – but she made it plain that they weren't to ask any more questions, and they haven't.

She couldn't bear their pity if they knew what day it was. She'd had a bellyful of pity last year, everyone looking at her with sad smiles pasted onto their faces, speaking to her with the kind of voice you'd use for a child with a bit of a want in him. Pity is useless; pity makes her want to throttle someone.

'Una's birthday today,' she says, to change the subject. 'Seventeen.'

They're aware she has a granddaughter but they've never met Una – she's never set foot in the shop. Daphne looks in from time to time, actually bought a skirt once, but Una doesn't come near the place. Youngsters wouldn't be interested in buying second-hand: they all want new and fashionable. You can understand that.

'Is she having a party?' Martha enquires.

'No, she's not bothered. She might go out with the pals after school, that's all. I'm going over there for dinner later. We'll make a bit of a fuss.'

Gretta pulls a T-shirt from the bag. 'You get her something nice?'

'Voucher for that shoe shop on Connolly Street.' Mo hasn't got it yet – she'll pick it up when she clocks off. The shop, whose name escapes her, has awning in fat green and white stripes, and shoes of every colour imaginable in the window, and music blaring from giant speakers on either side of the door. It strikes Mo as the kind of place a teenage girl would like.

'My granddaughter Charlene for her sixteenth,' Gretta says, 'and half a dozen of her pals, they got one of them make-up people to come to the house, did them all up, an' then they went out on the town. She didn't get home till three. Jean didn't sleep a wink till she heard her comin' in. This won't sell – look at the rip in it.'

'Sixteen is far too young to be out till that hour,' Martha puts in.

Gretta sniffs. 'Try tellin' that to Charlene, see how far you'd get.'

'Neighbours of mine,' Martha goes on, as if Gretta hasn't spoken, 'took their daughter to Italy when she turned sixteen.'

Gretta yanks a yellow shirt from the bag. 'I wouldn't go to Italy if you paid me. Can't stand the heat in them places, an' all them mosquitoes. Gimme a week in Dingle any day. Another one for the iron here.'

Martha takes a biscuit, snaps it in two, deposits half back on the plate. 'You've been to Italy, have you?'

'Wouldn't go if you paid me, I said.'

Mo thinks back to Una's sixteenth. She remembers them driving from the morgue to the bowling alley where they knew she'd gone with friends after school. Daphne sat white-faced and silent in the back seat of Jack's car. *I'll go in*, he said, *I'll get her* – but Mo climbed out on legs that barely worked. Couldn't let Jack be the one to tell her.

She remembers pushing open the door of the bowling alley, walking through the voices and the music and the clatter of falling pins – so loud, everything unbearably loud – until she found her. *Come outside*, she said, watching Una's face as it turned from happy to puzzled.

What for?

Just come, Mo said, and she saw the fear in the girl's eyes then, her birthday forgotten, pushed away to make room for whatever was to come.

They must try to make today better for her. Mo will send her a text, that's what she'll do. She gets to her feet and takes her bag from its locker – but the phone isn't to be found in it. Left at home again, forgets it more times than she remembers it.

She tucks the bag under her arm, takes her jacket from its hook. 'Going out the back for a pull,' she tells the others. She turns the key in the rear door, pushes it open and steps into the small yard. The chill is shocking after the warmth of the shop, but she won't be long.

She sits gingerly on the rusting garden seat someone had thought to position there and takes a pack of cigarettes from her bag. Her secret vice, nobody outside the shop knows about it. Gave them up when she married Leo, didn't look at them for forty-six years. Bought a pack the day they took him away from her, started up again just like that. One a day is all she has now though, for old times' sake. Daphne has no idea; neither did Finn.

She lights up, drawing the hot smoke deep inside. She pictures it billowing into her lungs, filling up all the spaces there. Leo never smoked, never even took a puff as a teenager when all his pals were trying them out. He didn't ask her to give them up when they got together, but she knew he wanted her to, so she did shortly before they were married. She'd have done anything for him.

Finn didn't smoke either: she was always glad of that. He was healthy, hardly ever sick as a child, and strong from the cycling. She's grateful she can think about him now without wanting to die … Took long enough for that to happen. Not that she'd care if she did die – what difference would it make to anyone? Who'd miss her? – but she doesn't *wish* for it any more, which she supposes is a good thing.

She leans her head against the seat back and regards the sludgy sky. Saw a plane crossing it earlier, pulling what looked like a long white flag in its wake. Writing on the flag she couldn't read: an ad for something, she supposed. Ads wherever you look these days.

She catches a sound in the lane beyond the low wall at the end of the yard. She sits up and sees a hooded figure walking by rapidly, blowing on his or her hands. Female, Mo decides. Something about the gait: too light, she thinks, to be masculine. Could be Una, similar height and figure, except she's at school. All the young ones look alike now, afraid to stand out from the crowd.

The person passes a parked blue car with twin white ribbons strung across its bonnet – wedding car, must be – and approaches a gate that leads into one of the back yards of the houses that are lined up on the opposite side of the lane. Immediately a dog sets up a noisy barking, shattering the peace of the lane. Mo stubs out her cigarette and goes back inside.

'What kept you?' Sadie says, tapping buttons on the cash register. 'I'm gasping for a cuppa.'

'I'm here now,' Mo replies, finding a carrier bag for trousers that lie waiting on the counter. Sadie spends most of her time in the shop drinking tea, only comes in for the company.

Left on her own, Mo tidies the bric-à-brac shelves, repositioning the chipped vases and worn leather wallets and mismatched candlesticks and soap dishes. She straightens the books and sweeps the floor and glares at a teen well known for his habit of forgetting to pay, keeps her eye on him until he eventually leaves, empty-handed and scowling. As the morning drifts on she sells a few more bits and pieces.

Just before noon she hears the repeated honking of a car horn in the street outside. She gets to the front door in time to see the blue car she observed earlier emerge from the lane a few doors up and turn in the direction of the charity shop.

As it makes its leisurely way along the street, horn honking repeatedly, the bride in the back seat catches Mo's eye and waves at her, smiling. Mo lifts a hand in return, thinking back to her own wedding day.

Never stopped raining from early morning. Her mother fed her two poached eggs with warm griddle bread and gave her a miraculous medal – something blue – that Mo pinned inside the bodice of her dress. Her cousin Therese played the organ as Mo walked up the aisle on her father's arm.

The look on Leo's face when she approached, the way he took her from her father. The way he thanked him, like she was a gift he was being presented with.

Her mother had made her wedding dress. It was shiny and

white with short puffed sleeves, and when Mo took it off that evening its elasticated waist had imprinted a puckered pink line on her flesh that Leo kissed softly, all the way around.

She stands and watches the car moving slowly down the street, its driver continuing to beat out a cheerful tattoo. She waits until it vanishes around a bend before she turns back inside.

Minute by minute her shift draws to a close.

◆

In the end she gets Una a gift box of shampoo and conditioner in the health shop near the train station. *Organic*, it says, and *rich in seaweed nutrients*. Amazing that it costs ten times as much as the shampoo she buys for herself in the supermarket – she would have thought seaweed was a free commodity.

Conditioner was unheard of when Mo was growing up. Her hair was washed once a week in rainwater scooped from a barrel outside the kitchen window, with shampoo that came in a big green bottle and smelt like trees, and stung like mad if it got in your eyes. In between washes, a more sinister liquid was scrubbed vigorously into her hair and left there for what seemed like an eternity before her mother dragged a fine-tooth comb painfully across every inch of Mo's scalp, wiping the black smudges she unearthed onto a page of newspaper, and that was it as far as keeping her hair clean went.

Things are different now, of course, new fancy ways to get rid of lice, and any amount of bottles and potions and whatnot for hair. Hopefully Una will like this fancy stuff, nestling in a bed of shredded gold paper inside a bronze box.

'Would you like me to gift-wrap it?' the impossibly tall sales assistant asks. Lashes tipped with silver, brows plucked so thin you can barely see them, nails sludge-green with awful square ends.

'I would.' Least they can do is make it look nice, the price Mo is paying.

'It'll be one thirty extra,' the assistant adds.

Mo looks at her in disbelief. 'One *thirty*? You'd get a roll of it for that.'

The assistant blinks, a silver flash. 'So you don't want it, then.'

'I do not,' Mo replies tartly.

The rest of the transaction is conducted in silence. Mo takes the plain brown bag and pockets her change without a word. Cheek of them, charging an extra fortune to put a bit of fancy paper on it. She'll find something at home: tinfoil will do fine if there's nothing else.

On the street her stomach rumbles. She normally eats her sandwich in the shop before she leaves, but today she'd had enough of Gretta and Martha, couldn't face another minute of them. She'll head to the park, have her lunch in peace there. The rain might hold off for another while.

Just as well, anyway, to delay the sandwich a bit – she won't be eating again till eight. At home she has dinner at seven, always has done since the days of herself and Leo in the shop. She'd leave work soon after five to get organised; he'd be home at half six, time to have a wash and a beer before she dished up. Still, she's not one to complain. And Daphne, it has to be said, is a good enough cook when she puts her mind to it.

As she approaches a café she feels a sudden urge to urinate. A less accommodating bladder, she's discovered, is one of the trials of getting older. She pushes open the door and steps inside, makes a show of scanning the faces of the people seated at the scattered tables as she strides across the floor towards the door that says *Toilets*. Look as if you have every right to be there, meet everyone's eye and nobody will challenge you.

On her way out again, whatever look she gives across the room, she spots a woman seated alone at a table to the rear of the place, the kind of table you'd choose if you didn't want to be interrupted. The woman's face is in profile, head bent as she reads the menu. What looks like an untouched glass of red wine sits before her.

Her ash-blonde hair is prettily cut, falling almost to her chin at the front, becoming shorter as it moves around to fluff out gently above her hairline at the rear. She wears a dress the colour of the nasturtiums that bloom every year outside Mo's kitchen window, and what look like black suede ankle boots with thin, pointed heels. A sky blue patterned scarf falls over the back of her chair. From the top of the dress her long neck emerges, white and graceful as a swan's. The first time they met, Mo envied her that neck.

Isobel, the woman said. *Delighted to meet you*. Extending a cool maroon-nailed hand in Mo's direction, her pale hair longer then, pinned up to show off the neck, and the high cheekbones that Daphne had inherited.

Her mother ran off with someone else when Daphne was six, Finn had told Mo – and it wasn't until his and Daphne's wedding that Mo first encountered the runaway mother and her second husband – not, she could gather, the same man who had spirited her away from six-year-old Daphne and poor cuckolded Jack. Isobel was popular with the gentlemen, it would appear.

Not hard to see why men would find her desirable, with all that fragile femininity, those almost-silver eyes. Difficult to fathom, though, how a woman could possibly turn her back on her child: rabid dogs wouldn't have kept Mo away from Finn when he was growing up. Had the woman no maternal instinct? Had she never bonded with her daughter?

Coincidental that Una and Daphne had both been deprived of mothers at exactly the same age, even if the circumstances were very different. You'd think something in common like that would have drawn them together – but as far as Mo can tell, all is not as it should be with them. They seemed to get on well enough while Finn was around; it's only since his death that Mo has become aware of a difficulty, a gap in communication that neither of them seems inclined to bridge.

What can Mo do, though? She's hardly an expert when it comes to breaking down barriers – on the contrary, she has no trouble putting them up. Anyway, it's not her place to butt in; she'd surely be seen to be interfering if she brought the subject up with Daphne. They're not given to that kind of conversation, never were.

Still, it's a shame to see Finn's widow and his daughter not close. A shame, too, to witness Daphne's all but non-existent relationship with her mother. Understandable, maybe, given their history, but a pity nonetheless.

Isobel had come to Finn's funeral, of course. It had taken Mo a few moments to place her. 'So sorry,' she whispered, her mouth exactly the same red as the scarf draped about her neck, her hands pressing Mo's briefly between them. Wafting a perfume that smelt like gooseberries.

Her husband was there too. Mo couldn't remember his name; he had to tell her. She can't think of it now either. Andrew? Max? He had one of those handshakes that nearly broke bones: she remembers that all right. Cold eyes, too, eyes that had held no sympathy despite his murmured words.

She looks again at Isobel, wonders belatedly what she's doing here alone. Mo should say hello, be civil.

She advances towards the table. Isobel continues to stare at the menu – but Mo gets the sense as she approaches, from some stiffness of the other's pose, that she's well aware of her presence. Was she hoping to avoid an encounter? Too late for that.

'Isobel,' she says – and the head lifts.

'Oh,' Isobel says, a hand reaching up to touch her hair. 'Oh, it's – Finn's mother, isn't it?'

Forgotten her name. Mo isn't about to enlighten her. 'That's right. How are you keeping?'

'Oh, I'm fine …' She trails off, hand resting now on the few inches of skin above the neckline of her dress. 'And you? How are you?'

Ill at ease is how she comes across to Mo. Embarrassed about it being the anniversary maybe, struck dumb as so many are in the face of another's troubles.

'As good as I can be,' Mo tells her. Shouldn't have come over, really. Should have left well enough alone. She catches the glance Isobel darts at the front door. Well, well.

There's a small, awkward silence. To break it, Mo raises the hand that holds the present. 'Una's birthday,' she says.

'Una's ... ? Oh, yes, Daphne did mention it. Is she ... having a party?'

A party, on her father's anniversary. How can she possibly imagine the girl would want a party? 'No,' Mo replies evenly. 'She's not inclined to celebrate today.' Putting just enough emphasis on the final word.

Isobel flushes a delicate pink. 'No, of course not,' she says quickly. 'Sorry, I wasn't thinking.'

Mo makes no response, begins buttoning her jacket.

'Chilly, isn't it?' Isobel goes on, indicating her glass of wine with a small forced laugh. 'Thought it might warm me up.'

Of course she did. Far more chance of a glass of red putting the roses back in your cheeks than, say, a cup of hot coffee. 'I won't keep you,' Mo says. 'Enjoy your drink.' *And whatever tomfoolery you're up to.*

'Yes, goodbye then ...'

And still she hasn't remembered Mo's name: bet she's kicking herself with those fancy boots. As Mo leaves the restaurant and heads left for the park she passes a young woman, still a teenager by the look of her, cradling a tiny baby. Catching a glimpse of his infant face – full pursed lips, pale pink knob of a nose, unafraid moist blue eyes – Mo recalls the sheer joy she felt when Finn was handed to her for the first time, parcelled up too neatly in a thin blue crocheted blanket.

She remembers unwrapping him, gazing down at the tiny perfect creature she and Leo had created. She remembers the miracle of Leo's eyes looking back at her, the Darling genes being carried on through their firstborn son.

She wanted more babies, of course she did. She wanted to fill their tiny place with children, but Finn was the only one she got to hold in her arms. On five more occasions she conceived, and one after another they slipped from her hostile womb before their time. Five tiny lost ghosts, each one adding another layer to her rage, each one making her sicker with loneliness. Sharpening her tongue, hardening her heart, pulling all the softness out of her.

But whenever the anger and heartbreak threatened to overpower her, she would remind herself that she had Leo and Finn; she had a lot more than some women. Her little family brought her happiness, undoubtedly it did, even if it was a more brittle joy than it might otherwise have been.

And when Finn met and married Susan, and Una became part of their lives, Mo found herself torn. Finn's choice of wife, it had to be said, dismayed her initially: why couldn't he have found someone less ... tainted? And while of course Susan turned out to be a perfectly adequate wife, and while it was certainly pleasant to have a child about the place again – Una was a personable little creature, despite her inauspicious start – what Mo hungered for was her own flesh-and-blood grandchild, a baby who would truly belong to Finn.

It would happen. She just had to be patient. And as she waited to become a grandmother she found herself smiling again at babies in buggies, like she used to when she was a young bride. She watched Finn's face for news each time he came to visit her and Leo, impatient for the small, satisfying weight of a newborn in her arms again. She'd turned sixty the January after his wedding; most women that age had at least a couple of grandchildren – but months turned into years, and no announcement was made.

In time Mo had to adjust her expectations and remind herself, once again, to be content with what she'd been given. She and Leo did their bit with Una, helped out with the babysitting, turned up for the birthday parties. Life shifted track, and eventually found its new momentum, and turned them into a family of sorts.

And in due course, as is the way in life, contentment morphed once again into tragedy. Susan died shortly before Una's seventh birthday – and later that terrible week, the discovery by Mo of Leo's wallet in the fridge marked the beginning of his decline.

The months that followed were heartbreaking in the extreme. While Finn was struggling to come to terms with his bereavement, Leo was slipping away from Mo like her lost babies; almost every day she saw fresh evidence of his crumbling mind, and she was gripped once again by rage and terror and helplessness. She felt pulled in every direction, doing what she could for Finn and Una, needing also to tend her husband.

She had plenty of energy though, and being busy was therapy in itself. She kept a grip on the accounts in the shop, looked after Una when school finished, cared as best she could for her disappearing husband. She even had Finn and Una around to dinner several times a week – as easy to cook for four as for two, and they all had to eat, regardless of whatever else was happening. They managed, after a fashion.

But time continued its usual relentless march. Within two years Leo's disintegration was complete, and he was entirely lost to them. If they'd been close before, she and Finn became closer as they supported one another through the aftermath of this loss and inched together towards a fresh, sadder equilibrium.

Despite her grief, Mo forced herself to remain as indispensable to Finn as she could, looking ahead to the time when she would no longer be able to manage on her own, and he would take her in to live with him, Una by then presumably having left to live her own life. As long as she and Finn had each other, they'd cope with anything.

And then Daphne had come along.

Mo recalls the day Finn limped into the bicycle shop with a buckled front wheel, a bloody nose and a face full of cuts. *I'm grand*, he insisted, as she clucked around him. *She didn't mean it, it's easily done* – but Mo was furious. Pure carelessness, some featherheaded driver not bothering to look behind her before she swung her door open. Easily done, maybe – but just as easily avoided if you had an ounce of wit about you.

So when Daphne showed up the following day – bringing a cake, if you please, as if that made everything all right – Mo was strongly tempted to give her a piece of her mind. Would have too, if Finn hadn't appeared with his ruined face. He opened the box, all smiles, said as long as she'd gone to the trouble of making him a cake he'd better introduce himself – and, of course, Mo was introduced too, so she'd had to be civil.

They'd already taken to one another: that very first day Mo could see it in their faces, in the soft smiles they gave to one another. Daphne was a lot younger than him – sixteen years younger, it turned out – but that didn't seem to bother either of them. Finn walked her to the door that first day and they stood talking on the path outside for several minutes. Out of earshot, none of their conversation reaching Mo, but she'd had a fair idea that another meeting was being arranged and of course she was right.

It wasn't long before Finn was rushing off to meet her at lunchtime, leaving Mo to eat her sandwich alone in the back room. They went out in the evenings a bit too, with Una dropped around to Mo's house or Mo making her way to Finn's to babysit.

The more they got to know one another, the happier Finn became, and while of course Mo wanted him to be happy – of *course* she did – she found it hard to warm to Daphne. Not Daphne exactly, she was harmless enough once you got to know her, but the *idea* of her.

Everything had changed when she'd come on the scene. Finn didn't need Mo anymore; that was the stark truth of it. Daphne took him away from her; that was the ugly truth of it. Oh, she knew she shouldn't let it get to her – she was still his mother; there was nothing Daphne, or anyone else, could do about *that* – but she couldn't help feeling resentful.

When they told her within six months of their meeting that they were getting married, she genuinely tried to look on the positive side, tried to focus on the fact that it was a second chance for Finn, another chance to hold his own child in his arms – but all she could see was him being snatched out of her reach; all she could see was the future she'd envisaged being wiped away.

Of course she went along with it; she didn't have much choice. She made the best of it, wished them well, bought a hat (second-hand) and clapped along with the others when the priest pronounced them man and wife. Then she sat back and waited for Daphne at least to provide her with a grandchild.

There was no reason why it shouldn't happen. Daphne was a young woman, still in the prime of her childbearing years. Surely it was only a matter of time – but once again Mo's hopes were to come to nothing. She watched the months go by with increasing frustration, each one bringing no good news at all.

Daphne had her career, that was it. Despite her rush to the altar, she was in no hurry to have babies, and she must have persuaded Finn to wait a few more years.

But of course he hadn't had a few more years. When he died, all Mo's hopes died with him. And it was Daphne who had stolen him away, who had claimed him as hers for his last few precious years on earth, and given Mo nothing at all in return.

She tries not to dwell on it – what use are regrets, what good will come of grudges? – but sometimes it's all she can do to be civil to her daughter-in-law.

She reaches the park and turns in through the gate. She walks slowly along the path until she reaches the lake. The water is slate grey, the swans huddled in a mass by the little island in the centre. Not too many people around, not exactly strolling-in-the-park weather, and today Mo is glad of the solitude.

She sits on a bench and unwraps her cheese and tomato sandwich – but at the first bite her appetite deserts her, and she feeds most of it to the swans that glide across at the sight of the bread floating on the water. She watches them bumping gently together, long necks curving, tail feathers twitching, heads swooping towards the food – descendants, she imagines, of the ones that lived here when she and Leo strolled past, newly engaged and then newly married.

She gets to her feet, brushing crumbs from her lap. She'll do the cemetery, then head home. Her knees ache in the cold: they've been at her all morning. 'You're doing too much,' her doctor tells her. 'Slow down, take it easy.' But she's never been one to take things easy, and she's not about to start now. Always better to keep busy; always safer to keep busy.

The walk from the park to the cemetery takes her forty-five minutes: when she was younger she'd have done it in thirty, no bother. The faster the years are slipping by, the slower she's becoming.

The sky darkens: she wonders how long it will be before the heavens open. She never brings an umbrella – would only lose it – but she keeps a plastic rain bonnet in her pocket in case she's caught. She'll take the bus home afterwards: enough walking done today.

There are flowers on Finn's grave. Yellow roses; cost a bit by the look of them. No card that she can see, but it must have been Daphne. She must have been in already. Mo should have brought flowers, never thought of it. Never thought beyond coming to say hello to him.

She rests a hip against his headstone. 'Still here, my darling,' she tells him. 'Still barging my way along, upsetting everyone. Nothing much has changed. Still miss you,' she says, 'as much as ever. Still wish you were here, that'll never change.'

There's nobody around; it's as deserted as the park was. Bleak here always, a wind whistling just now past the gravestones. She rubs her arms, trying to coax some heat into her, the padded jacket not nearly warm enough despite the cashmere layer beneath it. She'll wear her good coat tonight – it's like a blanket.

She shifts her weight from hip to hip. 'Getting old,' she says to him. 'Few aches and pains, not as much energy as before. Keeping busy, though. Not giving up, not till I have to. Three mornings a week at the charity shop, same old few coming in. Not exactly a laugh a minute, but it's something.'

She traces the shapes of the letters hewn into the stone. Hard to believe poor Susan is dead over ten years. Time rushing onwards, stopping for nobody.

'I've been thinking,' she tells Finn, 'about the bicycle shop. It's time something was done. I'm ashamed we've let it go this long. It's just … I couldn't face it up to now, couldn't face going in and not seeing—'

She breaks off, overwhelmed without warning by a wave of sadness, a familiar sensation of utter bleakness draping itself over her. What's the point? What's the point of any of it? Why is she still insisting on carrying on? Why is she so determined to keep going when the two people she loved most have been taken from her?

She regards Finn's headstone again, his name chiselled under Susan's into the granite. What's she doing here, talking to a ghost? He's gone, he can't hear her. He'll never hear her again.

The darkness settles around her, extends its claws and sinks them deep into her. She lifts her head, tries to push it away, but it refuses to leave. *Give up*, it urges her. *It's easy: just let go. You have nothing to live for, nothing—*

No. NO. With an effort she straightens her back, tightens

her grip on the handle of her shopping bag. She will *not* give up, she will not do that. She will never give up.

'I'll come and see you tomorrow,' she murmurs to Finn. 'I'll be here again tomorrow, son.'

She turns and walks away, fighting the urge to throw back her head and howl like an animal. She knows where she must go.

❖

The best thing about him, she has decided, is that he never tells her it's going to get easier. He never talks about time healing all wounds, or any of that rubbish. He never says anything much really, which suits her fine, because she has plenty to say. She saves them up, all the things she can't talk about with Daphne or Una, and out they spill as soon as she sits on the brown leather armchair in his butterscotch-coloured little room that always smells of cooking meat, and mint.

He's good at listening. He'd want to be, in his line of work. The things he must have heard over the years, the regrets and the anger and the frustration that must have been dumped at his feet. He listens when she talks, and occasionally he nods, and sometimes he tilts his head a bit as if he's trying to figure her out, and mostly that's about it.

That's as much as she wants.

He seems unfazed by the awful things she says sometimes, when she can't stop the fury escaping. The language that comes out of her then, she who never curses normally, swearing like a fishwife sometimes in that poky little place, her rage when it blooms seeming to demand that kind of frowned-upon language.

He never objects, hardly seems to notice the obscenities she sends flying around. He doesn't mind either when words fail her, and she can only glare at him with particular ferocity. He gives no sign of being put out today as she sits bawling her eyes out yet again, yanking tissues from the box on the table between them, soaking them with her grief.

Today isn't even her day. Her day is Tuesday. It's been two o'clock on a Tuesday afternoon for the past eight months, ever since she met him, literally went barrelling into him as he stood on the street ahead of her, about to push a key into a lock. Would have fallen if he hadn't caught her.

Sorry, he said immediately, even though it was her fault. Not looking where she was going, mind a thousand miles away. *Are you all right?* he asked, a strong hand cradling her elbow, steadying her. *Did you hurt yourself?* His voice deep, his words measured, despite the abruptness of their encounter. *Are you sure you're OK?*

Mo found herself leaning into his supporting arm, wanting to be looked after, craving the sensation of someone taking over after four months of being the one who coped, four months of never letting a crack show. Four months of trying to be strong for Daphne and Una when they collapsed.

The following day she walked again along that street until she came to the door he'd been about to open, right next to a Greek restaurant. She saw a brass plaque with a man's name on it, and underneath, Counselling Services.

Counselling. Telling your troubles to a stranger who sent you back to your childhood and raked up more muck, often left you worse off than you were at the start. She wanted help, she knew that, but it wasn't advice she was after. She carried on walking.

Three days later she returned and stood before the door again. It wouldn't commit her to anything; she would say she was just making an enquiry. She'd know in a minute if he could help her.

She pressed the brass button above the plaque and waited. Thirty seconds later she pressed it again, and again it went unanswered. She left.

Two days after that she was back again, and this time he was in.

I'd like a word, she said, *if you have a minute* – and he led her upstairs and into the little room she's come to know so well.

She met his eye. *I'm not looking for counselling*, she told him. *I know what your sign says, but I don't want anyone trying to fix me. I just need someone to listen to me, that's all I'm after. I need a place where I can talk, without anyone talking back.*

I see. He regarded her politely, his face revealing nothing. If he remembered her from their collision of five days earlier he didn't let on. If he thought she had a screw loose he kept that quiet too.

So what do you say? she asked.

I'm a good listener, he replied.

No hypnosis, or any of that nonsense? No sending me back to my childhood?

Absolutely not.

Just listening, nothing else.

If that's what you want.

His voice was as calm and steady as she remembered from

their first encounter. Some instinct, the same one that had brought her back to his door, told her that she could believe him. They made an appointment, and the following Tuesday afternoon he brought her into his office for the second time — and as soon as she sat down she began to cry.

For over half of her allotted hour she sat hunched in a ball as four months of tears rolled out, and all he did was push the box of tissues closer to her. Without saying a word, he had given her permission to stop holding everything in, and out it came.

And when she finally managed to stop she blew her nose and began in a rusty voice to tell him about Finn and Leo, and true to his word he listened, and never once interrupted.

The relief was immense. Every word she uttered made her feel lighter. The tears came back once or twice, but she talked around them, kept on telling him about the husband and son she had lost.

When the clock on the wall told her the hour was up she stopped talking and got to her feet, although he had given no sign that he needed her to finish. She wasn't one to take advantage.

She's been seeing him ever since, every Tuesday without fail. She wouldn't miss it: he's her safety valve. Today was the first time she'd turned up without an appointment.

He was on his way out when she arrived. About to pull the street door closed behind him, car keys in hand, umbrella under an arm.

You're off home, she said, but her face must have given her away, because he shook his head — *No, no, come on in* — and

brought her upstairs, and excused himself to make a phone
call. Cancelling or postponing whatever appointment she'd
interrupted.

I won't stay long, she said when he reappeared – and that was
the last thing she was able to say before words deserted her and
the tears came flooding out, just like the first time with him.

Now, finally, she wipes her eyes.

'Sorry,' she says. 'Sorry for barging in.'

'Don't be.'

'I don't know why that happened. I was fine this morning.'
And though he surely recognises this for the lie it is, he doesn't
contradict her.

He asked her last week if she wanted to change to Friday
because of the anniversary, and she refused, determined to
weather it on her own. Stubborn old fool that she is.

She feels better now, though. It's bearable again, like it
always is after time spent with him. She lays it at his door in all
its ugliness and pain, and he takes it without complaint and gets
rid of it.

It's thanks to him she's working at the charity shop. He
admired a jacket she was getting into at the end of a session,
maybe a month after she'd begun seeing him.

Charity shop, she told him, like she'd tell anyone.

He smiled. *Never have guessed.*

I get most of my things there.

You'd be good behind the counter so, he replied. Just like that,
no more than a bit of a joke – but the remark stayed in her
head. A fortnight later she offered her services at the shop.
Undoubtedly, it's helped her too.

She levers herself to her feet. 'I've delayed you.' Nearly half an hour she's stayed.

'Don't worry about it.'

He doesn't want to take payment but she insists. He's her only gift to herself in the week, and worth every penny.

'You want to leave next Tuesday off?' he asks, and she tells him no, she wants to see him as usual. Today was different. Next week will be back to normal, and he's part of her Tuesdays now.

She wonders how long more she'll need him.

❉

She welcomes the cold air on her flushed face as she makes her way to the bus stop. She wonders can people tell she's been crying, and thinks by the way nobody meets her eye that they probably can.

The rain begins as she reaches the stop, and she fishes the bonnet from her pocket. She tucks in her hair and ties the plastic straps under her chin. Not exactly the latest fashion but it does the job, and she's never been one for following trends.

As the shower turns heavy she longs again for her green coat, maybe the only thing in her wardrobe that was bought new. It was a gift from Leo, or rather the money was, on her sixty-fifth birthday.

'Get yourself something nice in the sales,' he said. 'A good winter coat, or a suit.' It was January, two months after Susan had died, and Mo was putting his little memory lapses down to the after-effects of that. He'd been fond of Susan, he was upset she was gone; that was all there was to it.

By April, that excuse wasn't working any more. The dread

had planted itself in her head, and each time he forgot to brush his teeth, or went to the supermarket with his slippers still on, or left his key in the front door all night, her fears increased.

The rain is getting heavier. The drops smack like popping corn onto her bonnet. There's no seat or shelter here, just a pole topped with the bus-stop sign. Two others wait with her: a youth of about sixteen, shoulders hunched within a black hooded top that's making a terrible job of keeping him dry, and a man in a flat tweed cap, hands shoved deep into his raincoat pockets, whose enormous reddish beard makes it impossible to put an age on him.

Traffic is building up, wipers slicing across windscreens, tyres hissing on the wet road as they pass. It'd be a night for the fire and the telly if she wasn't going out. She could murder a dinner now, but she has nearly four hours still to wait. She'll make Bovril when she gets—

Something pokes her in the side. She turns, affronted.

The bearded man gestures with the same elbow he used to nudge her. 'Someone wants you.'

She hadn't noticed the car that has pulled up next to them, the passenger window halfway down. She ducks her head and peers inside.

'Climb in,' one of her neighbours says, pushing open the door, and Mo gets in gratefully, even if it'll be non-stop talk all the way home.

❖

The house is chilly. She plugs in the two-bar heater she keeps in the kitchen and switches on the radio while she fills the kettle and spoons Bovril into a mug. Nothing like Bovril to warm the bones.

She must parcel up Una's present. She gets up to rummage in drawers but all she finds is old Christmas wrapping paper, so she tears a length from her roll of tinfoil and uses that instead. What does it matter? It's what's inside that counts.

When the kettle boils she fills the mug, inhaling the savoury steam. The rain has persisted: she watches drops race one another to the bottom of the windowpane. No sign of Cheeky, next door's cat who calls around occasionally for the few scraps she usually finds for him: more sense than to be out in that rain.

She plods upstairs and locates her phone on her bedside locker. She picks it up and sees a missed call from Daphne at 5:14, just two minutes earlier. No message, can't have been important. Hardly any need to ring back, she'll see her soon enough.

She opens a text box, selects Una as the recipient. *Happy birthday*, she types carefully, wishing for the umpteenth time that the keys were bigger. *See you soon, love Mo*. She sends it off: better late than never.

She shucks off her damp sneakers and tracksuit bottoms. She takes her black trousers from the back of the chair and pulls them on. The sneakers she replaces with black loafers, the only other pair of shoes she possesses. There: she feels smarter already. She balls up newspaper and stuffs the sneakers with it, leaves them propped on their heels against the wall.

In the bathroom she splashes her face with water and dabs it dry. She squeezes foundation from a tube, brushes on blue eye shadow, strokes pink across her lips as steadily as her hand will allow.

As she works, she tries to focus on the separate sections of her reflected face – curve of cheek, slant of forehead, dip of eye socket, rise of nose – rather than see it in its entirety. It disconcerts her, that wrinkled old thing. She doesn't want to be reminded of it.

Back in the bedroom she fumbles for ages with the clasp of her pearl necklace before managing to get it closed: why on earth do they make them so tiny? She dots eau-de-Cologne on her wrists and temples and behind her ears.

She takes her coat from the wardrobe and pulls it on. So dressed-up she feels in it, worth every penny, still going strong after ten years. Will undoubtedly outlive her – not that Daphne will think to recycle it. Straight into the bin, no doubt, along with all her other clothes.

At ten to six precisely she steps out of the house and closes the front door. Thankfully, the rain has stopped. She retraces the route they took coming home in the car till she reaches the river, not far. She turns and walks along by the bank, just half a block, until she comes to the wrought-iron double gates.

She turns in, the familiar mix of anticipation and apprehension settling over her, like it does every evening. In less than a minute she'll see him – and her heart will break all over again.

◆

'A chocolate cake,' she says. 'From a bakery that's not long open – where Hegarty's camera shop used to be, you know, a few doors up from the charity shop where I told you I work now.

The bakery is very fancy – I dread to think what Daphne paid for the cake. I just hope Una appreciates it.'

She lifts a forkful of mashed potato, and his mouth drops open to admit it, his eyes never leaving her face.

'I was caught in the rain earlier,' she says. 'I was waiting for the bus home from town. I was very lucky though, Nancy came along – I've told you about Nancy, married to Neville O'Keeffe, they live two doors up from me. Their eldest lad, Barry, would be about Finn's age. Nancy was telling me he's just after taking early retirement from his job, imagine.'

Another forkful, another silent mouthful. She keeps going.

'Nancy gave me a lift all the way home. I was very glad of it, wet old day. She and Neville are off on holidays next month – they're going to stay with some relatives in France. Well for some.'

In fact she has no idea if relatives in France exist, let alone whether Nancy and Neville are going to pay them a visit – but the accuracies don't matter here. What matters is that she talks to him.

The things she makes up sometimes. You could fill a book with them.

She wipes a fleck of potato from his chin, and immediately he frowns and swats her hand away. 'No, dear,' she says gently, 'it's OK, love, I'm just keeping you nice and clean. You'll have another bit of broccoli. You like broccoli, don't you?' Spearing a floret and feeding it to him. 'Good … that's nice, isn't it? You like that, you always went for broccoli when I made it. That and cauliflower, you loved them.'

Like a child. Like how she used to feed Finn when he was

small. Sometimes Leo grabs the fork from her and stabs the food with it, makes a right mess until she manages to reclaim it. Just like Finn used to do.

'Daphne's doing roast chicken tonight – it's Una's favourite. You like it too, don't you? And stuffing, you always wanted extra stuffing when I made it, remember? The sausagemeat stuffing with onions – your mother gave me the recipe when we got married. "Lots of onions," you used to say. "Don't spare the onions."'

He makes no sign that he hears her, never reacts to anything she says. He eats mechanically, chewing and swallowing with no indication of enjoyment. But he looks at her, he watches her face all the time. He must recognise it. It has to be familiar to him, whatever the doctors say. However empty his eyes seem.

She lifts the cup to his lips and he drinks noisily and unselfconsciously. She wipes the trail that dribbles out, and again he swats crossly. 'Ssh,' she says, picking up the fork, feeding him a little square of pork chop.

Every evening she comes. Six o'clock on the dot they serve up the dinner, and she feeds it to him. Every evening she makes herself nice for him. He's still her husband, he'll always be that, even if he can't talk to her any more or live with her. Even if his mind has betrayed him, his memory plundered by the cruellest of illnesses.

They sit at right angles to one another in the day room, he in an armchair, she on a wooden kitchen chair. His plate is on a table by her side, out of his reach – he can't be trusted not to send it flying. He's given to sudden bursts of anger, forgotten as quickly as they occur.

'I got Una fancy shampoo for her birthday,' she tells him. 'You remember Una, don't you? She used to come and see you. There's a nice smell from the shampoo, like lavender. It cost a bit, but I didn't mind. I hope Una likes it. She has lovely hair, all curly and golden. I used to wish my hair was curly when I was young – did I ever tell you that? My mother used to put it in rollers for me – a nightmare, trying to sleep in them – and after all that the curls would last about ten minutes.'

Finn would bring Una to visit him in the early days. If the weather was good they'd wheel Leo into the garden; otherwise they sat with him in here. But by the time Una's ninth birthday came around, Leo no longer recognised her, and Mo asked Finn to stop bringing her, fearing it would be too upsetting for the child.

He still came himself after that, of course, sometimes with Mo, sometimes alone. And Daphne, when she joined the family, accompanied him now and again. She'd never known the old Leo; all she saw was the husk he'd become. When his mood swings became a problem, one of the nursing-home staff had taken to hovering nearby whenever Daphne was in his company.

They'd wanted to do the same when Mo visited – *It's not safe to be alone with him*, they told her – but she was having none of it. *I'm his wife, I can manage him*, she said, in the sort of voice people didn't tend to argue with, so a compromise was reached: she leaves the door open when she's with him, and they don't bother her.

After Finn's death she asked Daphne not to come to the nursing home any more. *There's no need*, she said. *He's gone beyond knowing who comes to see him, it won't make any difference to him* – but the truth was more selfish than that. The truth was that he was all she had now, and she wanted him to herself.

'I bought a new top yesterday,' she tells him now. 'Three euro, like new. I would have worn it only it's in the wash. I'll wear it for you tomorrow. I think you'll like it. It's blue.'

Blue is your colour, he'd told her once, before they were married. *Matches your eyes. Always wear something blue.* So she'd bought blue eye shadow – as a joke, really, but she likes it. She only puts it on for him now; she doesn't waste it on anyone else.

'Woman came into the shop today,' she says, moving the empty dinner plate aside, picking up the bowl with jelly and custard in it. 'She bought a teddy for her little boy. He's in a show at his school. You know that song, "Ten in the Bed"? They're doing a little play about it.'

He hit her once, just once, about three months ago now. Brought his arm up without warning, walloped her across the face with the back of his hand, sent her flying sideways out of the chair. She scrambled to her feet, nose and cheek throbbing, elbow stinging where it had hit the floor, heart doing cartwheels inside her.

Thank God nobody came in – they mustn't have heard. Leo looked blankly at her as she resumed her seat, no trace left of the rage that had erupted out of him.

'Oh, don't do that,' she said, searching her face with wobbling fingertips, feeling for blood. 'Don't do that again, love.' And so far he hasn't. She wasn't cut; he hadn't done any lasting damage. Her elbow was black and blue for a week, but nothing was broken or sprained. She'd been lucky, had got off lightly.

She didn't say anything about it to the staff. He didn't mean it, it wasn't him. If she told them they'd sedate him more, turn him into a zombie. She's more careful now: she watches his movements, keeps an eye out for anything unexpected.

He doesn't know about Finn: she won't have him upset. *Don't tell him*, she's said to the staff, *don't let on*. She knows they think she's being ridiculous, and maybe they're right – Stephen, the man in the next room, died a couple of months back, and Leo didn't react when Mo made a mention of it a few days later – but still she can't bear the thought of him hearing that his son is dead. What father, whatever his condition, could hear that news and not be affected by it?

He eats his dessert with the same lack of emotion he displayed for the dinner, but she remembers how he used to enjoy it. Baked apples, he'd have been happy with one of those every day if she'd given it to him. Loved the way she did the baked apples, a knob of butter and a pinch of cinnamon and a spoon of sugar stuffed into the middle.

And gooseberry crumble with a scoop of ice-cream: the minute the gooseberries appeared in the shops he'd be at her to make crumble. And of course rhubarb tarts, with buttery pastry and a dollop of whipped cream. Just as well he didn't tend to put on weight – three or four helpings he'd have sometimes.

Her stomach rumbles, the sound clearly audible above the small clink of spoon on bowl. She gives him a smile he doesn't return. The loss of his sense of humour has been one of the hardest things to bear. He used to have her in stitches – a quizzical expression, a lift of an eyebrow, a jut of his chin was all it took sometimes. Even after she'd lost the babies, he'd do everything he could think of to put a smile on her face. Gone now, all gone.

She spoons up the last of the custard. 'Now,' she says, 'all gone.'

Nine years it'll be in June. She was sixty-six, Leo a month off his seventieth birthday when she'd finally had to admit defeat, after so long trying to cod herself that he wasn't so bad really. Telling herself, and Finn, that she could manage fine, when in reality she hardly closed her eyes some nights, so terrified she was of what he might try to do without her watching him.

Nine years she's been without him, nine years since she sold the big house they'd inherited from his parents and moved into the small redbrick, chosen not least because of its proximity to the nursing home. Every penny of the difference going towards his keep here, to boost the money from the insurance policy he'd taken out as soon as the shop had started to show a profit.

Eight years or thereabouts since he's looked at her with any glimmer of recognition, nearly three since he uttered his last word to her, or to anyone.

Shutting down: that's how the doctors describe it. His faculties leaving him, piece by piece. No longer able to use the toilet, no longer able to feed himself, or groom himself. His walk nearly gone too, reduced to an unsteady shuffle. Seventy-nine in July, his quality of life, to all intents and purposes, as non-existent as Finn's is.

But he's still here, he's still alive and breathing. He's still eating, still able to chew and swallow. And he's still her husband, in sickness and in health, for however long he continues to breathe. The doctors don't talk about how long that might be, and she doesn't ask them. What's the point of knowing? What would she possibly do with that knowledge?

But one day she might look into his eyes, one day when she's guiding a piece of food to his mouth, or telling him about something that happened in the charity shop – and she might catch a glimpse of the man she fell in love with. She might see a spark of recognition in his face – he might find a way to let her know that somewhere inside, in some still miraculously intact part of his brain, he remembers her.

She might see it – you couldn't rule it out. You could never rule it out.

◆

By seven she's home again. She'll have to leave for Daphne's in a few minutes. She longs to change back into her sneakers – the black shoes aren't half as comfy – but they're still too damp.

In the bathroom she reaches for the bar of soap, about to wash off the make-up. She always washes it off if she's going to Daphne's for dinner afterwards, can't have them pitying her for getting all dolled up to go and visit a man who looks at her and sees a stranger.

But then she stops. Tonight is different: tonight they have to commemorate a day they'd rather forget. Tonight needs all the help it can get to feel special. She'll leave the make-up on; let them think what they like.

She redoes her lipstick, dabs more perfume behind her ears, pouts into the mirror at the old woman with the thinning grey hair. 'Get a move on,' she tells her, 'before you die of starvation.'

Cheeky has shown up: he sits on the kitchen sill, his unblinking golden-syrup eyes turned into small torches by the kitchen light. 'Back again,' she says, opening the door, and in he hops. She tips milk into a saucer – no scraps today – and he lowers his head and laps. She heard somewhere that milk is bad for adult cats: clearly nobody's told him.

As he drinks, his tail gives an occasional flick to and fro. He's company of sorts: if she wasn't heading out again she'd let him stay a while, but as soon as the saucer has been licked clean she nudges him towards the door with her shoe.

'Go on – out you go.'

He blinks up at her, offended. He plants his paws on the floor, refusing to co-operate. She has to slide him across the tiles and bundle him out as he mews hoarsely in protest.

'I know you're cross, but I'm in a hurry. See you tomorrow.' He'll be back: he won't hold a grudge as long as there's something on offer.

Thank God the rain has stopped. Not a bad evening now, dry and calm, a few thin slashes of pink cutting the grey out of the sky. Might give them a better day tomorrow. It's far from warm, but the green coat keeps her reasonably snug. Her knee is complaining again – she walked a bit more than usual today – but the bus stop isn't far, just the end of her road.

The bus is early for once: she's barely landed when she sees it rounding the corner of the green. Good, she could do with a sit-down. She clambers on, pulling herself up the steps with the rail. 'Take your time,' the driver says. He's young enough to be her grandson, looks like he's barely out of school. He hardly glances at her pass, knows well she's entitled to it.

She takes a seat by the window, in front of a man eating an enormous sagging pizza slice. The herby, cheesy smell wafts tantalisingly in the air, sending saliva gushing into her mouth and reminding her again that she's eaten hardly anything since breakfast.

But she's not a fan of pizza, or any of those other things they didn't grow up with – pasta, rice, noodles, hard-to-pronounce grains that come from God knows where. Give her a couple of slices of bacon or beef and a spoonful of veg any day, healthiest food you can eat.

Susan used to do a lot of that stuff: pizza with garlic bread, bowls of pasta, herbs and spices, cheese that smelt like a teenage boy's well-worn socks. Finn used to wrinkle his nose when she produced the cheese, but she'd laugh and say he didn't have to eat it.

Mo didn't taste a mango till she was well over forty, or a pomegranate. Wouldn't give you tuppence for either of them, prefer a nice Cox's Pippin or a juicy orange. Melon isn't bad though; the creamy-coloured one, not the pink watery thing.

Daphne's been known to serve up something like quiche or lasagne, but she never tries to be too way out. Finn wasn't a fussy eater growing up, cleaned his plate whatever Mo put on it. Just as well: she'd have had no patience with a child pushing his dinner aside.

A loud, prolonged belch erupts behind her. She waits for an apology, isn't too surprised when none comes. Manners a thing of the past – not the done thing any more to show consideration for your fellow human beings.

The bus climbs a hill and rounds a bend. It pulls to a stop just outside the school where George teaches, and as new passengers clamber on, Mo watches cars manoeuvring into the parking spaces in the school grounds, and remembers Daphne saying something about a concert there tonight, otherwise George would be at the dinner too.

He'll be on Easter holidays after today, two weeks of no work on full pay. Two weeks of youngsters kicking a ball in the street outside Mo's house, booting it into her front door every so often just to annoy her.

She sees a woman she recognises emerging from the passenger side of a silver car, opening the rear door to unbuckle the belt of a child who bounds out, something dangling from one of his hands. Mo recognises the teddy his mother bought for him in the charity shop this morning. Small world: he's probably in George's class.

A man gets out at the driver's side, another familiar face. Mo watches the three of them walk towards the school entrance, the little boy skipping along between the adults. So the guard and the counsellor are a couple: small world indeed.

Before they reach the door the little boy points suddenly upward, and Mo follows his finger to find two kites in the sky, pulling and diving along with the breeze. She wouldn't have thought it was windy enough for kites; maybe it is, higher up. She's never flown a kite; presumably there's a bit of a skill to it, keeping them up like that.

The pizza eater leaves his seat and ambles down the aisle, pausing to hitch his trousers over his substantial hips. No sign of the packaging his food must have come in – left on his seat, no doubt, for someone else to dispose of.

The bus meanders through the city, picking up and dropping off as it goes. When it has passed the stop before Daphne's Mo reaches up and pushes the button on the pole by her seat. Getting off, she thanks the driver as she always does, and he gives her a cheery wave before pulling away.

She covers the short distance to the corner and turns at the shop that sells the Macaroon bars Daphne buys her. They're not her favourite: she liked them one time, but now the coconut gets trapped under her plate. Still, the thought is what matters, and they never last long when Mo adds them to the plate of break-time biscuits in the shop.

She walks up the road, quickening her step when she gets to the point where it happened. She hates passing it, but the bus leaves her with no choice. At least she was spared seeing him there, unlike Daphne. Every morning they drive past it, Daphne and Una. Every morning they're reminded.

She stops in front of the house, rests against the gate to catch her breath. She recalls Finn buying it, a single man still, a few years before he took up with Susan. Got a bank loan for it that scandalised Mo: how on earth would he ever repay it? Looking back, it wasn't that big at all, not compared to the huge mortgages people had to get afterwards, when house prices started to go mad. Finn was lucky: he got in before all that.

She remembers helping him to paint it: she could do so much then, all the energy in the world. Didn't cost her a thought to spend the afternoon up a stepladder running a roller to and fro across a wall after a morning of doing the books in the shop with Leo. Gave a hand in the garden too, shopped with Finn for shrubs, helped him to put them down after they'd cleared the weeds away.

And she'd donated things for the house: an armchair, a kettle, a rug for in front of the fire. A few cups, a saucepan, a frying pan. Most of them have gone now, have worn out and been replaced, but the chair, she's glad to see, is still in the kitchen.

She pushes open the gate. She walks up the path and rings the bell.

Daphne is dressed in jeans and a jumper, a pair of thick grey flecked socks bunched around her ankles, her hair pulled into a heap with a big tortoiseshell slide. You couldn't say she'd made much of an effort.

She makes no comment on Mo's made-up face; maybe she doesn't notice. She waits until Mo is in the kitchen before she drops the bombshell.

Mo can't believe it. Una not eating with them? Not bothered turning up for her own birthday dinner? Worse, Daphne doesn't appear particularly put out. On the contrary, she attempts to defend the girl, implying that they should feel sorry for her.

Mo sips the sherry that's poured for her, fuming. The idea of marking this day with anything other than sorrow is abhorrent to her – but she's *there*. For Una's sake, she's shown up. More fool her – and more fool Daphne for splashing out on a big cake: no doubt it'll be far too rich, have Mo awake with heartburn half the night. No sign of it, must be in the fridge. It can stay there for all she cares.

The sherry slides down, its heady sweetness welcome, hitting her empty stomach before moving up to drift around in her head. Despite her annoyance, she can feel herself relaxing. Oh, she knows Una's not a bad girl; she wouldn't have realised the ingratitude of her actions. Mo will rise above it, she won't allow it to ruin the evening.

She fills a jug with tap water when Daphne asks her to. She puts cutlery on the table, takes out serviettes and salt and pepper. She drains her sherry glass, wondering if she'll be offered a refill. For once, she wouldn't say no.

She remembers the first alcohol she ever tasted, the day Leo went into the home. She remembers seeing his room for the first time, the room she knew would more than likely be his last. The single bed, the floor that you might think was wood if you'd never seen a real wood floor. A painting she didn't recognise – a river, a boat, a humpbacked bridge – on the dull green wall. Why did institutions so often seem to favour green as a wall colour?

But it was the single bed that broke her heart. The days of them sleeping side by side were over; she was never again to lie in the dark listening to the rhythm of his breathing, never again to wake in the morning within the warmth of his arms. As she and Finn removed his clothes and put him into pyjamas, she kept up a ridiculous cheerful monologue, determined not to let him see how broken-hearted she was, even though he was pretty much gone beyond noticing by then.

On the way home she asked Finn to drop her at the shopping centre. *I need to get a few things*, she told him. He said he'd wait; she insisted he left her there, said she wanted the walk. When his car had vanished she went into the off-licence – the first time in her life she'd stepped through its doors – and walked slowly along the aisles before settling on a small bottle of Baileys. The ad on telly was nice, and she had a weakness for cream.

On the way out of the shop she stopped. She turned and walked back in, and went straight to the counter. *Twenty Benson & Hedges*, she said, reaching a second time for her purse.

Back home she put Leo's beloved Mozart on the CD and poured an inch of the drink into a glass. She dipped in a finger and brought it to her mouth; it tasted of fiery chocolate. She eked it out in tiny sips as the music washed over her. When the glass was empty she held it suspended above her mouth and waited for the last precious drops to roll down and fall onto her tongue.

Every day, she resolved, she would do this. Every evening after dinner, Baileys and music would be her consolation. Just an inch, she wouldn't overdo it – and a single cigarette every day. Every morning, the time she'd always enjoyed them the most.

She's tried sherry too, just for a change. She likes both, but Baileys feels more special. She'd prefer a Baileys now, but sherry is what Daphne always offers, so sherry it is.

The bottle is offered again and she extends her glass, noting her daughter-in-law's white face, her tired eyes. The first anniversary has taken its toll – but maybe once they're over it, things will pick up. If Mo has her way, this time next year could see them in a very different place.

Towards the end of the meal – which it has to be said is perfectly fine – Mo decides to broach the subject. With Una not here, it's the ideal opportunity.

But it doesn't go well. 'I've been thinking,' she says – and straight away she observes the wariness that comes into Daphne's expression. Resistant already, before Mo has even begun. Sure enough, Daphne refuses even to contemplate resurrecting the shop, making it clear that she thinks the whole notion is cockeyed, and that Mo must be out of her head to be suggesting it. Within minutes they're glaring at one another across the remains of their dinner.

Mo isn't altogether surprised, but she remains resolute. She'd known Daphne wouldn't jump at the idea – it would mean a big change for all of them, and a lot of work, and not a small degree of risk – but she can't be allowed, she *won't* be allowed, to dismiss it out of hand. She must be persuaded that they need to reclaim the premises that Leo had worked so hard to acquire, and that had provided a livelihood for Finn in his time.

So she persists with her arguments, she pushes her case – maybe pushes a little too hard. At any rate, she achieves nothing. By the time they're finally out of words, the room is crackling with tension. Mo's head begins to thump – the sherry, or maybe the whole fraught day, taking its toll. And just then Daphne's phone, sitting by her plate, begins to ring.

She looks at the screen. 'I have to take this,' she says flatly, and something tells Mo that it's Isobel calling. She pictures the orange dress in the café earlier, the blue scarf slung over a chair. The failed mother drinking red wine – and quite possibly awaiting an illicit assignation. She feels a sudden dart of sympathy for Daphne, regrets badgering her today of all days. Blundering in, as ever.

Left alone, she begins to clear the table: might as well do her

bit to make up. She tips open the lid of the bin to scrape the last
of Daphne's dinner into it – but what she sees makes her stop
short. She sets the plate on the worktop, retrieves the box and
frowns at the intact cake she discovers inside. This has surely
come from a supermarket shelf, not a bakery – what happened
to the other? And why on earth was this one thrown away
before it was even cut?

She checks the fridge and opens presses, but finds nothing
else. Daphne must have changed her mind and cancelled the
bakery order – but it still doesn't explain what this one was
doing in the bin. She takes it from its box, finds a plate for it and
gets a knife to reposition the pink icing that has slid sideways.
Daphne, no doubt, will explain when she reappears.

Getting on for nine o'clock, and still no sign of Una.
Something will have to be said when she appears, birthday or
no birthday.

❧

'Four euro in Mulligan's,' Daphne says. 'I never got to collect
the other.' And then she goes on to tell Mo why.

The news of the theft knocks her sideways: that lovely little
red car stolen, today of all days. Again she feels remorse for
her earlier haranguing – but Daphne makes little of the whole
business. Most stolen cars turn up was what the guards had told
her, she says. Expect some damage, they'd said.

She also seems to have forgotten their argument – or decided
to put it behind them. She tells Mo to collect the other cake,
bring it to the charity shop for the tea break. A nice gesture,
particularly after their harsh words. Nobody in the shop will

care that it's a day old. Mo will tell them there was a mix-up: Daphne and herself thought the other was collecting it, bakery closed by the time the mistake was discovered. She'll say Una wasn't a bit upset, on a diet like all teenage girls, just as well pleased without it.

She'll get them to sing 'Happy Birthday' in the back room — they'd enjoy that.

They finish the washing-up, the atmosphere somewhat easier between them. The subject of what to do with the shop will have to be revisited, but Mo is content to leave it alone for the present. The seed has been sown: it's enough for now.

As Daphne stows the roasting dish under the sink, the doorbell rings.

'That'll be Una now,' Mo says.

'No — she has her key. It's Dad. I told him to call around after work.'

'I heard there was cake on offer,' he says, when Mo opens the door to him.

'You heard right.' Better not mention it was fished out of the bin. 'And your timing is perfect; we were just about to cut it. Come in.'

He wears grey trousers that bag at the knees, a jacket the colour of porridge, and shoes that go with neither. His rapidly vanishing hairline and the brown-framed glasses that perch halfway down his long nose lend him a vaguely academic air.

He holds a package wrapped in proper gift paper, gold stars on dark blue. Box of chocolates, Mo guesses. The safe bet: he's not a taker of risks. Could well be why his wife walked out, wanting someone maybe with a bit more of an edge to him.

But during the scatter of years they've known one another Mo has warmed to him. He's solid, he's completely dependable – and from what she can gather he raised Daphne practically on his own after Isobel left. No help to speak of from his older sisters, both living in Munich with their pair of German husbands. And his parents, by the sound of it, not much better, miles away on a farm on the other side of the country, occasional visitors at best.

His in-laws did pitch in a bit, apparently – but they were the parents of the woman who'd abandoned him: can't have been an easy alliance.

'I'm afraid Una isn't here,' she tells him, as he wipes his feet carefully on the mat inside the door.

He looks at her in astonishment. 'Not here?'

'No – she's decided to skip her birthday dinner. She's eating at a friend's house instead.' She gives him a what-can-you-do look.

'Well,' he says, and she waits for more as he slips off his jacket and hangs it up, but no more comes. Playing it safe again, not wanting to say the wrong thing.

Daphne meets them at the kitchen door. 'Where's your car?' is the first question he puts to her, and Mo sets out cups and cuts the pink cake into slices as Daphne recounts her story again.

Twenty past nine: surely not long more till Una shows up.

❖

But she doesn't show up.

By half nine, pitch dark outside, they decide to ring her – but when Daphne tries, the girl's phone goes unanswered. Mo feels her earlier annoyance returning: in the middle of some antics with the pals, too busy to bother with home.

Turns out Daphne doesn't have a phone number for the pal Una was having dinner with. Turns out she doesn't even know her last name. Mo does her best to hide her incredulity – talk about careless. Wouldn't that be the first thing you'd make sure of with a child in the house, that you had numbers for all the pals? Finn would have had them, that's for sure.

But she says nothing, keeps busy trying Una's mobile phone while Daphne rings the principal of the school – the principal! – and manages to get the information she wants. And that's when the real worry sets in.

Turns out she hasn't been seen all day, not since Daphne dropped her off at the school before nine o'clock this morning. Turns out she claimed in a text to be at home sick today, but a check of her bedroom finds it empty.

She's missing. They stand in the kitchen, trying to decide what to do.

'We should phone the guards,' Daphne says, making no move to phone anyone, looking as if she might throw up at any minute.

'You phone,' Jack tells her, already heading for the hall. 'I'll go out and look for her. Mo, you'll stay here, will you? I can run you home afterwards.'

Something pulls at the edge of Mo's consciousness, some memory she can't grasp hold of. Something about Una, she thinks – something that she saw or heard today … She casts her mind back, retracing events as best she can, but whatever it is refuses to come.

Twenty to ten. Black as coal outside. Her fear increases.

ISOBEL FRANKLIN

Sixty.

In a few months she will be sixty.

The number has been squatting quietly at the outskirts of her consciousness since the year began, malevolent and terrifying as a Brothers Grimm witch, biding its time until 12 September when it will advance and take up residency. Sixty is the real start of old, the first stage of the slow decline.

She moves the gloomy thought aside and stretches, relishing the cool slide of the silk sheets on her bare skin. She flexes her toes, tenses her calves and squeezes her buttocks in turn.

She breathes slowly and deeply, inhaling the scent of her own body, exhaling the last traces of sleep. She yawns, opening her mouth wide, raising her arms above her head, imagining everything inside her elongating and narrowing. She turns her head to one side and the other, pressing her nose to the pillow, sniffing the traces of coconut and almond that her shampoo has left there.

When she was thirty she ran away from her marriage. She ran from stability and routine and security; she ran from everything that Jack Carroll wanted to give her. She left her husband of eight years, her home and her daughter to be with a man who told her that she was the most beautiful creature he had ever seen, and that he would die without her. The drama of it had appealed to her: she was hungry for drama.

There's a light tap on the bedroom door. She sits up, pulling the sheet with her as Alex enters, carrying a small tray. Her peppermint tea, her natural yogurt, her little dish of goji berries and pumpkin seeds. 'Morning,' he says, placing it on the locker, turning to open the curtains.

He smells of the cologne she gave him for Christmas, citrus and vetiver. His white shirt is immaculate, his charcoal suit single-breasted, his maroon tie perfectly knotted. His greying hair is well cut, his teeth realistic enough to fool most people. He looks good.

'Chilly today,' he says, looking out.

'Is it?' She sips tea. 'Oh dear, and yesterday was so nice.'

'Looks like it might rain.'

'Does it?'

'Meet for lunch?' he asks, as he does every Friday – his day for showing her off to clients — but this time she shakes her head.

'Not today, I'm afraid. Phyllis wants me to do an extra couple of hours.'

'Ah.' He checks his watch. She can anticipate his every move. *I'll be off so*, he'll say.

'I'll be off so,' he says, bending to touch his lips briefly to her forehead, and again she inhales the aftershave.

'See you for dinner,' she replies as he crosses the room. She tips the berries and seeds into the yogurt, listening to the sounds of his departure. Steps on the stairs, pause while he puts on his coat and takes his keys from their drawer, soft click of the front door shutting. Car door opening, pause while he gets in, car door closing. Engine on, pause while he puts on his seat belt — the *click* sounds in her head — and off he goes.

He's unfailingly polite. She wants for nothing. In ten years of marriage they've never had what you could call a proper row.

He is distant, and emotionally absent. She is dying of loneliness.

Why did she marry him? A thousand times she's asked herself the question. Was love ever part of the reason, or was she frightened enough of ending her days alone to snatch at the security he was offering without dwelling too much on whether she was in love or not? Maybe in the early days she loved him: so hard to recall now.

She finishes her breakfast, throws the bedclothes aside, pads across the carpet to the en-suite. Just as well they have it — she could hardly parade naked to a communal bathroom with George around. As it is, they don't meet in the morning:

by the time Isobel is out of the bath and dressed he's left for school.

George is sweet. In the ten years they've lived under the same roof she's grown quite fond of him.

I have a son, Alex had told her, fairly soon after they'd met. *He's sixteen* – and with a sinking heart Isobel pictured a sullen, spotty youth with smelly trainers and a mobile-phone addiction.

He was planning to be a teacher, Alex went on. He was diligent in school, got on well in his exams, had never been in any trouble. Certainly sounded good on paper. Isobel regarded the photo of the serious, dark-haired boy Alex had taken from his wallet as she tried to phrase her goodbye. Hunting for the right words, wanting to let him down gently.

Not another child, however well behaved. Not a second child, when she had failed so profoundly with the first.

But Alex had refused to listen to goodbye, refused to let her walk away from him. *You've been on your own too long,* he'd said. *Don't turn your back on this chance to be happy again. George isn't looking for a mother – he's practically an adult. You don't have to meet him until you want to.*

And Isobel, just five months away from the unsettling milestone that was her fiftieth birthday, had found herself agreeing to carry on seeing him. He was well-off and generous, and she was enjoying the sensation of being looked after again, after nearly two decades of short-term relationships with men who inevitably disappointed on some level.

And George, when they were eventually introduced, proved to be quite a relief.

A few spots, but not at all sullen – on the contrary, touchingly shy and polite. Decently dressed, no offensive footwear, no evidence of being particularly attached to his phone. When they told him, two months later, that they were to be married, he wished them well with what seemed to be no resentment at all. He stood beside his father in the registry office as Isobel walked towards them in her burgundy Paul Costelloe trouser suit, and later, after the elegant dinner, he tapped a fork against a glass, blushing, and welcomed her to the family with a short speech that she guessed he'd agonised over.

And so she became a stepmother, years after turning her back on her own daughter for what had turned out to be a preposterous mistake. Con Pierce – what in the name of God had possessed her?

She thought he'd give her what Jack couldn't. He was good-looking and passionate and persuasive, and seemed more than happy to desert his wife and children for her, so she'd accepted the way out he was offering.

Leaving without Daphne had been monumental, but what was she to do? Taking her with them would have killed Jack – and, let's face it, Con wouldn't have thanked her either. He wanted a lover, not a mother and child.

And looking back now, considering the swerves her life has taken, didn't she do the right thing in letting Daphne go? From the start, Jack was the one who had got up in the night when their infant daughter cried, in those first few hectic weeks and months when Isobel was struggling to come to terms with all the messiness and frustration and confusion of motherhood, all the bewildering selflessness it demanded.

And as the years went by it was Jack who had taken time

off to nurse Daphne when she was sick, who'd brought her to the puppet shows and the birthday parties, who'd driven her to school each morning. In Isobel's defence it made more sense for him to do it – being his own boss left him with far more freedom than Isobel, who was working at the time behind the reception desk of a major hotel.

But when she scandalised the neighbourhood, when she alienated her own parents by abandoning her marriage, she'd bet anything that everyone had nodded, folded their arms and said she was never much of a mother anyway. What none of them understood was that she wasn't running away from Daphne, she was running from Jack and all he represented, and leaving Daphne in his capable hands.

But God, she missed her. She was floored by how deeply she felt the loss of her little daughter. Daphne's absence was a constant jagged pain, like an infected cut that never stopped throbbing. A hundred times a day, a thousand times, she thought, *I'll ring, I'll talk to her* – aching for the sound of her little daughter's voice.

But then she imagined Daphne begging her to come home – and what could she do about that? She couldn't go back: that simply wasn't an option after what she'd done. Even if Jack was willing to forgive and forget, she couldn't return to a relationship that didn't exist any more for her.

A phone call would be selfish. It would only upset the child, make their separation harder. And undoubtedly Isobel herself would find it distressing too, however much she hungered for any contact with Daphne. So the weeks passed and she stifled her longings and never rang.

But of course she saw Daphne everywhere. Every female

child of a similar age, every skipping little figure ahead of her on a street, every small head of light brown hair caused a pang. She'd hear 'Mammy!' in a shop and swing around. She'd search school playgrounds for Daphne, even while she knew she couldn't be there.

Once she tailed a mother and child for three blocks just to listen to the little girl, to soak up the cadence of the chattering voice that was so eerily, so poignantly, reminiscent of Daphne's.

And by the time she and Con had run their course, by the time he'd packed his bags and gone back to the wife he'd turned out not to have forgotten after all, nearly four months had passed. Not so long in an adult's life, but an eternity, as she was to find out, for a six-year-old.

How is she? she asked, when she'd finally plucked up the courage to phone Jack, ten days after Con's departure. After she'd told him it was over with Con, after she'd said she was sorry for having hurt him, and he'd listened without comment. *How is she doing?* Another few endless seconds of silence followed before Jack told her, in a voice that held no discernible emotion, that Daphne was doing just fine.

Can I see her? she asked, the fingernails of her free hand pressing painfully into her palm as she pictured him standing in the hall where the phone was, as she imagined Daphne sitting at the kitchen table, listening to his voice through the open door. *Can I meet her somewhere?* He didn't want to go along with that: she knew well he didn't, and she couldn't blame him. But being the decent man that he was he eventually agreed, and Isobel came face to face with her daughter again.

The sight of Daphne, wearing an unfamiliar and unflattering green and white dress that was at least a size too big, almost reduced Isobel to tears. She ached to hug her but the child hung back, pressing into her father's side, so Isobel crouched before her instead and kept her hands to herself.

Hello! she'd said brightly, her voice all wrong. *Look at you — you've grown!* And Daphne stuck her thumb into her mouth — a new phenomenon — and looked dispassionately at her mother, and showed no sign at all that she was glad to see her again. How could four months have made such a difference?

And all through the encounter in that cheap little café, while Isobel and Jack worked out an arrangement for the future, Isobel was aware of the child's furtive glances from across the table. When she saw the little hand creep at one stage in her direction her heart leapt, and her own hand extended out to meet it — but Daphne reached instead for the scarf that Isobel had draped on the vacant chair beside her.

It would be all right, she'd told herself. They'd meet again regularly, they'd reconnect. Eventually, as she got older, Daphne might even opt to spend half her time, more than half, with her mother. So a schedule of visits was arranged — *Every other Saturday,* Jack said, sounding resolute for once, and Isobel felt she had forfeited the right to look for more — and for a long time she tried hard to reclaim her child.

She painted on a smile when Daphne emerged from Jack's car, she bought her little treats, she took her to the cinema — the last place Isobel herself wanted to be, stuck behind its ticket desk five days a week as it was, the only job she'd been able to find. She did everything she could to make up for her absence, but the hoped-for reconciliation with her daughter never happened.

Daphne endured the fortnightly outings, that was all. She greeted her mother cordially enough, but held herself aloof while they were together. She showed no enthusiasm for any part of their afternoons, accepted whatever trinket Isobel bought her with murmured thanks, responded to questions but never asked any in return. Watched each chosen film expressionlessly, thumb stuck firmly in her mouth.

And her relief each time Jack appeared to collect her was heartbreakingly plain to see. Her face would light up at the sight of him standing in the doorway of the café. She would greet him eagerly, pushing aside the largely uneaten plate of food that her mother was paying for. Pushing aside Isobel, it felt like, until she had to endure another afternoon in her company.

In the end it became too much. Sometime during Daphne's teenage years Isobel allowed the visits to dwindle, and finally to stop altogether. *I'll phone you*, Daphne said, cancelling another visit with another excuse, and Isobel knew they would never get back to how they used to be, and the thought was accompanied by a stab of bitter regret.

These days, all the contact they have is a brief weekly phone call and an occasional lunch that's always at Isobel's instigation. Daphne offers to share the bill each time, but Isobel insists on paying: that much, at least, she can do.

Like the phone calls, their conversations during these lunches skip and hop, and never land on anything significant – and Isobel is painfully aware that Daphne is only there because accepting is easier than explaining why not. The knowledge is something she must live with. She turned her back on her child for a while and in the process, lost her.

She runs water into the bath, thinking how sad today will be for Daphne. Now there was a match made to last – you only had to look at her and Finn together. Not that Isobel had seen that much of them; she hadn't laid eyes on Finn until Daphne was already his fiancée, and introducing him to her mother became pretty much unavoidable.

But she'd been to their wedding; she'd witnessed the pure happiness blazing out of Daphne that day. She'd seen the way Daphne had looked at her new husband as they were joined together.

She'd seen it and she'd been glad, even as she acknowledged the sad truth that no man had ever made *her* feel that happy, caused *her* to glow like that. Maybe Jack had briefly, in the early days, but those were long gone. And none of the men after him had lived up to expectations – not Con, or any of the men she'd dated and slept with and holidayed with in the months and years that followed her split from Con – and tragically not Alex either, her husband by then of six years.

But for all its intensity, Daphne's happiness didn't last: it was snatched away abruptly in the middle of an April afternoon. How cruel that had been, how inexplicably, savagely cruel.

Isobel's phone had rung that evening, and she'd seen Jack's name in the display, and she'd known it must be something to do with Daphne, for when else did he ring her? But Daphne's birthday and wedding anniversary were still four weeks away; too soon for the call to be about that. And Isobel had suddenly thought, *She's pregnant* – and that thought had collided with *Why isn't she telling me herself?*

And then she answered.

Are you at home? Jack asked. And without waiting for her response, he added, *Is anyone with you?*

Isobel sensed instantly that something was badly wrong, and she clutched at the edge of her chair in terror. *Daphne*, she said, hardly able to get it out – but he said quickly, *No, no*, and then he told her it was Finn, not Daphne, and while the news of her son-in-law's death had shocked her deeply, the relief that it was someone other than Daphne was almost overwhelming too.

Her first instinct, of course, was to be with Daphne.

Where is she? she asked, and Jack told her they'd just left the morgue – the word ghastly, the sound of it obscene. He gave her directions to Mo's house, and Alex drove her across the city to the narrow street of little terraced redbrick houses.

And Daphne's face, her devastated face, when Isobel arrived. Her hollow, empty eyes, the light gone from them. So still, so white, so completely ruined now that Finn had been taken from her. Slumped against her father on the couch, wanting only him. Nodding at Alex and Isobel when they entered the room but not really seeing them, seeming unaware of any of the people who were crowded into Mo's little sitting room, most of whom were unknown to Isobel.

George called around to Daphne's house later, after Jack had brought her and Una home from Mo's. He took a bottle of gin and a tub of ice-cream with him; he stayed there pretty much the whole night. Isobel heard him coming in around five the next morning, only to disappear again as soon as he rose before noon. Such a big, generous heart he has.

Today will be so hard for Daphne, the date dragging all the memories back with it. And Una: how does the girl endure the fact that she lost her father on her birthday? Sixteen today, or is it seventeen? Hard to keep track when they meet so rarely. Quiet child, Una; nice-looking. Wonderful hair: she could have modelled for Botticelli. She could be advertising shampoo.

Isobel will get flowers when she's in town. She'll visit Finn's grave today. It's not much, but she'll do it.

She pours oil into her bath. She wraps her head in a towel, applies a cucumber mask to her face and steps carefully in: fifty-nine-year-old bones mightn't knit back together that easily if she were to slip. She lowers herself into the scented water, lies back, closes her eyes.

Maybe she should call Daphne this morning, see how she's doing. But today is Friday: she'll be calling her later anyway. She'll wait till then – Daphne might prefer it. Still walking on eggshells with her daughter all these years later, still putting on a front when they talk, making believe that everything is fine between them. A long punishment she's enduring.

She reaches for the soap and begins to wash, listening to the drone of some engine – a plane? a helicopter? – outside the bathroom window.

◆

Stefano's, she types. *Near the railway station. A quarter to two. I'll wear orange.*

Less chance of them being seen there, not a place she'd expect to bump into any of her friends, or any business associates of Alex.

Less than a minute later, his reply blinks up on her screen: *See you then, looking forward to it.*

He'd wanted them to meet in a hotel – presumably so he could book a room – but she'd said no. Not on a first date: she's not like that. She's never been like that. And he didn't run away when she said no, which is a good sign.

She clicks on his profile picture, the one that prompted her to send the first message, over two months ago now. It pops into a larger format, and she studies his features. Grey eyes, biggish nose, pleasant smile. Teeth hidden; mightn't be perfect but hopefully not awful.

Hair so short it's little more than a bristly covering on his head. White, it looks, or light-coloured anyway. She has no objection to short hair – better gone than receding – and his face is presentable enough to carry off the bare look.

Presentable, but not young. Craggy jawline, a fan of creases on either side of his eyes, deep grooves from the base of his nose to the outer edges of his mouth, a network of broken veins scribbled across his cheeks. Quite a few years older than the fifty-two he's claiming, she'd put a bet on it. Not that she's in a position to criticise – she put fifty on her profile. They all do it.

She wonders what kind of lover he'll make, if she decides she wants him. Jack was sweet in bed but too submissive, too eager to please to keep her interested. Con, it has to be said, was gratifyingly enthusiastic between the sheets but lacked finesse – and for all his avowals of passion, was a stranger to the finer points of seduction.

Alex had been promising at the start. He'd had plenty of experience, knew what she'd like without her having to ask for it – until she married him and he got what he really wanted: someone to keep house for him and meet his physical needs as they arose. Someone who would look good on his arm, who could hold her own in an intelligent conversation, and host a sophisticated dinner party. Once he was assured of that he stopped trying to impress her, both in and out of bed. He let the mask drop and became himself.

She was a replacement, that was all, for the wife he had divorced less than two months before he and Isobel had been introduced. The wife whose departure he refused to discuss, passing smoothly onto another topic whenever Isobel brought her up. Maybe that should have warned her – what was he hiding? – but she was lonely, and not inclined to look for warning signs.

She's aware that other women envy her. Alex is rich and successful and attractive. He writes her generous monthly cheques; he gives her expensive birthday and Christmas presents. He takes her on city breaks to Rome and Paris and Berlin.

But the money means nothing to him, and the presents are so impersonal she knows his secretary bought them. And he spends most of their weekends away on the phone while Isobel wanders alone through galleries and parks.

And when he visits her bedroom once or twice a week – they've never shared a room: he claims to be insomniac and not suited to sharing – he rarely speaks as they couple, never stays to hold her for more than a few minutes afterwards. He never wants anything from her that isn't useful to him.

By the time she met him she was forty-nine, and weary of dating men who inevitably disappointed her, and wondering if she was destined to end up alone. The physical attraction to Alex was immediate when her date at the time, a rather overweight but amusing architect called Samuel, introduced them to one another.

Alex is my old college buddy, he told her, little imagining that his old college buddy would arrange to meet Isobel again before the night was out, and would propose to her within months.

And foolishly − still foolish at almost fifty − Isobel allowed herself to be swayed by his polished looks and suave manner, his professional background and his expensive gifts. He would do, she thought, he would be someone to grow old with − so she said yes, and made what was arguably the biggest mistake of her mistake-filled life.

And now, a decade later, she has finally decided to leave him. Nobody will understand, of course. He doesn't beat her, and as far as she knows he's not unfaithful. He doesn't drink too much, or take drugs, or gamble his salary away. When she leaves, all people will see is a woman walking away from her second marriage. Her second failure.

She won't let that stop her: they can think what they like. But at nearly sixty the prospect of being alone again is too daunting, so she won't leave him until she can find a viable alternative − and ironically, it was Alex who provided her with the perfect wherewithal.

He presented her with a laptop for Christmas, one of his typical detached gifts. She hadn't used a computer in years, not since her days of working the ticket desk at the cinema, but when she switched it on a few days later she discovered that the principles hadn't changed much. After a few minor teething problems, she worked out how to join an online dating agency, and towards the end of January she had her first encounter.

He was an Italian chiropractor living in Ireland. He was shorter and older than his profile picture had suggested, but he was pleasingly attentive and easy company. They met half a dozen times, and went to bed on three occasions – *Speak Italian*, she ordered, and he murmured words that sounded like music as he removed her clothes gratifyingly slowly, and she closed her eyes and told herself he meant them.

But after their sixth date, when she was beginning to imagine future summers in Tuscany, he vanished abruptly. His profile, still her only means of contact, disappeared overnight from the site. It was like she'd conjured him up.

The second man she met, a forty-one-year-old architect, had amused and aroused her in roughly equal measure, and their one and only physical encounter, which took place in his expensively furnished but rather dirty apartment, left her with bruised upper arms and a bite mark on her inner thigh that took weeks to fade. She deleted his messages and blocked him as soon as she got home: too much, too forceful.

And now it's April, and this is the third. This one may be different; he may be third time lucky. His name, to all intents and purposes, is Joseph. Hers is Amanda. She enjoys the play-acting: it's entertaining, and quite arousing. She can be anyone she wants, until she decides she wants to be herself.

She logs off, shuts down the website. She'll arrive at Stefano's at two, make sure he's there ahead of her. She regrets the lie to

Alex about having to work longer today – she's not a fan of lying in reality, avoids it where she can – but in this instance she could hardly have told him the truth.

She removes her towel and drops it into the laundry basket in the bathroom. She checks the time: ten past nine. Better get a move on – Phyllis hates her to be late, and she has dessert to make for tonight before she leaves.

She applies body cream, slips on underwear and sits at the dressing table. She considers the array of jars and tubes and brushes and pens laid out before her.

She picks up a jar and unscrews the lid. Time to take ten years off.

•

'I have to leave on the dot today,' she tells Phyllis. 'I have an appointment.' Her boss isn't above taking advantage if you let her.

'No problem,' Phyllis replies, writing in a small green notebook. 'Anything exciting?'

'Getting the hair done, nothing too adventurous.'

'Lovely.'

It's not a proper job, it's more like a hobby. Five mornings a week, ten till one, on duty behind the counter of Phyllis's little health-food shop, selling vastly overpriced organic quinoa, brown rice flakes and semi sun-dried tomatoes to people with more money than sense.

She quite likes it, though. She enjoys the company, and she has no qualms about bringing home the odd bag of goji berries, or half-kilo of the organic spicy couscous that George likes. She sees these little non-purchases as a supplement to the pittance Phyllis pays her.

She saw the ad in the shop window, a year into her marriage. She'd had to give up her job in the cinema, of course – marrying Alex meant moving back to the city. He didn't seem bothered about whether she found another, so for the best part of a year she kept his large house spotless, cooked dinner for him and George and made sure she was bathed and scented when he got home. She refused to accept, for as long as she could, that anything was wrong.

But eventually she'd had enough. One morning she waited until father and son had left the house, then she scanned the jobs section of the newspaper and began applying.

Three months and countless applications later, she realised that fifty-one-year-old women weren't exactly in demand. She lowered her standards, lied about her age, dressed to suit the job and delivered applications in person – but nothing worked. And then she was passing Phyllis's shop one day and saw the ad stuck in the window. *Part-time help needed*, it said. She pushed open the door and walked in.

Phyllis came right to the point. *The pay isn't great. You'd want more, but I can't afford it.*

The money doesn't bother me, Isobel replied. *Give me a week, try me out. I just want something to do.* Phyllis agreed, and took her on.

That evening she told Alex she'd found a job. He lowered his newspaper and looked at her in surprise. *Do you need more money?* he asked.

No, she replied, *I just want something to do. You're at work all day and it gets lonely here.*

He considered this for a second or two, then shook out his paper and went back to it.

It's in a health-food store, Isobel added. *It's on Reilly Street.*

Is that right? His eyes never leaving the page.

Just in case you were interested, she said lightly, and this got no response at all, so she left it at that.

The work is simple; a trained baboon could do it. Isobel's weekly salary is less than each morning's till takings – of course Phyllis could afford to pay more – but for the past nine years the job has kept her sane. She'd happily do it for nothing.

Alex has never once visited the shop – Phyllis probably thinks Isobel made him up. Her husband Ron appears every so often, usually on an errand for Phyllis. He's tall and cheerful, with more foxy hair growing on his chin than on his head, and he has the belly of a man who prefers a pint of beer to a plate of quinoa.

The morning passes in the usual way. Isobel sells coriander and wheatgrass and vanilla pods and flaxseed and oat bran and a variety of essential oils and homeopathic remedies. A woman buying aloe vera gel and a bottle of cider vinegar admires Isobel's orange dress. 'The colour is perfect on you,' she says.

Phyllis returns at a minute to one. 'Chilly out there.' She shucks off her leather gloves. 'Rain on the way, I'd say.'

Isobel gets into her coat, winds her blue and white scarf round her neck, tucks her bag under her arm. 'See you Monday,' she says, and Phyllis hands over her wage packet and tells her to enjoy the weekend.

As she leaves the shop a small blue car drives past, a pair of white ribbons fluttering along its bonnet, the driver sounding the horn repeatedly. Isobel glimpses a smiling, white-veiled bride in the rear: their eyes meet for a split second.

Good luck, she thinks.

❀

She parks the car in a side street and makes her way on foot to the hair salon, half a block away, where Damien is waiting for her. 'Careful with the make-up,' she tells him. 'I have a hot date for lunch.'

He laughs – assuming, of course, that the hot lunch date is with her husband. She could tell him the truth – he thrives on intrigue, and has never met Alex – but some things are best kept to oneself.

'A tidy-up,' she tells him, 'and lots of conditioner.'

Her hair doesn't need a tidy-up – it's not three weeks since her last cut. But a fresh going-over from Damien with his scissors, however minimal, will make her feel good, and she needs to feel good when she walks into Stefano's. That's what almost-sixty does: it pulls at your confidence, makes you less sure of yourself.

'Won't feel it till summer,' he says, wrapping her in a gown. 'Planning any holidays this year?'

She nearly laughs: the quintessential hairdresser question. 'Oh, I don't know. I might run away someplace, not sure yet.'

He smiles. 'Sounds interesting,' he says. 'You dark horse.'

He has no idea.

She leafs through a magazine and drinks the peppermint tea they always bring her as Damien snips millimetres from her hair. She looks at photos of improbably beautiful celebrities sitting on designer couches in their perfect homes, usually accompanied by equally attractive spouses and a pedigree dog or two. She wonders how happy they are, or if any of them dream of escape.

She and Jack were happy at first. She was twenty-one: the driving lessons had been the birthday present she'd requested from her parents. Jack was a little older, nice-looking, and an infinitely patient instructor. He always arrived punctually at her house to pick her up, and while he was perfectly pleasant during each lesson, he gave no sign at all that he was attracted to her. She found this unusual – men generally showed an interest – and a little challenging.

And then, as he was dropping her off after her final lesson, as she was opening her door, he spoke.

'I was wondering if you'd let me take you out to dinner sometime,' he said – and she realised that she'd been hoping for just such an invitation. And really, their courtship was very charming: Jack was thoughtful and generous and made her feel cherished. She was lucky, she decided, to have found him.

Her parents loved him, were thrilled when she told them he'd proposed. 'He's exactly the kind of man I would have chosen for you,' her mother said, which should probably have made Isobel sit up and take stock – but she went ahead and married him. She was twenty-two by this time, and she liked the idea of being the first of her friends to have a husband, and Jack Carroll was eminently suitable.

And for a while all was well. He loved her, and she loved him, she was sure she did. He was just so nice, how could you not? And then, less than eighteen months into their marriage, things started to change. Little things about him began to irritate her: the way he'd hum up and down a scale as he gargled his mouthwash, the way he had to mash potatoes before eating them, the way he'd say *excusez-moi* after a belch.

It wasn't long before all the qualities she'd admired while he was teaching her to drive – his patience, his punctuality, his courtesy – annoyed her as much as an out-of-reach itch. His congeniality made her want to scream.

He was useless to pick a fight with, too. 'Those trousers do nothing for you,' she'd tell him. 'They're like something a ninety-year-old would wear' – and he'd look at her in hurt bewilderment before going to change them, instead of telling her to mind her own business, he'd wear what he wanted. Insufferable.

Yet she still responded to him physically. The nights, if a little predictable, were still gratifying, so attentive he was, so obedient to all her orders. The nights made the days bearable, just about – and then she became pregnant.

They'd discussed it, of course. Isobel wanted to wait, having no immediate desire for a child. She was young, she had plenty of time. She knew Jack was eager for fatherhood, but he agreed to put it off for a couple of years. So she was careful, and two years passed – and then one night after a few glasses of something or other she forgot to be careful, and shortly afterwards she realised she was late, and Daphne was on the way.

While the realisation didn't exactly fill her with maternal joy, it didn't dismay her unduly either. She was twenty-four, her friends were all getting engaged and married and pregnant

– and Jack had given her the two years she'd asked for. Maybe it was time.

The labour was twenty-three hours of relentless agony, a horror-filled day and night of pain that sliced her in two, over and over and over until she could barely see with it, until her throat was raw with screaming. Never again, she vowed, when Daphne, squirming and bawling, was placed in her exhausted arms. Never, ever again.

She did bond with her tiny daughter, though – after the hell of labour had receded she was able to admire the perfect little creature they'd created. Even so, she found motherhood exhausting – but, predictably, Jack made it as easy as he could. He scheduled his driving lessons to suit whatever daytime running around was needed; in the evenings he took over the nappy changes and the lullabies, and he invariably got up in the night while Isobel slept.

All this had the effect of softening her towards him, and for a while things ran more or less smoothly. Their sex life was eventually restored, and Isobel was careful to keep the packets of contraceptive pills well hidden. When Daphne was three months old a minder was found and Isobel returned to her job behind the reception desk of a local hotel.

Being back in the real world suited her, and if life wasn't brimming with excitement, it was perfectly fine. Excitement, she decided, was overrated: what mattered was what she had – a loving spouse and a healthy child.

But as the years went by the old discontent wormed its way back, and Jack began to scratch at her nerves again. She knew it was unjustified. He had done nothing untoward; he was a wonderful husband and father. If only she could stop wanting more.

She determined to live with it. Maybe this was the norm, maybe all wives felt short-changed. Maybe nobody was truly happy in a marriage. And she'd married him for better or worse; nobody had forced her into it.

And then one day when Daphne was five, Isobel went to her dentist for a check-up. And as he examined her teeth, his face close enough to hers that she could feel the heat of his exhalations, he said, in a matter-of-fact voice, *I have to say that I find your scent bewitching*.

And while she was digesting that, and searching for an appropriate response, he removed his little mirror from her mouth and pulled down his mask and peeled off his rubbery blue gloves, and smiled. *Sorry*, he said, *that wasn't very professional*.

And Isobel lay in bed that night and thought about a man who would use a word like 'bewitching'. Not professional, not at all. She knew his wife by sight – they lived in the same neighbourhood – and his children. Two, she thought, or was it three?

Shame they were both married. Who knows what might have happened otherwise?

A week later she left work early, claiming a headache. She walked past his dental surgery around the time she knew he finished work, and when he didn't appear she circled the block and passed it again a few minutes later.

Isobel. This time he was coming out, his jacket slung across an arm. *Don't tell me it's time for another check-up already*.

She smiled. *Hardly*. She indicated the café a few doors away. *I was just about to get a coffee.*

It was so easy. Men were transparent, most of them. Pity Con had turned out to be such a disappointment. Pity every one of them disappoints her eventually.

'There we go.'

Damien shakes out the black gown and presents a mirror to the back of her head. Isobel thanks him and slips him the usual fiver, and he makes the usual show of reluctance before pocketing it.

'Nice dress, by the way,' he says, as he retrieves her coat. 'Colour is great with your skin tone.'

'Thanks.'

She wonders how Joseph will react when they meet, if he'll make any comment about her dress. One forty-five: time to make her way to Stefano's and find out. If he's punctual he'll be there by now, watching the door for a woman wearing orange.

Driving through the traffic-clogged streets, she feels the same mix of anxiety and anticipation that she experienced when she was meeting the other two. Those first few minutes, the sense that every word, every gesture, every hair on your head is being assessed ... and seeing him for the first time can be disconcerting too, adjusting to a voice you'd maybe imagined differently, an accent you mightn't have been expecting, a face that looks older or heavier or more pockmarked than you were hoping for.

She finds a parking spot and walks the short distance to the restaurant, the breeze cold against her face, the clouds packed tight overhead, full of unshed rain. A minute to two: perfect timing. As she approaches Stefano's she unbuttons her coat, lets a slice of orange show through. She pushes open the door and walks in, feeling warm air, smelling melted cheese.

She stands on the threshold, taking stock. Less than half of the tables are filled, the lunchtime rush on the wane. Only two are occupied by men on their own, neither of whom resembles the photo on her laptop, neither of whom looks in her direction. One taps at a mobile phone, a cup sitting on the table before him; the other reads a newspaper.

A waiter approaches. 'Table for one, *signora*?'

She hesitates. He's clearly not here: she should leave. Permissible for the woman to be late, unforgivable for the man. Then again, everyone deserves the benefit of the doubt.

She indicates a vacant table to the rear. 'Perhaps I could sit there?' Visible from the front, but discreet enough not to attract particular attention.

'Certainly, *signora*.' He leads her across the room, takes her coat, hands her a menu. 'You like a drink?'

'A glass of Shiraz, thank you.'

She doesn't normally drink during the day, would have chosen sparkling water if her date had been here. Now she feels she needs some ammunition.

She unwinds her scarf and drapes it across the back of her chair. She'll give him a few minutes, bide her time – and if he turns up with a damn good excuse and sincere apology she may overlook this.

The Shiraz is fractionally too cold. She takes a tiny sip and glances towards the door – and sees an elderly woman whose face looks vaguely familiar entering the café and crossing the floor. Who is she? Grey padded jacket above what looks like the bottom half of a tracksuit, hideous trainers beneath. The woman goes through to the Ladies – and as soon as she vanishes, Isobel remembers.

Just her luck to pick the same café as Daphne's mother-in-law for lunch. What is she called? Some funny little name that escapes Isobel just now. Always looks grimly determined.

She opens the menu. Better not be spotted when the woman emerges from the loo: she may feel she has to come over and say hello, and Joseph may arrive in the middle of it. Awkward.

Bruschetta, carbonara, ravioli, pizza: as predictable an Italian menu as a politician's election promises. Her appetite is fading anyway, along with her expectations. Five past two now, twenty minutes late. She'll give him five more minutes.

From the corner of her eye she sees the toilet door open. She keeps her head down, prays she won't be spotted – but to her dismay the woman turns and looks straight in her direction, and approaches. Lord, can she be about to suggest that they eat *together*? What then?

The ensuing conversation is awkward. Isobel, preoccupied with dread that her date is suddenly going to appear, struggles to find the polite small talk that usually comes so easily to her. In consequence, when her companion makes a reference to Una's birthday, Isobel enquires unthinkingly about a party.

She's immediately mortified – sounds like she's forgotten Finn's anniversary – and judging by the other woman's tart response, that must be exactly what she's thinking too. How clumsy, how badly done – and too late now to offer sympathies, which would sound horribly belated.

Flustered, Isobel makes some inane remark about the

weather, and how the wine is an attempt to warm herself up – now she sounds like an alcoholic making excuses. Thankfully, the other woman takes her leave at that stage, obviously having had enough.

Isobel watches as she heads straight for the café door: not staying to eat after all, then. Bit cheeky, coming in from the street just to use the loo. And the state of her: you'd take her for homeless if you didn't know her. Granted, she's had a lot to cope with – Finn, the husband with Alzheimer's – but, honestly, she could take a bit more care with her appearance.

After another minute or so Isobel gets to her feet: enough of this. She raises an arm and catches the eye of the waiter who took her order. 'My coat,' she says, 'and the bill.' She pays and walks out, leaving most of the wine behind. Let him think what he likes.

Making her way back to the car, she feels horribly conspicuous. She wonders if Joseph, or whatever he's called, is parked somewhere, watching her. Maybe he's been there all the time, waiting to see how long she'd wait for him, getting his kicks by observing her humiliation.

She drives to a multiplex cinema and chooses the least offensive of the offerings. She sits in the dark, each small movement of her head bringing a waft of the honey-scented conditioner Damien uses.

She thinks about being stood up at the age of fifty-nine by a man who calls her Amanda.

She thinks about her only child, and the distance between them.

She thinks about living every day with someone who feels

nothing for you, and who would not be at all heartbroken if you died.

Jack might miss her if she died. Oh, not in a my-world-is-going-to-end kind of way, not any more, but it might affect him on some level. In the middle of doing something else – driving to pick up a customer, maybe, or grilling a chop for his dinner – he might find himself thinking about her; he might remember a time when they were happy together. It might cause him a momentary pang.

She wonders if Daphne would miss her at all.

❋

A little bell tinkles as she enters the florist's. It's a few minutes after four. 'Something to put on a grave,' she tells the plump young woman behind the counter, 'whatever you think' – and the woman gathers together a collection of white flowers and a bit of trailing greenery.

In remembrance, Isobel writes on the card for a man she barely knew, and about whom she remembers very little. She places the bouquet in the boot of the car and drives the short distance to the cemetery.

Almost a year since her last visit. She pictures the group they made that day as they stood around the freshly dug grave, Finn's coffin lying on the grass beside it. Daphne, drained and hollow-eyed, the tears running silently down her face while Jack holds her about the waist. Una sobbing continuously, clinging to George. Finn's mother dry-eyed, glaring straight ahead at nothing. A huddle of Daphne's work colleagues, a scatter of friends, relatives, neighbours.

Susan Darling, Isobel reads on the headstone that was already in place when Finn was buried. *Beloved wife and mother* – and, beneath it, Finn's name. How hard it must be for Daphne to read that every time she comes here, to see them coupled on stone, husband and wife in perpetuity. Where will his second wife lie, when her time comes? She must have thought about it.

Isobel lays her bouquet on the grassy mound, alongside the bunch of beautiful yellow roses wrapped in pale green tissue already placed there. From Daphne, no doubt.

She stands at the foot of the grave, hands pushed into her coat pockets. It began to rain lightly a few minutes ago, as she made her way down the gravel path towards Finn's section, and it's getting heavier. She left her umbrella at home, her head is uncovered. Damien's careful blow-dry will suffer, but it hardly matters now.

And then, without warning, she feels a tear roll down her cheek. What's this? Crying for Finn? She hardly knew him.

Another tear follows, and another. They roll one by one down her face. She finds a tissue in her bag, presses the tears away but there are more, and now she's really crying for the first time in God knows how long, and it's not stopping, she's sobbing into the tissue, her shoulders are heaving, it's all coming out now, all the loneliness and sadness and regret, all the wrong turns she's taken, all the mistakes she's made, Jack and Daphne and Con and Alex, all the pain she's caused, all the hurt she feels, it's all pouring out now, here in the middle of a cemetery on a chilly wet April afternoon, and she is powerless to call a halt to it so she lets it out, lets it all out as the rain pours down on her, uncaring.

Eventually, she has no idea how much later, the tears lessen, and she is able to draw a deep, shuddering breath, then another and another. She blots her swollen eyes with her drenched coat sleeve, the tissue long since sodden and useless. She lifts her head and looks around. Nobody is nearby, nobody has witnessed her falling apart.

She pushes up her sleeve with a hand that trembles lightly, and sees a quarter to five on her watch face. Better get home, put on the dinner. Grilled mackerel with tomato salad, lemon posset in the fridge since this morning. Cheese and biscuits to follow, and port for Alex. Port gives her heartburn.

George isn't eating with them, some end-of-term event at the school, some theatrical performance by the little children he teaches. *Don't count me in for dinner*, he told her yesterday. *I'll do my own thing.*

She feels shaky and tender and emptied out, as if she's come through a long, debilitating illness. Her eyes burn, her cheeks are tight with salt: she tilts her face up to the rain, feels the plash of the drops as they land on her skin. Their coolness is welcome.

The rest of her is cold. The rain has soaked through her coat, her shoulders are damp, her hair ruined – but she's past caring. She makes her way slowly out of the cemetery, her steps fragile on the gravel. She reaches the car, gets in and sits, watching the rain trailing down the windscreen, blurring everything beyond it.

She thinks about what just occurred, turns it over and looks at it. It didn't come out of nowhere: it's been inside her for a long time. It's been sitting there quietly, feeding on her sadness and isolation, growing fat on her failed attempts to find forgiveness, to be loved – and today it all spilt out.

And now, curiously, she feels … unblocked, as if the tears have dislodged the mass that was clogging her thinking, as if they've washed it away, left her seeing things clearly for the first time in years. She knows what must be done now, and she must find whatever courage and strength is needed to do it.

As she's driving home, the name of Finn's mother pops abruptly into her head: Mo, like something out of *The Three Stooges*.

❖

'The little guy I picked for the main part, his name is Josh – he had a strop yesterday when we did a dress rehearsal, refused point blank to use his own teddy. His mother promised to get another one today.'

He's talking more than normal. He's wound up, she thinks, about this school concert. Taking it so seriously, putting his heart and soul into it, bless him. She watches him slapping butter on a slice of brown bread, topping it with ham, slathering a second slice with wholegrain mustard and pressing it down.

'There's cheese,' she tells him, 'I got nice vintage Cheddar' – but he shakes his head as he cuts the sandwich in two. He takes an enormous bite and reaches for his glass of milk. She likes to watch him eat: there's something touching about the vitality he imparts to it.

'Starving,' he says, his mouth full, and she smiles at him.

He was here when she got home; she heard him moving about in the kitchen but went straight upstairs and stood under the shower until she felt able to face him. She's dressed now in loose trousers and a cable-knit cardigan. She wears no make-up or jewellery, and her hair is still damp from the rain because she didn't bother drying it like she normally would.

She feels at peace now, and very calm. Very calm. Beyond being hurt now, beyond lies and deceit now. It's a good feeling. She refills George's glass without being asked. She likes looking after him.

'Looking forward to the holidays?' she asks.

'Yeah, the break'll be good. I'll do some house-hunting.'

'You should ask Daphne: she might find you something.'

'I will, yeah.'

It pleases her, the friendship that bloomed between her daughter and her stepson when they became siblings after a fashion. Nine years between them and no mutual parent, but they've found a connection. Isobel has no idea who instigated it, or how; all she knows is that they're often in contact – they meet up for lunch or coffee.

She knows this through chance remarks of George's; Daphne has never mentioned their friendship.

'I went to the cemetery,' she tells him now. 'I visited Finn's grave.' *I broke down: I cried my eyes out in the rain.*

'I should have gone, never thought of it.'

'No – you were busy.'

She takes the two mackerel from the fridge, already gutted by the fishmonger. She washes them and pats them dry. She slices vine tomatoes and drizzles them with oil, and sprinkles sugar, salt and pepper over them.

George brushes crumbs from his jumper, picks up the second

half of his sandwich. 'Tough on them today, Daphne and the others.'

'Yes, it is.' She takes crusty bread from the press and cuts slices from it. 'Poor things,' she says, arranging the slices in a basket. As she puts it on the table she hears a key in the front door. She glances at the wall clock: five to seven, punctual as ever.

The kitchen door opens and Alex appears. 'Hello,' he says. 'All well here? George, you set for your big night?'

'I am, all set.' He eats the last of his sandwich, gets to his feet and places his glass and plate in the dishwasher.

'Dinner in fifteen minutes,' Isobel says to Alex. He nods, disappears. They hear his tread on the stairs.

'There's lemon posset,' she tells George. 'It's in the fridge.'

'Might have some later, thanks.' He pats his pockets, finds his phone. 'I'll be off, just give Daphne a quick call before I go.'

'Good luck,' she says – but he has already left the room. She takes a bottle of wine from the fridge and opens it, remembering the glass of Shiraz she left largely untouched earlier. This is French, a white Bordeaux full of baked-apple creaminess. She prefers the lighter zest of a Pinot Grigio, but Alex buys the wine.

After her shower she closed her account on the online dating agency. There were two messages sitting in her inbox. She didn't open them or look to see who'd sent them.

She hears water running upstairs. She turns on the grill and sets it to high. She lays the table, lights the candles. She brushes the fish with oil and slides it under the grill. She snips chives for the tomato salad.

She stands by the window, watching the day seeping from the sky. She sees two birds in the distance and admires the grace of their flight before she realises after a few seconds that they're not birds at all but kites, swooping and dancing together in the fading light. Too far away to make out the colours, their twin tails barely visible, fluttering along behind like tin cans racing and tumbling after the car of a newlywed couple.

She drinks wine. She feels the icy stream of it running down inside her. She thinks about what lies ahead, and fear courses through her, every bit as cold.

She waits until he has finished his fish, until he has mopped up the last of the juices with his bread.

'Alex,' she says, her hands in her lap, two glasses of wine and not much food making her head feel light, 'I have something to say.'

He looks at her.

'I'm not happy,' she says quietly, aware of a quickening inside her. 'I haven't been happy for a long time.'

There. No going back now.

A small crease appears in his forehead, in the inch of skin between his eyebrows, but otherwise his face remains unchanged. 'What's the matter?'

'This,' she says simply. 'Us. We're the matter.' Her hands curl of their own accord into fists. Her toes press against the soles of her shoes. 'Aren't we?'

He tilts his head slightly, examining her as if he's trying to puzzle her out. She imagines him making the same face when he talks to clients, when he's preparing them for their upcoming trials, and trying to decide how much of the truth they're telling him.

'We're not working,' she says steadily. 'Our marriage isn't working.'

The eyebrows lift. '*Working?*' A world of disbelief in the single word. A tiny movement of one side of his mouth, the smallest suggestion of an incredulous smile.

'Alex,' she says slowly, 'please *listen* to what I'm saying. We don't have a good marriage. I don't think we ever did, not really. We don't ... *connect*. We're not close.'

For the first time she sees a narrowing of the eyes. No hint of a smile now. 'Connect?' he asks icily. 'We *connect* every day. We live together, we eat together, we have a healthy physical relationship.'

She shakes her head. Why won't he understand? Her fists tighten, pressing into her thighs. 'Alex,' she says, keeping her voice low and steady, 'do you love me?'

Something twitches in his face, there and gone so quickly she can't be sure exactly what it was. His gaze is locked on hers now. There's dead silence, three or four seconds of utter silence. It's all she needs.

He speaks, too late. Much too late. 'What kind of a—'

'I'm leaving,' she breaks in. 'I'm leaving you, Alex.'

His expression doesn't change. His eyes remain fixed on hers. 'You're what?' he asks quietly. Menacingly, it sounds to her.

She must not weaken. His face, his stare, frightens her. She must be strong. Her hands hurt: she loosens her fists until the pain stops. 'We're finished, Alex. I'm sorry, I just can't do this any more.'

She forces herself to hold his gaze. She must be brave. Her heart is pounding: she can feel it in her throat. Her neck is burning, it's on fire. Her shoulders ache, so clenched they've become. She must not weaken.

'I can't live in this marriage any more. It's killing me.'

'It's *killing* you?' he asks, lips curling into a sneer.

'Alex, please—'

'You have everything you could possibly want.' The words snapping out now, his voice rigid with anger. 'I've refused you nothing. *Nothing*.'

'Love,' she says, the heat spreading up into her face. 'You never gave me that.'

He rubs a hand across his jaw, still watching her. She hears the whispery rasp of his stubble.

'Alex,' she asks softly, 'when was the last time you called me by my name?' Her heart thumping so hard in her ears that she can hardly catch her own words.

'Your *name*?' The words dripping with scorn and disbelief. '*That's* what you're bothered about, that I don't say *Isobel* often enough?'

She shakes her head. 'Alex, that's just a—' She breaks off. What's the point? He's not listening. He won't hear.

He grabs his drink, tips his head back. The relief when his gaze leaves her is immense, like a dead weight rolling off her, allowing her to breathe again.

When he lowers the empty glass his lips are glistening. Without warning he lunges for the bottle that sits between them, making her flinch. He empties what's left into his glass – it half fills it – and drains it in one long swallow. She watches, feeling a fresh clutch of fear.

She thinks of the women whose husbands throttled the life out of them, or battered or stabbed them to death. Is he working himself up to an attack, planning to beat her about the head with the empty bottle – or break it against the table and cut her throat with it? She wishes George were here.

Alex's knife rests on his plate: she daren't look at it. Could you stab someone with a fish knife? Should she make a run for it? No use: he'd catch her before she had half a dozen steps taken.

He's never been violent towards her, never.

She's never given him cause before.

His first wife left him; he let her go.

Or did she? Was Alex the one who ended it?

Her thoughts zigzag madly as she waits for whatever is coming.

He finishes the wine. He wipes the back of his hand across his mouth, staring at her again. Then, without taking his eyes from her, he brings his arm forward and she recoils for the second time – he's going to hit her with the glass – but instead he hurls it away, sends it sailing across the room to smash against the opposite wall.

He pushes back his chair and gets to his feet, and everything stiffens a notch more tightly in her. Convinced that he's going to strike now, waiting for the weight of his fist against her body, or her head. Anticipating the pain it will cause, everything braced in preparation for it.

He stands looking down at her for several seconds that feel

like forever. She keeps her gaze trained on the table, every bit of her trembling violently now, more frightened than she ever remembers. He must see it, must realise the effect he's having on her.

'I'm going out,' he says finally. Voice perfectly controlled, no sign now of the rage that caused him to slam a glass into a wall less than a minute before. 'You've got two hours to pack your bags. Make sure I don't find you here when I get back.'

The relief floods through her, releases her from her terror. She looks up at him. 'Alex,' she says – but he's gone, the door slamming behind him.

She sits unmoving. The front door opens and bangs. His car starts up, roars out of the driveway. Most of a bottle of wine inside him – but he's not her problem anymore.

After a few minutes she begins to unlock herself, piece by piece. She turns her palms upwards, sees the small pink crescents her nails have made in the skin. Her hands are shaking – she can't stop the tremor.

Time passes. She hears a distant siren, a blackbird's beautiful trill. A sudden snatch of piano music, abruptly cut off.

The end of a marriage. Ten years it lasted, less than five minutes to finish it.

When she ran away from Jack she left him a note, couldn't find the courage to face him. *I'm sorry*, she wrote. *I can't do this any more. It's not you* – the hackneyed phrase mocking her even as she put it on the page – *it's me. I'm the problem.*

He loved her, and still she left him. She was loved, and she'd thrown it away. At least this time she has a good reason to leave. This time she's not the problem.

Eventually she gets to her feet, moving slowly. Moving like someone twenty years older than almost sixty. She takes the dustpan and brush from its corner and sweeps up the pieces of broken glass. She tips them onto a sheet of newspaper that she bundles together and drops into the bin.

She clears the table, fills the dishwasher and switches it on. She stows the empty wine bottle in the recycling bag. When the kitchen is tidy she goes upstairs to pack, every bone, every sinew, every muscle aching with weariness.

●

'Daphne,' she says, 'how are you feeling?'

It's a quarter to nine. It hasn't taken her long to fill two suitcases with what she wants to take from this house. Nothing he gave her, none of the jewellery, none of the perfume. The laptop she unwrapped on Christmas morning still sits on the desk beside the window.

'My car was stolen,' Daphne replies.

It's so unexpected it takes a few seconds to process. Isobel draws a breath. 'God – when? Where?'

As she listens to Daphne's response, she becomes aware that the day has taken on a quality of unreality. She looks about the bedroom and everything – her coat thrown across the bed, the suitcases by the door, the emptied-out dressing table, the wedge of light thrown onto the carpet by the open bathroom door – everything looks unfamiliar, as if she has wandered into someone else's bedroom, someone else's house, by mistake.

She crosses to the window and looks out. The encroaching darkness has washed the colour from the garden, but the kitchen light casts a yellow rectangle on the lawn. She tries to take stock.

Her marriage is over.

She doesn't know where she's going to sleep tonight.

Daphne's car has been stolen.

Finn has been dead a year today.

She becomes aware that Daphne has fallen silent. She pulls herself back. 'Really awful, I'm so sorry. Have you reported it?'

'Of course.' A little tartly.

'Let's hope they find it.'

Silence. Isobel searches for a more positive topic: they both need it. 'How's the birthday going?'

'Una isn't here. She's having dinner in a friend's house. It's just me and Mo.'

'Oh ... well, do wish her a happy birthday from me when she gets home, won't you?'

'I will.'

She can make out the clematis, clambering over the garden wall. It will be good this year, its third. She won't be here to see it bloom.

'Daphne,' she says.

'Yes?'

She could ask; Daphne would surely say yes. She could make it clear that it would only be for a few nights, until she got herself sorted.

'Hello?'

'I'm still here ... I was just wondering ...'

She stops. She can't do it; the words won't come. What if Daphne says no, what then?

'Wondering what?'

'Well, I ... Look, can we have lunch, sometime next week? There's ... something I need to talk to you about, something I need to tell you.' Daphne will have to know; Jack too.

A tiny pause. 'Can't you tell me now?'

'No, not really. At least, I'd rather do it in person, if that's alright. Maybe Monday?'

More silence. 'OK,' Daphne says eventually.

They make an arrangement. There's another brief pause. Stop, start, always the way with them.

Isobel thinks of something. 'George is house-hunting,' she says.

'He told me.'

Of course he told her. Daphne probably knew before Isobel did.

'I was at the cemetery earlier,' she says. A long time ago, it seems now, since she stood in front of Finn's grave and wept bitterly. 'I saw the beautiful yellow roses, I presume they came from you.'

Nothing.

'Daphne?'

'I didn't get to the cemetery today,' Daphne says, her voice sounding peculiar. 'I was too late, with the car—'

'Oh, no—'

'By the time I got there, it was closed.'

'Oh, my dear, I'm—'

'It's OK, I'll go tomorrow.' She sneezes. 'Sorry,' she says. 'I got a ducking earlier.'

'Me too. Horrible weather.'

Pause.

'Well …' Daphne says, and Isobel takes her cue.

'I'll let you go … give me a call if there's any news about the car, won't you?'

'I will.'

'Bye then, love. See you Monday.'

'Bye.'

After hanging up she brings her cases downstairs, one at a time, and loads them into the boot of her car. She goes back inside and walks slowly through the house, thinking, *I will never be here again*. She touches walls, straightens a painting, pulls a wrinkle out of a rug with her foot. In the kitchen she empties the dishwasher and puts everything away.

She climbs the stairs a final time and stands on the threshold of the bedroom that was hers for nearly ten years. Ten years in October, it would have been. She married him a month after her fiftieth birthday, and she's leaving him on the cusp of her sixtieth.

She wonders if he will remarry, and thinks he probably will. A man of his age, used to being looked after, won't fancy going it alone. And by the sound of it, George will be moving out in the not too distant future.

She'll miss George.

She will more than likely spend the rest of her life on her own. The prospect, she finds, is not unwelcome right now. Her own place, nobody to please, no hopes to be dashed. Could be alright – plenty of others do it. Plenty of widows, plenty of women who never walked down an aisle with a man.

She might enjoy a few dalliances, if any come along before

she's past it, but she won't look for them. She won't be going online again. Never again; not that.

She might take up painting, or golf. Neither occupation has ever tempted her in the past, but maybe she should give one of them a go. Or bridge maybe, she could try that.

'Right,' she says aloud. She closes the bedroom door and goes downstairs. She leaves her house keys on the hall table and pulls the front door closed behind her. They'll have to be in touch: things will need to be sorted out before the marriage can be brought to an end, but she'll never use her keys again.

She walks to her car.

'Isobel!'

Pat from a few doors down has stopped by the gate, accompanied by a little dog on a leash.

'I'm glad I caught you,' she says. 'I'm having a coffee morning on Tuesday, in aid of Alzheimer's. Hope you can come.'

'Sorry,' Isobel replies, 'but I'm not going to be around.' The dog cocks a leg at the gatepost.

'Oh, too bad. Going anywhere nice?'

Isobel opens her bag, finds a tenner. 'Not sure yet.'

'Ooh – a surprise trip?'

'Something like that.' She hands over the money. 'My contribution,' she says.

'Oh, aren't you—'

'Must dash,' she says, turning away.

'Thanks, Isobel. See you now.'

She gets into the car. She starts it up and reverses carefully out of the driveway and moves off.

The room is about a third the size of the bedroom she's just abandoned. The walls are white, apart from the one that faces the bed, which has been papered in cream with fat taupe stripes, their uneven edges presumably meant to suggest that they were each created by hand with a single careless swipe of a roller. A small television on a bracket is positioned too high up to watch with any degree of comfort.

A laminated page has been screwed to the back of the door. *Escape route in the event of a fire*, it says, above a sketch of the corridor outside with a highlighted pink line running along it. A bottom corner of the page curls up, and resists Isobel's attempts to press it back down. No matter: she's made her own escape route.

A round white tray on the dressing table holds a pair of cups and saucers, sachets of tea, coffee and sugar, little plastic tubs of milk and twin packs of biscuits in cellophane. A drawer beneath holds a hairdryer, another an iron. A trouser press sits in a corner; an ironing board hides in the wardrobe.

The bed is softer than she would like. The pillows have not been filled with feathers. There is a shower but no bath in the en-suite, and the shower gel, in a dispenser that's attached to the wall of the shower stall, smells medicinal. Running across the toilet, wrapped around both lid and seat, is a paper strip that reads *Sealed after cleaning for your peace of mind*.

'Two nights,' she told the man behind the reception desk, and gave him her credit card to swipe. Sixty-seven euro a night, practically an entire week's salary to spend her weekend in that sad little room.

She hangs two of her dresses in the wardrobe, stows shoes underneath. She sets her toilet bag on the shelf above the bathroom basin, props her toothbrush in the water glass. Someone pushes a cart, or pulls a suitcase, along the corridor outside; the wheels rumble past her door and fade away.

She stands at the window and looks down at the street, four floors below. She watches cars sweep by, their headlights making the wet road glisten briefly. She hears the shrill two-note song of a fire engine, or is it an ambulance? She sees a group emerge from the hotel, six or eight of them. One couple breaks away – waves, calls – the rest head off in the opposite direction.

It occurs to her that nobody at all knows where she is, not a single person in the world, apart from the man who checked her in. She thinks of her passport, in a side pocket of one of her cases. She could fly away – she could simply disappear. Go somewhere with a kind climate, live gently by the sea.

Phyllis would be cross when she didn't show up for work on Monday morning; Daphne would wonder where she was at lunchtime. Alex would no doubt find a way to divorce her, with or without her co-operation. There'd be talk among the neighbours when it became apparent that she was gone for good: Pat of the coffee morning would earn some notoriety by being the last person in the neighbourhood to speak to her.

By and large, depressingly few lives would be disrupted if she never appeared again.

She turns from the window. Enough of this self-pity: she'll make coffee, read her book for a while – but suddenly she can't bear the idea of spending another minute in this sad little room. She takes her handbag from the bed and finds her lipstick. She'll go downstairs, get herself a proper coffee in the bar. Get used to being on her own again.

❀

The lift doors whoosh open. Three people stand inside. Two adult females – mother and daughter, have to be – and a tall moustachioed man in a raincoat and trilby hat. Isobel gives a general nod and steps inside. The doors slide towards one another and they descend to the ground floor in silence.

Someone is wearing Chanel No 5. The older woman wheezes gently with every inhalation. The man clears his throat. Isobel feels his eyes on the back of her head. The lift stops at the second floor, the doors slide open but nobody is waiting. They stand unmoving as the seconds tick by, before the man reaches forward to extend his arm past Isobel – 'excuse me,' he murmurs – to jab a button once, twice. The doors close and off they go again.

The younger woman leans in to say something in a low voice to the older.

'What?' At the increased volume of the hard of hearing.

'The invisible man just got on,' the other repeats, loudly enough for the others to hear, and the man chuckles.

They reach the ground floor. The doors open again to reveal a bustling lobby, busier than when Isobel was checking in. She skirts several knots of formally dressed people and makes her way to the bar, where more women in party frocks and men in suits are milling about.

She spots an unoccupied barstool and claims it, eventually catching the eye of the lone, harried barman.

'Is there some function on?' she enquires.

'There was a wedding earlier,' he replies, pouring coffee from a pot. 'This is the tail end of it.'

She shows him her key and signs the tab, scans the room as

she raises her cup. Yes, a few look like they've been here a long time. The stocky man with the pointed shoes, hair tumbled, tie askew; his companion in a red sequined dress that's too young for her, tipping her head towards him, smile a little lopsided. Another younger group by the window, erupting into uproarious laughter every few seconds.

'Wasted.'

Isobel turns. A man leans against the counter a few feet away. Forties, average height, average weight. Average everything.

'I beg your pardon?'

'Youth: wasted on the young,' he says, one side of his mouth turning up, forming a crease in his cheek.

Isobel smiles back. 'I suppose it is.'

He lifts his glass. Dark amber liquid, half an inch left. Has he been there all the time, or did he move closer when he spotted her?

'I had a wasted youth,' he says. 'Don't remember half of it.'

'Maybe that's just as well.'

He drains the glass – she's reminded of Alex tipping back his head in exactly the same way earlier – and sets it down gently on the counter. 'Maybe so,' he says. 'Maybe so.'

Her room key sits by her saucer – he can't have missed it. He'll offer to buy her a drink, and she'll say yes. Where's the harm in it? They're both adults, and he seems normal. Might go some way towards redeeming an otherwise disastrous day.

'Well,' he says, 'have a nice evening.' He raises a hand in farewell and walks off. She watches him go, home to a wife probably. Not looking for company, or anything else, after all.

She sits on her stool and sips coffee. Alex will be home by

now, watching something worthy on television, or poring over whatever case he's working on. George might be home too, his show surely over at the school – but maybe he was heading out for an end-of-term drink afterwards with the rest of the staff.

At some point, tonight or tomorrow, he will ask his father where she is. She wonders what Alex will tell him, how much of the truth he'll choose to reveal. She hopes George won't turn against her, won't think badly of her. She wonders about ringing him in a few days; she wouldn't want to put him in an awkward position.

Nobody else approaches her, she talks to nobody. As she finishes her coffee the barman approaches her with the pot but she shakes her head and slides off the stool: more than enough to keep her awake tonight without an overdose of caffeine. She makes her way through the thinning crowd back to the lift, back to her room on the fourth floor.

She's brushing her teeth when her phone rings. Alex, she thinks. She drops the brush, spits into the sink, crosses to where the phone sits charging by the bed.

It's Jack. She looks at his name in surprise. She checks her watch: nearly ten.

What could he want at this hour? She feels a slither of anxiety as she picks up the phone, remembering his call to tell her of Finn's death.

She sits on the bed, presses the answer key. 'Jack,' she says.

'It's Una,' he says, without preamble. 'She's missing. She's been gone all day but we didn't realise till a little while ago. I thought we should let you know. I'm at Daphne's. I'm just going out to look for her.'

'Have you called the guards?'

'Daphne's doing it now.'

'I'm coming over,' she says, getting to her feet. 'Tell Daphne I'll be there in fifteen minutes. Tell her I'm coming.'

Her child needs her. She takes her car key from the dressing table, energy flooding back into her.

UNA DARLING

'Thanks,' she says, getting out, slinging her rucksack across a shoulder. 'See you later.'

She doesn't look back. She never looks back. She hears Daphne's car idling at the kerb as she walks off – why does she always hang around, why doesn't she just *go*? Una can feel her watching, pretending to everyone that she can't bear to part with her precious stepdaughter.

She works her way through the knots of chattering, jostling, flirting people in the yard, hoping not to be spotted by anyone, praying for her name not to be shouted. Better if she escapes notice this morning, better that way.

She reaches the side of the building and keeps going around to the back, making for the sports field. If anyone meets her now she's looking for her glasses, or maybe her locker key, which she lost there yesterday.

Behind the equipment shed she kicks off her shoes, pulls off her jacket and jumper and unbuttons her shirt, shivering as the chilly air hits her skin. She opens her rucksack and rummages around until she finds the top that Daphne got her. She shakes the creases out of it.

It's the blue of the lapis lazuli bracelet Ciara gave her last Christmas. She recognises the brand – it wasn't cheap. Three green buttons at the neck, three-quarter-length sleeves that end with a thin green band. She has to admit she likes it. She pulls it over her head, feels its softness as it slides down.

She upends the rucksack. Books and more clothes topple onto the grass. She hurriedly gets into her sweatshirt and jeans, slips her feet back into her school shoes. She gathers the books together and packs them up again, stuffs her uniform in on top.

She transfers Daphne's tenner from her jacket to her wallet. *Get an ice-cream*, she said, as if Una was a child. She'll buy him flowers with it. She'll spend every bit of it on flowers. She pats her other pocket to make sure her phone is still there.

She hoists the rucksack over a shoulder again and begins making her way along the sports field, half walking, half running along the grass, keeping well in to the edge but still feeling horribly conspicuous, with so many windows overlooking the field. She's alert for the sound of a whistle or a shout – not that she'd respond, she'd just speed up – but she hears neither. Looks like she's getting away with it.

She reaches the far end of the field and stands panting before the old stone wall that borders it. She hitches her rucksack over both shoulders and regards the wall. It's nearly twice her height, she reckons about ten feet, but she's often seen boys clambering over it. Can't be that hard.

She grips a jutting rock, searches for another to grab onto. Her fingers are frozen – why didn't she bring gloves? She clambers up a few feet before losing her hold and slithering back down, grazing the heel of one hand painfully. She swears and rubs her hand hard until the stinging lessens, and then she tries again.

Her second attempt is better. She gets almost to the top before her foot slips, and again she plummets to the ground, banging her chin on the way and landing on her back with a thump that knocks the breath out of her.

She sits on the ground and waits till her heart has stopped slapping like a fish inside her. She feels her chin gingerly: it's sore, but there's no blood. She doesn't think any real damage is done.

She'd be better able to climb without the rucksack – but flinging it over the wall is easier said than done. After four failed attempts she opens it, takes out the books and flings them over, one by one. The lighter rucksack finally follows: she hears it land with a distant thud on the other side of the wall. She hasn't a clue what's there – hopefully not someone's back garden with a big dog in it.

She brushes grit from her hands and launches another assault on the wall – and this time she gets to the top, despite a heart-stopping moment halfway up when a foot slithers and she almost loses her grip. She straddles the wall to catch her breath, looking down at the laneway where her splayed books and rucksack are lying. Good job it's not raining. At the other side of the lane is another wall, a couple of feet lower than the one she's on, and beyond that the back gardens of a row of semi-detached houses.

A woman is hanging clothes on a line, no more than twenty feet away: Una would be clearly visible to her if she were to turn her head a few inches to the right. Una leans forward slowly until her upper body is resting on the top of the wall, her face turned towards the garden, and waits.

The woman bends to take a shirt from the laundry basket and shakes it out: the damp cotton snaps loudly. A spider darts across the top of the wall, inches from Una's face: she squeezes her eyes closed, trying not to imagine it crawling into her ear.

Eventually – three minutes? Ten? – the woman lifts the empty laundry basket and goes back inside. As soon as she hears the door close, Una sits up. She eases her other leg over the top of the wall and, grabbing onto what she can along the way, she slithers to the ground, bringing dust, grit and a few woodlice with her.

She brushes herself down rapidly, flings the books back into her rucksack and flies down the lane, her injured hand and chin still smarting, the chill of the day forgotten with the adrenalin that's galloping around inside her.

When she reaches the end she stops, out of breath again.

She's on familiar territory now, the school to the right and her destination the other way.

She hears the drone of an engine in the sky and looks up. It's a small plane trailing a banner that reads *Congratulations Charlotte and Brian*. She hadn't known they were planning to do that. She wonders whose idea it was, and how much it cost.

She tucks her hair into the hood of her sweatshirt and walks on. A few people pass by, nobody taking any notice of her. After a few minutes she increases her pace, the cold biting at her face now. She checks the time: Daphne will have got to work.

Her phone beeps. She takes it from her pocket and sees a message from Ciara: *Where r u?*

She types back: *Sick, tummy bug*

The lie causes a worm of discomfort in her gut but she can't tell, not even Ciara. Not until it's over.

Aw, happy bday. U OK? xx

OK, c u 2moro xx

She carries on, rubbing her hands together. She knows this route so well, could do it blindfold. Cycled it every weekday afternoon for years.

Come to the shop after school, Dad had told her when she started at the comp. *You can do your homework in the back room and leave with me when I close.* And that was what she'd done, delighted to be finished with the primary-school routine of being collected each afternoon by Mo and brought to her house on the bus, waiting there until Dad came to pick her up on his bike. Homework done at Mo's little kitchen table, trying to ignore the smell of cabbage that she always got there. Now she was allowed to cycle to school on her own bike and come home with Dad.

Things didn't change towards the end of first year, when Dad married Daphne and she moved in with them. *I could run you to school in the mornings*, she'd told Una. *It's on my way to work. We could take your bike in the boot, and you could still go to the shop after school* – but Una opted to keep the old arrangement. Cycling to school woke her up, and rainy days didn't bother her: she had all the wet gear.

Of course, eventually she grew out of going to the shop in the afternoons – she still cycled to school, but went downtown with Ciara and the others after. Her and Dad's Sunday cycles didn't stop, though, it was still the thing she shared with him. It was their time together, with no Daphne to come between them. Daphne wasn't interested in cycling.

But now it's completely different. Una hasn't got onto a bike in the past year; she just can't. Daphne drives her to school now, and her bike sits gathering dust and rust in the garage, just like his blue one is doing in the shop. Useless now, both of them – and yet she can't let hers go.

And his death brought about another change, one that nobody knows about. Daphne assumes she still hangs around with Ciara and the others after school; they think she goes straight home. They're all wrong.

A couple of weeks after he died, still broken in bits with loneliness and hungering for what she'd lost, Una hunted down the shop keys. She went through the house one day when Daphne was still at work and eventually found them pushed to the back of the wardrobe in what had been his and Daphne's bedroom. She had copies made and replaced the originals exactly where she'd found them.

She lets herself in the back way every day after school, keeping an eye out in case Sean from next door is around. She turns off the alarm and makes her way to the little room at the rear of the shop where she does her homework. It's always cold: she leaves her jacket on.

As she works she pretends Dad is there on the other side of the door, selling bicycles and helmets and pumps and puncture-repair kits like he always did. She tells herself he'll appear in a minute to tell her it's closing time. He'll lock up and they'll cycle home together, maybe stopping first for a quick chat with Sean, who would always stand at his door when he had no customers.

It sort of works. She fools herself for a while, as she bends over her books in the silent room. It's the only small comfort she can find, the only way to feel close to him again. Of course it stops the minute she packs up her things and walks out into the shop and finds it dark and empty, and without him.

She hates the way it is now: a layer of thick dust settled over everything, over the counter top he kept so shiny, over the rows of new bicycles, over the silent cash register. Cobwebs dangling from shelves, spiders spinning their houses uninterrupted. The place permanently gloomy because of the shutters she can't open.

Horrible to have it like that, like something out of Dickens, like a place where creepy Miss Havisham might sit in her falling-apart wedding dress, or Scrooge might crouch to eat his gruel. Horrible that Daphne and Mo don't seem to care about it any more – it feels like they don't care about *him*.

On the other hand, she can't bear the thought of it being sold, of strangers coming in and changing it all. It would be like wiping the last of him out, scrubbing him away like chalk from a blackboard.

She reaches the street where the shop is located and turns down the lane that leads around to the back. Outside the shop's rear entrance she lifts the red brick where she stashes the keys. She opens the door and presses the familiar code on the alarm box inside to silence its beeping. She stands in the dusty gloom for a few seconds, sniffing the oily, metallic smell she knows so well. She puts out a hand and finds his ancient blue bike, leaning against the wall where he'd left it a year ago. She runs her fingers along the bar where she'd sat so often as a child, before she was old enough to have her own bike.

No time to hang around today: she drops her rucksack on the floor, sets the alarm again and leaves, replacing the keys under their brick before scurrying back down the lane to the street, keeping her hood up, her face averted from the butcher's shop as she crosses to the other side.

●

The scent, so rich and gorgeous you can almost taste it, stops her for a few seconds on the threshold. She breathes it in, fills her lungs with it. Must be wonderful to work here, to be surrounded by that scent all day – although you might get so used to it you wouldn't notice it after a while.

'Can I help you?' a woman behind the counter calls, and Una lets the door swing closed behind her as she steps forward.

The woman is overweight with a round, pretty face. Her

peach blouse is tied with a bow at the throat. Her wedding ring, embedded deep in the flesh of her finger, looks like it will never again come off.

'That looks sore,' she says, nodding in the direction of Una's chin, which is still smarting.

'It's fine,' Una tells her. 'I just bumped it – it looks worse than it is.' She wonders what it looks like. 'I want to buy some roses,' she goes on. 'Yellow, if you have them.' He liked yellow roses.

'I certainly have.' The saleswoman indicates a bucket of opening blooms in a glorious shade of bright lemon. 'Aren't they gorgeous?'

'How many can I get for a tenner?' Una asks.

The woman smiles. 'Let's call it ten,' she says, and wraps them in pale green tissue paper. 'Whoever they're for will love them.'

'They're for my dad,' Una tells her.

'Ah – isn't that nice? Fathers don't often get flowers. He'll be delighted with them, I'm sure. Would you like a card?'

'No, thank you.' Far too sad, writing him a message he'll never read. She considers revealing the flowers' true purpose, but decides against it: talking about death makes people awkward, and saying the words out loud might just bring on her own tears again.

She pays and leaves the shop, the bouquet cradled against her chest. In the doorway she takes out her phone and checks her email: no message. The cold is sharp, she's glad the cemetery isn't far. She dips her head into the roses, but to her disappointment they smell of nothing.

Ten minutes later she walks through the iron gates. The place is quiet, just a few people standing in front of headstones, a few more strolling along the paths. She makes her way to Mum and Dad's grave, reads the words she knows by heart.

She comes here once a month, drawn by a yearning for what they had, the three of them – although after more than ten years her memories of Mum are all but gone. Not her face – she has photos to make sure she never forgets that. It's more her voice and her smell, it's her gestures and habits, and the way she moved.

It's like Mum stood up one day and walked away from them, and all Una could do was watch her getting smaller and smaller, until she became little more than an infinitesimal speck, then nothing at all. Now she's just a smiling half-stranger in a photo album.

But Dad is still so real to her. She can still hear his voice, she can recall the feel of his arms around her, the reassuring warm, buttery smell of him. *My beautiful girl*, he'd say, holding her tight.

Except that she wasn't his girl, not really. He'd claimed her when he married Mum, he'd treated her like his own, but she never really belonged to him, even if she felt like she did. Even if she wished every night that she did, like she used to when she was younger. Screwing up her eyes tight in bed, whispering the words to whoever or whatever might be listening. Stupid wish, as if she could turn the clock back and change everything. As if anyone could do that.

She crouches and lays the yellow flowers in front of the headstone. She stands silently in the cold, hands shoved deep into her pockets, and talks to him in her head.

She tells him everything.

It's gone half ten, later than she'd planned, by the time she turns up the alley that leads to the rear of the terrace of narrow little houses, blowing on her hands to warm them and thinking of Mo in the charity shop just across the way. If she only knew.

She sees Kevin's blue car parked by the wooden gate, white ribbons already in place. As she approaches the gate, a volley of enthusiastic barks erupts from the tiny yard. She reaches over to slide back the bolt, and submits herself to the usual welcome as soon as she steps inside.

'Hey!' She stoops to make a shelf of her thighs for the front paws, rubs the head that butts into her chin, offers her face to be licked. 'Good girl.'

Dolly's provenance is uncertain. The pendulous ears of a spaniel, the long nose of a collie, the round barrelly middle and spindly legs of a terrier, the goofy soul of a Lab. Una was slightly disappointed when she discovered that everyone, even total strangers, gets the same enthusiastic welcome. As a guard dog, Dolly is a total disaster.

The back door opens. Una looks up.

'Thought it was you,' Judy says.

She wears a blue dressing gown, her hair bumpy with brightly coloured rollers, her face unfamiliar with eye liner, lipstick, foundation – the first time Una has seen her with make-up on.

'Come here to me,' she says, and Una crosses the tiny yard, Dolly trotting along beside her. Judy opens her arms and Una steps into them, inhaling the familiar savoury smell of her as they embrace. Day or night, Judy always smells of food.

'Good to see you,' she murmurs into the side of Una's head. 'Delighted you could come.' As they draw apart, she frowns. 'What's that on your chin?'

'I bumped it, it's nothing ... I saw the plane,' Una says, 'with the banner.'

'Oh, did you? That was Brian's boss – he has a pal who does those things. Wasn't it nice of him? Charlotte hadn't a clue – he never said a word. Now, get in before we both catch our deaths. *No*,' she adds sharply, 'not you, missy' – and instantly Dolly's tail stills, and her rear end thumps down in disappointment.

'Oh – can she not come in?' Una wouldn't normally question Judy, but she hates the thought of the dog stuck out in the cold.

'Not today she can't – what if she jumped up on Charlotte? She'll be fine, don't you worry about her.'

The kitchen is warm, and smells tantalisingly of sausages. Charlotte sits at the table in pink fleecy pyjamas, eating.

'Hi there,' she says, through a mouthful of food, and Una smiles back. She doesn't know Charlotte well – she's hardly ever here when Una comes around.

Kevin stands at the worktop, rubbing a brush over and back across a black shoe. He wears yellow rubber gloves and a long-sleeved vest that was probably white once upon a time. One of Judy's aprons – red and green stripes with a red frill – is tied around his waist, over grey trousers. His hair is shorter than the last time Una saw it.

'Here she is,' he says. 'What's that on your chin?'

'I banged into something. It's OK.'

'Florrie can cover it with concealer,' Charlotte says.

They don't know she had to sneak away from school today.

They think Daphne knows about the wedding, they think she knows that Una comes to visit them. All the lies she's had to tell.

'Have you eaten?' Judy asks, and Una remembers the couple of bites of toast earlier.

'Well …'

'You'll have a couple of sausages. They're made already – I threw them all on. Make room there, Charlotte. You want an egg to go with them, pet?'

That's the thing about them. They haven't got much, but they share everything. 'No, thanks,' Una says. She's taking their sausages; that's enough. She's glad they don't know it's her birthday – they'd definitely want to make a fuss.

'Sit,' Kevin says, indicating the chair opposite Charlotte with his brush, and Una pulls it out and sits as Judy bustles from press to cooker.

OK? he mouths over Charlotte's head, nobody else to see it but Una, and she gives a small nod and bites her lip, feeling tears nearby again. He returns immediately to his polishing, and she keeps her eyes on the table till the urge passes.

'I saw the plane,' she tells Charlotte then.

Charlotte grins as she reaches for the butter. 'Gas, wasn't it? He never said a word.'

'Flew so low I thought it was going to come in the window,' Kevin puts in. 'Thought it was the Twin Towers all over again.'

'Shut up, Dad; that's terrible.' But she's still smiling.

'How're you feeling?' Una asks her. For someone getting married in a couple of hours she seems remarkably cool.

'Grand. Probably get the jitters later. I'm waiting to have my make-up done – Florrie's upstairs doing Gaby's now.' Gaby is her cousin, and her only bridesmaid. 'What d'you think of Mam?' she asks, pointing her fork at Judy. 'She was the first to get done.'

Una smiles. 'Nice.' Although looking at Judy is disconcerting today: she's like someone Una almost knows, but not quite.

'I think I look a bit ridiculous, to be honest,' Judy says, placing a plate with three sausages in front of Una, 'but they insisted.'

'You look gorgeous, Jude,' Kevin says. 'You're like Maureen O'Hara, only better.'

She flaps a tea towel at him. 'Listen to that for rubbish — haven't you those shoes finished yet?'

'Not till I can see my face in them,' he tells her, brushing placidly, turning to wink at Una.

Judy gives an impatient puff. 'Take some bread, pet,' she says to Una. 'I made it this morning. Charlotte, pour tea. Kevin, get out the blackberry jam for Una. You're coming to the church with me and Theo, love — we're going in Donie's car.'

Una has no idea who Donie is but she nods. The sausages taste wonderful; she hadn't realised how hungry she is. She helps herself to a slice of the still-warm soda bread and spreads it with butter, then spoons on Judy's homemade blackberry jam. 'Where's Theo?'

'Upstairs, getting dickied up,' Kevin replies. 'I think he's out to impress someone today.'

'Stop that, you,' Judy says, but Una can feel her face getting warm. She doesn't mind the teasing, though — they know she and Theo are just friends. It's his family, or more precisely his parents, she's fallen in love with. Who would have thought it, of all the families in the world?

It was Theo Quirk's father, Karen O'Doherty said, a few days after Una had gone back to school. A week after the funeral. *Just thought you'd want to know.*

Una looked at her. She didn't hang around with Karen; they rarely talked despite being in the same class for most subjects. There was no animosity between them, just a mutual indifference.

What are you talking about? she asked, although she didn't really care. It didn't matter; nothing mattered any more. Dad was gone. That was all she could think about.

It was Theo Quirk's father who was driving the bin lorry, Karen said, watching Una's face closely – and it was all Una could do, as the words sank in, to keep it from changing.

I knew that, she lied, taking books from her locker and banging it shut. Walking away from Karen, holding her head high, although it nearly killed her. Not giving her the satisfaction of seeing how close to breakdown she had been brought by the spiteful little piece of information.

Theo Quirk. She knew him to see: he was two years ahead of them, in Leaving Cert. To the best of her recollection they'd never spoken. Una had no idea how she even knew his name.

For the rest of the day she turned the information around in her head. Theo Quirk's father had driven the bin lorry that had killed her father. She didn't doubt that it was true – Karen was going out with a boy in Leaving Cert; he must have told her.

All that night in bed she lay awake, trying to digest it. Theo Quirk's father had killed her father. And even though she knew the lavender bicycle was mostly to blame, the accident wouldn't have happened if the bin lorry hadn't been there. He'd played his part, Theo Quirk's father. She wished him in Hell, along with the rest of his family. She prayed she wouldn't come face to face with Theo Quirk before he left school in June.

Her prayers weren't answered. Two days later she was rounding a bend in the corridor on her way to the science lab when she almost ran into him. He was with two friends, and his face as soon as he saw her told her he knew. Of *course* he knew.

Hey— he said, but she kept going, almost running to get away from him. They had nothing to say to one another – there was nothing he could say that she might possibly want to hear.

But there he was at the school gate when she came out that afternoon. Standing alone, obviously looking for someone. Looking for her.

Una, he said as she approached. She walked past him, quickened her pace. Heading straight home, like she did every day now.

He followed. *Listen*, he said, *please* – but she was deaf to him. She broke into a run, kept running until her heart felt like it was going to burst. She sped across streets, heedless of cars, she raced around startled pedestrians – she narrowly avoided tripping over a baby's buggy on her flight to escape him.

She stopped on the point of collapse and slumped against a wall, trying to catch her breath – and there he was, behind her all the way. There was nothing she could do; she was too exhausted even to tell him to get lost.

Look, he panted, *I know you don't want to talk to me, I understand that*—

She turned her back on him, tried to blot him out as she pushed away from the wall and forced her legs to move again.

It was an accident, he called after her. *My dad is in bits over it, we all are—*

She closed her eyes against the tears that suddenly threatened, bit down hard on her lip. Kept going, kept stumbling away from him.

Honest, if you knew how bad he feels about—

She stopped then, wheeled around. Glared at him, outraged, her heart still going mad inside her. *Your father is alive*, she panted back at him. *Mine is dead. I don't give a damn about how bad he feels. I wish he was the one who was dead — I wish you were all dead.*

He made no response, just stood there. People were listening, heads swivelling to stare at them. Let them, she didn't care. She turned away and marched off, trying to swallow a huge lump in her throat, knowing he wouldn't follow her this time.

She told nobody what had happened, not even Ciara. For weeks after that she hurried from class to class, determined to blank him if they encountered one another, but there was no sign of him — he must have been equally resolved to avoid her.

In the meantime she found the shop keys and began revisiting there, trying to fool herself through her homework each afternoon, yearning for the sound of her father's voice, for the weight of his hand on her shoulder, the whirr of his bicycle wheels, the music of his laughter.

But as the days wore on, as the fierce intensity of her grief began to subside, she found herself straying back to the awful words she'd spat at Theo Quirk. *I wish he was the one who was dead*: had she really said that? It wasn't true. She *did* hate him for what he'd done, but she didn't wish him dead. It wouldn't bring Dad back; no good would come of it. It was a hurtful thing to say, something a child would throw out in a temper. She was ashamed of it.

It preyed on her mind. She resolved to apologise, and put it behind her. She didn't need anything to make her feel any worse than she already did.

A week before school finished she stood at the gates watching for him, just like he had for her, and praying that nobody she knew would spot her and come over. When he emerged from the building in a group, her nerve almost deserted her. He might tell her to get lost, to shove her apology. He might ridicule her in front of his friends. But she had to do it, for her own peace of mind.

Theo, she called when she spotted him, the first time she'd used his name.

He turned, stopped dead, stared at her. She was conscious of others looking, of his friends stopping too. He muttered something to them and walked over.

Can we talk, just for a minute? she asked, and he nodded. She led him a little way down the street, away from the crowds.

I wanted to say I'm sorry, she said quietly. *I was … upset, last time, I didn't mean—*

To her horror she felt her eyes fill with tears. She'd cried a river since Dad died, and still out they came with half an ounce of encouragement. She couldn't seem to stop them. She scrabbled in her pockets for a tissue, and when she found none she scrubbed her face hard with a sleeve.

It's OK, he mumbled, *forget it. I know how I'd feel if I lost my dad.*

You don't, she replied bleakly, thumbing away fresh tears. *You don't have a clue, until it happens.*

She turned away. They had nothing more to say to one another.

Listen, he said rapidly. *I know this is a lot to ask, but you wouldn't … meet him, would you?*

She stopped. She turned, frowning. *Meet who?*

My father, he said. *Could you — would you meet him?*

She mustn't have heard right. She stared at him. She *couldn't* have heard that right.

Say no if you want, he went on. *I'll understand if you say no, but he's in a really bad way. He still blames himself for what happened. He hasn't gone back to work since. My mother's afraid he—* He broke off, mouth clamping shut, face reddening, gaze dropping to the ground.

Una couldn't believe it. Was he serious? He wanted her to *meet* the man who'd taken her dad away? What planet was he on?

You have got to be kidding, she said flatly. She hitched her rucksack onto her shoulder, began to walk away again, willing him to shut up.

He didn't shut up. *If you came*, he said, *if he could … just tell you how sorry he is, I think it might help him.*

Once more she turned back, unable to let it go. *It might* help *him? You expect me to* help *him, after what he did?*

His face tightened. *It was an* accident, he said quietly. *An* accident.

She glared at him, more angry words on the tip of her tongue – and then, out of the blue, a memory slipped into her head.

They were having breakfast, just the two of them. It was after Mum and before Daphne. Dad was reading the newspaper. Una, who must have been eight or nine, was eating cornflakes.

Listen to this, Dad said, and he read to her about drivers in California stopping at a motorway toll booth and paying twice, once for themselves and once for the driver in the car behind. *Random acts of kindness, they're calling them*, he told her. *Isn't that cool, doing something nice for a complete stranger?*

Una didn't think it was cool. It sounded naff to her. *Why would you pay for someone you don't even know?* she asked. *They couldn't pay you back, even if they wanted to, cos they wouldn't know where you lived.*

He smiled. *Because it would make them happy, it would brighten their day. And it wouldn't have to be something that costs money – you could help people out in other ways, like letting someone share your umbrella in the rain or ... helping someone across the road, or carrying their shopping. It could be anything at all. I think it's a great idea.*

She didn't think it was a great idea at all. Maybe people wouldn't *want* to share a stranger's umbrella – maybe they'd think you wanted to rob their shopping if you offered to carry it. But Dad had raised the newspaper again, so she said no more and went back to her breakfast.

And after that she began to notice him doing them, these random acts of kindness. He'd pass on a parking disc if there was time left on it, offer directions without being asked to tourists holding maps. He'd allow someone with just a few groceries to go ahead of him in the supermarket checkout queue. Once he found a travel pass and cycled across town to return it to the address printed on it. And, yes, he carried a person's shopping more than once.

She noticed these things – it made her half embarrassed, half proud when she witnessed one – but she never thought about doing the same herself. She'd feel a bit awkward, approaching perfect strangers. And Ciara and the others might laugh at her.

So what did it mean, remembering all this now? Could it be some sort of a *sign* from him? Was it his way of saying, *Now's your chance?*

But this was different. This was nothing like the things he did. For a start, it wasn't random: she was being *asked* to do it. And the things he'd done had been small, and simple to do, and this was big, this was huge, and there was nothing simple about it.

But still the doubt scratched at her, the question remained: was Dad asking her to do this incredibly difficult thing? Did he think she was capable of coming face to face with the man who had killed him, accident or not? The notion of meeting the bin-lorry driver filled her with dread, made her churn inside.

But reverse the situation, put Dad in her shoes, and she knew he'd do it: she'd known him well enough to be sure of that. He'd want to help. He'd want to forgive the other man and brighten his day. She knew this to be true, even as she shied away from it.

And maybe that was reason enough to say yes, if she could dig deep enough and find the strength.

She became aware of Theo standing silently by. She met his eye. Neither of them spoke for what seemed to her like an awfully long time. He was taller than her. His tie was askew. Anyone observing them would probably think they were eyeing each other up for quite a different reason.

I'll think about it, she said, and walked off – and in the week that followed, the last week of school before the summer holidays, it was all she thought about. As she sat alone each afternoon in the little back room of the shop, trying and failing to concentrate on her homework, she returned to it again and again.

What would he be like? He drove a bin lorry for a living – what did that make him? She didn't know anyone with a job like that: all her friends had parents who worked in banks or offices or shops, or ran their own businesses.

He might be fine – Theo seemed OK. But what if he wasn't? *He's in a bad way*, Theo had said – what if he turned up drunk to meet her? What if he didn't want to meet her at all, what if this whole thing was just Theo's idea? What if his father was horrible, and sneered or swore at her?

At least once a day she decided she couldn't face it, she wasn't strong enough. But then she'd think of Dad – and she knew that if she was ever to find peace again she'd have to go through with it.

The following day, the second last of the term, she watched for Theo at the gate again. He spotted her and came straight over.

I'll meet him in the park near the bus station, she said. Nobody she knew lived around there. *Just him and you, nobody else.*

Thank you, he said, with what sounded like real sincerity. *I know this can't be—*

Tomorrow, three o'clock, just inside the main gate.

We'll be there.

Walking away, she was already dreading it, already kicking herself for having agreed to it. She didn't sleep a wink that night, visualising the scene in several different ways, none of them good.

It'll be nice to have the holidays, Daphne said at breakfast, in the too-bright voice that was all she seemed to use now. *Just half a day to go. Any plans?*

Una wondered what she'd say if she knew the plan for that afternoon. *Not really*, she replied, spreading peanut butter on toast she didn't want. *Nothing much.*

There was no sign of him at school. She went with Ciara and a few others to a café for lunch afterwards, but it was all she could do to get halfway through the Caesar salad she had ordered.

You OK? Ciara murmured, when they were queuing up to pay. *You're very quiet.*

I'm fine, Una told her. *I didn't sleep well, I'm just a bit tired* — because she had to keep this to herself. Ciara wouldn't understand, she'd try to talk her out of it; and Una suspected that might be easily done.

Want to come around later? Ciara asked.

Yeah, maybe — I'll give you a shout.

Ciara hadn't been to her house since Dad died; none of her friends had. It wasn't planned, it had just turned out that way. For the first few weeks, of course, she'd wanted nobody around. She'd gone to school like a robot, hovered at the edges of conversations, tried not to look too pathetic.

After school — before she started returning to the shop — she'd made her way straight home, no more going downtown with Ciara and the others. They were probably just as well pleased not to have her trailing after them, bringing her misery along with her.

And even when that stage had passed and she began to feel halfway human again, she still found herself reluctant to bring friends home. It wasn't really Daphne's fault, she knew that: it was nobody's fault that they'd ended up living together – it was just the way they'd ended up – but she wished Daphne wouldn't feel she had to keep pretending that Una meant anything to her. She didn't want her friends to see that, and pity her.

Three o'clock took forever to arrive. She passed the time drifting in and out of shops, running a hand across rails of clothes she didn't want, riffling through magazines she had no intention of buying. At five to three she stood in the bus station, stomach gripped tight with tension, mouth dry.

She could just not turn up. School was out for the summer – except for his exams, Theo Quirk had officially left. He wouldn't be back in the autumn; she might never meet him again. If she did she could just blank him, or say she'd been sick. He'd never know.

She watched the second hand of the big clock above the ticket desk make its jerky way past the numbers. Two minutes to three. She could still walk away, she didn't have to do this.

And then she thought again of her father, and she knew it had to be done. She left the station and walked the two hundred metres or so to the park gates.

And there they were.

He was small; that was the first surprising thing. He was only about her height, a foot shorter than his son. And he was skinny, not burly like she'd pictured. Just a little man with not much hair in a black jacket and baggy blue jeans, with eyes that were rimmed with red and shadowed beneath, and the same little red scratches on the lower part of his face that Dad used to get when he put a new blade into his razor.

They were awkward, all three of them. *My father Kevin*, Theo said, and the man put out a hand – and after a brief hesitation Una took it, and he clasped it tightly. *This is Una*, Theo told him, as if there could be any doubt about who she was.

Do you want to get a cup of tea? his father enquired, in a voice that trembled a bit. He seemed to be looking at something over her shoulder, and she said no quickly, still wanting to be anywhere else but there. There was a brief, charged silence before Theo and his father both began to speak, their words crashing into each other until both of them shut up again.

It was awful. She wished she hadn't come. Nobody knew what to do, nobody had a clue what to say.

And then Theo's father cleared his throat, and this time he looked her in the eye, and she made herself look back. *I wanted to say thank you* – haltingly, voice still unsteady – *for giving me this chance, to tell you … how sorry I am for what happened, sorrier than I can say. Not a day goes by, not one single day, that I don't … think about it, and wish I had … called in sick that day, or been put on a different route, or—*

He stopped, his face reddening, and for a few appalling seconds Una thought he was going to cry. Instead he turned his head aside and cleared his throat again a couple of times, and rubbed a hand hard to and fro across his mouth. Una was rooted to the spot, unable to speak or move. Theo stood stock-still, looking off to the side: for all the help he was, he might as well not have been there.

Eventually his father turned back to her, still clearly struggling to compose himself. He drew air in, puffed it out. *I didn't know your dad*, he said then, his voice more controlled, quieter and lower, *but I know he must have been a good man because of what you're doing now*. He paused. *I don't blame you if you hate me, and I'm sure this is the last thing you wanted to do, but you did it.* Another cough. *You must have been brought up right, and that would be down to him. I'm so very sorry I took him away from you, and I thank you with all my heart for letting me tell you that.*

He was sincere; it was obvious from his face and his voice. The accident had damaged him too. He had taken a man's life without meaning to – what must that have done to him? For the first time, Una found herself feeling a trace of sympathy for him. It had happened, it was terrible, and he felt responsible.

And then she spoke, without thinking about it. *It was my fault,* she said – and they both looked at her in astonishment.

And after that the words just tumbled out, as if she'd been waiting for just that day to say them. *I know he was knocked down, but it was my fault because he was riding a bike he was giving me. He was cycling it home to give it to me, and it was too small for him, that's why it happened, his foot must have slipped or something, he wasn't used to it, it wasn't his own bike, it would never have happened if he'd been on his own bike, he was a brilliant cyclist, it was all my fault—*

She broke off, horrified that she'd said them out loud, the

words that had been burning inside her since he'd died. She became aware that tears had started spilling from her eyes and were running down her face. She dug in her pockets but Theo's father was there before her, shoving a giant hanky into her hands.

She pressed it to her face, not caring how clean it was, and held it there, cried bitterly into it for what felt like ages. Hating that they were witnessing this, but totally unable to do anything about it.

She couldn't look at them then. She thrust the hanky back and Theo's father took it. *Anyway*, she said miserably, her eyes on his rather battered brown shoes. Her cheeks stung, her throat throbbed, her eyelashes flicked wetly against her hot skin when she blinked. So much for making him feel better.

Now you mustn't think like that, he said quietly. *That's the last thing you should be thinking. A cat ran out, you know that. It wasn't your fault, no way was it your fault.*

All she could do, still powerless to look at him, was shake her head silently. The cat he could have handled on his own bike.

Look, he said then, almost briskly, *we don't live far from here. Why don't you come home with us and have your tea? I know my wife would like to meet you too.*

His *wife*? She lifted her head slowly then and blinked at him. She glanced at Theo, whose shoulders were hunched, hands thrust deep into his pockets. The second time she'd cried buckets in his presence – bet he was glad now he'd asked her to meet his dad. Bet he couldn't wait for this to be over.

No, she said uncertainly, *I should be—*

We're not five minutes from here, Theo's father said. *Just a cuppa then, just till you feel a bit better. We'd be honoured to do that for you.*

He wasn't the monster she'd imagined him to be: he was a lot different from that. A cup of tea with him wouldn't kill her. And she'd said it all, there was nothing more she could say to embarrass herself.

With tears threatening again she gave a quick nod, and he picked up her rucksack and began to walk from the park. She followed silently, falling into step with Theo, grateful that neither of them tried to make conversation with her.

The short walk had an unreal quality about it. What was she doing? She tried to imagine Daphne's face, and Mo's, if they knew. They'd be horrified, they'd think she'd lost her mind.

But her father would understand and approve: she was sure of this, and the thought made her feel marginally better. She walked on, past terraced houses that faced a small scrubby green where runny-nosed boys scampered after a football, next to a lone horse that pulled at the grass and ignored them.

The street they turned onto after a minute or two housed a scatter of shops – among them the charity shop where Mo was to start volunteering a few months later. Theo's father turned up a lane that led off the street and Una halted, feeling for the first time a touch of fear. Where exactly were they taking her?

It's just around the corner, Theo said, *we always go in the back way* – and she walked on with him. She'd come this far, she'd take her chances. Not much choice anyway, with Theo's father carrying her bag – how would she explain its absence to Daphne if she turned tail and ran now?

They walked down the lane that swung around behind the street, backing onto a line of low redbrick houses on the other side, each with a little yard to the rear. Halfway up the lane

Theo's father opened a gate, and immediately a dog set up a furious barking.

Una stopped again – was she about to be attacked? – but beside her Theo said, *It's OK, it's only Dolly. She wouldn't harm a flea.*

His father had caught the dog by its collar and was beckoning Una in. *I won't let her near you,* he said, *shush, Dolly* – and Una entered the little yard and walked past the dog that strained to leap at her. *Shush,* Theo's father repeated, more firmly. *Theo,* he said, *open the door.*

But before Theo could get to it the back door of the house was flung open by a very round little woman – as round as her husband was spare – who was wiping her hands on a blue apron and smiling broadly at Una, as if she'd been expecting her.

Introductions were made. The woman was called Judy. Una offered a hand to be shaken – and instead found herself enfolded in the woman's arms, pressed to her very ample chest and held there. She hadn't hugged anyone, or been hugged, since her father's funeral, when so many people had clasped her in an embrace that the gesture had eventually become utterly meaningless, each one over almost before it had begun, as if it was something that had to be got out of the way as quickly as possible.

This was different, this was comforting. She was gently rocked, the woman's hand cradling the back of her head. *Thank you, pet,* she whispered, *thank you.*

And even though they'd only just met, there was nothing forced or awkward about it. You could tell by the unselfconscious way the woman did it that she was well used to hugging people.

You could tell that putting her arms around someone came very naturally to her.

Now, she said, loosening her hold but still with a warm hand encircling Una's waist, leading her into a small kitchen that smelt delectably of fresh-baked bread, *you'll have tea and a scone. They're just made.* It wasn't a question. *Kevin, pull out that chair. Theo, get the milk. Do you need to wash your hands before you sit down, love?*

The bathroom at the top of the stairs was tiny. It didn't have a bath, just a shower with a flowery plastic curtain around it. On the windowsill sat a handle-less cup that held a clutch of brightly coloured toothbrushes, like a bunch of flowers, and a crumpled tube of toothpaste without a lid, and next to it a can of shaving foam and a razor, and a curve of pink soap sitting in a small puddle in a little white dish.

Una's face was a mess, all blotchy cheeks and swollen eyes. She splashed it with cold water a few times, ran fingers through her messed-up hair, scrutinised herself in the little spotted mirror above the basin. No better, but it would have to do.

She made her way down the narrow stairs and back into the kitchen, feeling horribly self-conscious: what was she *doing* there? Theo and his father were already at the table. *Sit*, Theo's mother ordered, pouring tea, and Una sat beside Theo, who immediately placed a scone from a dish on the table onto her plate.

Blackberry jam, he said, indicating the pot on the table from which he was ladling a large spoonful onto his own scone. His father, who sat across the way nursing a mug of tea, nodded encouragingly at her. *Help yourself*, he said.

She had the sensation that this wasn't really happening – but she was also, she realised, incredibly hungry. She split the scone, releasing curls of steam. She spread butter that immediately melted into each half, and topped it with jam. She took a bite – and it was like the best thing she'd ever tasted.

Warm, sweet, light, buttery, the tartness of the jam a wonderful contrast. *Mmm*, she said involuntarily – and immediately felt herself reddening, but nobody seemed to notice.

Aren't they good? Theo's mother said, settling herself beside her husband, reaching for the milk jug. *Nobody can resist my scones. I add a bit of cream; that's the secret.*

Una noticed that Theo's father wasn't eating very much of his, just cutting it into tiny pieces, most of which still sat in front of him. Nobody remarked on this, although the other two must have seen it. She wondered if he'd become as thin as he was now in the two months since the accident. Maybe before that he'd eaten plenty of scones.

The mother did most of the talking, and while her remarks were addressed mainly to their visitor, to Una's relief they didn't demand much in the way of a response. She told Una about Theo's Leaving Cert exams. *He's hoping to get enough points for catering college. He loves to cook, don't you, pet? And he's very good at it – you should taste his spaghetti Bolognese.*

She spoke about a week in a cousin's mobile home in Wexford that the family was planning in August. *They let us have it every year. It's right on the beach, although I get a desperate heat rash if I sit in the sun for too long. Not like Kevin, he goes brown as a nut. I tell him he must have some African blood in him.*

She talked about Theo's sister Charlotte's wedding, scheduled for the following April. *They've had the hotel booked since Christmas, imagine. She and Brian grew up together – he's from just over the road, beyond the green you would have passed. Not that he was her only boyfriend, mind you. But I always thought they'd end up getting married, and wasn't I right? He's a nice lad, we're very happy.*

It was constant flowing monologue – half of it delivered through a mouthful of scone – and designed, Una suspected, to put her at her ease. The few direct questions she was asked were the kind that didn't need more than one-word answers – *Are those beautiful curls natural? I always wanted curls as a girl ... Were you ever in Gorey? It's a nice little spot, I must say, and piles of lovely beaches nearby ... Don't some weddings go on a bit long, though? I sometimes think they'd be better if they were half the length.*

Have another one, she urged, when Una finished her scone, *go on, they're only small* – so Una had another. Theo was on his third, while his father across the table from her still played with his first. He caught her eye a few times, and each time he gave her a small, encouraging smile. She decided she liked him. Who would have imagined it?

Eventually she pushed back her chair and rose. *I'd better be getting home*, she said – and immediately Theo's mother got up too. *Theo, you'll walk her back*, she said, but Una said hastily, *No, no, there's no need* – what on earth would they talk about? – and thankfully the offer wasn't pressed.

I'll see you out, Theo's mother said instead, and opened the door into the hall. *We'll go out the front*, she said. *I can't believe Kevin brought you in the back.*

Oops, Kevin said, smiling weakly at Una. *Sounds like I'm in the doghouse again.* He shook hands with her. *Thanks for coming*, he said. *It means the world, it really does. Drop in and see us some other time, if you want.*

OK, she said – but she doubted they'd meet again. She was glad she'd done it, but making a habit of it would be too weird. She turned to Theo. *Good luck with the exams*, she said, and he thanked her. He was OK.

She picked up her rucksack and followed Theo's mother out through the hall to the front door, which led straight onto the path, like Mo's house.

She got another hug on the doorstep. *You can't know how much good you've done for us, coming here today*, Judy whispered. *I know it'll help Kevin no end. Your daddy would be so proud of you.* The first time she'd made any mention of him – and the words were as welcome to Una as the warm feel of the woman's arms around her.

They drew apart. Judy's eyes as they met Una's were sparkling. *Would you come back to see us?* she asked. *Next week, maybe, would you come for your tea? What about Wednesday? It's shepherd's pie night.*

And Una looked at her round, anxious face and imagined sitting at that table again, eating what she guessed would be a tasty shepherd's pie. And she thought of the alternative: having dinner with Daphne, both of them going along with the façade that all was well.

If she came she'd have to lie to Daphne, say she was going to a friend's house. Shouldn't be too hard – Daphne was hardly going to check up.

Yes, she said, *OK* – and a time was set for her return. And walking home, she realised that she *wanted* to go back, that she was looking forward to it.

That's good, Daphne said when Una told her she was having dinner with Ciara. Relieved, probably, to be having a break from her. Imagining, no doubt, that Una was getting over things, moving on. If she only knew.

And on Wednesday they invited her to come again the following week, and she accepted again, and so it began. She visits them once a week, occasionally more often. Usually it's just the four of them, sometimes only three – Theo can't always make it home from catering college in time for dinner, which they call tea – and now and again Charlotte drops in too.

They're easy company. The event that caused them to come together is never mentioned. Invariably Judy does most of the talking: she never runs out of things to say. Little by little Una has got to know them, and to feel comfortable with them. She's become attached to them, she's come almost to need them.

Kevin eats better now; his face has filled in a bit. He's back at work too, went back a few weeks after Una's first visit to them. And he's funny: it took her a while to notice that. He can make them laugh, even if it's usually by poking gentle fun at Judy, who never seems to mind.

They're helping one another, Una and the family she'd been determined to hate. A random act of kindness, or whatever it was, has brought her far more than she imagined. And nobody knows, not even Ciara.

Of course, Mo nearly messed everything up when she began working in the charity shop just across the lane, a couple of months after Una began visiting the Quirks – but when it turned out that she'd be doing mornings only, Una relaxed. Today is the first time she's been at the house by day – but even so, there's no danger. The two places are back to back, and what would bring Mo out to the rear of the shop?

So her secret has remained safe from Mo and Daphne. As far as Daphne knows, Una is eating at a friend's house each time she misses dinner at home – and as far as Una is concerned it's true. They *are* her friends: at this stage, they're almost her family. And today she's going to Charlotte's wedding, just like a member of the family.

It's the date of your daddy's anniversary, Judy said a few weeks ago, when it was just the two of them in the kitchen, sitting over mugs of tea and slices of Judy's tea brack. *It was booked way back. Charlotte said they could change it, after ... but I said no. I thought it might be good to have something to take Kevin's mind off it. We were wondering if you'd like to come. We'd love to have you, we really would.*

A wedding, on what Una knew already would be the worst day in the year for her.

Of course, Judy went on, *we'll understand if you'd rather not, given the day that's in it* – but it seemed to Una all the more reason to go. Take her mind off it too, help her to forget, if that was possible.

Yes, she said. *I will – I mean, I'd like to. Thank you.*

It was a gift, and she accepted it gratefully, and made her plans. And now the day is here.

●

She finishes her sausages. Kevin continues to polish his shoes — surely only to annoy Judy at this stage. The kitchen door opens. A stoutly built woman she doesn't recognise comes in wearing a figure-hugging strapless dress in a purple so deep it's almost black. 'Your turn,' she tells Charlotte, who pushes away her plate and takes her mug and leaves.

'I'm Gaby,' the newcomer says, putting out a hand. 'You must be Una.' Her dark blonde hair is piled on her head. Her eyelashes are spiky with purple mascara. The dress shows a dangerous amount of cleavage. She takes Charlotte's seat, begins to eat what food remains on the plate in front of her. 'Any more sausages, Jude? I've a head on me after last night. I need feeding.'

'There she goes,' Kevin puts in, 'eating us out of house and home again' — but Gaby only laughs as she helps herself to a slice of bread and spreads it thickly with butter. 'That's because I'm a growing girl, Kevin — growing more beautiful every day. Pass over that jam there, Una.' She brushes crumbs from her hands before grabbing the top of the dress to hoick it higher on her chest. 'God, I wish this thing had straps — I've an awful feeling I'm going to let it all hang out today.'

'Might liven things up a bit,' Kevin says, and Judy shushes him as she adds sausages to the plate that used to be Charlotte's.

The door opens again and Theo enters. Una has never seen him in a suit: it makes him look older. Like his father's, his hair has been recently cut, and the lower half of his face is smooth and pink.

'Ah, you look so handsome, son,' Judy says, spreading her arms. 'Come here and give your old mother a hug.'

He bends and embraces her briefly – 'Mind my suit, Ma' – before plucking a sausage straight from the pan and eating it with his hands, leaning against the windowsill. He meets Una's eyes briefly and gives her what looks like a rather strained smile. She smiles back as she gets to her feet.

'I'd better get changed,' she says.

'Your things are in Charlotte's old room,' Judy tells her. 'First left, across from the bathroom.'

The dress Una brought over on her last visit is one she found in a charity shop – not Mo's – a couple of weeks after being invited to the wedding. It's the rich bright green of new grass, a wraparound dress that falls to just above her knees, and it's silk. She's never owned anything made of silk before. It slithers like liquid over her skin, and it cost eight euro.

She found the shoes on sale, twenty euro, down from seventy-five because of a little nick on one of the heels that you can hardly see. They're cream patent with pointed toes and a thin ankle strap, and narrow heels that are four inches high, far higher than anything she's owned before. She's not sure if they go with the dress: she had nobody to ask.

She's been wearing them in her bedroom in the evenings, trying to get used to walking in them. She thinks them wonderfully elegant, loves how much longer her legs look in them – but she wonders how her feet will feel several hours from now.

Her jewellery for today is the little gold five-pointed star on a delicate neck chain that Dad gave her on her twelfth birthday, a couple of months before he crashed into Daphne's car door. There's a tiny diamond set into one of the points, invisible until the light catches it. She wears it every day, hidden under her school uniform during the week.

Upstairs she slips first into the bathroom and examines the red mark on her chin, about the size of a thumbnail. She runs water on the grazed palm she's managed to keep hidden from them, and pats it dry. She hunts in the small press above the sink and finds a tub of Sudocrem, and rubs some in.

She stands on the tiny landing, listening to laughter coming from Charlotte's bedroom. She's never been in it before. She taps lightly on the door and pushes it open.

The room is small, like the others in the house. The air is thick with hairspray. Charlotte sits at the dressing table while Florrie brushes something onto her face. Florrie isn't a make-up artist, she's Brian's sister. Una has met her just once before.

'Come in,' Charlotte says, meeting her eye in the mirror. 'Your stuff is on the bed. Florrie, pour her a drink there. It's just Prosecco,' she tells Una, 'very light.'

'Thanks.'

Una takes a sip. It's warm and a bit flowery, and not as tasty as West Coast Cooler. The bag with her stuff sits on the single bed. She places her glass on the windowsill and opens the bag, and lifts out the dress.

'Here, Florrie,' Charlotte says, watching Una in the mirror, 'wouldn't you kill for hair like that?'

Florrie, stroking on eyeliner, doesn't look up. 'Yeah, it's divine. Is it hard to manage?'

Una removes her sweatshirt and pulls off the top Daphne gave her earlier, wishing she had a fancier bra. 'Not really – I just comb it with my fingers.'

'Divine.'

A small silence. Una gets into the dress and ties the sash, feeling the others watching.

'Oh, that's lovely on you,' Florrie says, glancing up. 'Fabulous colour.'

'Thanks.'

She shrugs off her shoes, shimmies out of her jeans, takes tights from the bag and eases them on. The small cream clutch that Charlotte is lending her for the day sits on the bed: she transfers her wallet and lip balm into it.

'Here,' Charlotte says, 'what about Ursula Foley saying that to Marie last night? Jesus, I didn't know where to look.'

'I know: cow. Poor Marie was gutted – it's not as if she hasn't been trying to lose the weight. Look up … now look down. Course if she gave up the pints it'd help.'

Una steps into the shoes, takes another sip from her glass. It's actually not that bad. She folds the clothes she took off and stows them in the bag. She stands by the bed, not sure whether to stay or leave.

'So, you and Theo,' Florrie says then, glancing back at Una, mascara wand in her hand.

Una feels her face getting hot. 'No,' she says, 'we're just friends.' She takes too big a gulp of Prosecco so it goes down the wrong way. She catches the look the other two exchange in the mirror as she coughs and splutters.

'Don't mind her,' Charlotte says. 'She's only teasing.'

'I am – don't mind me.'

But she knows they're wondering all the same.

●

Two glasses of Prosecco later, there's a mild pleasant buzzing in Una's head. Florrie hid the mark on her chin with concealer and patted a little powder on her face — *That's all your skin needs, it's so clear*. She applied eye liner and mascara, and lipstick that's darker than Una would have chosen — she rarely wears any lipstick — but she thinks she likes it.

When Judy saw the end result, she was predictably enthusiastic. *You could be a model*, she insisted, which made Una laugh. Kevin, dressed in his suit finally, told her she looked smashing, and Theo, busy pinning on his carnation, didn't say anything at all.

Judy wears a powder blue jacket and skirt, with a little cream feathery hat perched to one side on her head. *Got the suit on sale in the autumn*, she told Una. *The hat isn't a bit much, is it? It's a loan from a neighbour's daughter. I'm not mutton dressed as lamb, am I? I don't want to make a show of myself as mother of the bride.*

The bride better not get a divorce, Kevin remarked. *We can just about afford one wedding.* Judy told him to shush, weren't Charlotte and Brian paying for most of it?

A navy wool wrap has been found for Una, who hadn't thought about an outer layer — *Charlotte*, Judy said, *that lovely shawl thing you got me last Christmas will be perfect over her dress*. Una isn't altogether sure the colours go together, but the wrap is beautifully warm so she says nothing.

They're assembled in the kitchen now, preparations done. Kevin and Theo wear ties in the deep purple shade of Gaby's dress beneath their pale grey suits. 'Don't they look gorgeous?' Judy asks, and Una says, yes, they do, wondering why Theo seems to be avoiding eye contact with her today. Maybe he's nervous – although as far as she knows he has no particular role to play. He's not the best man, he doesn't have to make a speech. Could he be annoyed with her over something?

The beep of a car horn is heard out the back. 'That'll be Donie,' Judy says, practically leaping to her feet. 'Come on, you two. Now, Kevin, you leave here on the dot of five to twelve, not a *minute* later, you hear? I don't want poor Brian waiting any longer than a quarter of an hour – he'll be nervous enough. You hear me now?'

'Yes, ma'am.'

'And take your time going down the street. I promised everyone you would; they're going to be out waiting.'

'Yes, ma'am.'

'Stop *saying* that. And fix your tie, it's gone all crooked again. Charlotte, make sure to check it before he walks you up the aisle. Have I tissues? Who took the tissues I left on the ironing board? And Kevin, don't go without feeding Dolly – it'll be all hours before we get home. Oh, and someone come out and hold her now, so she won't jump up on us.'

'I can do that,' Theo says – but his father goes ahead of them, and Dolly is corralled while the three of them cross the yard and get into the waiting car. 'You go in front,' Judy tells Theo. 'Una, we'll sit in the back like ladies. God, I shouldn't have eaten those sausages – my stomach is turning somersaults. I'm feeling very jittery, I don't mind telling you.'

Donie turns out to be a friend of Brian's, living on the outskirts of the city. As he drives them to the church, Una notices him glancing at her a few times in the rear-view mirror. Wondering who she is, no doubt: all Judy gave him was her name. Trying to figure out how she's connected with the family – or maybe he assumes she's Theo's date, like everyone else seems to be doing.

She turns her face away when they drive past the charity shop, just in case. Not that Mo would be likely to recognise her – her sight isn't that great – but she isn't about to take any chances. She glances at her watch: a quarter to twelve. She hasn't thought of the anniversary since she reached the house more than an hour ago. She feels under the wrap and finds the little gold star. She holds on to it and keeps her smile in place.

❀

It's the first wedding she's been to since Dad married Daphne. Una was thirteen and trying to be happy for him, trying not to resent Daphne for coming between them. Because she *had* come between them, whatever Dad said.

You'll always be my number one lady, he'd told her, right after he'd broken the news of their engagement – but that wasn't really true, not any more. He loved her still, of course he did, but he had Daphne now, and Daphne had made him laugh again. And Una *did* like her, she couldn't say she didn't: she just wished she'd married someone else, and left her and Dad alone.

But if Dad hadn't married Daphne, what would have happened to Una after his death? She'd have had to move in with Mo, probably. Mum's parents wouldn't have wanted her, she's sure of that. They live in England – they're English, like Mum was – and send cards to Una with ten-pound notes in them at birthdays and Christmas. There's probably one waiting at home for her today. *Best wishes*, the cards always say, and their two names below in the same handwriting, and nothing else.

The only time they met her, the single time in her whole life that they met her, was at Mum's funeral, and they didn't exactly act like grandparents then. She doesn't remember much about them: she was only six, and missing Mum like anything. As far as she recalls, they were both tall — but then, everyone is tall when you're six. They were both dressed, she thinks, in black trouser suits, but that could be wrong too.

Una, the woman — her grandmother — said, when Finn introduced them, and she looked like the word tasted bitter. They examined Una without smiles, hardly spoke to her throughout the day, or to anyone.

She wonders what they did with the photos of her that Mum used to send them, if they kept them or threw them into the bin. She wonders why you would blame a child for something they hadn't done.

No, they wouldn't have wanted her when Dad died.

The church is chilly. She gathers Judy's wrap more tightly around her as she sneaks a look at the other guests. Not a very big crowd, about fifty, she reckons, mostly couples who look around Charlotte's age, some older people she assumes are family. A few small children, fidgety in shiny dresses and miniature suits, a couple of bored-looking boys of ten or eleven.

Judy's sister Miriam sits next to Una, in a tight red dress that sparkles when she moves, and a streak of matching lipstick on one of her front teeth. *So you're Una*, she said, when they were introduced, her gaze travelling unhurriedly from Una's face all the way to her shoes. Her husband Robbie, in pointed shoes and with hair that seemed a bit too black, looked straight at Una's chest as he shook her hand. She's glad he's sitting on Miriam's far side.

Charlotte and Brian stand before the altar as the priest — a family member too, she's forgotten whose — binds them together for better or for worse. In the seat directly ahead of Una, Judy blows her nose loudly, and Una watches the back of Theo's head and wonders again if she's done something to annoy him.

Normally they get on fine. They're hardly ever alone; Judy is pretty much always in the kitchen when Una visits, and Kevin is rarely far away — but she and Theo seemed to have settled into an easy familiarity. Up to today she would have said he was the closest thing she has to a brother. Now she's not so sure.

Occasionally her visits have coincided with days that he brought home something he'd made in catering college: a lamb tagine, a chicken or fish pie, a rhubarb and custard tart. He endures his father's teasing as Judy doles it out — *You'll make someone a lovely wife one day, son* — and if there are leftovers Judy parcels them up for Una to take home. This isn't a problem: Una tells Daphne they came from whatever friend she was supposedly having dinner with. It's only half a lie.

Daphne has suggested, more than once, that Una bring her friends home so she can cook for them. *We should return the favour*, she says, *you're always going to their houses* — and whenever this happens Una says, *Yeah, sometime*, knowing Daphne won't try to fix a date. Daphne goes through the motions, that's all.

The organ starts up: there's a rustle among those assembled.

Una gets to her feet with the rest of them as the newlyweds emerge from the sacristy and parade down the aisle, Charlotte being ambushed for an inevitable hug from her tearful mother.

Her bridal dress, bought on eBay and adjusted by Gaby's friend, is white and lacy, with tiny pearl buttons pattering up the back, and sleeves that come to a stop just below her elbows. When she moves, the train of her veil slides along behind her like the ribbon of foam that follows a cruise ship. Gaby, bringing up the rear beside the best man, gives Una a wink as she passes.

The guests leave the church in a slow, chattering mass that forms itself into little knots outside. People cluster and regroup around the bride and groom, who stand together on the steps. Cameras flash, confetti flies, laughter erupts. Shoe straps are adjusted, hats are straightened, children exclaimed over.

Judy moves from group to group, her equilibrium restored, Brian's relatives as familiar to her as her own. All of them, it appears, have grown up within the same half a square mile. Everyone, it seems to Una, knows everyone else. Everyone except her.

She stands alone in the church doorway, trying not to shiver. A tiny headache taps at her temple – the consequence, no doubt, of the Prosecco. Her shoes, predictably, have begun to pinch: she slips each foot out in turn and wriggles her cramped toes.

She sees Theo standing with Brian and a few others. He must have spotted her, she's in full view, but he makes no effort to approach or draw her into the group. Maybe he feels she's taking over his family, claiming his parents for her own. Maybe he wishes he'd never introduced her to them.

She sneaks a look at her watch: half past one. Lunch over at school, double history usually on Friday afternoon but classes finishing early today because of the Easter holidays. Ciara and Emma will go into town, like they always do. *We'll treat you to a birthday hot chocolate*, Ciara had said to Una yesterday – only of course that's not happening now.

Jennifer, the fourth in the group, won't be with them: she's flying to France this evening with her mother and sisters. They're spending Easter in a hotel that overlooks the beach in Cannes. Jennifer's parents split up last year, a few months after Una's dad died. Since then it's looked like they're in competition to see who can spoil their kids the most.

It's a pain, Jennifer said once, *having to spend every weekend with Dad in his stupid apartment.* And then she glanced at Una and her face went bright red, and suddenly none of them knew where to look or what to say.

'Sorry, love, you're all alone.' Judy appears, clamping a hand to her hat to keep the wind from catching it. 'Where's that Theo? Why isn't he looking after you?'

'It's OK,' Una says quickly – but Judy has spotted him and is beckoning him across. He walks over to them, jacket flapping in the breeze.

'Yeah?'

'I found poor Una all by herself,' his mother scolds. 'She knows nobody here except us. You need to look after her.'

'I'm fine,' Una says – it's plain the last thing he wants to do is have her hanging onto him – but Judy has vanished again, leaving them alone. They stand side by side in the porch as conversations continue all around them. She wants to ask if

he's cross with her – there's definitely something up – but the
question sounds silly in her head, so she leaves it there.

She shifts her weight from one aching foot to the other,
holding her wrap tightly around her, wishing she could sit
down, wishing this part of the day at least was over. Maybe it
wasn't such a good idea to come; maybe she should have turned
down the invitation.

'I have kites,' Theo says suddenly.

She looks up at him. He's turned away from her, staring out
into the crowd. He must be talking to someone else, although
nobody seems to be paying them much attention.

He turns to face her, looking at her properly for the first time
that day. 'Kites,' he repeats. 'Two. I got a loan of them from a
guy in the college. His uncle makes them.'

His cheeks are pink with the cold. His eyes are green as a
cat's. His nose is slightly too big for his face, but she thinks that
adds to it a bit, gives it character. He is, she realises suddenly,
quite good-looking.

'Kites,' she says, because he seems to be waiting for some sort
of response. 'Right.' What's he on about?

'Have you ever flown one?'

'No.'

'They're brilliant. We could do it later. They're in the boot
of Dad's car – I put them in last night.'

She regards him with astonishment. Fly kites in the middle
of his sister's wedding – what's got into him? And then it strikes
her that he's joking – he must be – and she laughs.

He doesn't join in. 'Just an idea,' he says, looking away again.
'I thought you might fancy it, that's all.'

It's not a joke. He really was suggesting that they fly kites. He actually seems disappointed that she's not jumping at it. She shifts again from foot to foot, trying to find the right response.

'It's just — wouldn't you need lots of space for that, like … a park or something?' *Not to mention that we're at a wedding*.

He shrugs. 'There's a big garden at the hotel … Doesn't matter.'

Silence resumes. She sees Charlotte throwing back her head in laughter at something Gaby has said. Confetti is strewn about on the ground, like breadcrumbs from a fairy tale.

Theo sighs, shoves his hands into his trouser pockets. Una feels she's let him down in some way — but honestly, how could he possibly think it's a good idea today? Running after a kite — or is it the other way around? — in a silk dress and shoes definitely *not* designed for running seems like the height of idiocy to her. And yet, if he brought them along with her in mind, is she being mean not to at least consider it?

'We're moving,' he says suddenly, and walks off without waiting for her, and now she sees Judy beckoning to them from the church gate. She follows him gingerly, every step a challenge by now.

'Your shoes are at you,' Judy says, as she approaches. 'Gaby has plasters; we'll get some from her at the hotel.'

The skin beneath her eyes is spotted with black. Her lipstick has all but disappeared. One of the feathers in her hat is bent and drooping. She looks completely happy.

'Isn't this an absolutely wonderful day?' she says — and immediately afterwards her mouth falls downward in an almost

comical expression of dismay. 'Oh, my God,' she says, hands
flying to her cheeks, 'oh, God above, I'm so sorry, love—'

Una shakes her head. 'It's OK,' she says, 'really' – and, oddly,
it is. It is OK.

* * *

The plasters are helping a lot, and so are the gel cushions Gaby
gave her to slip under the balls of her feet.

I've been there, girl, she told Una. *I have shoes that cripple me no
matter how often I wear them. They're a curse: don't know why we do
it to ourselves.*

It's the middle of the afternoon, and the rain that's been
threatening has so far held off. Scores of photographs have
been taken in the hotel gardens, mostly around the giant horse
chestnut tree that grows beyond the tastefully designed and
beautifully kept shrubberies and flowerbeds. Behind the tree is
a huge, manicured lawn, easily the size of a football field, and
bisected by paved walkways that are dotted here and there with
benches.

Plenty of room to fly a kite, if you had a mind to.

Since their odd little conversation in the church porch, Theo
has kept well away from Una. They've been positioned close to
one another for various photos – Judy ignoring Una's reluctance
to be included – but that's as much as she's seen of him. Instead
she's been befriended by Ellen, a first cousin of Brian's, and her
husband Paul.

'Weddings are horrible on your own,' Ellen says, when Una
confesses she knows only Charlotte's immediate family. 'They
should have let you bring a boyfriend' – and Una doesn't want

to admit that she doesn't have one, or elaborate on how exactly she came to be invited, so she says nothing and lets them think a boyfriend would have been available if he'd been called upon.

Over the past few years she's been kissed by various boys. From time to time she's indulged in a little more than kissing. She's allowed occasional hands under her top, has felt the thrill of someone else's touch on her bare skin, and the hot itch it has generated lower down. She's been aware of the answering arousal of the boy in question when he has pressed against her.

But she's drawn the line at going further, despite other girls' hints at the excitement to be had, despite the increasingly graphic love scenes she's seen in films on Netflix. It's not time, she thinks, not yet. She wants it to be special, not just a coming-together of two bodies. Also, she's a little bit scared.

She wants to be in love, however old-fashioned that might sound, and she's still waiting for that to happen.

She excuses herself and visits the hotel bathroom. In a cubicle she takes her phone from her bag and checks her emails – and there it suddenly is, the one she's been waiting for all week. She races through it.

I have the information you want. I can meet you this evening, say 8.30, in the lobby of the Charles Hotel. It's nice and quiet, we can talk there. I'll wear a brown jacket so you'll know me.

She stares at the screen, rereading the few sentences, trying to take them in. *I have the information you want* – can it be true? She hardly dares believe it.

Meet him, though – she wasn't expecting that. She assumed he'd just email her with whatever he'd found, but it appears she was wrong. He wants to meet her. Maybe he wants to see her face when he tells her, and maybe he deserves that much.

She's never been in the Charles but she knows where it is. The other side of the city, not far from an Irish-dancing school she and Ciara used to go to when they were younger. She'd have to get a taxi there – it's not on any bus route she knows. Dad or Ciara's father used to take it in turns to drop and collect them from Irish dancing. Una always preferred when it was Ciara's father's turn: Dad drove so slowly, and they weren't allowed to put on the radio.

She puts a fingernail between her teeth and nibbles it as she reads the email again. He's told her his name is Dave. He's mentioned a wife, but she could be a figment of his imagination. There mightn't be a word of truth in anything he's told her.

But it might be true, he might have found something. *I have the information you want* – and she does want it, oh, she wants it so badly. The thought of getting it tonight, in just a few hours' time, is tantalising. And meeting him in a hotel lobby should be safe enough, shouldn't it? Even if it's quiet, like he says, there would still be people coming and going – and surely at least one receptionist behind the desk.

But by eight-thirty she'll be at home, eating her second dinner with Daphne and Mo. She can't do it, she can't not turn up for the special meal Daphne is cooking – even if Una hadn't asked for it, even if it's the last thing she feels like facing this evening.

She leans her head against the cubicle door and tries to think. She could ring Daphne now and explain, come clean about what she's been doing. She imagines Daphne's surprise, her shock maybe, the endless injured questions that are bound to follow.

She can't do it.

She won't tell, not yet. She'll send Daphne a text in a while, say she's having dinner at Ciara's. It won't go down well – Mo *definitely* won't like it – but they'll get over it. It won't be the end of the world.

She'd love to have someone with her when she meets him, though – because of course she's going to meet him: she realises the decision was made as soon as she read his email. But there's nobody she can bring with her, nobody at all. Obviously not Daphne or Mo – and certainly not Theo or any of his family, not today.

And not Ciara either, not after Una claiming to be sick. And, anyway, Ciara knows nothing about this – nobody knows anything about it except Una, and the man who may or may not be named Dave. She can't call Ciara.

George, she thinks suddenly. George would come, she's sure. She could swear him to secrecy, promise she was going to tell Daphne soon – but as she scrolls through her contacts she abruptly remembers his school show. Last weekend he told them about it, he wished Una a happy birthday in advance because he'd be busy on the night. So George is out too.

She'll go alone, then. She'll take a taxi to the hotel – no way can she walk across town in these shoes, even with Gaby's remedies. She'll have to trust that this Dave is on the level.

I can't pay you, she'd told him, and he'd assured her that he wasn't looking for money. *It's like a hobby of mine*, he wrote. *I get a kick out of tracking people down, makes me feel like a real private detective. It drives my wife mad — I'm like a dog with a bone sometimes — but I tell her there are worse things I could be doing!*

She hadn't looked for his help, not specifically his. She'd just asked for information. *I'm trying to trace my birth father*, she'd posted a month earlier on Boards.ie. *All I know about him is his first name and his nationality. Anyone got any ideas?*

It had come to her out of the blue a few months ago, sitting in the back room of the bike shop one afternoon. She hadn't thought about him in years, literally years. She'd always known Dad wasn't her real dad; she knew she was already born when he and Mum had met. She knew this because Mum had told her, lots of times.

He came along like a handsome prince, Mum would say. Usually at bedtime, when the subject of handsome princes was generally on the agenda. *He met us when you were just a baby, and we fell in love, like Cinderella and her prince, and then he asked me to marry him, and I said yes, and he became your dad. Not your real dad, but your new dad — and we all lived happily ever after.*

And where is my real dad? Una would ask — but the question was more automatic than anything, because when Mum shook her head and said, *Gone away*, which she always did, Una accepted it without asking any more. Her new dad was so good at being a dad, she didn't feel the need to investigate further. And then Mum died, and Dad became even more important in Una's life, and any thoughts of another father were forgotten.

Until one day when she was at school — she must have been nine or ten at the time — Ursula Conroy told the class that she was getting a new dad, and Una said, *My dad is a new dad too*, but they all thought she was joking, because Dad had been around for as long as they'd known her.

So where's your real dad? Ursula asked, just like Una used to ask – and she had to admit that she didn't know.

What's his name? they asked, and again she shrugged. She could see they didn't believe her – even the teacher was looking at her doubtfully. *It's true*, she insisted, but her lack of evidence didn't do a lot for her credibility. So when she got home from school she asked Dad, the first time she'd brought up her other dad with him.

And he told her.

He was French, he said. *Your mum met him in England when he went there on holidays. His name was Victor.*

And what happened to him?

Nothing.

She was puzzled. *So where is he now? Why did he stop being my dad?*

And Dad explained as best he could that Victor and Mum were just holiday friends, and Victor had gone back to France before Mum knew she was going to have a baby, and she couldn't tell him because she didn't know where he lived or even his last name.

That's why Mum came to Ireland, Dad said. *Her mum and dad were a bit cross because she was having a baby before she got married, so she thought it was best if she went away. But I'm glad she came here because I'd never have met her, or you, if she'd stayed in England.*

Una had felt her way around this new information. *You mean*, she said eventually, *my real dad never knew I was even born? He never knew he was my dad?*

That's right, love.

She thought some more. *So he's never going to find out.*

No, probably not.

It disconcerted her for a while, but then she pushed it aside and forgot about it. Later, of course, she understood the whole thing better, when she found out where babies came from, and learned what a holiday romance was. She thought it sad that there was a man called Victor out there somewhere, probably in France, who never knew he'd fathered her, but there was nothing she could do about it. Impossible to track down a man who'd spent a couple of weeks in England years ago, when all she knew was his first name. Anyway, she'd done all right in the dad stakes, hadn't she, in the end?

But then Dad died, and Daphne was left with Una to look after. Una, who had come as part of the package when Daphne married Dad. Just like she'd been part of the package when Dad and Mum had got married, except that Mum had been her real mum, which made it different. When Mum died, Dad was left with her real daughter. When Dad died, Daphne wasn't left with *his* real daughter, just his stepdaughter. Una was Daphne's dead husband's stepdaughter.

Pretty tenuous connection, when you thought about it.

And slowly, the idea of looking up her real father began to occupy space in her head, began to seem like something she should try to do. Imagine, just imagine, if she found him. He'd probably be shocked at first to discover he had a daughter, but once he got used to the idea he might decide he really wanted her. He might think it was the most wonderful thing that had ever happened to him. She might have a French family of half-brothers and sisters who would be delighted to discover her.

It was a long shot, she knew that. She also hadn't a clue how to go about it – but it was worth a try, wasn't it? Surely now with all the DNA information available there might be a way to find him. It would let Daphne off the hook completely: she would never have to bother with Una again, and Una would make sure she knew there were no hard feelings.

Lots of people responded to her Internet enquiry, but Dave was the only one who didn't tell her she hadn't a hope. He seemed friendly – and now it sounds like he might have found something.

She'll take a chance, and trust that he's genuine.

●

When she leaves the hotel bathroom it's to find that they're all finally being summoned in for the meal. It's almost half past four, and it's raining. They take their seats at the impeccably decorated round tables – Una has been put at one with three couples, all relatives of Brian's, and an elderly woman with her coat still on.

After a bit of small talk Una is largely ignored as the others chat among themselves, which suits her fine. She kicks off her shoes under the table and eats every bit of the prawn cocktail in the wine glass that's placed in front of her, even the bit of parsley that everyone else leaves on the saucer. She can't remember the last time she was this hungry.

'Red or white?' a waitress asks, showing her both wine bottles, assuming she's old enough – but Una shakes her head and fills a glass with water instead. Bad enough coming home late on her birthday, but coming home smelling of drink would be asking for trouble. Daphne mightn't give out much, but Mo would have plenty to say.

Anyway, there's the encounter with Dave before she gets home: she wouldn't want to meet him smelling of drink either, wouldn't give him a very good impression of her. She'll wait till after eight to leave the hotel, instead of the quarter past seven departure she was planning; that should get her to the Charles in good time.

Outside the full-length windows the rain continues to fall steadily. From where she sits she can just see Theo, seated at the top table between Brian's mother and a man she doesn't know. She thinks of the two kites he put into the boot of his father's car: no way could they fly them now.

Mightn't have been so bad if she'd had the right clothes on. Might have been fun, actually. Maybe she'll ask him to borrow them again another time — they could take them to the park or something.

That's assuming he'll be back to normal next time they meet.

She's in the middle of the beef she chose over salmon — bit tough, she should have gone for the fish — when she hears a text message coming through on her phone. She slides it from her bag under the table, squints down at the words.

Happy birthday. See you soon, love Mo.

She'd completely forgotten her birthday. *See you soon*: she feels a flick of guilt. A quarter past five, her phone says. Daphne will be leaving work soon, going home to put the chicken into the oven, chop up vegetables, peel potatoes.

Una will have to text her, tell the next lie of the day. She'll wait another while, no point in doing it too soon. She puts her phone on silent and slips it back in the bag as she turns to one of Brian's cousins who's asking her something about her hair.

❀

By seven the rain has petered out. The speeches have been made, the last of the baked Alaska cleared away, the wedding cake cut and doled out in fat fingers that sit unwanted and uneaten on plates. Cups and glasses and crumpled napkins dot the white tablecloths that are stained now with sauce splashes, smudges of cream and overlapping red wine circles.

Guests migrate between the tables, new groupings are formed and re-formed. Some have vanished, presumably to the hotel bar. A four-piece band is assembling at the end of the room; tables are being moved aside by the hotel staff to create a space for dancing.

Una sits on, picking raisins from her piece of cake as she watches the rest of the room. *Come to the bar with us*, Florrie had said, passing with a group by Una's table, but she assured them she was fine where she was, not wanting to be a nuisance.

She spots Kevin, still seated at the top table, in conversation with the priest. Judy is nowhere to be seen – gone to the bar too, maybe. Charlotte and Gaby have relocated to another table; Gaby sits on the knee of a man in a dark suit, her arm thrown around his neck, letting out an occasional whoop of laughter, one time mock-slapping him across the face.

Theo – where is he? She casts about, sees no sign of him. She takes up her bag and slips her shoes back on, and makes her way to the Ladies in the corridor outside. When she emerges there he is, a little way down the corridor, leaning against the wall, head bent towards his phone as he types.

She stands watching him, waiting for him to look up, wanting to see what his face does when he sees her.

At length he finishes, stows his phone in his trouser pocket, glances up.

'Hey,' he says, one side of his mouth turning up in a smile.

She smiles back, relieved, and walks towards him. 'I was wondering where you'd got to.' Sometime during the meal he must have got over whatever was bugging him.

'Having a good day?' he asks.

'I am.'

Although the day has been an odd one, not without its anxieties. And this morning, when she was unwrapping her present from Daphne, seems a million light years away.

'Today is my birthday,' she says then, the words coming out of nowhere, taking her by surprise. At exactly the same time, he says, 'Sorry—'

They break off. 'What?' he asks, frowning.

She makes no response, kicking herself. What on earth made her blurt it out like that? No way was she planning to tell him, or any of them.

'Did you say it's your *birthday*?'

'I wasn't going to mention it, it just …'

'Why not? Why didn't you want to tell us?'

'I didn't want a fuss. I suppose it … didn't seem important. And it's Charlotte's day.'

A beat passes. She waits, looking at the wall behind him.

'He died on your *birthday*?' he asks softly.

She nods, turns it into a headshake. Blinks hard. 'It's OK, I'm OK.'

'Una,' he says, and something in his voice when he says her name makes the blood rise to her face. She can feel its heat in her cheeks.

'Look,' he says quickly, glancing to left and right, but nobody who passes is paying them the least bit of attention – 'I'm really sorry I was … a bit off with you earlier. The kites, it was a stupid idea.' He shakes his head. 'I just, I thought––' He makes a face, sticks his hands into his pockets, studies the patterned carpet beneath their feet. 'I don't know what I thought. Anyway, I'm sorry.'

And suddenly, unexpectedly, flying a kite with him seems like the best idea in the world.

'Can you get them?' she asks.

He looks up.

'Can you? The kites, can you get them?'

He laughs. She loves his laugh: it's like music. It's like musical happiness.

'What – you want to fly them now?'

She nods.

'Are you serious?'

'Let's do it,' she says – so he collects his father's car keys while she waits in the corridor, and they slip out of the hotel.

And as soon as they reach the grass, she takes off her shoes.

❖

It's hopeless. *She*'s hopeless.

Run with it, he said, *throw it up, let the wind catch it* – but each time she tried – *Now, let it go NOW!* – her kite flopped to the ground and dragged along behind her. After twenty minutes she's disheartened and breathless and frozen, even though he's given her his suit jacket to wear – and her feet in their tights are soaked from the wet grass.

He's at the far side of the lawn, his red kite sailing high in the air, tail fluttering. He shouts something, but she can't hear him.

She drops her kite on the grass and plops down on the bench where she left her bag. She pulls out her phone and finds Daphne's number. She types as rapidly as her nearly numb fingers will allow: *Sorry, having dinner at Ciaras, her dad will drive me home, hope thats OK, c u later*

'Here.'

She looks up and there he is, offering the taut string of his still-airborne kite to her. His face is flushed and shiny. She sends off the text and shoves her phone back into the bag. 'Don't let it go,' he orders, placing the string in her hand, waiting until her fingers close around it.

She can feel the tug of it, doing its best to get free. She holds it tightly, watching as the breeze lifts and drops it, feeling the dance of it in the pull and release of the string. She turns to see Theo running back across the lawn, and the blue kite taking off at last, soaring up in a wide arc, and the sight exhilarates her, as if she was up there swooping and dipping along with it.

'Run!' he shouts, and she runs towards him, laughing, hair bouncing out behind her, dress blotchy with sweat. And when they meet he scoops her up and swings her around, and she screams that she'll let go of the kite but she doesn't, she manages to hang on, and when he lowers her to the ground her heart is racing, and the kites are still dancing together high above them, and he hasn't let her go, and his head is dipping towards her, and she's rising up on tiptoe to meet him – heedless now of the wet grass, her frozen toes forgotten – and she's closing her eyes for his kiss.

◆

'Thanks a million,' she says to Judy. 'It was great.'

It must be written all over her face, everyone must see – but incredibly, nobody is laughing or whispering or nudging their neighbour, or even looking in her direction. They're too busy dancing, or drinking, or chatting.

Amazing. Astounding.

Judy gives no sign that she's noticed anything either. 'You'll get a taxi home,' she says, and Una crosses her fingers and promises that she will. 'And you'll come and see us next week sometime – what about Thursday?'

'OK.'

She'd replenished her lipstick in the loo, after they'd replaced the kites in the car boot, after they'd made their way, fingers interlocked, back to the hotel. *He kissed my lipstick off*, she told the mirror, and giggled. *He's a good kisser*, she told the mirror, because she had to say it out loud, it was bursting to come out of her, and a rather spotted hotel mirror was all she had. *I could have kissed him all night*, she told it, the feel of his mouth on hers still vivid, the taste of him still on her tongue. Astonishing, amazing that nobody can see the change he's wrought in her.

I'm mad about you, he told her between kisses. *I've been mad about you for months*. She was sitting on his lap on a stone bench, the kites in the grass beside them.

I could hardly look at you today, he said, his hands cradling her face, *you were — you are — so beautiful. I was afraid you'd see by my face how I felt, and I thought you mightn't want to see it.*

I've had the kites for weeks, he said, tucking her hands under his shirt to warm them. *I wanted to ask you to come and fly them — I thought it mightn't seem like a date. I thought if I could get you away from my family you might actually notice me, and I might grow on you, or something. I shoved them into the car last night, but this morning I thought it was a stupid idea, and it was too late to take them out again, everyone would have seen, so I had to leave them. I wasn't going to mention them, and then it just ... came out when we were standing in the church porch.*

I love your hair, he said, touching it, pushing his fingers into it, lifting handfuls to press to his face. *I love your hair, it's beautiful.*

I'll call you in the morning, he said, after he'd added her number to his phone, after he'd placed a call to her so she'd have his. *I'll call you first thing.*

Incredible that it should have happened today. Incredible that it has happened at all.

Theo Quirk, of all the boys in all the world.

After saying goodbye to Kevin — there's no sign of Charlotte and Brian — she collects her bag of clothes from the reception desk and changes in the bathroom while Theo waits for her outside. She laughs when she realises she's left her runners on the floor in Charlotte's bedroom, socks stuffed into them — who cares? She slips her feet back into the heels: she'll tell Daphne she borrowed them from Ciara, she'll collect the runners over the weekend.

She folds the green dress — it's so thin it fits into Charlotte's clutch bag — and slips her phone into her jeans pocket. The navy wrap she drapes loosely around her neck.

Theo walks to the door with her. 'I wish you'd stay longer,' he says, but she tells him Daphne will be expecting her. She hates lying to him, pretending she's going straight home, but she can't tell him about Dave: it's too complicated for now.

He kisses her again on the street, in full view of everyone passing. He wraps her in his arms, just like his mother does, and whispers goodnight, his breath warm in her ear. She closes her eyes and clings to him, drinking in his scent.

The first taxi they hail pulls up, and she squeezes Theo's hand before climbing in. She shuts the door and smiles out through the window at him.

'Where to?'

She turns. 'The Charles Hotel, please.' They pull off and she sits back, her head full of all that has happened as they cross the city. She remembers again that it's her birthday, and that she should be at home.

She takes out her phone and sees a missed call from Daphne, no voicemail message. Sent directly after she'd got Una's text, it must have been. By now they're having dinner without her, Daphne and Mo. She can imagine how Mo took the news.

She opens the clutch bag, sniffs her dress and smells the tang of Theo's aftershave. She checks her watch: already twenty to nine. Too much time spent saying goodnight. She smiles down at her lap.

'Here we go,' the taxi driver says, and charges her fifteen euro, which sounds expensive, but she pays up. Only five left, not enough to get a taxi home after this; she hadn't bargained on needing two. She'll have to take a bus, whenever she finds a stop. She's quite far from home so she'll be late back — there'll probably be hell to pay. Can't be helped.

She regards the hotel façade, fifty yards or so from the road. A bit more flash than the hotel she just left. A man in the act of getting into a car, another standing under the awning by the hotel entrance. She tucks the clutch bag under her arm and walks up the paved pedestrian pathway, her high-heeled shoes clacking loudly, her earlier apprehension creeping back.

She wishes Theo was here. She should have told him: he'd have come, he'd have understood. Why didn't she tell him?

'Una?'

She stops, thrown. The man under the awning takes a step towards her. 'Are you Una?'

'Yes.'

He's older than she imagined him to be. At least fifty, maybe a lot more. Short speckled hair grows on either side of his head, the top of which is completely bald, freckly and shiny. He's not tall — an inch or so above her, that's all — but his shoulders are as wide as a wrestler's, his brown jacket tight across his chest. His neck is as thick as a tree trunk.

'Dave,' he says, offering her his hand so she feels obliged to take it. Why is he out here? Didn't he say they'd meet in the lobby?

'I'm afraid I've been an awful clown,' he says, smiling, spreading his palms. 'I've only gone and left my wallet at home.'

She looks uncomprehendingly at him. Why would he need his wallet?

'It's just,' he goes on, 'they mightn't look too kindly on us sitting in their lobby without buying a coffee or something.'

Is he hinting that *she* should pay? Is he waiting for her to offer? She thinks of the fiver in her pocket. 'I only have enough money to get a bus home,' she says.

He laughs, shaking his head. 'Oh dear, no, I didn't mean that, I didn't mean for you to fork out at all. No, what I was going to suggest –' gesturing to the right, so she looks and sees a line of parked cars '– was that we head to my house. It's only down the road, not five minutes away, and my car is just over there.'

His car? He's asking her to get into his car? She feels a fresh stab of alarm.

'Joan – my wife – made apple tart earlier,' he goes on, the smile still broad on his face as he pulls keys from his pocket. 'And I have to tell you, her apple tart is legendary. What do you say?'

Una feels trapped. He seems OK, but he's still a stranger. 'Why can't you just tell me now? We don't have to go in. We can talk out here.'

He hesitates. 'I wish I could, Una, I know how anxious you must be to hear what I found out, but it's not that simple. There's quite a bit to tell you, actually, and it's fairly complicated. That's why I didn't want to put it in an email. We really need to sit down and do it properly.'

Still she demurs, reluctant to take a chance on trusting him. 'It's just that I haven't got long. My stepmother is expecting me home.' She immediately regrets 'stepmother': she should have said 'mother'.

'Not a problem,' he says immediately. 'I'm literally a few minutes from here, and I can run you home afterwards, no bother. You can ring your stepmother and explain. I could talk to her, if you wanted.'

Talk to Daphne? Una can imagine how that would go. She looks towards the cars again, playing for time as she casts about for the right thing to do.

'Look,' he says, 'I can see you're a bit nervous, which is perfectly understandable. Let's leave it for now. We can make a new arrangement. It's just that I'm away all next week and the soonest I could meet you again would be the week after. So will we say same time, same place next Monday week? Would that suit you?'

He sounds reasonable. His wife is called Joan, and she's made apple tart. The thought of having to wait more than a week to find out about her father is deeply frustrating. Why can't he just tell her what he knows now? What could be so complicated that they'd need to sit down and talk about it?

'Is he dead?' she asks, the thought jumping into her head. 'Is that what you don't want to tell me?'

He shakes his head quickly. 'No, no, he's not dead, it's not that. But ... like I say, Una, it's a bit complicated. I really don't want to go into it like this. It just doesn't feel right, you know?'

She makes up her mind. She can't wait: she has to trust him.

'OK,' she says. 'Where's your car?'

❁

'You'd better buckle up,' he says, turning onto the main road. 'Can't be too careful.'

His breath smells of whiskey. Why hadn't she noticed it before now? She pulls the seat belt across and clicks it closed.

'Won't be long,' he says, drawing to a stop at a pedestrian crossing to allow an elderly man to shuffle across. 'Just a few minutes, that's all.'

She pulls Judy's wrap more tightly around her. He hasn't switched on the heat: the air in the car is icy.

'You got holidays from school today, yes?' he asks.

Una nods, her mouth dry. She shouldn't have got into the car. That was a mistake. Her toes curl inside their too-high shoes.

He drives off again, glances at her. 'You must be in … what? Transition year, yes?' He makes a left turn onto a side street, leaving the shops behind. 'Or maybe you didn't bother with that.' Houses, more houses, a green, a church. She's never been this way before.

'Fifth year,' she says, watching the road disappearing under the car.

From the corner of her eye she sees him glance over again. 'Don't worry,' he says. 'You needn't be afraid of me, Una. We're friends, aren't we? Friends help one another, don't they?'

His voice sounds different. She nods again, frightened now, heart thudding.

He begins to whistle, some tune she doesn't recognise. Again she gets a whiff of alcohol. He makes another turn. More houses, less densely packed. They must be nearly there. She shivers, wishing he'd put on the heat.

He stops whistling to glance at her again. 'You cold?' he asks. 'Not to worry, Jean has a lovely fire on, soon be cosy.'

Jean.

Una forces herself to look at him. 'You said her name was Joan.'

He smiles, not taking his eyes from the road. 'Oops,' he says, turning the car into what looks like an industrial estate.

'Where are we going?' she asks, watching low buildings fly by as they lurch over a speed bump. Wrong, all wrong, her insides knotted in fear.

'Just a little shortcut,' he answers lightly. 'Soon be landed.'

Every muscle tense, something hard lodged in her throat, making it difficult to breathe. Fingers clutching Judy's wrap so tightly her hands ache.

'I love your hair,' he says then. 'Beautiful.' They pass more buildings. He makes another turn, slows down. Moves a meaty hand from the steering wheel to place it, almost absently, on her thigh.

She jerks away but he hangs on, clamps his fingers around her leg. She clicks open her seat belt, presses herself back against the car door. 'Stop,' she says, a pulse banging in her neck, thumping in her ears. 'Stop the car.'

He laughs, pulls in beside what looks like a warehouse. 'Thought you'd never ask,' he says, turning off the engine, twisting in his seat to lift a handful of her hair with his free hand. 'Beautiful,' he repeats, pulling it towards his face, forcing her head to follow, closing his eyes as he inhales loudly. 'Mmmm,' he says softly, 'smells like strawberries.'

'Please ...' She's fighting to keep her voice steady, rearing back from him as much as she can. 'Please let me go.' She tries to pull her head away, feeling the pain in her scalp as he maintains his grip on her hair. It's black beyond the windows: she can see nothing but the giant blacker shapes of the warehouses all around. Nobody there, nobody to help her. 'Please,' she repeats.

He laughs again. 'Oh, come on now, sweetheart,' he says softly, his hand moving swiftly up from her thigh to find the waistband of her jeans. 'Don't be like that,' he murmurs, fumbling at the button, popping it open. 'Be nice to me, darling.'

She shrieks, scratching at his hand, slapping at it, wriggling her hips in an effort to shake him off but he's strong, too strong for her as he releases her hair to wrench with both hands now at her zip. She hears the sharp sound of it ripping apart.

'Good girl,' he breathes, his mouth pressing into her ear now. 'I like a good fight, makes it twice as spicy ...' Sliding her towards him, forcing her down in the seat as he tugs at the jeans, trying to pull them past her hips.

'Come on,' he pants, his breath hot on her face, 'that's the girl, that's it ...'

She reaches down with her left hand and scrabbles around frantically till she succeeds in yanking off one of her shoes. She grabs it by the toe and jabs the pointed heel blindly at his face. He lifts a hand, laughing, and tries to grab the shoe from her – but miraculously she manages, in her wild swipes, to connect with her target.

He howls and jerks his head back, hands flying to his eye. With all her strength she shoves him away and turns to feel in the darkness for the door handle as he curses her loudly, hands still clamped on the stabbed eye. She pushes the door open and half-falls from the car, palms and knees slapping onto the road.

She stumbles to her feet, sobbing with fright. She pulls

off her remaining shoe and throws it aside, then breaks into a hobbling run, one hand holding closed her ruined jeans as she makes her escape, waiting all the time to hear him in pursuit, waiting for the sound of his car starting up.

Her breath tight in her chest, the air coming out of her in ragged, painful gasps, she reaches a corner and darts down another road, trying to remember the route they took, heedless of the tights that are being ripped to shreds under the soles of her flying feet, heedless of Charlotte's bag, with the silk dress inside, that still sits in his car.

She runs on, knowing where she has to go, knowing she must make her way to the only place she'll be safe.

DAPHNE AND MO

She hangs up, shakes her head at Mo. Voicemail, for the umpteenth time. Where is she? Where in God's name is she?

How can a day last so long? How is this still the one that began with her waking to the knowledge, before she'd even opened her eyes, that it was Finn's anniversary? The morning feels like it happened in another lifetime – breakfast, Una's present, dropping her to school, going to work – yet here they still are, inhabiting the same interminable twenty-four hours. How can that be?

And where *is* she?

We'll find her, Louise said, the same Louise who had made Daphne a cup of tea when her car was stolen a million years ago. Louise, who was miraculously still working the same shift at the police station, who picked up the phone when Daphne rang. *She can't have gone far* – but, of course, Una can have gone far. Since nine o'clock this morning she can have gone very far indeed.

Find her passport, Louise said, *see what clothes are missing from her room* – but while the passport was quickly located in a drawer by Una's bed, figuring out if any items of clothing were gone was impossible. Daphne doesn't know all the clothes Una has, she doesn't *know*.

Her birthday top, Daphne's present, is nowhere to be found – but that's not much help. One blue top, not nearly warm enough on its own today. If she's wearing it, she must have another layer at least on top. She *must*.

And without a passport she could still have left the country, couldn't she? She could get on a boat to England without a passport, couldn't she? And where are the guards Louise promised to send to the house? What's taking them so long?

'Stop biting your nails.'

She rounds on Mo. 'Leave me alone,' she says sharply. 'I'm worried sick.' *Stop, don't take your guilt out on her, she's done nothing*.

The photo of Una she has found for the guards sits on the table. *A recent one*, Louise said, *a clear one of her face. We'll scan it and circulate it*.

Finn had taken the photo in March of the previous year. He and Una had just returned from one of their Sunday-afternoon cycles. Daphne heard them laughing about something in the garage as she basted the root vegetables she was roasting to go with the leg of lamb.

A minute later the back door opened and in they came, bringing a blast of cold air with them. Una was still giggling, cheeks flushed from two hours of pedalling the roads on a frosty day. Daphne can't recall what the joke was – did they tell her? – but she remembers Finn, also in high good humour, taking out his phone and snapping his daughter as she peeled off her outer clothes.

She's standing by the table, her cycling helmet and scarf already shed, in the act of unzipping her jacket. Her hair has been gathered into a fat bunch from which several tendrils have escaped. Her smile is mischievous as she looks at Finn.

Less than three weeks later he was dead, and there were no more smiles. And now she's disappeared.

Mo gets to her feet. 'Tea,' she says firmly, and fills the kettle. As if tea will help.

'I don't want any.'

'Well, I do.' She plugs in the kettle. 'Have you any biscuits? I'm sick of that cake.'

Biscuits – who can think about biscuits at a time like this? 'Don't you *care*?' Daphne demands. 'Are you so unfeeling that this doesn't mean *anything* to you?'

For a minute it seems Mo isn't going to respond. She takes two cups from the draining board and sets them on the worktop. She empties the pot, still warm from its last outing, and drops in new teabags. And then she turns to face Daphne.

'Let me tell you something,' she says quietly.

And still standing by the worktop, hands dangling by her sides, she tells Daphne about her babies.

●

She was never going to tell, it was never on the agenda. She had planned to go to her grave without sharing that secret with anyone. In all her sessions with the counsellor, she never spoke of the babies. And of all the people she wasn't going to tell, Daphne would probably have been top of the list.

But when she heard, *Don't you care? Are you so unfeeling that this doesn't mean anything to you?* something cracked open — maybe something that had been loosened by the counsellor, who knows? — and here it is now, all falling out. Here she is, telling Daphne everything.

The months each of them lasted in her womb, the names she'd picked out in her head for them. The tiny bootees and cardigans and vests and nappies she'd hung on to from Finn's babyhood, hung on to through all five of her miscarriages. Unable to let them go, unable to give up hope.

And as she speaks, as it all tumbles out, all of it, she's aware that a part of her feels horrified — what are you *doing*? — but there's another part that feels like she's shedding something, like it's dropping away like a length of rope that was wound tightly around her, now suddenly cut.

'They did something to me, the miscarriages,' she tells Daphne steadily. 'They closed me up. They locked everything up tight in me. It's not that I don't feel — I feel everything. It's that I can't show it, I can't let it out, for fear of what it might do to me.'

All the while she's speaking Daphne remains unmoving, her elbows resting on the table, her eyes locked on Mo's face. Her mouth is half open, but no words come out. She makes no effort to interject, simply waits to hear what there is to be said.

When Mo finally stops there's silence in the room, broken only by the soft *chick-chick* of the kitchen clock, and the singing of the almost-bubbling kettle. And then Daphne lets out a slow breath, as if she were the one who'd been doing all the talking, still looking all the while at Mo.

'Why didn't you tell me this before?' she asks quietly. 'Why did you never tell me about this?'

Mo lifts a shoulder. 'Why would I?' But she puts no meanness into the words – she feels no antipathy towards Daphne.

'Finn never said anything.'

'Finn didn't know. Nobody knew except me and Leo, and the people at the hospital.'

'Mo, I'm so sorry—'

'Don't be,' she replies brusquely, turning to lift the kettle from its base. 'It's in the past. It's over. I just ... I don't know, maybe it was time you knew. Why I am the way I am, I mean.' She fills the teapot, brings it to the table. She doesn't want tea, it was just something to do.

She checks the clock again, clicking her tongue with impatience. 'What's keeping those guards? And your mother's taking her time too – I thought she was to be here in fifteen minutes.'

She's beginning to regret it. She shouldn't have spoken, shouldn't have let it out. She feels exposed, she feels her raw edges are showing. Why did she open her mouth? What possessed her?

'Mo,' Daphne says.

Mo brings the cups to the table, busies herself stirring the tea in the pot, pouring for both of them. Spooning sugar into her cup, stirring, stirring. When the silence stretches she raises her head.

'I have something to tell you too,' Daphne says, pressing palms to her cheeks as if to cool them. 'Sit down, please.'

Mo sits.

Daphne speaks slowly, taking her time to settle on each phrase, as if she's assembling it in its entirety before letting it out. 'We wanted children, we did, Finn and I ... We both wanted them ... but it didn't happen, it just ... and I know it's not the same as what you went through, it's not the same at all ... but I wanted you to know ... it wasn't that we didn't want any.' She stops, looks up. 'Just in case you were ever wondering. I wouldn't want you to think ...'

She lets it drift away. It's like a gift she's offering, a confidence in exchange for the one Mo shared earlier. Mo studies her hands as she feels her way around Daphne's words, picks at the sense of them, thinks about what they mean.

Finally she nods slowly. 'I did wonder,' she says. 'I thought maybe you didn't want children.'

Daphne closes her eyes briefly. 'I did,' she whispers. 'I did want children, *his* children, so much—' She presses a hand to her mouth, and Mo sees a tear make its way out and roll unstopped down her cheek.

Who would have thought it? How wrong had she been to assume that the lack of babies had been Daphne's decision, all Daphne's fault? Clearly very wrong indeed.

Daphne hadn't been denying Finn anything: she'd wanted his child, his children, as much as he surely did. What kind of cock-eyed God decides to give babies willy-nilly to ones who don't want them, and refuse them to the most deserving?

And to Mo's dismay, she feels the heat of incipient tears in her own eyes. She blinks rapidly several times until the impulse has passed. No cause for two of them to be bawling.

⚬

It's a lie but a permitted one. It's a kind lie, born of the need to cause no pain. Maybe less of a lie than a tweaking of the truth. What's the difference, after all, between 'it didn't happen' and 'it couldn't happen'? A hair's breadth at the most. Mo doesn't need to know that her son, her dead son, had been incapable of fathering a child. Not with all she's going through with Leo, with all she went through in the past.

Despite her preoccupation with Una's disappearance, Mo's confession floored Daphne. She listened with growing disbelief to the account of the lost babies, the facts made all the more poignant from being delivered in Mo's trademark no-nonsense way. *It's not that I don't feel – I feel everything.* You'd never think it from her.

How did she bear it, though? To lose one baby must be horrendous: how could any woman cope with losing five? And as Daphne listened, she was reminded of her own heartache. They weren't, she realised, so dissimilar after all. Both with secrets, both denied the thing they most wanted: Mo to have more than one child, Daphne to have any at all.

But Mo had shared her secret, and Daphne owed it to her to

do the same. And now they sit across the table from one another, with nothing left to tell. It's a relief of sorts, she supposes, to have told Mo: it felt like something she should do – but where do they go from here? What are they to do now with one another's intimacies? She has no idea.

And just then, as she lifts the cup Mo has pushed towards her – might as well drink it, now that it's made – the doorbell rings, making her start. Making her remember, with a lurch of fright, what the real business of tonight is.

ISOBEL AND DAPHNE

There's a squad car parked outside the house. Isobel pulls in behind it, praying there's no bad news. As she hurries up the path the front door opens and two uniformed guards emerge, one of them still in conversation with Daphne.

'… keep you posted,' is all Isobel catches, but it's enough. The story still ongoing, thank the Lord. She nods as the two men pass. 'I'm Daphne's mother,' she tells them, although they haven't asked.

She steps into the hall and faces her daughter, who regards her silently and unsmilingly.

'I take it there's no news,' Isobel says.

'No.'

'I'm later than I said,' she goes on. 'It took me longer than I thought it would. I wasn't at home when Jack phoned,' she adds, when no response is forthcoming. 'I was ... somewhere else. I forgot it would take me longer.'

Daphne plucks her jacket from the hallstand. 'Can we go and look for her?' Her voice trembles, and it becomes apparent to Isobel how frightened she is. 'Mo is here, she'll stay. Can we go?'

'Of course we can, love.' Isobel aches to put her arms around her daughter, wishes it were possible.

As Daphne pulls on her jacket the kitchen door opens and Mo appears, a somewhat smarter version of the woman Isobel encountered earlier in the day. Her face made up, albeit a little garishly. Better clothes, better shoes. Isobel wonders if she's told Daphne about their meeting in the café. Such a long time ago it seems now, so much changed since then.

Mo nods at her, as solemn as Daphne. 'You're heading out so,' she says, to no one in particular. 'I'll be here if she turns up.'

Daphne moves swiftly towards her and enfolds her in an embrace, over as soon as it's begun but not so fast that it doesn't cause a whip of jealousy in Isobel. Mo doesn't react – she hasn't time before Daphne is out of the door. Isobel follows, pulling it closed behind her. They walk down the path in silence. At the gate Isobel presses her key fob and the car lights wink an answer.

They get in. Isobel looks at Daphne as she turns on the heater. 'Where to?'

Daphne frowns. 'I don't know – she could be anywhere. I

don't—' She breaks off, bites her lip, turns away from Isobel to look out of the window.

Isobel starts the car, executes a three-point turn. She drives quickly to the corner, turns onto the road that leads back to the city centre. Retracing the journey she's just taken, passing the same houses and shops, crossing the river again.

'Have you called her friends?'

'... Yes.'

'And they've no idea where she might have gone? None of them?'

'No.'

'And she's still not answering her phone?'

A not quite concealed sigh. 'No.'

Isobel drives on, meandering through the dark streets, passing knots of people on their way home, or maybe on their way out. What time is it? She's lost track. She can still taste the coffee she drank in the hotel bar. She should have taken the refill when the barman offered it; looks like none of them will be getting to bed for a while.

A lone man stumbles against a wall; a pair of women, arms linked, give him a wide berth as they overtake him. A small dog scurries down a street, stopping to cock a leg briefly against a lamppost. A couple embrace – or maybe get up to a bit more – in a doorway.

It all feels removed from Isobel, or her from it. The whole evening has taken on a surreal quality. What are they doing, driving around in the dark? What hope do they have of finding Una, who in all likelihood doesn't want to be found? But what else can they do, other than sit uselessly at home?

A small breathy sound to her left makes her glance over. Daphne's face is shiny with tears. Isobel reaches across instinctively to place a hand on her arm – but at her mother's touch Daphne pulls away to lean against the window.

Isobel withdraws, stung. They drive on, Daphne continuing to weep quietly. After a minute or so Isobel pulls into the kerb, switches off the engine. *Now*, she thinks, with no rehearsal, no prior plan. *Now*, because she's had about all that she can take today.

Daphne turns, runs the back of a hand across her eyes. 'Why are we stopped?' Her voice is clogged with misery.

Isobel turns to face her squarely. 'Are you ever going to forgive me, Daphne?' she asks, as calmly as she can manage.

Dead silence for a second, two seconds. Then Daphne shakes her head impatiently. 'This isn't about you – this isn't the time—'

'It'll never be the time,' Isobel says. 'Will it?'

'We have to find Una—'

'Yes, we do. And we also have to sort things out between us. Or at least stop avoiding them. We have to *talk* about them.'

Daphne draws a ragged breath, then scrubs her eyes again, this time with a sleeve. Isobel finds a pack of tissues in the door pocket and hands it over. Daphne accepts it silently, pulls one out.

'You left me,' she says, dabbing her eyes. 'You just *left* me. You didn't even say you were going.'

Isobel sighs. 'You think I don't know that I behaved abominably? I thought it was for the best. I thought you'd be better off with your—'

'You didn't want me tagging along. You knew I'd be in the way.'

Isobel opens her mouth — and closes it again. What can she say to that? A car whooshes by, another. What can she say to that?

She looks into her daughter's blotchy, beautiful face. 'I'm sorry,' she says. 'I'm very sorry for what I did. I deserted you, and I regretted it almost immediately, and I missed you unbearably. But it's years ago, it's decades ago. Just tell me how long you're going to go on punishing me.'

'I can't think about—'

'Or tell me what I can do to make amends, because I am really, really tired of being punished, Daphne. I'm so tired of it.'

Silence. Story of their lives, silence. Unspoken words, unvoiced sentiments. Not any more.

Isobel studies her hands, realises with a jolt that she's still wearing her wedding ring. How could she have forgotten it? She slides it off, lays it soundlessly in the little nook by the steering wheel.

'I've left Alex,' she says then. Why wait until Monday?

Daphne raises her head slowly. 'What?'

'I left him, just a few hours ago,' Isobel says. 'Our marriage was a mistake, and now it's over.'

A trio of young people saunter past the car, two females hanging on to the man between them. 'You *never*!' one says — and for an instant Isobel thinks she's been overheard but they walk on, paying no heed to the car or its occupants.

'I was in a hotel,' Isobel says, 'when your father rang. I booked in for the night. I came from there.'

'What are you going to do now?' Her voice so low that Isobel barely hears the words.

'I'll find a place, I'll rent somewhere probably. I'll get by.'

In the ensuing silence Isobel watches a runner coming towards them on the opposite path, striding along effortlessly, arms swinging easily. He could be George – same build, same hair – except that George isn't a runner.

Daphne's phone rings suddenly, causing Isobel's heart to jump. Daphne jabs at the answer key.

'Is she back?' Tersely.

Silence, during which Isobel can hear the faint quacking of the other voice, which she assumes to be Mo's. The subject is closed between them for now – but at least she's opened it. At least that has happened.

'*What?* You *what*?' Pause. 'Where?'

Another silence, after which Daphne hangs up abruptly. 'We have to go to the charity shop,' she says.

'Which charity shop?'

'Where she works, where Mo works. Turn around.'

Isobel waits for a car to pass before executing her second three-point turn of the evening. She won't ask, she'll wait.

'She saw her.' Daphne is nibbling at a nail, something Isobel has never seen her do. 'Mo saw her this morning. Go left at the end. She thinks it was Una. We have to check.'

'Well, why didn't she say so before?'

'Right at the lights. She didn't remember till now.' Daphne leans forward in her seat. 'Next right. Can't you go any faster?'

They negotiate the streets, Daphne issuing directions, still hunched forward as if this will propel them sooner to their destination. Isobel has never set foot inside a charity shop, has no idea which of them Mo volunteers in – and by the look of her, where she picks up most of her wardrobe.

'Here,' Daphne says suddenly, and Isobel spots the shop, its window filled with mannequins. She brakes and pulls in – and has barely stopped before Daphne leaps from the car and strides off, turning into what appears to be some kind of alley a little way up the street.

Isobel shoves her bag under her seat and climbs out. She locks the car and glances around at the deserted street, gloomy between its occasional pools of light. Not the most auspicious part of town, not a place she'd choose to be after dark. She walks to where the alley begins, its tarred surface, what she can see of it, pockmarked with holes. 'Daphne?' she calls, peering into the darkness.

'Here.'

Already quite a bit ahead. Isobel advances cautiously, pulling her coat around her as she skirts dustbins, a heap of bricks, tattered scraps of what looks like clothing. Where on earth are they headed?

'There was a dog.'

Daphne's disembodied voice startles her. 'Where *are* you?'

'Here.' Isobel makes out a sharp turn ahead where the alley becomes parallel with the street they just left. Daphne stands waiting around the bend.

'There was a dog,' she repeats. 'Mo saw her going into one of the houses, about halfway down' – a row of them tied together, about a dozen, Isobel guesses, backing onto the far side of the lane. Windows lit here and there.

A dog doesn't seem like much to go on. They walk slowly along, picking their steps in the near darkness.

'We should knock on a door,' Daphne says, but her voice holds little hope. What are they to say to whoever responds? They're looking for a teenage girl who may have visited one of the houses this morning – it seems a pitifully inadequate reason for disturbing a stranger at this hour.

Suddenly they hear barking up ahead. Isobel instinctively reaches out to clutch Daphne's arm. 'Hold on—'

But Daphne isn't there, she's moving swiftly towards the noise. And as Isobel follows reluctantly – what if it's a guard dog, trained to attack? – Daphne's phone rings again.

'Una!' More of a gasp than a word. 'What? Slow down – where?' And then, after just a few seconds, 'We're coming.' In a new voice. 'Hang on, we're coming.'

'Where is she?' Isobel asks – but Daphne has already turned back.

'At the bicycle shop,' she says, rushing off through the darkness, heedless of the barking that follows her back down the lane.

UNA AND DAPHNE

She sits on the floor in the dark next to his bike, her back against the wall. Her legs are drawn up, arms wrapped tightly around them, head resting on her knees. Daphne is coming, she tells herself. Daphne is coming. It's nearly over.

Her feet ache. When she breathes in, her chest hurts. Every bit of her is heavy with weariness but she dreads sleep for fear of what it might bring. And she's cold: in the unheated shop she's frozen, she's shaking with it.

She's wrapped Judy's shawl around her feet, which are filthy and probably cut but she hasn't investigated them properly. She should have asked Daphne to bring socks and shoes, but she forgot.

Getting here took forever. Terrified all the time that he'd follow her, she zigzagged her way back into the city through unfamiliar streets, pressing herself into doorways or crouching behind rubbish bins when any car approached.

The few pedestrians she encountered, when she finally reached civilisation again, gave her funny looks. Of course they did – walking barefoot in this weather in the dark, her wrap knotted around her waist to keep her ripped jeans closed – but she ignored them. They could have helped her, but she was still too shocked to think clearly. All she could hold in her head, all that concerned her, was getting to the bicycle shop.

And when she finally got here, she nearly set off the alarm. For a few seconds her stupefied mind refused to supply the code. She stood, frozen with panic, as the insistent beeping continued – and at the last minute the numbers she needed flew into her head.

What will happen now? Will Daphne be angry? Of course she will. So much explaining to be done, so many new lies to be concocted. So many missed calls from Daphne and Mo when she finally checked the phone she had silenced hours ago. She must think, she must be ready when the questions come.

She'll tell Daphne she came here this morning; she'll say she spent the day here, she'll admit that she made up the bit about having dinner in Ciara's. She'll make no mention of the Quirks, or of the wedding. She'll say nothing about what happened afterwards.

But how can she explain the loss of her shoes and socks, and the state of her feet? What can she possibly say that Daphne will believe?

And then she hears a car pulling up in the yard outside. She undoes the wrap around her feet and struggles to a standing position as hurrying steps approach the rear shop door that she's left ajar.

'Una?' Daphne's voice.

She says, 'Here,' but it comes out as a whisper. 'Here,' she repeats, 'I'm here' – and suddenly there's a snap, and the shop is flooded with light. And there's Daphne, hand still on the switch.

Their eyes meet. 'I'm sorry—' Una begins, but by the time the words are out Daphne has reached her, and she's enveloped in Daphne's arms – she nearly topples backwards with the surprise of it – and she almost can't breathe, she's being clasped so tightly.

'Oh, my *God*,' Daphne wails, 'I was so *worried*, why did you just *disappear* like that? How could you *do* that to me? How could you just go off like that? I thought you were – I didn't know *what* to think, I just, I was so *frightened* that you might have – I just thought something *awful* must have happened to you – and I understood, I really did, when you sent a text to say you weren't coming home for dinner, but when I rang Ciara and she said you hadn't been to school I got such a *shock*, I couldn't understand it because I'd *driven* you there, it made no sense, and then for you to be gone for the *whole* day, where did you *go*, you shouldn't have *worried* me like that, it wasn't *fair* to do that today, and I *know* you're upset, I under*stand* that, and I know it's your birthday and it's horrible too, and we're *all* upset about it, but still, to just *disappear* like that – and why are you not wearing *shoes*, what's *that* all about, but I'm just so *relieved* to have you back safe, you must *never* do that to me again—'

And all the time she's sobbing and her words are coming out in ragged jumps, and Una has to wriggle a bit to breathe, and Daphne is taking no notice whatsoever of her mother, who's appeared in the doorway and looks like she doesn't know where to put her eyes while Daphne is having hysterics. Where has *she* come from?

And the weirdest part of it all, the one thing that is clear to Una as she's held so tightly, as Daphne cries real tears into her hair and keeps telling her how worried and frightened she was, and keeps demanding to know how Una could have *done* such a thing – all Una can really understand on this day, which has been filled with so much emotion, so much confusion, all she can marvel at is how totally and completely wrong she was about Daphne.

❖

'You can stay here,' Daphne says, 'until you find a place to live, I mean.'

She sees how the words change her mother's face.

'Don't cry,' she warns. There's been more than enough crying today. 'It's no big deal. I'm just offering you a room while you get sorted.'

Isobel nods. 'I'll come tomorrow,' she says. 'If that's all right.'

'That's fine. Any time after eleven.'

Are you ever going to forgive me? The question had angered her, coming as it did in the middle of her desperate anxiety about Una. But now, with Una home, safe and well, all she wants to do is give thanks – and this gesture, this reaching out, feels like the right way to go about it.

She'd never thought of it as punishment. Until tonight, until Isobel used the word, Daphne would have called it keeping her distance; she would have said they had a strained relationship because of their past. Was it punishment, though? Had she really been that bitter, that unforgiving, for nearly thirty years?

She can't think about it tonight. All she can do is offer her mother a place to sleep, and take it from there. Tonight needs to be about Una.

They stand on the doorstep. Mo has already gone home with Jack, who was alerted on their way back from the bicycle shop. Daphne had sent him and Mo packing as soon as he'd shown up, well aware that Mo was none too pleased at being dispatched. It was clear she wanted to hang around to hear what Una had to say for herself, but Daphne was having none of it. *I'll fill you in tomorrow*, she said, giving Mo no choice but to do as she was told.

Isobel stayed – somehow she'd earned the right, as the one who'd brought Daphne to the bicycle shop. She filled a basin with warm water for Una's feet and waited around until the guards arrived, the same two who'd called before. She tidied the kitchen while Una and Daphne spoke with them in the sitting room and now, just after they've left, she's leaving too.

'See you tomorrow then,' she says. Thankfully she doesn't attempt to embrace her daughter. They have a long road to travel before that.

Daphne closes the front door and returns to the kitchen,

where Una sits wrapped in a quilt with her feet in a fresh basin of water and a cup of coffee before her on the table, next to a slice of the pink-iced cake.

'Sure you don't want a bath?' Daphne asks, and again Una shakes her head, so Daphne pulls a chair up close and cradles one of Una's hands in hers. No more hiding for them, no more avoiding what needs to be said. Tonight has been a night for speaking out, and it's not over yet.

'Now,' she says gently, 'I know you told the guards, but I want to ask you again. Did that man hurt you?'

'No.'

'You're positive? Promise?'

A ghost of a smile passes over Una's white face. 'Promise.'

'Is your coffee gone cold? Will I make more?'

'No, it's OK.' But she makes no move to drink it.

So pale, still so pale. Daphne hangs on to her hand, presses it between her own. 'So,' she says, 'we need to talk.'

Una says nothing, drops her gaze to the bundle their hands are making.

'We need to sort a few things out,' Daphne says. 'Don't we?'

'I suppose ...' The smile has vanished, an expression of wariness on her face now.

Daphne pauses, hunting for the right words, trying to find a way through the barrier that still exists between them, in spite of all that's happened tonight.

'It's just,' Una says faintly, glancing up, 'there are things ... You might not want to hear them.'

'I do want to hear them,' Daphne assures her. 'Whatever they are, I really do want to hear them.' And even as she speaks, she's aware that she's bracing herself for what may come, for what *must* come now.

The seconds tick by. Una eases her hand from Daphne's, finally sips coffee. 'OK,' she says, continuing to cradle the cup. 'I'll tell you.'

And there, in the silent kitchen, she begins to talk.

First, she tells Daphne about the bike shop. 'I go there after school every day. I do my homework in the little room at the back, where I used to do it. I found his keys a few weeks after he died, I got copies made for the back door ... I'm not sure why I go, because I hate to see it all empty and dark and dusty, that makes me really sad, and it's cold all the time, so I have to leave my jacket on, but I think I go because it's where I remember him best, where I can picture him clearly.'

And that's only the start of it.

'I've met him, the man who was driving the bin lorry. His name is Kevin Quirk — but you know that. His son went to the comp, he was two years ahead of me. He ... asked if I'd meet his dad, a few weeks after it happened. He told me how sorry he was about the accident. I didn't want to meet him — I hated the thought of it, I said no — but ... then I thought Dad would want me to, so I changed my mind. I met him in the park near the station — his son was there too — and he ... wasn't a bit like I'd thought he'd be, the father I mean, and I went back to the house with them, it wasn't far, and I met his wife. They gave me scones, they were really friendly, they kept thanking me for going to see them, and asked me to come back, and I said yes, I'm not sure why ... I visit them a lot. They're the ones I have dinner with, not Ciara or the others. I didn't tell you because

I thought you might be angry, because of who they are and everything.'

And there's more, oh yes.

'I was with them today. I went to their daughter's wedding. I wasn't in the shop all day like I told the guards. I did call in there first, I left my school things there, but then I left. I went to a florist shop and bought flowers for Dad – with the tenner you gave me this morning – and I brought them to the cemetery, and after that I went to their house, the Quirks. I got a green dress for the wedding in a charity shop – it was silk, it was lovely – and shoes. And the wedding was good—'

She breaks off abruptly, and Daphne sees a flush drifting up her face. 'Well, anyway ...' she says. 'And then I took a taxi from the hotel where the wedding was, and ... well, you've heard the rest.'

Daphne picks a bit of icing from the cake on the table. Lying to the guards: that'll need to be sorted – hopefully Louise will be on duty tomorrow. But for now Daphne will deal with the more pressing issue of why Una felt she had to lie, or not reveal the truth, about anything. For now, *that* is what needs to be sorted out.

'You know,' she says lightly, 'you could have told me about wanting to find your birth father. I wouldn't have minded – I *don't* mind. It's perfectly natural that you'd be curious about him.'

Una doesn't meet her eye. 'I just thought,' she says, 'it might be better if you didn't have to worry about me all the time, if I wasn't your responsibility. I thought if I could find my birth father he might want to ... adopt me, or something.'

She thought she wasn't wanted. She thought Daphne didn't want her. Daphne's fault, entirely her fault, for not making it clear that Finn's daughter, birth or otherwise, is precious to her. Observing the girl's stricken face, Daphne is deeply ashamed. 'Una,' she begins, 'you mustn't think—'

But Una hasn't finished. 'I feel so guilty all the time, about Dad's death I mean. I feel it was my fault – that it wouldn't have happened if he'd been cycling his own bike home that day. I know it wasn't all to do with that, but his own bike might have made a difference. It *might* have.'

And when she sits back, finally out of words, neither of them says anything for what feels like an awfully long time. The clock above the fridge gives a little whirr. Somewhere outside, an animal – a cat? – emits a long, plaintive yowl.

And then Daphne shifts in her chair. 'Right,' she says. Praying that what she has to say, what must be said, will come out the way she wants it to.

'First of all,' she says, 'I haven't exactly been looking after you like I should. When your dad was alive I was happy to leave the parenting to him – he was so much better at it. I hadn't a clue. I had no experience of looking after anyone. When he died I tried, I did try, to pick up where he'd left off, but I still didn't know what I was doing, and he wasn't around to ask. So I told myself you were almost grown-up anyway, and you probably didn't want me trying to be a parent, so ... I made sure you had enough to eat, and I bought you clothes when you asked for them, and I gave you money when you needed it, and I hoped for the best after that.'

She stops. Una remains silent.

'It's become clear to me tonight,' Daphne goes on slowly, 'that I messed up. I was grieving, of course. I was shocked and sad and completely lost without your dad, just like you were – but that's no excuse. I was the adult, and you were in my care and I failed you, and I'm sorry.'

Una begins to speak, but Daphne lifts a hand to stop her. 'Hang on a minute,' she says, so Una hangs on.

'My car was stolen this afternoon,' Daphne tells her, in so matter-of-fact a tone that the words take a few seconds to register with Una. When they do, her mouth drops open and her eyes widen.

'No, but listen,' Daphne says earnestly, as if she'd been interrupted, 'I was valuing a house at the time. It took about ... oh, about an hour, I think, I can hardly remember, and it doesn't matter anyway. When I finished, I went back to where I'd left the car, but it had disappeared. Naturally, I was very upset. I was late getting to the cemetery as a result, so I never visited your dad's grave – and in all the fuss I forgot to collect the cake I'd ordered for your birthday. That's why we have this one. I picked it up in Mulligan's.'

They both turn to look at the remains of the cake, sitting forlornly in the centre of the table.

'My point,' Daphne goes on, 'is that lots of things went wrong today, and I was feeling really *rotten* when I got home, but none of that mattered – *none* of it – when I discovered that you were missing. When I realised that you'd been gone all day, it just, I just – I don't know, it just ... took over. It was the only *important* thing, you know? I was so completely terrified that something might have happened to you, I could hardly think.

And when I saw you in the shop, looking so miserable, I was just so—'

She breaks off, pressing her hands into her thighs and shaking her head, trying to banish the image of her hysterical outburst in the bicycle shop. 'Well,' she says, 'anyway … you saw how I was.' She attempts a smile, but isn't sure how it comes out.

She leans forward. 'Listen, I'll help you to look for your birth father, if that's what you want, but don't do it because you think I don't want you here because I *do*.' She finds both of Una's hands, and captures them between her own. 'I *do*,' she repeats. 'OK?'

A beat passes.

'OK?' she asks again.

'OK.'

'OK,' Daphne repeats, nodding several times, holding Una's gaze. 'Now,' she goes on, 'I need you to listen carefully to this next bit. Are you listening?'

'Yes.'

'What happened to your dad was not your fault,' she says steadily and gently, watching the girl. And again: 'What happened was not your fault.' And again: 'It was not your fault.' Three times she recites it, all the while holding Una's gaze, keeping Una's hands tight in hers.

'I want you to tell yourself that every day,' she says. 'You must keep on telling yourself that until you believe it. Your dad died, and it was a terrible thing, but it was nobody's fault, least of all yours. You have to let yourself believe that.'

And she sees Una listening to the words, she sees her wanting to believe them. Maybe one day she will.

Silence falls briefly in the room, and then Daphne speaks again. She has to speak of it, she has to speak of him. 'As to your meeting the lorry driver,' she says slowly, 'that's certainly a bit of a surprise.' She pauses. 'I do think it's a good and courageous thing you did. I don't think I would have been as brave if someone had asked *me* to meet him.'

She stops again, her gaze roaming around the table, the almost-eaten cake, the neat piles of cups and plates, washed and dried by Isobel while Daphne and Una were talking to the guards. The milk jug, the fanned-out spoons.

'I'm not sure that I can forgive him, you see,' she says, in the same deliberate way, 'even though I know he didn't do it on purpose. I do know that. That's awful, isn't it?' She looks back at Una. 'That I wouldn't want to meet him.'

Una shakes her head. 'It's not awful. I didn't want to meet him at all. I hated him. I didn't feel a bit brave, I was really scared. I felt sick, I was so scared. I nearly didn't go.'

'But you did.'

'Yes ...'

Daphne feels her face relaxing, feels the tightness of the day falling away. 'I hope Finn knew,' she says softly, 'what a very good job he did with you.'

Una gives her a wobbly, watery smile.

'Mo's picking up your cake tomorrow,' Daphne goes on, 'the proper cake. I told her to bring it to the charity shop – I didn't think anyone here would want it – but maybe I should ring her in the morning and ask her to keep some for us. I think,' she says, 'we deserve some chocolate, both of us.'

'I hope it wasn't too dear,' Una says.

Daphne flicks her head to dismiss the comment. 'There's one more thing,' she says, releasing Una's hands to push her fingers through her hair. 'It's about the bike shop. There's something you should know about that.'

And then she tells her about her earlier conversation with Mo. This whole day has been so strange, so full of frights and surprises and revelations, she may as well throw another one into the mix. It won't commit her to anything if she runs it by Una – and there's the tiniest chance, isn't there, that Mo's completely ridiculous idea just might have something in it?

❁

Una lifts her head, turns her pillow over and sinks back into its cool cottony softness. So much to think about, not a hope of getting any sleep tonight – but she's on Easter holidays, no getting up for school tomorrow, so who cares?

She thinks about the man who attacked her. She thinks of rushing from his car across town, in the darkness and in her bare feet, all the way to the bike shop, never even considering going home instead, which would have been nearer. She closes her eyes and remembers the surprise of Daphne's embrace, and how it felt every bit as warm and real as Judy's.

She recalls Daphne's tears, her almost incoherent tumble of words as they stood entwined in the shop as Una realised, to her utter amazement, that she was cared for – *is* cared for – after all.

She thinks about how she lied to her best friend, and how she involved her in another lie to Daphne, and the trouble that lie caused. She thinks of the visit she'll have to make to Ciara's house tomorrow in an effort to explain, and hopefully to be forgiven.

She thinks about the dark, dusty space that is the bike shop and imagines them bringing it to life again. Scrubbing it and painting it and filling the shelves with … well, anything. She pictures a new name on the outside, and a bell that gives a musical tinkle when someone opens the door, not like the old one, and her standing behind the counter, maybe in a cool uniform in a colour that suits her. Maybe she could design it.

She thinks about Kevin and Judy, how they'd fed her scones and made her feel welcome, and invited her to their daughter's wedding. She remembers the day she met Kevin, remembers him saying her father would be proud of her. And while the thought of that doesn't come close to mending her broken heart – she still wants Dad back, she'll always want him back – there is some comfort in it. There is.

She thinks about Daphne, and the thing she said three times, each time like she believed it: *What happened to your dad was not your fault.* She imagines how great it would be if it really were true.

Maybe it is true.

She thinks about racing across wet grass in a silk dress, the string of a kite pulling in her hands as she flew straight into the arms of a boy who picked her up and whirled her around and kissed her. She thinks about him ringing her tomorrow like he said he would, and her insides do a happy little flip.

She thinks about Daphne, who hugged her again when they were finally saying goodnight on the landing, who whispered, *We'll try to get it right from now on, OK?*

She thinks about the father she's never met, the French father she will probably never meet, even with Daphne's help. She thinks it's sad that he'll never know he has a daughter, but her sadness is soft, and manageable. Anyway, she'd had all the father she needed: she just didn't have him for long enough.

It wasn't much of a birthday, was it? Daphne asked at one stage, and Una shrugged and told her it wasn't all bad.

And Daphne assumed, no doubt, that she was talking about the wedding.

Friday, 29 April
(a year and a bit later)

DAPHNE

As soon as she enters the kitchen she sees it, a yellow paper carrier bag that sits in the centre of the table.

She closes the door softly behind her and sweeps the curtains back. The morning looks promising, the sky an uninterrupted expanse of palest blue. She tiptoes across the floor so her heels won't clack on the tiles. She stands by the table and regards the bag, not touching it yet. Wanting to draw out the sight of it.

Poking from the top is a wooden skewer, a triangle of white card stuck to it like a flag. *Happy birthday*, it says, in Una's round handwriting, in green ink.

Happy birthday, Mrs Darling, Finn said. It was five years ago today, she was thirty-two, and she had just married him. His left arm encircled her waist, her upraised palm resting against his. They were waltzing, or trying to, around the floor, with forty-seven people looking on. *I love you*, he told her, and she echoed it back to him, never happier than at that moment.

Two years on his absence is still an ache inside her. The memory of his voice, his smile, can still bring occasional late-night tears. But it's getting better: the piercing sting of his loss is softening. Time, it would appear, is not without some healing power after all.

Of course, it's had a little help.

She pulls out the flag, parts the top of the bag. It's filled with tissue-paper packages of varying shapes and sizes and colours: lilac, lemon, pink, peppermint, blue, apricot. Every package has been secured with several strands of thin white ribbon.

One by one she unwraps them.

A pair of lavender and green striped gardening gloves.

Two chunky wooden bookends painted orange, one a giant A, the other a Z.

A set of four cookie cutters – star, crescent moon, palm tree, gingerbread man.

A small, soft, blue leather coin purse – and, squeezed inside, a bag of Daphne's favourite Maltesers.

A silver bangle, slender as piano wire.

The final package, the apricot one, is the shape and heft of a thin paperback book. She removes the ribbon, opens the folds of tissue – and looks down at herself and Una.

Finn took the snap: she remembers the day clearly. It was

the weekend, it was autumn, a few months into their marriage. The three of them travelled in Daphne's Beetle to a forest a few miles outside the city, with a picnic Daphne had prepared as sunshine streamed through the kitchen window – but they'd hardly reached the outskirts of the city when the sun slipped behind a bank of cement-coloured clouds that had loomed out of nowhere.

They unpacked the picnic – chicken wings, carrot salad, flapjacks, apple juice – and they ate it sitting in the Beetle, listening to the rattle of rain on the roof, feeling the car shudder every now and again when a sudden gust caught it, watching the trees thrash and shiver outside. Afterwards the three of them played Twenty Questions in the car, in no hurry to turn around and go home again, happy to wait all afternoon for a sun that didn't bother reappearing.

Finn, sitting in the back seat, caught both of them in mid-laughter. It's slightly blurry – he wasn't a great photographer – but their good humour is almost palpable. They were happy that day, all three of them, despite the weather. It was a good day, storm and all.

She hasn't seen the photo in ages, in years; she'd forgotten all about it. It's been framed in plain, bone-coloured wood. Did Una search through albums for it? Did she look for the happiest photo she could find of the two of them?

Daphne places it on the windowsill behind the sink, next to the caddy that holds the washing-up liquid, the rubber gloves and the pot scraper. She slips on the silver bangle. She folds the sheets of tissue, rolls up the ribbons and replaces them in the yellow bag, then transfers the rest of her presents to the worktop. She sets the table and makes tea, and as she drops bread into the toaster her phone beeps.

It's George. *Happy birthday, see you later, bring your appetite x*

It'll be a lot of work, she told him when he'd made his suggestion a week ago, offering to host the dinner originally planned for Mo's house. *There'll be quite a few mouths to feed.*

No worries — call it payback for all the meals you've made me. And, anyway, I'll have my trusty assistant.

He'll have Louise, he meant, the policewoman on duty when Daphne reported the theft of her car over a year ago. Louise, who had called to the house the following morning to tell Daphne the good news about her car.

It's been found, she said. *In Galway, of all places. It's fine, no damage. You'll get it back this afternoon, when we've taken prints.*

Louise, whose son just happened to be in George's junior infant class at the time. Louise, who has since taken up residence in George's generous heart.

George is in love with Louise, and it's just the sweetest thing to see.

The mystery of Daphne's car turning up sixty miles away in Galway was never solved. The prints found didn't match any on file and nobody came forward to admit they'd taken the Beetle for a spin — but that's what seemed to have happened.

Some young lad probably, Louise said, *on his way to the station to get a bus or a train, passes your car with the keys in it. Looks on it as his chance to save a few bob. You were lucky.*

She *was* lucky. There wasn't a scratch on the car, and nothing left behind by whoever had brought it to Galway. She got it valeted, put the whole business behind her and vowed to be more careful in future.

Her phone beeps again.

Happy birthday, hope your day is happy. See you later. T x

T, followed by an x.

T, which stands for Tom, who just happens to be Louise's older brother.

Small world.

❂

I heard about your car, he said.

It was Monday, three days since he and Daphne had met for the first time. He arrived without warning at the estate agency: it had taken her a second or two to place him.

Louise is my sister, he said. *The guard you met at the station when you reported the car stolen. I hope you don't mind that she told me what happened – she knew you were with me at the time.*

Daphne wasn't bothered that Louise had told him. The car was back in one piece: its recovery was hardly a state secret. *All's well that ends well*, she said. Bit of a coincidence that those two were related, all the same – and that Daphne had had cause to be in contact with both of them on Friday.

But what was he doing here now? Had he simply come to congratulate her on the car's reappearance? No, of course he hadn't – he was one of their clients. He was there to talk business, find out what value she was planning to put on his house. Mentioning the car was his polite preamble.

Have a seat, she said. She recalled the journey in his car to the cemetery, her abrupt departure from it. Had she even thanked him for the lift?

He remained standing. *I won't stay*, he said. *I have an appointment. I just wanted to say I'm relieved the car was found.* He smiled. *I felt a bit responsible, after keeping you waiting like I did.*

Not at all. She felt abashed that she'd assigned an ulterior motive for his visit – and ashamed that she'd also blamed him a little bit for the loss of the car.

Nice of him to drop in. Not many would have thought of it.

The bungalow isn't mine, by the way, he added. *I should probably have mentioned that. It belonged to our uncle – he died a few months back and left it to us. It hasn't been lived in for over a year – he was in a nursing home.* Which would account for the state of it. Not the neglected home of a recently separated man, as she'd imagined, but the abandoned home of a dead man. Explained a lot.

She watched the door close behind him. She should have mentioned that she already had a prospective buyer – she and George were due to view it that afternoon. No matter: she'd phone him later.

But the viewing never happened. George phoned to cancel, saying he'd changed his mind about looking for a house. *I've decided to put it off for a while*, he told her. *Just for a few months. I feel I should stay with my father for a bit.* Typical of him to put someone else first.

Daphne is so glad he found Louise, or Louise found him. She was touched when he confided in her, around November. *A parent in the class*, he said, *or she was, until June.* Delightfully shy about telling her, shuffling his feet, rubbing his grinning face. *It's going well*, he said, the grin widening. *We'll see*, he said, looking mighty pleased with himself.

In the meantime there was plenty of interest in the little bungalow, although the smallness of it put some viewers off, and the absence of a proper back garden was another sticking point. But enquiries continued to come in, and Daphne became accustomed to travelling to Bridestone Avenue, where she was always careful to remove her car keys from the ignition.

And sometimes Tom was there before her, having plugged in a heater or two. And on one occasion, after the viewers had left, he suggested coffee in the little hotel a few streets away, and although Daphne didn't take him up on it – another appointment waiting – she found herself considering his offer later that evening, and thinking that he mightn't be the worst to spend an hour with.

Not that she was looking for anyone, for coffee or anything else. And maybe he wasn't either: maybe he'd simply made the offer out of politeness. For all she knew he already had a partner.

And then one afternoon, around the middle of July, when the bungalow had been on their books for a little over three months, her phone rang and it was him, and the sound of his voice caused a funny little jump that she assumed had more to do with the coffee she'd just had.

You're not going to like this, he said, and she thought he was going to reject the offer that had just been put on the bungalow. Couldn't blame him, well below the asking price.

We've decided not to sell the house, he went on. *In fact, Louise is going to move into it with Josh, her son.*

*Oh … * Ridiculous to feel deflated – that kind of thing happened all the time. *Well, thank you for—*

I wondered, he said, *if you'd let me buy you dinner, or lunch or something. Just to say thanks for all your help.*

Oh, there's no need—

But I'd like to.

And so, it seemed, would she, because she found herself agreeing to let him take her out. No harm in it, just a meal with a friend. Probably never clap eyes on him again.

They live with me, he told her over bowls of pasta. *Louise and Josh. The father isn't on the scene, he never was. He did a runner when she got pregnant so I moved her in with me. It wasn't a problem – I live alone, there was plenty of room – but at this stage they should really have their own place.*

I wanted her to take the bungalow when Uncle Stephen died, but she was adamant we should sell. She had this daft notion that she'd be doing me out of my inheritance. Now she's changed her mind, which I'm glad about. Makes perfect sense for her to take it.

After dinner, he walked Daphne to her car. He shook her hand. *We should do it again sometime*, he said, and she didn't object, so they did it again about ten days later, and again a week after that.

So wary she'd felt to begin with though, so afraid of venturing down that road for the second time. So understanding he'd been, so patient when she'd turn away as he moved closer, not ready for that. Not yet.

So wonderful to allow herself finally to accept that what she thought she'd never feel again was making its slow, steady way back to her. He's not Finn, he'll never be Finn – but she never expected to find another Finn.

Funny how things turn out. Wonderful how things can turn out.

The kitchen door opens.

'Morning,' Daphne says.

'Happy birthday to you,' Una replies. 'Going to be a nice day.'

'I think so … Thanks for the presents, they're wonderful.'

'Glad you like them.' Una takes a mug from the draining board, spots the photo on the windowsill. 'You remember that picnic?' she asks.

'I do. I'd forgotten it until I saw that.'

'We played Twenty Questions, remember?'

'I do.'

'Dad was hopeless, kept asking the wrong kind of questions. I knew he was doing it on purpose.'

She talks about him now, she often mentions him. There's a lovely fondness in her voice when she does. She isn't done missing him, any more than Daphne is, but she's coming along.

At the start of June last year, two months after her birthday, she told Daphne about Theo.

It just happened, she said. *We were friends, that was all, and then, I don't know … it … changed. He's nice. He's lovely … It's OK, isn't it?* Looking anxiously at Daphne, wanting very badly for it to be OK, so Daphne told her it was, not at all sure how she felt about it.

A year later they're still together. Daphne has met him – he's been to the house several times. On his first visit he brought a red geranium that's getting ready to bloom again; on his next, a box of very good fudge that he made himself. He never comes empty-handed.

He was ill at ease in Daphne's company at the start, his eyes sliding away from hers, his neck blotchy with embarrassment. Afraid she didn't want him there, probably. She felt sorry for him, as much a victim of circumstances as she herself was. He's still a bit shy with her, but not as much. He'll relax eventually, if he and Una last.

'The peanut butter's nearly gone,' Una says, scraping in the jar with her knife.

'I'll put it on my list.'

'I can do the shopping after school: you shouldn't have to on your birthday.'

Daphne smiles. 'It's fine – I have plenty of time today.'

A couple of viewings this morning, a visit to the cemetery, lunch with Joanna from work, some filing, some phone calls – and this evening, dinner served up by George in his new surroundings.

At twenty to nine she gets to her feet. 'Time to go,' she says, and Una finishes tapping at her phone screen and pushes back her chair.

'Can I drive?' she asks, as she's done every morning for the past week, and again Daphne tells her no, not yet.

As they pull up outside the school, Daphne's phone begins to ring.

'Get that,' Una says, opening the door. 'I'll see you later.'

'Happy birthday,' Isobel says. 'Everything all right?'

'Everything's fine, just dropping Una at the school.' Returning the girl's wave through the window, watching like she always does as Una disappears into the crowd. 'What about you?'

'All well, finishing my cuppa, getting ready to open up. I'm looking forward to the meal this evening.'

'Me too. Hope George isn't regretting his offer.' She thumbs at a mark on the dashboard. 'I would have been happy to switch it to my house.'

'Don't be silly, you can't host your own birthday dinner. George will be fine – I bet he's dying to show us all what he can do.'

It's healing too, the wound that Isobel's departure had opened up between them all those years ago, the running sore it had become. The first tentative step taken on the night of the anniversary, with Daphne's offer of a bed to Isobel, but it wasn't until a few months later, long after Isobel had settled into the apartment Daphne had found for her, that an opportunity presented itself that would allow a real reconciliation to take root. Because of the circumstances, Daphne likes to think Finn had a hand in helping them to bury the past – but Mo deserved a bit of the credit too.

Ask your mother, she said to Daphne, when the idea of reopening the bicycle shop finally began to take hold. *She's used to working behind a counter in that fancy place*. So the suggestion had come from Mo – but without Finn and his father, there would have been no shop to begin with, and no need for them to be casting around for someone to work in its new incarnation.

Despite things having thawed somewhat between them, asking Isobel to become involved with the shop hadn't appealed initially to Daphne. Such a big step – were they ready for it?

It's not as if you'd be there with her all the time, Mo pointed out. *You'd hardly have anything to do with her really. And we'd be keeping the business in the family, which would be good.* Whatever way you looked at it, the idea did seem to make sense – so Daphne put her reservations aside.

A craft shop, she told her mother the following night. It was a week before Isobel's birthday: hard to believe she was going to be sixty. *Knick-knacks, bits and pieces for the home, jewellery, knitwear, gift ideas, that sort of thing. Everything Irish, everything designed and produced here. Would you be interested?*

Her question was met with silence. Isobel, it would seem, wasn't interested in a new job, didn't fancy being under compliment to Daphne. She was working out how to say no.

You're opening a shop? she asked eventually.

Well, not me personally – I'm going to keep on working at Donnelly's, but we're using the compensation money to set it up, and Mo will handle the accounts. Una wants to work there on Saturdays until she—

And you want me to be involved?

Well, Mo thought you might be interested, yes.

You're asking me to work there? You're offering me a job?

Only if you're interes—

I am, Isobel said. *I will. I'd love it. Thank you. I'd absolutely love it. Thank you.*

And that was that: they had their assistant.

But Mo was wrong in thinking that mother and daughter wouldn't have much to do with one another. On the contrary, Isobel and Daphne were thrown together a lot more. They had to be: everyone had to pitch in to get the place ready. And

Isobel did as much as anyone else, helping to source products, using her many contacts to spread the word, doing her bit when it came to painting and decorating. Truth be told, she made herself pretty useful.

And little by little, she and Daphne are unpicking the past, filling in the blanks.

I worked there Monday to Friday, Isobel told her. *The cinema we used to go to every fortnight, remember? My job was behind the ticket desk. Terribly boring, but it was all I could get.*

I lived in a small flat, she told Daphne, *above a shoe-repair and key-cutting shop. The noise of those machines they used, the screech of them, was worse than a roomful of wildcats. I had one bedroom, and a kitchen-cum-sitting room. Miserable little place, tiny bathroom. Glorified bedsit, really, but it was cheap, and I could walk everywhere.*

They haven't discussed the intimacies. There's been no mention of how Isobel regards her two failed marriages, no talk of Con Pierce the dentist, or Isobel's abrupt departure from her family.

And in her turn Daphne hasn't talked about Tom, how he's helping her to be happy again. She and Isobel simply haven't reached that place yet.

But once, almost at the end of a lunchtime conversation, Isobel said, *I loved them, you know, those Saturday afternoons we spent together. I'd look forward to them so much* – and Daphne felt a sting of remorse as she recalled her dread of those same encounters, her endurance of whatever activities Isobel had lined up, her relief when the arrangement finally petered out.

They have a long way to go, a lot of making up to do. She thinks they'll manage it. She hopes they'll manage it.

Getting the craft shop off the ground wasn't all plain sailing. One promising supplier declared himself bankrupt, leaving them little time to find an alternative. Another dropped them with scant warning when a bigger customer came along. Road works on the street outside caused damage to a water pipe that created havoc for deliveries for more than a week.

And at the beginning of November, six weeks before the shop was due to open, the inevitable happened, and a new grave was dug in the cemetery. Poor Leo, at peace finally after his years of what must have been bewildered isolation. Mo, of course, was thrown into fresh mourning, which she battled with her customary vigour, still continuing with her shifts at the charity shop, still turning up afterwards at the work-in-progress that was the craft shop to tut over invoices and complain about redecorating costs.

But eventually things had come together, and as the grand opening approached, Daphne found herself wondering how Isobel and Mo would get along once the business was up and running. So different, the two of them, and Mo's legendary sharp tongue a challenge for any co-worker. But to her relief the two women trucked along, seeming to get on fine – or if they didn't, they weren't sharing it with their financial backer.

Using the compensation money to fund the new business made perfect sense, of course it did. *It's what Finn would have wanted*, Mo had insisted, back when they were still tossing the idea around, back when Daphne was still so unsure about the whole idea. *He'd have loved to see the shop open again, and his family still running it* – and eventually, when Mo was joined in her corner by Una, who had jumped at the thought of the shop reopening, Daphne gave in.

It had sat restlessly with her for a while, the fact that she was making use of the money she'd sworn never to touch. But seeing the closed-down shop slowly brought back to life, and the enthusiasm with which Una threw herself into the project, she had to acknowledge that Mo was right. It's what he would have wanted.

And after four months, despite everything, the shop is still there, still trading every day between the hours of nine thirty and five thirty – and, according to the accountant they had to call in to replace Mo, they ended last month in profit for the first time. A small profit, admittedly, but a milestone nonetheless. They're going in the right direction.

The name was Una's idea. *Dad's bicycle was blue*, she said, so The Blue Bicycle it became, even though bicycles are one of the few things they don't sell. But they're all agreed that it, and its accompanying logo of a bright blue penny-farthing – another of Una's creations – lend the place an appealing quirkiness.

So much has changed in a year. Not all of it for the better, of course – there was Leo, and then there was Mo – but on the whole it's treated them more gently than the one that went before. Time is marching on as it always did, but these days, most of the time, Daphne manages to march along with it, and to regard whatever may lie ahead with more hope than dread.

When she gets to work she finds birthday cards waiting on her desk from Mr Donnelly and Joanna. William, typically, is on the road, chasing up business somewhere beyond the city. The estate agency continues to putter along, each month bringing its share of fresh successes and disappointments.

At eleven Daphne leaves the office and travels across town to show a first-floor apartment to an elderly widow whose family home has become too large for her to manage. 'It's just the garden,' she says, following Daphne listlessly through the clutch of rooms, looking without enthusiasm at the tiny balcony. 'I don't mind giving up the house, it was always a bit draughty, but I'll miss the garden so much' – and Daphne, who has already shown the woman's house and its beautifully tended grounds to three interested parties, closes the file on the apartment and tells her about Mrs Clohessy's little cottage up the road from her, complete with small, neat back garden, that's about to be sold privately by the family. If Mr Donnelly heard her ...

She locks up the apartment and bids farewell to the widow and drives through the city to a familiar narrow street, lined on each side with redbrick terraced homes, each differently coloured front door leading directly onto the path. She pulls up outside number five and sits for a minute, listening to the soft ticking of the cooling engine as she looks out the house where Mo lived until six weeks ago.

She recalls the first time Finn took her there, a couple of months after they'd begun seeing one another. She'd met Mo just once before, the day she'd delivered the apology lemon cake to the bicycle shop, and the memory of the older woman's frosty reception on that occasion had made her approach their second encounter with more than a little wariness.

Don't mind if she's a bit cool, Finn said. *It's just her way, she won't mean anything by it* – but Daphne still prickled with anxiety.

With just cause, as it turned out: all through the forty-five-minute visit, during which Mo served a pot of dark brown tea and a plate of ginger nut biscuits in her little sitting room, Daphne was acutely conscious of a stiffness in her hostess's manner, a pursed-lips attitude that screamed disapproval of her son's choice of companion. Finn did his best, bless him, but his sterling efforts to keep the conversation going did little to lessen the tension that kept Daphne on the edge of Mo's tweedy couch throughout, nibbling the biscuit she'd felt obliged to accept – she wasn't a fan of ginger – and drinking tea that was much too strong.

In time, things had got better, of course. Daphne had grown accustomed to Mo's brusque manner: they'd learned to get along after a fashion. They never became close – too different, maybe – but they tolerated one another's company. On occasion, they even enjoyed it.

And on Finn's anniversary last year, when she learned of Mo's miscarriages, Daphne gained a new understanding of and sympathy for the bluntness and lack of warmth that had so often bewildered and hurt her in the past.

Poor Mo, silenced now.

She gets out of the car, standing back to allow a young woman with a buggy to pass by on the path before approaching the front door that Finn had painted the same shade of maroon every second year. Could do with a fresh coat now: maybe Daphne and Una will do it between them some Sunday.

She lets herself in, feeling the cooler air in the deserted little hallway. So empty it feels, so impersonal, without Mo clattering around. She takes off her jacket and makes her way to the kitchen, where she finds the spray polish and cloth sitting where she'd left them on the worktop after her last visit.

It's not much, but it's something. She works her way through the silent house, banishing dust from windowsills and tables, dado rails, shelves and mantelpieces. She wipes the glass fronts of the framed photos – Leo, Finn, Una, Susan, Daphne; the weddings, the birthdays, the Christmases – that pepper the walls of Mo's bedroom. She kept them close, all the important people in her life.

Daphne pauses at the most recent one, taken by George on the afternoon of the grand opening last December. There they all are, Isobel, Una, Daphne and Mo, grouped underneath the shop sign, arms interlocked. Huddled in coats and scarves and hats – it had been bitterly cold – but all dressed in their finery underneath, all waiting to begin the new adventure.

All over for Mo now, never again to check invoices or tot up outgoings or calculate tax returns. The adventure ended for her the day she collapsed in the back room of the charity shop, six weeks ago tomorrow. *Just finished her tea*, Daphne was told by Martha, one of Mo's fellow volunteers. *Stood up to go out the back for a smoke, and that was it.*

The last bit was wrong, of course – Mo didn't smoke. But Daphne said nothing. What did it matter now?

❀

The cemetery, on the way back to the office, is mellow in the late April sunshine, headstones gleaming. 'Still miss you,' Daphne tells Finn. 'Never forget you. Five years ago today, never forget that either. Happiest day of my life – but you know that already.'

She squints upwards, sees a pair of sparrows flit by. It was sunny on the morning of their wedding too, but by the afternoon the rain had arrived, trailing down the hotel windows as they ate their first meal as man and wife. Chicken she had, or maybe fish. Food the last thing on her mind.

She wonders if she'll marry again, like Finn did. He'd found love a second time too. Maybe it keeps going around, like the random acts of kindness he was so fond of. Maybe if you wait long enough it comes back to you.

Driving through the town, looking forward to her lunch with Joanna now, she stops at a zebra crossing and watches a straggling line of paired-up little children in uniforms of navy and white as they pass in front of her. Junior or senior infants, she guesses. Six years old at the most.

She watches them hopping and skipping their way over the stripes, hair and ribbons bouncing, sees one of the accompanying adults say something sharp to two little boys who have paused to examine an object on the road, causing the ones behind to bump and stumble into them. So unintentionally enchanting at that age, hardly out of babyhood, still all innocence and curiosity.

Thirty-seven. She's only thirty-seven. There's still time.

ISOBEL

The cuckoo springs from its clock and chirps twice as she turns the door sign from *Closed* to *Open* and undoes the latch, already regretting the spring onions in her lunchtime salad. She loves the kick they add to the tomatoes and cucumber, but the last thing customers need is a salesperson breathing oniony fumes all over them. Hopefully she'll find a few mints in her bag.

She remains at the door to watch a somewhat dishevelled line of little schoolchildren passing on the path, twenty or so of them, she reckons, bookended by a pair of adults. She follows them down the street, past the dry-cleaner's and the chemist and the bookshop and the new apartments, until they finally drop out of sight.

She recalls Daphne at that age. A few months past her fourth birthday when she started school, the hem of her blue pinafore dress landing on the skinny little knees, schoolbag heartbreakingly huge when they'd drawn her arms through the straps and fastened it in place.

Isobel's hand clasped tightly as they stood side by side at the classroom door that first day. Jack busy with pre-test driving lessons, Isobel's hotel shift not due to start till four, so the task had fallen to her to bring their daughter into school for the first time.

Daphne had looked up at her mother with eyes that swam. *Do I have to go in?* she asked, and Isobel, feeling like the worst kind of monster, told her yes, she did, and look at all the fun the other children were having, and didn't Daphne want to join them?

She didn't. *You come too*, she insisted, so in they both went – and within ten minutes Daphne had become engrossed with the dressing-up corner, and her mother was able to slip away. And from then on, she and Jack had taken it in turns to drop her to school and pick her up afterwards.

Of course, when Daphne was six, the responsibility had become Jack's alone.

She finds her bag, locates the end of a packet of mints. Mo was a terror for the mints: you couldn't leave a pack around or they'd be gone. Quiet without her on Friday afternoons now, her time for dropping in and doing her thing in the back room. Coming out when she had finished, pottering about the shop floor for half an hour or so.

Making a nuisance of herself at times, if the truth be told, moving things around, upsetting Isobel's careful displays, getting in the way when customers were trying to browse. Imagining she was helping, no doubt – and, in fairness, she *did* make herself useful in some respects, replenishing the stocks of bubble wrap, tissue and carrier bags when they were running low, sweeping up without being asked, emptying the bin.

But if an unsuspecting customer enquired about a product, Isobel would cringe at the responses. Mo would blithely admit that she couldn't see the point of chocolate stirrers for coffee – wouldn't something made of chocolate melt the minute you put it near a hot drink? She would be equally dismissive of coloured-paper lanterns, designed to hold a nightlight – don't tell *her* putting a lighted candle into a paper container wasn't asking for trouble.

The mantelpiece was good enough for us, she told a customer who enquired about miniature pegs to hang Christmas cards, barely a week after they'd opened. Another time she laughed, actually laughed, when a woman asked if they stocked pink toasters. Anyone who didn't know her would think she was trying to sabotage sales.

But of course she wasn't. Above all of them, Mo wanted the reincarnation of her precious Leo's shop to do well. Shame she seemed incapable of filtering what came out of her mouth; shame she couldn't be chained to her adding machine in the back room, and only let out when the shop was empty.

It had certainly taken the two of them a while to get along. Before Isobel had learned to accept Mo's presence on the shop floor – surely the accountant didn't have any business there? –

she would assign her various harmless tasks in an effort to keep her occupied and out of the way of the customers. It wasn't long before Mo objected.

I'll thank you not to order me around, she said tartly, after a simple request to move a few empty boxes into the back room one day. *You're the employee here, not the boss*. For goodness' sake, such a fuss she'd made. Isobel pulled back after that, anxious not to give Mo any cause to go complaining to Daphne. She learned to accept the older woman's forays into what she considered her territory, to grit her teeth when she overheard the tactless comments and over time, they achieved a tolerance of one another that was shaky at best.

Still, now that Mo is gone, Isobel almost misses her about the place. She doesn't miss the tea she'd make though – strong enough to stand a spoon in. The china mugs Isobel had provided for their breaks – after throwing out the awful chipped articles that had preceded them – needed a thorough scrub after a round of Mo's tea, so badly would they be stained.

Isobel drifts through the empty shop, plumping cushions, straightening boxes of notecards, refolding scarves, tweaking the paintings straight. She stands and regards the seascape that nearly sold yesterday, one of her favourites. It's a steal at seventy-five euro: the movement in it, the drama – but the artist's name is largely unknown, and after nearly two months on display, it's still for sale.

Mo, not surprisingly, didn't mince her words when it first appeared on the shop wall. *You're charging seventy-five euro for a few daubs of blue and white?* she asked, her expression almost comically disbelieving. *I could do better than that myself. A toddler could do better than that.* Isobel managed not to rise to the bait, knowing any argument would fall on deaf ears.

The woman yesterday appeared quite taken with the painting, but seemed to lose interest when she read the price tag. She said she'd think about it, and she'd need her husband to see it, but Isobel only heard excuses. Tragically, most people haven't a clue about art: one customer actually stated a few weeks ago that she was buying a painting – a beautiful watercolour of a yacht race – purely because some red sails in it matched her couch. Not a clue.

Admittedly Isobel didn't know much about art herself before she married Alex. She could recognise a Renoir or a Picasso or a le Brocquy – who couldn't? – and she was quite fond of Jack Yeats, Paul Henry and Vermeer, but that was about it.

When she first encountered it, the first thing that struck her about Alex's house was that it was full of paintings. They were scattered about the walls, the bulk of them by contemporary Irish artists, most of whose names were unfamiliar to Isobel. Some of the works appealed to her, more didn't, but she remained noncommittal, not wanting to reveal her ignorance.

Alex went to exhibitions; he read reviews. When he came home with a new painting Isobel would ask, *What do you like about it?* Wanting to learn, wanting to see what he saw – but more often than not he'd shrug and say, *It's hard to define.*

It took her some time to realise that he wasn't interested in art for art's sake. It was a commodity to him, something he could make money from, nothing more. But as long as she was surrounded by so much of it, Isobel thought she might as well try to learn a bit more about it. She began to attend exhibitions too, sometimes with Alex, other times alone. She began to see, and appreciate, and discern.

She'd been the one to suggest that they include a few paintings in the shop, back when they were hunting down craft suppliers and deciding what to fill it with. She'd taken on the job of contacting artists and agents, and gradually she'd narrowed her choices to half a dozen and arranged them in a corner. She's pleased with the result, feels they add to the quality of their offerings. Only two have sold since they opened, the yacht race and one other, but they'll all shift, she's sure of it, when the right people come in.

And if the seascape is still unsold when her birthday comes around in September, she might just treat herself to it.

Her birthday. Sixty-one this year, just another number. But that's the thing, isn't it? They're all just numbers. The trick, she's discovered, is to treat them with equal nonchalance, laugh them away when they come around.

She thinks back to this time last year, and how much she dreaded turning sixty. Like it was somehow going to change her life for the worse – as if it could have been much worse than it already was.

And in the event, by the time sixty happened, everything had changed. She'd left Alex, she'd moved into the apartment, she'd handed in her notice at Phyllis's shop – and finally, finally, she and Daphne were reconnecting.

You can stay here, Daphne had said, *until you find a place to live* – and Isobel had clutched at the offer, and the tentative hope it engendered in her. She'd moved in the following morning, stayed for ten days, cooked dinner for Daphne and Una each evening, and viewed several rental properties with Daphne, until the one-bedroom apartment behind the cathedral became available.

And now she wakes up to bells every Sunday, and she and Daphne talk most days, either on the phone or in person. Mistakes are being forgiven, resentments cast aside. It's slow and it's painstaking but it's happening: Isobel can feel it each time they talk, each time they exchange a smile, and she rejoices that it's finally coming to pass.

But vastly improved as her situation is now, it wasn't without its challenges. Being single again has taken plenty of getting used to. She's had episodes of loneliness, plenty of them, particularly at the start of her split from Alex, particularly at night – but on the whole it was such a relief, it still is, to have left her old life behind. How did she last ten years with so little love to keep her company?

Until now, the process of dissolving her second marriage has run smoothly. Her solicitor has done what was required, and spared her the details. A separation agreement was quickly reached; a divorce will be arranged in due course. She might have known emotion wouldn't feature highly in any negotiation involving Alex.

She's accepted every condition that's been set, yielded to every demand – who cares what she has to leave behind, as long as a line is eventually drawn through the misadventure that was their marriage? *You're entitled*, her solicitor keeps saying – he's inordinately fond of that phrase – but she wants nothing from Alex. She expects nothing.

They haven't met since the night she left his house, although she's caught sight of him a few times. Across the floor of a bookshop as he scanned the shelves in the new-releases section; pulled up at traffic lights, one finger tapping on the steering wheel in the way she remembered so well; emerging from a restaurant one lunchtime with a few of his work colleagues.

Quite possibly he's spotted her too on occasion, but so far they've managed not to come face to face. She's relatively certain it will happen eventually, the city being too small for them to avoid one another indefinitely. She'll deal with it when the time comes, greet him civilly and hope he does the same.

Her apartment is compact, but cleverly designed and perfectly adequate. She's learnt to put up with various neighbourly sounds coming at her from above and below; she's got the knack of earplugs at night. There are no obstacles that cannot be overcome: it took her long enough to learn that lesson.

And this job, this golden opportunity that landed like a gift in her lap a week or so before her birthday, has given her new heart. The hours are long; her feet ache after a day spent mostly standing, but it's nothing that a hot bath and a glass of wine can't cure. The wages are generous, and by and large the work is enjoyable.

Behind the counter her phone rings. She takes it from the shelf and sees George's name. So good that they haven't lost touch since she left his father.

'Hello, dear.'

'Isobel – can you talk?'

'I can.'

'We've just discovered we don't have enough cutlery for this evening. Any chance you could bring us three of everything when you come?'

'Of course I can.' His first proper dinner party: about time, twenty-eight next month. She must remember to get flowers on her way home. 'Do you need anything else? Plates, glasses?'

'Hang on, I'll double check—'

Her phone had rung one morning, about a week after she'd left Alex. *It's George*, he said, as if she might already have removed his name from her contact list. As if she might have left him along with his father.

I heard what happened, he went on. *I haven't called to ask why, I just want to say that I hope we can still be friends. I don't want to take sides in this.*

Relief washed through her. *I'm so glad*, she told him. *I wanted to call you, but I was afraid you mightn't want to keep in touch ...*

Of course I do, he replied, sounding genuinely surprised, and Isobel was ashamed of herself for doubting him.

She didn't ask him about his father. Alex's name wasn't mentioned during their brief conversation.

I'm going to stay on here for a while, George said. *There's no rush with my getting a house. It can wait.*

She felt bad. *It's because of me, you feel you have to stay.*

No, not at all – I'm just postponing it for a bit, that's all. I'm in no hurry. And in the event, he stayed on in the house with his father for an entire year – but look how it's worked out.

Maybe, all things considered, she did him a favour.

His voice is in her ear again: 'Isobel, we're OK for everything else, except ... would you have any of those long skinny candles?'

She smiles. 'I certainly would. Do you need candlesticks?'

'No – we found a load of flowerpots in the shed; they'll do nicely. Come a bit early and I'll show you around before the others get here.'

Isobel hasn't seen the house yet: George has only been living there for a week or so. *It's small*, Daphne has told her. *A bungalow, two bedrooms. Needs a bit of modernising but there's a nice little side garden, and a garage.*

Daphne knows the place well: she was the first of them to come across it. She valued it when it was put up for sale just over a year ago, had her car stolen from right around the corner on the very same day.

The house wasn't sold; it was reclaimed by one of the people who'd inherited it. She decided she'd move in after all, along with her little son who just happened to have George for a teacher. And at some stage romance blossomed, and now George has moved in too, leaving his father to live alone, for however long that will last.

'You busy?' George asks, and Isobel tells him it's been quiet so far this afternoon.

'But on the whole it's going well, right?'

Yes, she told him. On the whole, everything was going well.

●

'Does it come in blue?'

The woman holds an olive green cushion with an owl motif in rusty oranges and browns on the front. 'I don't care for the green, but I think I'd like it in blue.'

Her face is shiny and very pink. A dark brown fringe draws

a dead straight line across the tight skin of her forehead, an inch above her eyebrows. What appears to be a tiny diamond in her left earlobe winks when the light catches it.

'I'm afraid that particular one doesn't come in other colours.'

'Pity. I always think owls are mysterious.' Tracing the curves of its head with a slender finger. 'I think they should be witches' familiars instead of black cats.'

'Do you really?' Isobel asks. The things she has to listen to sometimes.

'Definitely. Those giant eyes, and the way they can twist their heads around, and that sound they make. Sends shivers down my spine when I hear it.'

And yet she wants an owl on her cushion.

'We do have a blue one, but it's got an elephant on it. Or how about the gorgeous Siamese cat in navy? I have it myself at home — everyone admires it.'

Isobel doesn't have the Siamese cat, or any of the other Creature Comfort cushions, in her apartment. Her couch is the pale yellow of wild primroses; the cushions scattered across it are in various shades of cream, with no motifs. But it's a lie that works surprisingly often: people are easily swayed.

Not this one. 'It was the owl I was after,' she says, her eyes sliding away, her gaze wandering over the shop as if other owls might materialise. Fly from the teapots, maybe. Pop out of the toasters, or spring from the cuckoo clock when its door opens.

When she's alone again Isobel goes into the back room and makes a pot of green tea. While the kettle sings she opens a press and sees Mo's ancient adding machine inside. Had it for years, she told Isobel. *Leo got it for me*, she said. *Better than any computer, never lets me down.*

They could well get rid of it now – their new accountant does all his sums on a tablet, would surely laugh at that contraption if they showed it to him. They could bring it to a charity shop – might catch the eye of some collector of antiques. Or they could simply bin it, but so far nobody's touched it. Not doing anyone any harm.

Back in the shop her phone beeps: a text from Jack. *You need a lift tonight?* he asks. *I'll be passing your door.*

Thoughtful as ever. She studies the screen, composing a reply. Composing a number of replies.

Thank you, she types eventually, *but I'll be travelling early to help with preparations. See you there, looking forward to it.*

After she'd left Alex, she phoned Jack to tell him. She's not sure why: it just felt like something she should do. She'd met him briefly at Daphne's on the night it happened, the night of Una's dramatic disappearance – but of course it wasn't the time or place, and it wasn't until four or five days later that she picked up the phone and dialled his number.

Daphne told me, he said, which Isobel had partly guessed. Still, she felt he should hear it from her too. *I'm sorry*, he added, and it didn't sound insincere.

There's nobody else, she told him, even though he hadn't asked, even though he probably wasn't interested. She wanted him to know that another man wasn't involved this time; for some reason, it seemed important that he know this.

There hasn't been anyone else since Alex. In over a year she hasn't gone on a single date. She hasn't shared her bed, or anyone else's, since she and Alex were man and wife. She's interacted with males in the shop; a few have even flirted mildly with her, but nothing more has come of it. And for now, she's fine with that. In lots of ways, being alone suits her — it's the thought of being alone forever that unnerves her.

She's happy to have Jack back in her orbit, however casually. For years, after she'd renewed contact with him and Daphne, their encounters had, not surprisingly, been strained, and Isobel had assumed that they'd never again achieve anything resembling a normal friendship. But over the past year, since she and Daphne have been repairing their damage, it seems that Isobel and Daphne's father are achieving their own resolution. Now when they meet, usually at Daphne's house, there's an ease between them that Isobel rejoices in — and if she senses a tiny occasional hesitancy in him, a barely discernible pulling back in his manner towards her, she considers it no more than she deserves.

For Daphne's sake, she's glad for her and Jack to be where they are, and for her own sake too. He's a good man.

The shop door opens to admit a couple, mid-thirties, with brightly coloured jackets and the healthy complexions of people who spend a good deal of time out of doors. Boating, maybe: Isobel can see them on a yacht in matching white trousers and striped jumpers.

'Great window,' the man says. American or Canadian; she can never distinguish the accents.

'My granddaughter is responsible,' Isobel tells him. Granddaughter is easier than trying to explain the relationship

– and now that she's getting Daphne back, she may as well lay claim to Una too. 'She changes the window every Saturday – she's very artistic.'

'I can see that. How 'bout the bike? Is it for sale?'

The question is regularly asked. Once again, Isobel explains that the bicycle in the window belonged to the previous owner, a relative of hers by marriage, and is not for sale. 'We keep it there for sentimental reasons,' she tells them. 'He wasn't old when he died.'

For whatever reason, the story tends to go down well. Finn's blue bicycle, and its constant presence in the window, usually adorned with items from the shop's supplies – an umbrella dangling from the handlebars, a birdcage sitting on the carrier, a throw draped over the saddle – gives the shop its character, makes people more inclined to bring something away from it.

As the pair wander along the aisles, the door opens again and Una appears, her school tie absent as usual from its official spot, her hair pulled into the high ponytail she's taken to wearing lately.

'Anything that needs doing?' she asks. She's dropped in most days after school since Mo's departure – not that she wasn't a frequent caller before that. 'Can I help in any way?'

'I was just talking about you,' Isobel tells her, and passes on the tourist's compliment. 'He was asking about the bike too.'

Una laughs. 'Another one.'

Wonderful to see how happy she is now, after the loss of both parents in her short life. She delights in the shop; it's as if she was born to work there. And of course, love helps. Love always helps, and Una is undoubtedly in love. Her choice of boyfriend might have been a little bewildering, but love doesn't always allow for choice.

Wonderful, too, how she and Daphne look after one another now, closer than many a mother and daughter. Lovely to see how Daphne, with no children of her own – and, it has to be said, no great memories of being mothered herself – has nurtured that relationship and built it into the fine thing it is now.

And of course Daphne has also had a little luck in the love department lately, which is good to see too.

Isobel checks under the counter. 'You could bring some bubble wrap out from the back room,' she tells Una, and off the girl goes.

'Say.'

Isobel turns. The Americans, or Canadians, are standing before the seascape.

'You might wrap this one up for us,' the man says. 'It's a little beauty.'

❖

Una stays for an hour or so, working her way along the shelves, lifting objects to dust carefully under them, replacing everything exactly as she found it. Watching her, Isobel wonders if she's ever reminded of the shop when her father ran it, if she ever thinks back to the time he stood behind the counter.

Of course, it's changed a lot since then – the renovations were pretty extensive – but one of the features they've retained is the old counter, sanded and varnished but still there. Does she ever see him as he was? Is she ever stirred by memories of him here?

'Are you looking forward to this evening?' Isobel asks.

Una smiles. 'Yeah, should be good.'

And before either of them can say more, a car horn toots outside the door. Una instantly blushes: he's here, the one she's been waiting for. The one who always collects her as soon as he finishes up at his catering college. She stows the duster in its place behind the counter and lifts her rucksack. 'See you later,' she says, slinging it over a shoulder. She strides across the floor and pulls open the door with the effortless grace of the young. Eighteen, and all to live for. Isobel was happy and hopeful too, at eighteen.

When the clocks tell her it's five twenty she cashes up, looking forward to Daphne's reaction when she hears that the seascape has been sold. Nice news to get on her birthday.

Mo would surely have something to say about it, if she could. One born every minute, or words to that effect.

UNA

S he listens to his phone ringing.

'Hello?'

'Hi, George. Kevin says the pups are ready to go. We could bring Josh's along with us this evening, if you like.'

Dolly had done what came naturally sometime in January. *We've no idea who the father is,* Kevin said, when it became apparent that the family dog was in the family way. *We'll have to wait and see what comes out* — and what came out, around the middle of March, was a glorious tumble of twelve oversized ears and six raggy tails and plump wriggling bodies in coats that ranged in colour from Dolly's black and white through caramel brown to chestnut red.

We need to find homes, Judy said. *Ask anyone you can think of* – so Una put it to George, who consulted with Louise. When the response was positive, Una took photos of each pup on her phone, and a chestnut male with a cream patch over an eye was selected.

'I'm being given the thumbs-up here,' George tells her now. 'Bring it along – he'll be delighted.'

'OK, see you later.'

She hangs up and passes the word to Kevin, who goes off in search of a box.

Charlotte spreads butter on a second scone. 'They'll have to think up a name,' she says, reaching for the jam. Charlotte has been eating for two since November. *Eating for half a dozen, more like*, Kevin remarked lately, and got a swipe with a tea towel across his rear end in response.

'I think they're going to let Josh name him,' Una says.

Josh, five since last August, hasn't been told of the pup's existence, let alone its imminent arrival. Una can't wait to see his face. She's been his official babysitter since just after Christmas. Their bedtime routine never varies: she tucks him in and reads him three stories, and then they sing songs in turn until he falls asleep.

And now that she has her own car, and is doing the driving test the very second she can, George won't have to drive her home for much longer.

She couldn't believe it when Daphne gave her the keys on her eighteenth birthday, four weeks ago. *It's too much*, she said.

Tom gave it to me for a good price, Daphne replied. Una didn't think people who were well on the way to forty could still blush.

You're getting it on condition you take lessons with my father, Daphne went on. *He's giving you six as his present* — and that was fine by Una.

The car is so retro: none of her friends had seen a Morris Minor before, and everyone is mad about it. It belonged to some old relative of Tom's, and even though it's pretty ancient it's in really good nick, and had less than forty thousand miles on the clock.

It stank of cigarettes when it arrived — the owner must have smoked like a chimney — but she and Theo scrubbed it and sprayed it until they banished the smell, and Una found a website that sold car stickers, and ordered four red flowers that look great against the black. *Hippie chic*, Theo said, when he saw them stuck on the left rear wing. He's so goofy sometimes.

She had her fifth lesson with Jack on Wednesday — he says she's got lightning reflexes — and Theo takes her out sometimes in his car. He brings her to the university campus where everyone goes to learn. He's had a full licence since he was seventeen — Kevin taught him to drive — and he bought a car at Christmas for five hundred euro, an eighteen-year-old dark green Nissan Micra that will do them until Una passes the test and Daphne finally has to let her drive. The Morris Minor is *much* cooler than the Micra — but she keeps that thought to herself.

She'll be finished school in two months, and she's taking a couple of weeks off before starting full-time at The Blue Bicycle.

She and Isobel will split the week between them, overlapping now and again at the busy times.

She adores working in the shop on Saturdays. She annoys Isobel during the week too – can't keep away from the place. She still feels Dad there, but it's in a good way now, not so sad anymore. He was happy there, and so is she. Sometimes she gets frightened, thinking that all this happiness can't last forever. And then she thinks, *Well, of course it can't*, so she's enjoying it while she can.

She doesn't know if she and Theo will last forever either – they're both young, they're one another's first love – but she hopes they will. She wants him to be her last love too.

She's told her dad about him. *You'd like him*, she said. *He's a good person, he's like you.*

'Here we go.' Kevin reappears with a box. 'Theo, get the scissors and poke a few holes in it.'

Judy removes her apron and sinks into a chair. 'I'd sell my soul for a cup of tea. Charlotte, how's that pot?'

'Empty.'

'I'll make more,' Una says, and brings the kettle to the sink. Perfectly at home she is here now, part of the family. For her birthday Judy baked a sponge cake, filled it with jam and whipped cream and wrote *Happy 18th* on the top in buttercream icing. *I wasn't sure I'd fit 'birthday'*, she explained. Seeing it, Una recalled the slices of chocolate cake she and Daphne had eaten the day after her seventeenth birthday. Banishing, with every sweet, delicious mouthful, the memory of the evening before.

The man who attacked her – Dave wasn't his real name, surprise, surprise – was traced through his computer. And there *was* a wife, only her name wasn't Jean or Joan, and she knew nothing of her husband's online activity.

At first he tried to deny the attack, said he'd never met Una, only spoken on the Internet with her – but under questioning he broke down, said it was the only time he'd done anything like that, he didn't know what had come over him, he was deeply sorry. The guards waited until he'd finished apologising and charged him with sexual assault.

Thankfully his guilty plea meant Una wasn't needed as a witness in court: she wanted never to lay eyes on him again. He's doing time now, and Louise has told them that he'll be put on the sex offenders' list when he gets out. *He'll think twice before he looks at another young girl*, she said.

Una hasn't told Theo, or any of his family, what happened. She told them she left Charlotte's bag behind in the taxi, and she found a similar one to replace it. They didn't need to know. Nobody needed to know the full story except Daphne and Isobel, and presumably Jack and Mo, who would have expected some kind of an explanation. She doesn't know exactly what they were told – the subject wasn't raised by either of them afterwards.

She doesn't think about it now; she doesn't let it into her head.

The pup is placed in the box, with a squeaky rubber bone and a bald tennis ball that he loves. When the lid is put on, Una pokes a finger through one of the holes, and immediately feels the small wet tongue lapping at it. She carries the box out through the front door – can't let Dolly see her taking one of the babies away – and Theo brings his car around.

It's half past six. The journey to Louise's house – George and Louise's house now – will take them a good forty minutes in the Friday traffic, still heavy at this hour. She sits in the passenger seat with the box on her lap. She slides her finger back into the hole, wiggles it and feels the baby teeth grab it.

'We won't stay too long, yeah?' Theo asks. 'After the dinner, I mean.'

He's wary at the thought of spending time with them. The only one he's met so far is Daphne, and only after Una practically forced him into it. This evening he'll be introduced to the rest of her family, and she's well aware that he's dreading it. She wonders if he'll ever feel at ease among them, if that will ever be possible for him. Even though he's entirely blameless, he'll always be the son of the man who drove the lorry that killed her dad.

'It'll be OK,' she says, hoping to God it will. 'We'll go as soon as you want to. I'm dying to see Josh's face,' she adds, to take his mind off it, but she can see by the set of his jaw that he's wishing they were going somewhere else. Anywhere else.

She slides a hand across, lays it palm up on his thigh. 'It'll be OK,' she repeats, 'honestly. They're fine, they're great' – and he shifts gear as they approach a red light.

'We could run away,' he says. 'We could go to Australia and never come back. We could go tonight – we could go right now.'

She laughs, loving the intimation that they'll spend the rest of their lives together, even if he's saying it in jest. 'We have no passports,' she says. 'No money, no clothes. And what about this pup? We couldn't bring him to Australia.'

'Hmm.' The light changes and they move off. 'Passports might be a problem all right.'

'And the pup.'

'And the pup.'

She leans across and kisses his cheek. 'They'll love you,' she says, 'like I do,' and he shoots her a soppy grin.

They carry on driving. It's twenty to seven.

EVERYONE

It's ten o'clock. They've finally got as far as the cake.

'Mostly wholewheat flour,' Louise tells Daphne. 'Just a small bit of white. And brown sugar, but not much, because the carrots are pretty sweet.'

Three small pink candles, recently blown out, sit on the plate next to the remainder of the cake. The six long white ones that Isobel brought have been dotted about the room – three on the table, one on a windowsill, two on the dresser, each pushed into a sand-filled terracotta flowerpot. Two floor lamps with twin deep-yellow shades provide the only other light in the room.

They've eaten Thai lamb curry and wild rice, and followed it with fruit salad and George's special brown-bread ice-cream. Daphne has taken possession of earrings, half a dozen crystal wine glasses, two books, homemade truffles, bath oil and a pair of red gloves in soft, soft leather.

Josh's head droops towards his largely uneaten finger of cake. Una gets to her feet. 'I'll put him to bed.'

She gathers him, unprotesting, into her arms. 'Bob,' he says drowsily against her shoulder, and Una glances towards the little pup, out for the count in the new pet bed beneath the radiator.

'You'll see him tomorrow,' she whispers, 'he's fast asleep now' – and Josh's eyelids slide down as she carries him out of the room.

'Go with her if you want,' Louise tells Theo, and he makes his grateful exit.

The seven remaining guests sit on. Coffee cups are refilled, more cake cut and doled out. Conversation breaks into splinters around the table.

❀

'Daphne looks happy,' her mother remarks.

'She does,' her father replies. A few seconds pass as they both observe their daughter, still in conversation with Louise. In their various pots the white candles flicker lazily, making shadows dance in corners.

'And you?' Jack asks then, turning to his ex-wife. 'Are you happy?'

Isobel looks at him in astonishment.

He waits. Time passes. She tilts her head, thinking.

'I am,' she says finally. 'Quite happy,' she adds. 'Probably more,' she says, with a small laugh, 'than I deserve to be.' Another small silence, but an easy one, falls between them. 'How about you, Jack?'

He smiles down into his coffee. 'I'm doing all right,' he replies eventually. 'I'm glad we've got to this. The two of us, I mean. I'm glad we can get along like this now.'

'Yes ... me too.'

She threw away her life with him. She's older and wiser now. It could have gone another way, it might have ended differently if she'd given them more of a chance. If she'd focused more on what she had, rather than what she didn't have.

'We might have a cup of tea sometime,' he says. 'Or lunch, maybe. Just us, I mean. For old times' sake.'

'I'd like that.'

Just us. He doesn't mean anything by it. They're parents together, they'll always have that connection. He's being friendly, keeping the door open between them. And for her part she enjoys his company; she likes being around him. That's all there is to it.

All the same, she'll wear her blue trouser suit. She always feels good in that.

◆

'My point,' Louise says, 'is that dogs and people's beds don't mix. All that shedding hair, not a bit hygienic.'

'Your sister is very harsh,' George tells Tom. 'Did you have no pets growing up?'

'We had a cat,' Tom tells him. He turns to Louise. 'Remember Sissy?'

'God – Sissy. He killed anything that moved.'

'Sissy was a he? A killer he-cat called Sissy?'

'Short for Sisyphus,' Tom says. 'That cat was lethal – remember the baby hedgehogs, Lou?'

'God, I'd forgotten them – and all the poor birds. Nothing was safe. And he terrorised that small dog up the road – poor thing would run a mile when he saw Sissy coming.'

George grins. 'Maybe we should get a Sissy,' he says to Louise. 'Spice up the neighbourhood.'

She looks at him sternly. 'No Sissy, just Bob.'

They turn in unison towards the sleeping little bundle that is Josh's new pup.

'Bob,' Tom says thoughtfully – and all three laugh.

❖

The burst of laughter is infectious. Seated on Tom's left at the head of the table, Mo does her best to produce a smile, but she can feel the lopsided thing that results. After seventy-six years of more or less faithful service, her body – or rather, half of it – has decided to call time.

Lie still, Martha said when it happened, when Mo's speech started all of a sudden to thicken and slur, when a terrifying sludgy numbness began to ooze its way down her left side, and an accompanying dizziness folded her to the floor just as she was getting to her feet to go out for her cigarette.

Lie still, Martha said, turning to throw a shout over her shoulder – *Ambulance! Quick!* – to whoever was there. *Lie still*, she repeated, holding on to Mo's hand, her suddenly useless left hand. *Don't talk*, she ordered, when Mo tried to say she wanted to get up. Nothing coming out but gobbledegook, nothing that you could call a word issuing from a mouth that didn't feel like her mouth any more. *Just lie still, the ambulance is coming.*

Someone pushing something under Mo's head. Someone loosening her shoes, unbuttoning the top of her blouse. A blanket that smelt of mouldy leaves being tucked around her. Martha kneeling on the floor, kneading Mo's hand like it was dough. *You'll be OK*, she kept repeating. *Help is coming, don't you worry.*

Gretta appearing to gape down at Mo, her face full of fright, asking what was wrong, Martha snarling something at her that made Gretta go away. The whole left side of Mo gone now, as if someone had sliced her in two and taken half of her away. A drumming in her head, Martha shouting for tissues, dabbing at Mo's chin. *You'll be fine, Mo. Help is coming, they won't be long now.*

The scream of the siren as the ambulance sped her to hospital. A racing trolley, white ceilings speeding by, lights shining too brightly, loud voices, faces bending towards her, questions she couldn't answer. Tests, X-rays, don't move, Mo, don't try to talk, Mo, just lie still, Mo, can you feel this, Mo? People she didn't know, strangers in blue overalls, in white coats, all calling her Mo. White sheets, too many pillows, drink this, Mo, dribble, dribble onto the white sheet. Don't cry, Mo, you're all right now.

Daphne, sometime later, looking fearful like Gretta. *You've had a stroke, Mo.* Sitting beside the bed, holding her hand in the way Martha had. The counsellor – Tom – standing by her chair, him and Daphne together now.

Mo had parted company with him, her last session at the end of October almost a year to the day since her first.

I think you don't need me any more, he said, and she realised he was right. He shook her hand and said she could always come back if she felt he could help her again, and off she went, thinking they'd probably seen the last of one another. Even when Leo died, just a few weeks later, she hadn't gone back: there was no anger this time, just a pure and simple sadness that she knew she could find a way through by herself.

But when they held a little party the evening before the craft shop had its official opening, there the counsellor was among the assembled press and invited guests, talking to Daphne as if they knew one another well.

Tom Wallace, Daphne said, and he shook hands with Mo and said hello like they'd never laid eyes on one another, and she didn't let on either. Turned out he and Daphne had met months earlier, when he was selling a house – this very house, as it happened – and it would appear that things had developed between them.

At first Mo had felt angry. Finn was being replaced, his marriage to Daphne cast aside like a used-up battery. But then logic prevailed: much as Mo would wish it otherwise, Finn's marriage had ended the day he died. And Daphne was young, and she deserved the second chance that Finn had been granted.

You'll come to us, Daphne said, sitting by the hospital bed. *As soon as you're ready, you'll come to Una and me. We'll look after you until you're able to go back to your own house.* And Mo could feel a hot trickle running down her good cheek – such a cry baby she'd become – and she opened her mouth to say thank you, but of course nothing intelligible came out.

The days and weeks that followed were full of therapy. Physiotherapy and occupational therapy and speech and language therapy, men and women manipulating her useless left side, encouraging her to make sounds, Mo, do exercises, Mo, urging her not to give up, to try again, Mo, I know it hurts, Mo, but try one more time. Try, Mo. Just for me, Mo.

Daphne came every day, sometimes with Tom, sometimes without. Una and Isobel and George came too, and Martha and a few others from the charity shop. They brought grapes and magazines and flowers and chocolates. They sat by her bedside and told her how well she was looking, how well she was doing. *You'll be home in no time*, they said, smiles stretching their mouths as they looked anywhere but at her twisted-sideways face.

Six weeks tomorrow it happened. Six weeks of torturously slow progress, six weeks of trying to teach her muscles and her vocal cords all the things they'd known before. *It'll take time*, they tell her. *You'll get there*, they tell her. *You're doing great*, they tell her.

Liars – but she's coping, like she's always done. Her brain is still intact, praise the Lord. She still sees what's going on, she can still make herself understood. It could be worse, as she well knows.

They're letting you come to my birthday dinner, Daphne said, a few days ago. The dinner Mo had been planning to host, Una coming to help her with the cooking, all arranged.

Tom and I will collect you and drop you back, Daphne said. *It'll be like a trial run, see how you get on, see how you manage.* Mo is out on loan tonight, her hospital bed waiting for her return.

The wheelchair came with her, folded up in the boot of Tom's car. Not yet able to get around without it, her left leg still learning how to hold her up again, despite the daily pulling and massaging, the painful bending and stretching.

Her talk hasn't come back, there's been no progress at all there. When she opens her mouth, some language that nobody can understand still issues from it. *Keep trying,* the speech therapist urges – but to tell the truth, Mo has no great desire to speak again. Living in silence, she has discovered, is so wonderfully liberating. No more foolish small talk, no more arguing, no more putting her foot in it and upsetting someone.

And if she wants to have a chat, there's always Leo. She's found him again, now that she's locked away like he was. And when she talks to him she can feel him listening. She can see his face turned towards her, his eyes really taking her in, his mind restored. He's the Leo she fell in love with, and it's such a comfort to have him back.

He understands her perfectly. He's the only one who does now.

It took a while to convince Daphne, but she came round. It's changed a lot since your day, mind; you'd hardly recognise it, but it's doing well. You wouldn't believe the things people will buy – toasters with flowers painted on them, spotty egg-cups, clocks with the numbers all jumbled up. And the prices – you'd feed a family of four for a week on what they're charging for a picnic basket. A picnic basket!

Daphne's mother is working there. You never met her, bit uppity, but good behind the counter, I have to say. Two broken marriages. Good looking I suppose, but can't keep a man. Hard to live with, I'd say. Too pernickety.

Una works in the shop on Saturdays. She loves it. Always hunting down new stock, she spends nearly all her time on the Internet – I'd say she's doing no study for that Leaving Cert. She says all she wants to do is work full-time in the shop when she leaves school, and how could we object to that, you and me? She's carrying on what you started, she's keeping it alive.

She's taking driving lessons, if you don't mind. Apparently Jack is teaching her. Not that I approve of her getting a car at eighteen – far too young – but she's delighted with it, and at least Jack can be trusted to make sure she learns right. It's a Morris Minor – remember the grey one we had, years ago when Finn was small?

She has a boyfriend now, imagine. He's been around for a while but I haven't met him yet. Someone from her school, I believe. Nice lad, Daphne says. Quiet.

Daphne has someone too. He's a good man, like you. He helped me after Finn, he listened to me when I needed someone. He'll treat her well.

There's so much to talk about. She never runs out of things to tell him.

She's tired now, her bad eye drooping. She listens to the conversations drifting around her as she reaches with her good hand for the last piece of cake on her plate. She transfers it carefully to her mouth, chews it slowly on her good side the way she's been taught. She wonders when they'll bring her back, let her go to bed.

She catches a look that passes between the guard – Louise – and George. Daft about each other they are, like herself and Leo in the good days. She's glad for George, he deserved someone nice. She's glad he got Louise, who hadn't forgotten Mo after all.

I knew who you were the minute I saw you, she told Mo last year, when George let it be known that he was part of a couple, and brought her around to Mo's to show her off. *It's not something you forget*, she said, when George was gone to the loo and she and Mo were alone. *You don't forget bringing someone that kind of news. I said nothing when we met again, I didn't want to go upsetting you.*

She'll be kind to George, she'll look after him. As for Una's young man, hard to have an opinion on him when he hardly opened his mouth all evening. But Una certainly seems keen, and Daphne hasn't objected. Watch that space is all they can do there.

And Daphne and Tom will surely walk up the aisle in time … and Mo wouldn't rule out a rerun of Jack and Isobel, if the sheep's eyes Isobel is making at him tonight is anything to go by. Poor man might well fall for her a second time, and good luck to him. Worse things have happened.

'Mo.'

She looks up. Tom lays a hand on her arm.

'You tired? You want to go?'

He knows, he always knows. She nods.

'I'll get your coat.'

While she waits she looks around the table, taking them all in. She scans the faces, sees the friendship and love, hope and forgiveness that they show. She must remember, so she can tell Leo tomorrow.

She must remember everything.

❖

Daphne, lowering her coffee cup, thinks how much Finn would have enjoyed this. He always loved dinner parties, people gathered around a table sharing food and conversation.

She glances at Mo, who looks tired. She sees Tom lean towards her, watches their brief exchange. He gets to his feet, meeting Daphne's eye: she nods in response to the question he hasn't needed to ask.

As she waits she regards her parents, seated across the table from her, side by side. Nice to see them at ease finally in one another's company, after their fraught history. Isobel looks well, as she always does. Tailored shirt in an apricot shade, hair freshly cut and gleaming, figure still trim at sixty. Watch her, tipping her head to one side with a half-smile on her face, considering something Daphne's father has said to her. You could almost be forgiven for thinking they were flirting.

'Daphne.'

She looks up. Tom has Mo's green coat draped across his arm.

'Stay,' he says, 'I can bring her back, you wait for Isobel or Jack' – but she gets to her feet: it's time to go home.

As she gathers her things Una and Theo reappear, ready to leave too. There's a general pushing back of chairs then, a jangling of car keys. Coats and jackets are found and donned, Mo's wheelchair retrieved from the hall. They move in a still-chatting mass towards the front door, where a flurry of thanks and goodbyes ensues.

Mo is installed in the front seat of Tom's car, Daphne sits behind. Just before they take off, Daphne meets Tom's eye for an instant in the rear-view mirror.

He winks. She smiles. So dear to her he has become.

She sits back and recalls the first time they met outside this very house, when he was late and she was caught in the rain, cold and cross and grieving.

She remembers the drop of her heart when she realised that the Beetle was gone, and the useless trip in Tom's car – this car – to the cemetery. She remembers the kindness of his sister Louise, making tea for her when she broke down at the police station. She recalls the forgotten fancy chocolate birthday cake, and its bright pink substitute. Into the bin, out of the bin.

She remembers Una's disappearance, the fright she got when Ciara told her she hadn't seen her at school. The wash of relief when she walked into the bicycle shop and saw her safe, making her realise that it wasn't just Finn she'd grown to love.

Such a day that was, a little over a year ago. Such a mix of good and bad, for each of them. Such a different year they've all had since then; a year of new beginnings, and laying the past to rest. Not that there aren't still challenges to face, obstacles to overcome – but the bulk of their sadness is behind them, she's sure of it. And Mo, with her indomitable spirit, will fight her current battle, and will win.

They're all looking ahead now. They all have everything to hope for now.

ACKNOWLEDGEMENTS

Huge thanks to all who contributed in any way, big or small, to the making of this book. In particular I want to give a mention to my very attentive and encouraging editor Alison Walsh and all the usual (and lovely) suspects at Hachette Books Ireland; my agent Sallyanne Sweeney of Mulcahy Associates who was there giving support at every turn; my copy editor Hazel Orme and my proofreading brother Aonghus Meaney, who both performed their usual miracles; the wonderful Tyrone Guthrie Centre in County Monaghan, which took me in for a week of final tweaking; my computer-savvy brother Ciarán Ó Maonaigh, my accountant friend Agnes Keane, marketing guru and pal Sharon Noonan, Helena Carey in Kerry and Mike O'Connor in Clare, who all helped me with my research – and most of all, a big thank you to you, kind reader. Without you, I'd be a bit redundant!

Roisin xx

www.roisinmeaney.com

Twitter: @roisinmeaney

Facebook: www.facebook.com/roisin.meaney

Don't miss
I'll Be Home for Christmas
by Roisin Meaney
Publishing in October 2015

It's days before Christmas and all is calm on the small island of Roone. The summer tourists are little more than a distant memory and everyone is looking forward to the peaceful festive season.

But things rarely go according to plan on the island.

As storm clouds gather on the horizon, a young girl arrives in Ireland determined to get to Roone in time for Christmas. And before the year is out, a resident of Roone will have her life thrown into turmoil once again …

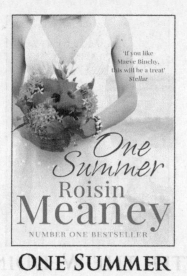

'If you like Maeve Binchy, this will be a treat'
Stellar

ONE SUMMER

This summer on the island, anything is possible ...

Nell Mulcahy grew up on the island of Roone – playing in the shallows and fishing with her father in his old red boat in the harbour. So when the stone cottage by the edge of the sea comes up for sale, the decision to move back from Dublin is easy. And where better to hold her upcoming wedding to Tim than on the island, surrounded by family and friends?

But when Nell decides to rent out her cottage for the summer to help finance the wedding, she sets in motion an unexpected series of events.

As deeply buried feelings rise to the surface, Nell's carefully laid plans for her wedding start to go awry and she is forced to make some tough decisions.

One thing's for sure, it's a summer on the island that nobody will ever forget.

Available now in print and ebook

AFTER THE WEDDING

Getting married was the easy part ...

After a bumpy start, Nell and James have finally said 'I do' and everything seems to be falling into place. Nell is getting comfortable in her new role as stepmother to James' sixteen-year-old son Andy, she's finally mending fences with her father and she's ready to look to the future.

Then Nell's ex-fiancé Tim – her husband James' brother – comes back to Roone, a place he's never liked, and she begins to feel uneasy. As the summer days roll by, and Tim seems in no hurry to return to his wife and daughter, Nell is finding it more and more difficult to enjoy her new beginning.

But when the little island of Roone is rocked by the disappearance of a young child, Nell realises that life can change in a single moment. Will happiness be restored before the autumn comes?

Available now in print and ebook

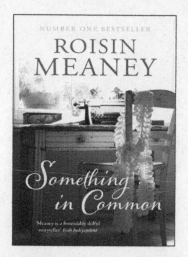

SOMETHING IN COMMON

The friendship starts with a letter ... from aspiring writer Sarah to blunt but witty journalist Helen, complaining about Helen's most recent book review. And there begins a correspondence that blossoms into a friendship which spans over two decades.

As the years pass, the women exchange details of loves lost and found, of family joys and upheavals. Sarah's letters filled with thoughts on her outwardly perfect marriage and her aching desire for children, and Helen's on the struggle of raising her young daughter alone.

But little do they realise that their story began long before Sarah penned that first letter – on one unforgettable afternoon where, during a distraught conversation on a bridge, Sarah changed the course of Helen's life forever.

This is the story of Helen and Sarah, and the friendship that was part of their destiny.

Available now in print and ebook